HAREM GIRL

Harem Girl

A Harem Girl's Journal

M. Saalih

iUniverse, Inc.
New York Lincoln Shanghai

Harem Girl
A Harem Girl's Journal

Copyright © 2004, 2006 by Mariyah Saalih

All rights reserved. No part of this book may be used or reproduced by any means, graphic, electronic, or mechanical, including photocopying, recording, taping or by any information storage retrieval system without the written permission of the publisher except in the case of brief quotations embodied in critical articles and reviews.

iUniverse books may be ordered through booksellers or by contacting:

iUniverse
2021 Pine Lake Road, Suite 100
Lincoln, NE 68512
www.iuniverse.com
1-800-Authors (1-800-288-4677)

Although many of the events depicted in this novel are based on historical writings and actual happenings and places, all the characters are fictional and any resemblance to people living or dead is purely coincidental.

Edited by Donna Jeffrey and Charis de Jonge.

COVER PICTURE

Jean-Léon Gérôme(1824–1904) painted the Slave Market in 1867. By permission of the Sterling and Francine Clark Art Institute.

Describing a similar scene in Cairo, W.J. Muller wrote:

"The slave market was one of my favorite haunts. In the center of this court, the slaves are exposed for sale and in general to the number of thirty or forty. I did not see the dejection and sorrow I was led to imagine, watching the Master remove the entire covering of a female and expose her to the gaze of a bystander."

ISBN-13: 978-0-595-31300-6 (pbk)
ISBN-13: 978-0-595-76117-3 (ebk)
ISBN-10: 0-595-31300-0 (pbk)
ISBN-10: 0-595-76117-8 (ebk)

Printed in the United States of America

Remembering Barry

1939–1997

Contents

❀

INTRODUCTION—*historical background*..................*xi*

PART ONE MY JOURNEY BEGINS
PROLOGUE 3
MY JOURNEY BEGINS.. 5
THE END OF CHILDHOOD................................... 8
ARABIA 11
BEYOND DECEIT 17
EXCHANGED—in the month of Shawwal 19
KASRE EL NOUZHA... 27
LESSONS.. 36
SANGARA... 45
HENNAED 50
THE BEDCHAMBER... 52
ERGASTULA 54
FIRST NIGHT.. 58
SETTLING IN.. 63
RING FOR SERVICE... 69
BEJEWELED DANCERS 72
SHEIK ALI... 75
TANTRA 78
PLEASURING.. 79
ENSLAVED CAPTIVES....................................... 84

THE DARK ART	89
WRITINGS DISCOVERED	93
BETWEEN DIGNITY AND DESIRE	95
TRAVELING COMPANION	101
SOHRAB	104
A SMALL GIFT	115
SLAVE MARKET	117
ENGLISHMAN	123
AT THE RACES	134
BAD NEWS	154
HUSSEIN	157
RETURN TO KASRE EL NOUZHA	160
CHANGE OF POSSESSION	165
MY JOURNEY ENDS—in the month of Safar	168
NADYA AND TOPAZ	180
FORBIDDEN	183
MARKED	189
GIRL SOUP	194
PIERCED	196
BOREDOM	199
SURPRISES FOR THE HAREM	203
HORTENSIA	211
FIRST CHILD	214
RELEASE	217
AL-KHOUTBA—the Engagement	220
HAFL AL ZIFAF—the Wedding Ceremony	226
WEDDING NIGHT	231
MATCH MAKING	234
RETURN TO RANYAH	236
RANYAH AGAIN	240
UMM ISMA'IL	243

TEARS—a poem for Isma'il 245

PART TWO CLOSING THE CIRCLE
DERELICTION. 249
YEARS 260
CONFESSION 265
NOW I UNDERSTAND 280
FOURTEEN 282
DO YOU REMEMBER ME? 284
CLOSING THE CIRCLE 288
ÉPILOGUE 309

THE HAREM *311*
CHRONOLOGY *313*
GLOSSARY *315*
ABOUT THE AUTHOR. *321*

INTRODUCTION—historical background

Inspiration to write this novel came from three sources: nineteenth century Middle East history, a visit to the Moorish Alhambra palace in Spain, and an imagined journal of a harem girl. As I ventured through the history, this imagined journal assumed a life of its own and at times I found it difficult to tell in my mind and writings where fiction ended and historical fact began. Nevertheless, I have kept as true as possible to the historical setting and overlaid and embellished it with the memoirs of Sapphira, my harem girl.

To write these journal memoirs, a young Arab woman masqueraded her way into a sheik's harem. She managed this by a deceitful ruse involving a sheik friend of her husband, who agreed to present her as one of his slaves and send her to a harem in exchange for another girl. Four months later the sheiks would undo the exchange—if nothing went wrong.

Slavery was widely practiced at the turn of the century, and I quote from two letters sent by Spanish priests to the Cardinal of Madrid giving account of pirate raids in the Philippines:

> *Abdulla then gave the town of Ilo-Ilo over to organized loot. Detachments of Moros looted the churches and rounded up the fleeing women and children. Krismen passed from house to house down narrow streets, ferreting out the frightened women.*
> *In the plaza of the ruined town, the plunder was collected in a great pile. White-skinned Spanish women mingled with brown Visayan girls in the long line assembled for the inspection of Abdulla. The fairest of the women were selected for the harems of Sulu—the male survivors of the conflict were put to the "kris".*

Again, in a later letter describing another incident:

> When Tagal wearied of the slaughter and raised his hand to turn the prows of the pirate vessels to the south again, 650 captives lay trussed like chickens in the hold.
> One hundred miles from Jolo, a Spanish fleet, operating from the base at Zamboanga, intercepted the victorious Tagal as he rounded the treacherous angle of rough water at Puenta Flecha. Hampered by the hundreds of captives in the holds, the garays of Tagal were slow and unwieldy, and in the naval engagement that followed the Moros suffered a crushing defeat. Three hundred Moros, including Tagal, were killed and 120 captives were set free. Tagal jettisoned many of the captives as the tide of battle turned against him, and the sharks at Puenta Flecha fed well on the bound bodies of Christian slave girls bound for the harems of Jolo.

At the time of the journal, Western nations had for many years abolished slavery and declared it illegal, but in the Middle East, it was a long held practice that continued well after prohibition laws were passed. This was due largely to the remote location, sparse population, the inhospitable terrain where the practice flourished, and the conflict in ideology between East and West. Additionally, Western governments were in no mood to upset the delicate commercial arrangements between the owners of the newfound oil of the Middle East, and their own commercial oil interests. It was not until 1935 that Somalia officially outlawed slavery, followed by Saudi Arabia in 1962—at the urging of President J.F. Kennedy—one hundred years later than the United States of America.

Our word harem is derived from the Arabic word harim—"sacred, forbidden place", which in turn comes from the Arabic word harama—"he prohibited". Now as then, it is a section of a house reserved for the women and children of the household, a quiet sanctum for the free—a gilded prison for the enslaved. Her narrative of course documented the latter.
The last officially sanctioned harem of record that I could find was that of King Abdul Aziz Ibn-Saud (1880-1953), the supreme ruler of Saudi Arabia. He had seventeen wives, four concubines and four slaves to satisfy his desire. He fathered forty-four sons and a similar number of daughters (it seems no exact record or count of daughters was kept!).
Spelling can be a dilemma because there is often no direct translation from Arabic script. For instance, the word for the female purdah garment is sometimes spelled burqa, burka, or burqua in translations. Even the spelling and pronunciation of the town of Jeddah (Jiddah) (Jaddah), the major seaport of Arabia, is unclear. Jiddah in Arabic means "seashore" and Jeddah (Jaddah)

means "grandmother"—the latter given credence by the belief that Eve lies buried just outside the city walls. All are plausible names. I have used Jeddah, probably incorrectly, nevertheless most commonly used nowadays by Westerners.

Also included as an appendix is a glossary of some words and terms that may be unfamiliar.

In her journal, which she called her *Journaux Intimes,* she mentioned many historical characters such as Sharif Hussein of Jeddah, and the towns and countries referred to all exist. And the hotel she stayed in, the Maison Dorée on rue de Hollande in Tunis, is still open for business today, though mature and tired, eclipsed by the Hiltons and Holiday Inns of our time, but no doubt grand accommodation in her day. These are just some of the facts that lend credence to the authenticity of her memoirs.

In what period is the novel set? When was her journal supposedly written? Many clues are scattered throughout the text: Reference to Burton's translation, *Tales of the Arabian Nights, 1001 Nights,* places the journal start after 1888, mention of the Suez Canal, officially opened in 1876, and the use of the telegraph to send messages, would support this. Finally, reference to *La Grippe,* the worldwide Spanish Flu epidemic, clearly places the start of her journal in the year 1900 when she is fourteen years old, and ends in 1926 when she is forty.

Mariyah Saalih

حريم بنت

PART ONE
MY JOURNEY BEGINS

PROLOGUE

It is unbelievable to me that I have written the first chapters of my journal for an audience I do not know and cannot picture. Nevertheless, I write regardless, it fills my time if nothing else. I write in French, slipping back to Arabic occasionally when lost for a word or phrase. Why do I write in French? Because to me it is easier and quicker than writing Arabic script, and here, in the harem, no one reads or understands French. If others found my journal, my words would remain a mystery, which at this time is the way I wish it to be.

Previously, my short stories and poems have been for family and close friends, but they are all now far away, and I find myself confused and wandering without their direction. Am I telling a story or writing a diary, and for whom? My style flows as the moment takes me, so please bear with me. It is after all, just a collage of thoughts and moments in the life of a harem girl—many trivial, some momentous.

From here onward, I shall add to my journal as my life unfolds. I chance that my experiences and writings will be worthy of your reading—whoever you may be.

To find a beginning I must go back to when I was fourteen, when I was neither a child nor an adult. I had stopped playing children's games such as pick-up-stones, dressing up in my mother's clothes, and reading books in the forked branch of the old olive tree. Boys had become exciting to me, they made me blush and feel uneasy, and I had my showings—but in my mind, I was not yet a woman. At that point, I had no plans for my life—what fourteen-year-old does? Certainly, I had romantic thoughts, love and marriage, and other dreams young girls have, even so, being a slave girl in a harem was not one of them. I was not seeking change; I was content in life to follow the path that unfolded before me.

MY JOURNEY BEGINS

My real name is Mariyah, Mariyah El-Abiad, but they have always called me Marie. Marie was a fair compromise—a Muslim name shortened to a French name. Neither a Muslim cleric nor Catholic priest could be offended.

My mother was the daughter of a senior French Embassy official and my father a Tunisian Government minister responsible for purchasing military supplies. I considered myself a fortunate woman to be born in Tunisia to a Tunisian father of Arab and Berber descent and a French mother. Although my Catholic mother embraced Islam within her marriage she never fully adopted all the customs and teachings, and insisted that I, unlike most women, be given that rarest of gifts—an education. It was my mother, by means unknown to me, who enrolled me in the private French Embassy School, although by the rules of admission I was not entitled to attend. I learned to read and write both Arabic and French and received instruction in the arts. My drawing and sketching skills were amateurish, but adequate for illustrating the short stories and poems that I loved to write. It was here that I met Jacqueline, the French Ambassador's daughter, my best friend and constant companion.

I shall remain forever indebted to my mother for what she gave me.

Two younger brothers, Mamoud and Amenzu, at this time more of a nuisance and of no significance to an older sister, completed my family. I loved them all dearly, my brothers included.

Looking back, I see my mother as a loving sensuous woman. At the time, I did not fully realize or understand the depth of her sensuality or the release she sought. Now, upon reflection it all falls into place. I can see her, now in my minds eye, cooking my father's favorite meal, Moroccan *tajine*, singing or humming a song, aware of herself, moving more slowly and gracefully than usual. These were signs that she was looking towards a special evening. Dressed in one of her French gowns, tight fitting at the waist, attractively low cut at the front, my mother would lean over unnecessarily low and close to serve my father, the fragrance of her closeness lingering in the air, suggesting things to come.

Often I peeked through the kitchen window after my father had come home from work, and on more than one occasion I saw him standing behind my mother as she went about her preparations, his hands feeling her through layers of clothing, while he nuzzled her neck and mussed her hair. She sometimes feigned rejection of his advances, pushing him away with a backwards thrust of her bottom, and then, as though forgiving him for his boldness, she would turn her face to his and peck him on his cheek.

He was her little *chou-chou* and I was encouraged about married life.

I was fifteen years old when I caught a glimpse of the book on the bedside table, open at a colorful illustration showing a turbaned man and a naked woman in a close embrace. It was quickly, yet casually picked up by my mother, closed and placed in a drawer—followed by a slight blush and forced conversation. We went about our bed-making chores, she hoping that I had not seen what I saw, I with my curiosity aroused.

A few weeks after this incident my parents took a short sojourn to the Tell Atlas mountains, and my friend Jacqueline stayed overnight with me. We had been close friends for many years, sharing the bonds of age, the French language, and the same school.

After dinner, we excused ourselves from the watchful eye of the housekeeper, and the bothersome squabbling of my brothers, and went to my bedroom, but only after I retrieved the book from the drawer in my mother's bedside table. It was an illustrated Guide to Burton's *Tales of the Arabian Nights, 1001 Nights*. Since it was written in English, I could not read it; however, Jacqueline could, having lived with her parents in London before her father's promotion to French Ambassador to Tunisia.

We lay side by side on the bed, leafing through the pages, pausing at the pictures, while Jacqueline translated the captions from English to French, and we posed, practiced and re-enacted each romantic scene, taking turns being the man and then the woman.

New awareness and sensations swept through our bodies—newly formed bodies—barely out of puberty. New awareness and sensations we could not control, feelings Jacqueline and I had not yet learned to take further. We were two cats in heat.

And we giggled and danced with each other in that scandalous European way, to imaginary music played in an imaginary crystal ballroom with a make-believe handsome prince in our arms.

Jacqueline showed me how to kiss the French way, with mouth open and tongue searching tongue, she saying beyond her years, "French girls kiss this way to show a man they have desire for him."

She also taught me to wink at the French boys as we passed by them at school. "If you open your mouth while you wink the power of love will compel them to come to you and kiss you on your lips," she said.

"Ugh," I thought at the time, and always winked with my mouth closed.

THE END OF CHILDHOOD

My father thought I was eligible at fourteen, my mother wanted to wait until I was eighteen, and in a compromise sixteen was agreed on. I was to be married at the age of sixteen, after my schooling was finished.

My mother had hoped for a love-marriage, but in Berber tradition, my parents chose my husband. I had no experience of men, I did not know the details of their being and therefore, even if it was proper and done that way, I could not draw up a list of qualities I wanted to find in my husband-to-be.

"*Maman*," I said. "When he parts my wedding veil, allow my eyes to look into those of a young man. I want to be the first wife of a young man, like it was with you and Papa, not the second or third wife of an old one, no matter how generous his bride-price may be."

"He will be a young man, and you will be a first wife. I promise you that," replied my mother, with tears rolling down her cheeks.

My parents conferred with his parents, I was shown to his parents and he to mine, but the two of us never met while the negotiations were taking place. I had to rely on my mother's judgment and assurance that I would find him attractive. They agreed on a bride-price and announced that a husband had been found for me. Despite my inquiry, they never told me the bride-price. Was I valuable, or given away for nothing? I would never know.

In strictest tradition, parents of the bride and groom ask them individually if they accept the marriage without the bride or groom first seeing each other, but my mother intervened. Shyly, I first saw him as a dinner guest and then more comfortably as a frequent visitor to our house. Jamaal al-Jubier was a handsome young Arabian with inviting Semitic features, nineteen years of age. I was encouraged to take walks with him, with my chaperone mother twenty paces behind us.

Much to my father's relief, I accepted the marriage. To me it was a family obligation. I would marry a man—I know now in hindsight—I would grow to be fond of and care for, but never love.

In the weeks before the wedding, we cut and sewed clothes, hired musicians and singers, made arrangements with others, and sent invitations. My husband-to-be and I could now be together, and given time to better know each other.

Jamaal was a horse dealer representing his father's Arabian stables—taking advantage of the closeness of Tunisia to Europe to sell his horses—I, a self proclaimed writer and artist. I thought he was good-looking, definitely well to do, and had no obvious shortcomings. On the other hand, he had no exciting or outstanding qualities worthy of note. Many a girl could marry him and be happy.

Over afternoon tea, my mother and I had the requisite pre-marriage mother to daughter talk. She spoke openly and sincerely about her marriage, the responsibilities of a married woman, and the bedroom duties of a wife.

"Never deny your husband's needs. Give yourself to him, even when you are of a different mind. And when your womb desires his seed, do not wait for him to notice. Invite him to lie with you, lead him to bed. Do not be bashful, for he will feel honored by your asking. Surprise him. Invite him when he is least expecting it, perhaps at an unusual time or place, not always in bed at night.

"A woman's breasts are irresistibly alluring to a man. Show them to entice and seduce, but do so privately with grace and discretion. And never forget, a woman is not a bowl of roses. Bathe frequently and give nature a helping hand with fragrances.

"Celebrate your love for him often, for the Prophet taught us that any woman, who dies in a state where her husband is pleased with her, shall enter *Jannah*."

In return for these well-taken snippets of advice, I asked the questions expected from an innocent girl, although confident that I knew the answers. "Does it hurt? How often will we do it? How will I know what to do? Will he want me in the ways shown in your book?"

She was visibly taken aback by the last question, and assured me that harems no longer existed, that her government had closed them—she always referred to "her government" when she meant the French government—and made slavery illegal. Besides, she said, the girls in the book were slave concubines; they had no say in the matter and had to bend to his ways.

"Nevertheless," I countered, "the man would only want to do those things if it was in his nature and gave him pleasure."

"Well, your father is not like that," was her defensive reply that told me otherwise.

My wedding was a joyous occasion, even if a little bewildering to me, for I was, in truth, unprepared for this abrupt end of childhood. Nevertheless, it was not unwelcomed. I looked forward to married life, and the challenge of making a home for my husband and myself. My mother and father, perhaps intentionally or otherwise, had taught me well, and I became eager and excited by the prospect.

In Berber ceremonies, the bride and groom retire to consummate the marriage, and only when they returned to the gathering and showed the bloodied bed cottons was the bride-price paid and celebrations commenced. My mother would have none of that! Nevertheless, I entered my marriage bed a virgin; there was blood and new smells.

We bought our own house in Tunis, the capital city of Tunisia, and settled down to married life with the unconfined enthusiasm of youth, happily caught up in the optimistic exuberance that comes with the first flush of marriage.

Two years later, Jamaal's father died. Islamic custom called Jamaal home to look after his mother and two sisters, and manage the Arabian stables. We packed our possessions, said a tearful goodbye to family and friends, and sailed for Arabia to live in his mother's house in the Red Sea port of Jeddah.

I dearly missed my family and Tunisia. I missed the scent of jasmine on the warm night air, almond blossoms in the spring, and red bougainvillea spilling over white walls. I missed the olive groves, date palms, forested hills and mountains, the Tells, the Madjerda River valley—and rainy days. That was my Tunisia.

Arabia—scorched by the oppressive heat of early summer—desolate, unforgivably dry, tiresomely barren…and not mine.

ARABIA

For me, my marriage started to unravel two years or so after we settled in Jeddah. Unquestionably, homesickness contributed to my growing unhappiness, although perhaps more troubling was an innermost feeling that I had never found love in my marriage, despite assurances from my mother and father that after marriage we would come to love each other. It was not my husband's fault; he kept his promises, and I held no complaint. I blamed myself. Perhaps my childhood dreams of idyllic and exciting romance were unrealistic—one of life's disappointing realities.

There were glimmers of love, but they always retreated under the unrelenting dark shadow cast by my inability to conceive a child. The air was poisoned, killing off what little love there may have been, giving it no chance to blossom, and I found myself more and more excluded from my husband and his family. To me I was a huge failure as a woman, and I brooded about the futility of being a wife and making a home if there were to be no children. The other women of the household saw me as a lacking foreigner, I was different, and they were inclined and willing to tell me so, and I saw myself as incomplete, damaged merchandise kept high on a shelf, taken down and dusted off, so to speak, only occasionally.

Jamaal, at the urging of his mother, took a second wife, and when she bore him a son, it clearly placed blame for my barrenness. My estrangement and disenchantment was sealed.

And as though all that was not enough humiliation for me, she again swelled resplendently with child.

Uplifting good fortune is the other side of depressing adversity, and for me it came from horses. Whether it was because Jamaal felt sorry for my not being wanted around the house, or because he sought a more harmonious household, I do not know. However, to my utter delight, and that of everyone else, he found something of great consequence and importance for me to do outside of the home—he broke with tradition, and took me with him to the stables most days. There he spent time with me and patiently taught me about the care of horses and camels and how to train and ride them. I became an accomplished horsewoman—and stable-hand!—something unheard of for a woman in this country, particularly a married woman. They were skills that pleased me immensely, and Jamaal seemed happy and enthused to have found something for me.

Although in our household I had become a secondary wife, my knowledge of the French language was a great help to my husband since much of the trading was with French horse fanciers and my marriage woes were no barrier to my accompanying Jamaal on many of his travels as an unacknowledged business partner.

I always wore Western style clothes and socialized in the European manner with his Arabian customers. They appreciated and enjoyed the exotic and unusual foreign atmosphere that I brought to our dealings. In return, the way of life of the Arab Sheiks we met captivated me. Exceptionally beautiful women often accompanied them—and I use the word women lightly, as many were young girls. I was astonished and shocked, yet intrigued, when I learned that most of the girls were slaves normally secreted away in their owner's harem, despite my mother's assurances about the noble actions of "her government".

Being a woman, I had the opportunity to be with these girls and hear their stories of intrigue, enticing dress, seduction, and busy nights. It sounded exciting and exotic—a life entirely different from what mine had become. I daydreamed about it—how I might take a peek into, or even experience, the life of a girl in a slave harem, reasoning that there I could find what I thought was missing from my life—the attentions of a man and the prospect of loving. It brought back images from my mother's bedside book and in my confident mind I imagined writing and illustrating a better one.

Entering a harem would not be difficult, slave traders would willingly assist and profit, but it would be a one-way journey, for life. To just visit or stay for a short while in such a place and then return home was impossible. I tucked the thought of it away in the back of my mind.

Nevertheless, I desperately wanted to enter into the world of love between a man and a woman where I could release my repressed womanliness and confirm my femininity. "How exciting it would be to once again have a man desire and choose me, and little by little defer to his wishes," I thought. I missed the bed-company of a husband and the things he did, and I was weary of waiting to be a woman again. To hear again the deep voice of a man, murmuring gentle thoughts and caresses close to my ear, was my longing.

The unexpected unfolded before me one evening during a conversation with Ahmad, a young sheik who was a worldly and well-traveled trader in carpets, spices and medicines.

My husband had purchased from him two expensive carpets for the house, and in gratitude, Sheik Ahmad invited us to dine with him that evening in his home in the inland town of Al-Ta'if.

We sat on cushions around a small carpet spread on the floor, my husband and I, Sheik Ahmad and his companion Kassim, an exceptionally pretty brown-skinned Asian girl. She was dressed in silk *chalwars* and *choli*—traditional harem trousers and bolero jacket—just as I had imagined harem dress to be, and adding to this exotic aura was a small jewel nestled in her navel. It caught the light and drew attention to her narrow waist and the smooth swell of her hips.

During the meal, I noticed more than once that my husband's eyes were paying attention to the young Kassim, and her shy downcast eyes told me that she, too, was aware of his scrutiny. After our meal, my husband rose and asked permission for us to walk about the grounds at which point Sheik Ahmad leaned over and whispered in Kassim's ear and then insisted that she accompany Jamaal on his walk and show him the gardens. They left the room together, leaving me sitting on the floor, not invited to join them.

I started our conversation quite bluntly, possibly rudely, by asking, "Sheik Ahmad, is Kassim your slave?"

He never answered the question directly. Instead, he told me, "She is a traveling companion. I brought her back with me after a voyage to India. She is under my care until I make other arrangements for her. She wants to be placed in a harem."

"An agreeable way of putting it," I thought, because I knew "will be sold into a harem," was more to the truth. I was far from naïve about harems by now—my travels and discussions had thoroughly enlightened me. However, burying my darker thoughts, I took advantage of this opportunity to tell him of my ambition.

"I would like that for myself; to be placed in a harem," I ventured.

Ahmad looked at me, amazed. "Your husband would not allow it. A slave harem is not the place for another man's wife. Furthermore, I can assure you it is not a place for a free-spirited woman like you, one who is worldly and knowledgeable about many things and other cultures," he replied.

"Yes, I am sure that what you say is true," I countered. "Nevertheless, I would like to be placed for a short time, or simply visit such a place. Could you arrange for that? I think my husband may agree. He has both a new wife and child and one more child to arrive shortly. I am unwelcome in his household these days and my presence distresses his other wife. It is important that peace and harmony exist for her at this time, or the baby will be born sickly and irritable. Jamaal is aware of this fact and is concerned about it."

His first response was immediate. "It would be impossible. Outsiders are forbidden to enter the interior of a slave harem, and if by subterfuge you gained entry and were discovered, you could never leave. You would be enslaved and forced to remain there, and then the only way out for you would be to either bear the master a son or be put to death."

My barrenness left me with death, however, Sheik Ahmad did offer some comfort. "You are too pretty and valuable to be put to death, instead you would probably be sold to another master if discovered. Salim the Turk pays a good price for girls like you, a very good price I should venture." He said this with a hint of brisk enthusiasm that I did not share, while he unashamedly looked me over from head to toe—a barely perceptible smile on his face taking away any comfort his earlier words had given me about not being put to death.

However, the idea of my entering a harem had obviously taken root; his mind was working, and I could tell that he found something intriguing about it.

After a long pause, he spoke again. "Perhaps there is a way for you that would pose no danger of entrapment or death." He went on to tell me that "On a recent visit to the town of Makram I saw an unusually attractive fair-haired slave girl belonging to Sheik Ali al-Saalih. He is a long-time friend of mine, and he offered her in service to me for a few months. In return, I agreed to send Sheik Ali an interesting girl for his enjoyment, and this was what I had in mind for Kassim before she is…placed in a harem."

He looked at me as if wondering if I had grasped the implication in what he had said, and whether to go on or not. Then he continued. "What if I sent you instead of Kassim? It would be for four months; you could then come back here and return to your husband. You would of course have to perform the duties of a harem girl while you were there, the nature of which you are surely well aware of, and would agree to."

I stared back at his slight smile, neither shocked nor uncomfortable.

After another long and thoughtful pause he continued. "A harem slave girl is kept for the sole purpose of gratifying one man, the master. A harem girl's duty is to allure, entice and arouse him using the five senses: sight, sound, smell, taste and touch, and then to offer herself to him in any way he desires so that he can spend the lusts aroused within him. Most harem girls are slaves; their thoughts and actions are completely subservient to those of their master. They accord him his every wish, and I may add, denial, aversion or deficiency in service is rarely taken lightly by the master."

He spoke as though reading from a *ferman*, and I remember well those words.

"If harems are closed to all except the master how was it possible for you to see this girl of your choice?"

"Ah, a good question. Grand harem baths have a screened wall or window behind which there is a darkened room. From there the master and his eunuchs sometimes watch the women bathe, unseen by them. My friend Sheik Ali invited me to sit with him late one afternoon and that was when I was attracted by the unusual fairness of this girl of his."

I had listened, fascinated. Then I spoke, quite calmly, saying, "I want to take this chance. Please talk to Jamaal about it."

My husband and Kassim returned and I could tell that in this short time, more than a walk had taken place—wives can tell these things. His flushed face glowed with guilt. He was ill at ease and quickly agreed when Ahmad suggested they retire and smoke awhile together. There he listened to Ahmad's words and then came and spoke to me.

"Marie, are you sure this is what you want?" he asked, his dark eyes firmly on mine.

"Yes. Please let me do it," I replied.

Perhaps he was ready to be free of me for a while. He was content with his new wife and son, and maybe he saw this as a chance to bring quiet harmony to the household for the occasion of the birth of his second child—who knows? Whatever the reason it suited him and he agreed to the plan with one condition.

"We will return to Jeddah. I will think this over for a few days to be sure it is what I want for you. It is a most unconventional proposal and I need to give more time to thoughtful consideration before I send a message to Sheik Ahmad with my decision, one way or the other."

Even though it was clear that the decision would be his, and his alone, his giving of thoughtful consideration delighted me. At least it wasn't outright rejection of the idea.

Sheik Ahmad would be delighted also if this plan worked. He could finish the other business he had in mind for Kassim, a profitable one no doubt, and then devote his attention to another journey to India or other distant places he had mentioned.

BEYOND DECEIT

I tell myself I never lied to Jamaal. Silence and secrets cannot tell lies, can they? What I did, or rather did not do, was merely a sin of omission, a silent obstruction of the truth.

Three days after we returned to Jeddah, Jamaal sent his reply to Ahmad:

> …I am pleased to inform you that I have given permission for my first wife Mariyah to assume the position of French tutor to the children of Sheik Al-Madr and I accept his most generous offer.
> I accept also your word that Sheik Al-Madr is an honorable man and that Mariyah's position will be one that will bring with it great respect and honor, and be held in high esteem by all who may hear of it.…

French tutor? Sheik Al-Madr? What had Ahmad told Jamaal when they retired to smoke together? It certainly wasn't the truth—but whatever it was, I could see that it served my purpose well and I delighted in the skill of the deception. At this point, I had time to change my mind, or say something in shocked amazement; I did not…and became a willing conspirator.

As the messenger rode away with the letter, an unnerving hollowness in the pit of my stomach replaced my earlier jubilation.

There was ample time to make arrangements, as the exchange was to take place after the holy month of Ramadan. Four months later, in the second month of the Arabian year, the month of Safar, I would return to Al-Ta'if and then to my home and husband in Jeddah.

I needed new clothes for my new role as a sheik's slave girl. It was out of question to seek advice from anyone in the household, and for a while, the task stymied me until I had sudden inspiration—I would talk to the brothel keeper. Ask her where she buys clothes for her girls—an idea I promptly acted on, much to my own surprise.

Being the month of Ramadan, I could not shop between sunrise and sunset, so after the sundown prayers I recruited the houseboy to escort me on my mission.

A somewhat puzzled madam directed us to a local seamstress whom, she derogatorily informed me, "specializes in clothes for dancing girls. She may be of help to you."

A wizened old woman, her back bent from years of sewing, answered my call. I told the aged seamstress what I wanted—three sets of clothes to create the scene of a young slave girl in a Sultan's harem. I needed them to "romance my husband and rekindle his flagging ardor," I said. With a knowing smile, she assured me that I had come to the right place.

While regaling me with promises that her clothes were of the highest quality and lowest price, she took my measurements and showed me samples of materials. Draping the flimsy cloth over her bared arm and hand, she showed me how much they revealed and how much they concealed. I chose dusty blue chiffon, and white gossamer silk—materials that were sheer and diaphanous—and a striking jade-green polished Bursa silk from Turkey that relied on its weight, shimmer, and clinging drape for effect. Following her advice, I ordered three chalwars with matching cholis, some with laces and others with buttons to close them, all to be finished with embroidery and gold thread.

I paid her in advance—"a generous amount," I thought, in view of her assertion about her low prices. But after I had half-heartedly protested, and she offered to make short sheer skirts, small caps, and *niqaab* veils from leftover materials, I agreed with her that sewing these delicate materials was exacting and time consuming, and the cloth itself expensive. We settled on a slightly lower price. A visit to the souk for two pair of slippers completed my shopping.

Two weeks later, I sent the boy to pick up my parcel.

In my bedroom, behind bolted doors, I excitedly opened the parcel of clothes and unrolled the cotton cloth that protected and helped preserve the shape and appearance of the delicate items. As though again a young girl I let my imagination roam as I tried on each costume, imagining with girlish vanity that I was a *haseki* parading myself before a handsome Sultan, who might choose to bed me. After putting on each ensemble I crawled to my imaginary Sultan, seductively undressed before him, and then kneeling upright and naked, offered my breasts and Mount of Venus to his eyes. Twice in my mind, he waved me away. After the third costume found favor he summoned me to lie on his bed, and I imagined him mounting me. I let my mind and fingers conclude my play.

EXCHANGED—in the month of Shawwal

We arrived just after noon at Sheik Ahmad al-Sabur's home in the town of Al-Ta'if, where the exchange was to take place. Jamaal would return to Jeddah that afternoon and I would spend the next two days with Sheik Ahmad as his honored guest before being escorted to my destination—the harem of Sheik Ali.

That evening, our first order of business was to make up a story about how I became a slave, and to give me a harem name. Ahmad recounted the history and traditional sources of slave girls and we agreed that to have been captured and sold into slavery by Algerian corsairs would best fit my background, and require the least amount of fiction to support. I was to be a nonbeliever at the time of my capture and enslavement, a requirement to conform to Islamic law that forbids enslavement of believers, though I had later converted to Islam, something that Sheik Ahmad said I would find of benefit in the harem, without offering any explanation. That was to be my story and Sapphira was to be my name. Sapphira had an exotic and precious ring to it—I liked it, and I could weave a story around it, although I had hoped for a more salacious name but could not think of one at the time.

We spent time rehearsing possible scenarios, he asking me questions to see if I could answer convincingly, trying to catch me off guard with clever questions that could bring my story into doubt. We found a weakness—my lack of experience and knowledge of the "ways of the harem". Therefore, I agreed to have him present me as a newly acquired girl not yet instructed.

A servant brought in a wrought iron stand. At first, I thought it was a candlestick, but it was a small iron anvil mounted on a tall stand. On a short side arm, several silver bangles of different sizes swung back and forth. Ahmad selected one, squeezed it tightly around my upper arm and raised it so that the silver band rested on the anvil. A small lead rivet, passed through the clasp and hammered over tightly, closed the bangle around my arm and prevented its removal.

Two girls served us that evening. Dressed in heavily embroidered silk *salwar-kameezes* they opened my mind and eyes to what lay ahead for me. Unbuttoned at the top, the kameezes showed more than a glimpse of their curves. I felt uncomfortable with this sensual display, and I sensed that all three of us shared this feeling, more so after Ahmad spoke.

"Let me show them to you," he said, beckoning the girls to stand before him.

With a brief hand sign from him, they took off their kameezes and stood before us, naked to the waist, eyes cast downwards. Another sign, a circling of his hand, and the girls turned around to show a striking single braid of black hair that fell down their backs almost to their waists.

"Let me show you the rest of them," he said, ordering them to turn around, loosen the drawstring of their salwars, and step out of them.

"Aren't they pretty? I have a sharp eye, don't you think?" he continued, proudly. "They come from the northern part of India. It is surprising what you can find beneath the rags of low caste peasants. My spotters in the port of Hochin found them for me—I paid them a generous finder's fee for their efforts. I gave their desperately poor parents a small amount of money to relieve their poverty, and a promise to look after their daughters for them. Told them I would place them as maids to regal daughters of royalty I knew. They were impressed.

"For the sail back to Jeddah, I cleverly dressed them as boys, hiding their long hair under Sikh turbans. You never know when the British navy might board you. Brought them up from Jeddah on a cart piled high with carpets, each of them rolled up in one to hide them from prying eyes," he said, sitting straight-backed and turning his head slowly from side to side as though trying to affirm to all how clever he was in his deviousness.

"And you can imagine my surprise when my physician reported that they were virgins—easily quadrupling their value—and you can also imagine their surprise when I had them *smoothed* and started their *tantra* instruction. I paid an old Indian merchant friend of mine to teach them a few words of Arabic and tell them in their own language that they had been sold by their parents to be slaves, not maids, and would be instructed in the erotic arts before being sold to a man."

Searching for something to say, I blurted out, "It must be difficult for you to instruct them with their small understanding of Arabic."

His answer sent a chill through me. "A camel whip speaks all languages."

Quickly changing the subject, I asked, innocently, "Sheik Ahmad, what is tantra?"

"Tantra is an ancient Indian teaching of spiritual and physical love. A girl knowledgeable in the tantric ways makes for an exciting night companion. We believers of the true faith have purged it of false faith and holiness and given it earthly practice, and for added measure, I include some Persian and Greek customs so that my slave girls are three ways ready. Yes," he said proudly, while again moving his head haughtily from side to side, "when one of Sheik Ahmad's girls goes to auction she is ready to serve her new owner whatever his lustful intentions may be."

He was obviously a trader in more than pepper-spice, carpets and medicines—and supremely proud of it.

"Knowing that you write, I assume that you also read," he continued.

"Yes, I can read."

"Good. I shall lend you some pages, a translation of some of the Asian tantric writings describing often demanded and unusual favors. They may be of help to you in your venture, but you must remember to bring them back with you. My precious secrets must not fall into the hands of other traders."

After thanking him kindly and seeking pause from the conversation, I asked, "Where is Kassim?"

"Sold," he replied, firmly, confirming my earlier suspicion that she was a slave and he an uncaring slave trader. Without offering further explanation, he quickly changed the subject. "Have you," he asked, pointing his beard with long strokes of his fingers, "been groomed in the style of the harem?"

"I think so," I replied, passing my fingers through my long shiny hair and then tossing it back over my shoulder, although I knew what he was alluding to, and had foolishly thought I could avoid it somehow by ignoring it.

"No, that is not what I meant. Have you been smoothed? Have you had your superfluous hair removed?"

"No, I am not groomed in that way," I admitted, blushing badly.

"You must be bared before you are presented to Sheik Ali, or our ruse will be exposed. We will do it tomorrow."

"Is it necessary? Could you not tell him…."

"No. As I said, it will be done tomorrow."

Smoothing was an ancient practice, dating back to the time of the Egyptian Pharaohs[1]. It later spread across North Africa, from Persia in the east to Morocco in the west, and north to Turkey and Rome. Today, it was still a common practice, particularly among brides and younger married women, although rarely spoken of. My husband's second wife arrived in our household already smoothed and I knew he found the sleek silkiness attractive. However, because he took me to his bed only on those few occasions when his second wife was indisposed, he never asked me to have myself groomed in that fashion. For me, he probably saw it as an unnecessary monthly expense, and I didn't encourage it.

In a slave harem, smoothing was *de rigueur*.

Next day Ahmad took me to his barber where I had a private early afternoon appointment.

Once I was inside the shabby establishment the barber bolted the door shut, and closed the latticed shutters over the window openings to keep out unwanted eyes, yet allow in light enough for him to go about his business.

Ahmad told me to remove my garments and sit in the padded barber chair, an ancient assembly of creaking wood and squeaking leather. In a show of modesty the barber, but not Ahmad, turned his back while I undressed—a needless gesture considering what he was about to do and see.

A small pillow, wrapped in a towel and placed under my hips, embarrassingly caused my thighs and belly to rise into view when the barber slowly lowered the back of the chair. Then, to my further embarrassment, he eased my thighs apart, wide enough so that my legs hung off each side of the chair.

Towels soaked in hot water and placed over my lower belly and between my thighs restored some semblance of modesty, and thoroughly softened and moistened the area before they enthusiastically worked in a generous dribbling of hot wax and sticky pine rosin over my mons and deeply between my thighs. Strips of muslin embedded in more layers of wax formed up a thick pad that was left to cool and harden, pulling at the hair with every slight movement—a harbinger of things to come.

"The pleasure is to be mine," said Ahmad, pushing aside the barber. Ahmad worked his fingers under the lip of the wax pad, his other hand pressing down flat on my stomach. With one smooth stroke, he tore away the hardened pad,

---

1. 'Priestesses of the ancient religion of Egypt shaved their entire person, in order that all roughness be smoothed and the skin have a beautiful polish, making them clean and pure in approaching the throne of God.'

taking with it the offending hair. The barber's hand, placed firmly over my mouth, muffled my cries as a fierce stinging swept down my groin. Ahmad, smug with satisfaction, waved aloft the expended pad like some sort of animal pelt trophy, while the barber plucked out a few hairs that had evaded the grip of the wax. My underarms received the same painful attention.

My ordeal, however, was not yet over.

Ahmad left the room, and then quietly reappeared proudly holding high a yellow striped jar. "This balm stops hair from growing back," he said, before he had the barber spread the foul smelling cream over my denuded areas. "You're a lucky woman; this is a great improvement over the old ways of monthly plucking or *threading*. I am being kind to you."

A slight tingling sensation swelled to a maddening burn as a triangle of fire spread over my groin, pushing away any thanks I may have had for Ahmad's kindness. I could not hold back my tears or find comfort regardless of how much I squirmed and changed position. Unconcerned with my suffering, Ahmad insisted on leaving the balm to do its work—for a full hour—otherwise, he said, it would be an expensive waste of money.

Over the foul smell of the balm, I occasionally caught a whiff of the pleasant aroma of coffee and tobacco and heard the two men laughing and chatting, interrupting their talk to briefly come to me and inspect their handiwork, apply fresh balm, but not to ask about my comfort or offer consoling words.

After an excruciatingly uncomfortable hour, the barber scraped off expired balm and wiped clean the bared mound and hollows with a cloth. The burning sensation died down, giving me some relief from my torment.

In a large polished metal mirror, I saw myself as others would see me. Although my skin still bore a rash from its ordeal, I was peculiarly pleased with my new appearance, and could understand why many men preferred their women groomed in this manner. I felt young, alluring, and confident that I could seduce my sheik when the time came.

"You have me to thank for the balm," Ahmad confided on our way back to his house. "I discovered that *mehndi* and I am the only purveyor of it. For many years, I brought back from the Orient a lotion to remove warts. I had one here on the side of my face," he said, parting his beard and pointing to a small bare patch. "The wart disappeared and so did the hair—neither grew back—and this gave me the idea for a profitable new use for the balm. I had to disguise its humble origin, so I added tiger bile to give it a strong overpowering smell, and put it in an expensive looking pot. Extremely clever of me to uncover money hidden away in an old remedy, don't you think?

"My Chinese apothecary must think Arabs have many warts," he chuckled[2].

On our return to Ahmad's house, he showed me into a small room with a quarter-bath set in the floor in one corner. Before leaving, he instructed me to "Wash thoroughly, at least twice. The smell of tiger bile is not easily washed away."

I emerged from the soothing water, wrapped a towel around me, and was startled to find Ahmad standing in the doorway. "How long had he been standing there, watching me?" I wondered.

"Follow me. I will escort you to your room," he said, bending down to scoop up my clothes from the side of the bath before I could reach them. Instead of clothes, I held the small towel about me, as best I could, and followed him.

Passing through the archway leading to the courtyard he reached out and unhooked the first key from a row of large iron keys hanging by the side of the door, before continuing briskly to my room. He stood aside to let me pass into the room, then, to my unease, followed in behind me and turned the key in the lock.

"Lie on the bed," he instructed, snatching the towel from my grip.

As though nothing unusual or untoward had happened, he smiled thinly, smoothed down his *djellaba* and said, "Dinner will be served at the sound of the bell."

I was sickened to my stomach and absolutely in no mood to eat anything, particularly with him. However, as the afternoon passed by my moral strength returned. From my tumultuous mind emerged the clear realization that leaving at this instance to return to Jeddah would be impossible and unwise. I could not be certain what Jamaal or his family would think about my raping at the hands of Ahmad. In this country, the reasoning of men and women towards a dishonored woman is unpredictable. Some blame the woman regardless of the circumstances, others understand and console, and I think Jamaal would understand—but not his wife and sisters. Would they not see me as a foolish woman, deservingly sullied, and further belittle and ostracize me?

Furthermore, I had no horse or camel to ride on, and beside, even if I did, traveling alone to Jeddah would be impossibly dangerous.

---

2. Some years later Sheik Ahmad al-Sabur was captured by the Emperor of Ethiopia and executed for the crime of selling arms to Somalian rebel forces, and the secret of the smoothing balm went with him to the grave.

Not surprisingly, I decided I had to keep this part of my life to myself, bury it in my mind as best I could, and reclaim my dignity. I would not be cowed by him or by his despicable doing. For the time being I would act as though nothing had happened, and quietly wait for the right time and place—for I was not above taking revenge.

A graceful and seductive dancer entertained us that evening. Ahmad had hired her to teach her art to the two Indian girls, but on this occasion, she was showing her skills for our enjoyment.

While serving "Tea from China" in delicate porcelain finger bowls one of the Indian girls nervously stumbled when her foot caught the edge of a carpet, sharply clinking the bowls together and spilling some tea. Sheik Ahmad examined the fragile bowls for damage and then apologized for the careless manner in which they served us. "I can assure you that their poor ways will be corrected before they are sold," he said coldly, before proudly informing me that he had "a hard earned reputation to preserve, as a purveyor of only the best and well-instructed slave girls."

At the close of the evening, Ahmad escorted me and the Indian girls back to the courtyard. As he led the way through the open archway, I casually reached out and took my room key from its hook. I walked to my room, and he disappeared into another room on the other side of the courtyard with the two Indian girls. I turned the key in the lock, and settled down for the night.

It was not long before the quiet stillness of the desert night carried their cries through the window and into my tense consciousness. He was no doubt "correcting their ways". How was he doing this? What was he doing to them that made then cry out like that? Surely, it was only Ahmad's way and not the way of others.

I spent a fitful night thinking about, and regretting, how foolish I had been to allow my blind curiosity to launch me on this journey. In the closed and secret world of the harem, would I find myself trapped and helplessly passed around an endless circle of masters, perhaps never to return? Used, and then discarded? And would my new master take pleasure in bending me to his ways, and be so demanding as to find reason to put a camel whip to me? What would happen if I displeased him, would he punish me harshly and cause the desert night to hear my cries?

My visions of romantic interludes with an enraptured sheik rapidly evaporated—and with Kassim gone, plans could not be undone. My course was set; the door had closed behind me.

Someone rattling and pushing against the door awakened me just before dawn. I heard only retreating footsteps when I asked, "Who is there?" Thanks be to Allah, I had the key safe beside me.

Before formally concluding the exchange, Sheik Ahmad handed me a letter of introduction to deliver to my new master and after I halfheartedly thanked him, I handed over his key. "Here is your key. I borrowed it last night," I triumphantly explained, before turning my back to him, and climbing onto the back of my kneeling camel.

As our entourage prepared to depart, my escort, a dark bearded man, pointed out to me a fair-haired girl Ahmad was leading away. "She is the slave Nadya, for whom you have been exchanged," said the man, who, I later learned, was Mustafa the chief eunuch of my new master's harem.

KASRE EL NOUZHA

We traveled by camel from Al-Ta'if to my new master's house in Makram, securely escorted for the overnight journey by Mustafa, the chief eunuch, and four armed guards. I carried with me a side bag of personal belongings: writing instruments, sketchbook, notepaper, clothes the seamstress in Jeddah had made for me, Ahmad's tantra notes, and his letter of introduction.

A camel, with its awkward rocking gait made for a tiring journey. I much preferred to ride a horse than a camel. I could move in the saddle to the stride of a horse, but not a camel. This cumbersome beast compellingly swayed me back and forth, hour after hour, and the monotony of the hot shimmering desert sands provided no distraction. Insidiously, the motion sickened me so much that it overcame my excitement, and when it was time to stop and make camp, I was thankful.

Before darkness fell, after I had rested and enjoyed a cooling drink, I reached into my side bag and took out the letter Ahmad had given me. Taking care that no one saw me, I tilted it to catch the last glow of sunlight, and read:

> *In the Name of Allah, Most Gracious, Most Merciful.*
> *My Tunisian slave Sapphira, who bears this letter to you, has recently studied the Qur'an and has embraced Islam. I ask that you treat her accordingly and reward her for her good diligence.*
> *I plead for your forgiveness and understanding for sending you a less experienced girl than you have sent me.*
> *In your wisdom, do not confuse her lack of skill with a reluctance to please. Her exotic beauty, freshness of spirit, and her eagerness to learn, I am sure, will be more than offsetting.*
> *I encourage you to find comfort with her to the full, with the expectation that I shall be fortunate to take back, to my benefit, a girl imbued with your teachings.*
> *I have recently acquired two unspoiled Pearls of Allah. Both are beautifully formed and eager to serve a new master. They answer well to commands.*

> *Because our long-standing friendship is something I value highly, I offer you first choice and a favorable price. I will be proud to bring them to you so your eyes may judge their virtues.*
> *Sapphira will vouch for your good fortune in being offered these pearls of the Orient.*
> *Please advise within the month of your intentions in the matter of my offer as others are anxious for their company.*
> *Peace be upon you and your brother and Allah's mercy and blessings.*

I passed the letter to Mustafa for safe delivery.

We rested briefly during the night snatching a few welcomed moments of sleep. A small fire kept the night chill at bay, and to catch the damp Mustafa spread a piece of muslin over me supported by poles at each corner. I appreciated his caring, but the efficacy of the cover was lacking and I awoke before dawn, cold and clammy, and moved to join the others around the embers of the fire. Nevertheless, I thanked him profusely, thinking it better to encourage his friendship rather than make complaint.

At daybreak, we quenched our thirst with hot mint tea and ate some dried fruit and *khobz*, freshly baked on the hot stones of the night fire, before we mounted our rides for the final leg of the journey.

Our traveling took us from the central desert plateau through a broad divide in the western coastal mountain range, and down to the shores of the Red Sea.

As we emerged from the low mountains our entourage halted, and with a broad wave of his hand Mustafa announced, "Makram." There in the distance, close to the shore of the sea, was a large spread of buildings—a fair-sized town laid out at the foot of a rocky promontory that jutted out from the coastal hills like a pointing finger, before tumbling into the sea. Along the promontory, lines of green trees traced sharply against the golden brown of the dry hillsides. Mustafa pointed out a large white building set high against the south face of the promontory that would give those looking out long views of the sea to the west, the desert to the east, and the town beneath. Two tall towers, capped with gilded domes, soared over the high surrounding wall, shimmering in the heat of the late morning sun. "That is Sheik Ali's palace, your destination."

I was both surprised and threatened by the enormity of the palace having expected nothing more than a large house and started to imagine how luxurious and colorful, or dark and foreboding, his *Kasre el Nouzha* might be within its walls. And the occupants—what were they doing at this moment, what did they look like, what were they wearing?

As our approach shortened I saw water—that rarest and most precious desert commodity—cascading from cracks and ledges in the rock face above the palace, the flow carefully diverted into a huge overflowing cistern. From there it streamed into irrigation ditches to nourish the long rows of fruit trees I had seen earlier from a distance, before it drained through the stony ground, to find, no doubt, a subterranean passage to the sea.

I welcomed the cooling sea breeze, the tamarisk and spreading acacia trees, and the gracefully tapered cypress trees spiking above them. It was a pleasant change indeed from the barren desert we had traveled through with its jagged rock outcroppings and endless *méréyé* sands.

Creaking wooden doors swung open before us, and our bedraggled and dusty band of travelers filed into the palace. The doors creaked and banged closed behind us with an echo of finality.

We reported at once to the man who was to be my master, Sheik Ali *bin* Shareef al-Saalih[1]. Mustafa found him in a secluded courtyard garden. Much to my disappointment, I was unable to see him clearly. He sat far back in the shade, and the full morning sun glaring in my face dazzled me. I had to be content at this time to hear his disembodied voice giving instructions. "Take refreshment, Mustafa, and then have her bathed. When I sound the gong bring her to the great hall."

Mustafa handed over Ahmad's letter and led me away.

We ate together, saying little to each other. Concerns about my venture and the cool indifferent way the sheik had greeted me, subdued me.

After we had eaten, an African slave woman bathed me under the watchful supervision of Mustafa, who afterwards dabbed fragrant oil through my hair and sat me naked on a bench to await his order. A gong sounded. He quickly wrapped a bright red cotton cloth around me and escorted me into the great hall of the harem. I clutched the cloth closed so it would not billow open as I walked.

Sheik Ali bin Shareef al-Saalih was waiting and reading the letter I had brought with me. After a thoughtful pause, he brusquely commanded me. "Slave Sapphira; reveal yourself, my eyes are curious."

I stood unmoving before him, bashful and restrained.

Mustafa interpreted my hesitation to obey as shyness, and quickly explained to the sheik.

---

1. Ali bin Shareef al Saalih—Exalted son of Shareef the Good

"If that is the cause, some help is required. Talil will encourage you," he said. He had no sooner spoken than the second eunuch rose to his feet, a whip in hand.

However, without lifting his eyes from the letter, the sheik held up his hand. Talil halted in his threatening advance, and I, unwilling to discover if he was prepared to use the whip to persuade me to do my Master's bidding, let the cloth slip off my shoulders and then to my side so that I stood naked before the sheik. Talil sat down.

Sheik Ali walked towards me slowly, casting over my naked body what I imagined to be appraising and calculating eyes—imagined, because I could not bring myself to let my eyes dwell on his. Nevertheless, as he came closer, I did exchange a furtive glance; a glance tinged with the unseemliness of my being there, and when he passed behind me, his *thobe* brushing against my legs, sent a tingling frisson up my spine.

Through lowered eyes, I again saw his feet paused before me, while he leisurely satisfied his curious eyes with what the barber had uncovered, and those other parts of a woman that call out to the eyes and thoughts of men.

Mustafa pushed me down onto my knees, and pressed my head to the carpet with his foot.

A long quiet pause followed, and out of curiosity, to see if they had left, I turned my head to one side and glanced upwards, and was startled to find the sheik looking down at me in thoughtful contemplation, a glimmer of satisfaction showing on his face.

"I look forward to knowing you better, though for now, I am placing you in the well experienced hands of Mustafa, who with his usual thoroughness will see to it that you are ready for that occasion. For your part, you will do as he commands, as though his words are mine," his compelling eyes settling on mine as he spoke, dark eyes set in a kindly bearded face that seemed strangely at odds with his strong commanding voice. Audaciously, I held his eyes with mine, dropping my head back down to the carpet only when driven by an insistent urge to blink.

Whispered conversation followed that I could not hear and then Sheik Ali clearly instructed Mustafa. "She is to have Katana's room, and show her the harem buildings and courtyard later in the afternoon. Bring her to the great hall after sundown. She will take part in the celebrations this evening."

Whether he was speaking to Mustafa or me I did not know, because I kept my head on the carpet, however, before he dismissed us Sheik Ali said, "Pleasing to the eye. Ahmad is a man of his word, a fair exchange indeed."

He did not know, of course, that he would be gazing down on a strikingly beautiful Indian girl, had I not intruded on his affairs. I stayed in that unladylike and submissive position, under the watchful eye of Talil, as Sheik Ali and Mustafa left the room.

Mustafa returned shortly, ordered me to stand up, and thrust a matching set of black harem chalwars and choli at me. "Cover your nakedness and follow me," he said, as though somehow I was responsible for my state of undress.

We passed through the only entrance into the harem—it led from the great hall, passing between an unoccupied guardhouse and the eunuchs' quarters before opening to a sunlit courtyard.

Down the middle of the courtyard ran a string of shallow oblong pools, connected to each other by narrow channels through which silvery water trickled from sparkling pool to sparkling pool reminding me of a Berber crystal necklace I had once seen and coveted. On a stone bench, circled around a pool, sat a beautiful woman unashamedly naked, having her hair groomed by a black woman dressed in colorful African garb. In the center of the pool a fountain spouted water and two naked girls ran in and out of its arching jets laughing and shrieking like excited children.

On each side of the courtyard, a colonnade of slender columns supported latticed Moorish arches, where in the dappled shade cast by the lattice sat other women of various nationalities. Two tended with mehndi the face and eyes of each other; others embroidered and sewed.

Mustafa paused, allowing silent and uncertain faces to dart more than questioning eyes at me, the unwanted intruder, but a friendly wave and a comforting smile from a girl with hair the color of polished copper warmed my welcome. Hesitant smiles from others followed her lead, pushing from my mind unsettling thoughts about the cool reception and the incident with eunuch Talil and his menacing whip.

In the walls set back deep in the shade of the colonnade were doors leading to small rooms. Mustafa led me into one—it would be mine for the next four months.

It was a colorfully furnished room, with a small bed set in an alcove, a long padded bench backed with silk cushions, and a table and chair under a barred window that was cut high in the wall, "but low enough," I thought, "to allow me to see out if I stood on the table." By the side of the bed, hung from the ceiling by three light chains, was a burnished metal cylinder. A rope ran down between the chains and through the cylinder. Some sort of lamp or bell, I reasoned.

The door through which we had entered was set in a large expanse of wooden mashrabiya shutters, to let in light without exposing to view those within. Below these shutters was the long padded bench, thoughtfully placed so that a slave girl could sit and pass the hours away with a view of the courtyard or simply savor any cooling breeze that managed to percolate through the screen.

Mustafa told me to take my rest—he would return in two hours to show me around as Sheik Ali had instructed. He left, sliding a wooden bar into place to lock the door behind him.

I lay down on the bed, exhaustion overcame my curiosity, and I fell asleep to the soothing sounds of the women's voices in the courtyard.

I jolted awake to the sound of Mustafa sliding back the wooden bar and opening the door, my eyes squinting against the burst of sunlight.

"It's dark in here—accept my apology, I should have attended to the shutters earlier," he said, as he moved to the window. He reached through the iron grill that barred them, unbolted them, swung them upwards, and propped them open with a wooden rod. A flood of light and fresh air filled the room.

"Come, I shall show you the harem buildings and facilities and later tonight I will take you to the celebration."

A high walled courtyard contained the buildings and rooms that made up the inner sanctum of the harem. In one corner of the courtyard, overlooked by the eunuchs' quarters, was a large outdoor bath, and inside an adjacent building there were two smaller baths. A domed ceiling, supported by blue and yellow tiled columns, spanned over these indoor baths, and a galaxy of star shaped openings in the domed ceiling cast down beams of misty sunlight that dappled the water with moving light.

Mustafa told me that the smaller of the indoor baths was for soaping and washing, and the larger one for rinsing and soaking. A short submerged tunnel connected the larger indoor bath to the outdoor one, and if the eunuchs raised the iron grill that normally blocked the tunnel, it would be possible to dive down and swim from one bath to the other.

Carefully tended flowerbeds, stone-covered pathways, pools and fountains, filled the rest of the courtyard. It was fabulously luxurious, far in excess of anything I had ever seen or imagined.

At the far end of the courtyard, several wide stone steps led up to a pathway in front of a low stone wall that served to screen a smaller courtyard from view. We mounted the steps and walked beside the wall to a narrow gap that opened to this inner garden. Ahead of me—a massive pair of wood and bronze doors—the entrance to the Master's bedchamber. I looked up, and could just see the gilded domes of the two towers I had noted earlier on my approach to Makram. It seemed to me that there was one at each far corner of the Master's bedchamber and the only entrance to them would be from within that room. Off to one side of this small private courtyard were four apartments and a private bath and toilet for his wives.

"Do you have any questions?" he asked, while escorting me back to my room without showing me the interior of the bedchamber, much to my disappointment.

"Yes Sir. Does the Master have wives?" I asked.

"No. There are no wives here. He has not seen the need to marry. The apartments are empty."

At dusk, Mustafa escorted me to the great hall and to the center of a large sunken floor, where Sheik Ali sat. He rose and stood beside me.

"Please welcome Sapphira into our presence; she is a slave, here to take the place of Nadya. She has traveled far to be here, from the country of Tunisia, and she is a stranger to our Arabian ways but anxious to learn. Patiently teach her, for she is without experience.

"Yasmeen, she is in your care."

A confident, pretty woman of petite stature stepped forward and led me to the side of the room where we sat down together on the padded bench that ran around the walls.

I was relieved with the shortness of my "showing" as I had heard vividly told stories of harem initiation ceremonies where the girl was made to do unseemly things and had unseemly things done to her. I was thankful to be safely at the side of Yasmeen.

"This is a special occasion; we have been preparing for it all day, and have chosen to celebrate with an Egyptian fantasy."

"All for my coming? That is kind of you."

Yasmeen smiled. "Slaves are not given such celebration. No, it is our Master's birthday, and we are honoring him."

Shamed by my naïve and conceited arrogance, my face colored beneath my mehndi. I wanted nothing more at that moment other than to take back my words and forget I had spoken them. Happily, my foolish presumption brought no further comment—Sheik Ali and the festivities claimed attention.

As I gazed into the room from my vantage point, an undeniable scene from the Arabian Nights unfolded before my eyes. I was enthralled. Here was a gathering of *houri*, each hanging on every word and gesture of a handsome and authoritative man, waiting for his commands, and eager to please. Two bare breasted girls sat on the floor, one on each side of him, leaning lightly against his legs. Possibly twins, certainly related—my cynical mind thinking, "matched pair of bookends."

Rings and dangling jewels graced nipples and ears, dark eyes flashed beneath gold sprinkled eyelids, necklaces swung about elegant necks. Taut bellies held brilliants tightly, and ankle bells and bracelets tinkled their beguiling tune. Sparkling *bindi* spaced along eye-lines gave shape and size to the eyes, with a line curving back from the corners adding an exotic Cleopatra look…and I saw the glitter of bindi in other places, places where I never expected to see the glitter of jewels.

Two black women, one I recognized as the harem servant who had bathed me, sat to one side making music by plucking the stringed *'ud*, shaking tambourines, and occasionally tapping gently on a drum.

Colorful sheer cholis and short sheer skirts, proudly worn and parted with deliberate carelessness, replaced the afternoon dress of harem pants and thickly embroidered cholis that I had earlier seen the women wearing in the courtyard. Now, loose diaphanous cholis cascaded over hazily outlined breasts, their draped smoothness disturbed only by the thrust of protruding nipples, and anyone with more than half an eye could see that nothing but woman was under the sheer skirts. The serving girls showed themselves alluringly this way, but only induced restrained touching from the Master. Occasionally he lifted a skirt, glided a hand over skin and under silk, or straddled a girl vulnerably across his knees—suggestively, if nothing more—and from the sultry pace of the girls I knew that they were thinking about less restrained behavior later in the quiet of his bedchamber.

A magnificent feast ensued, with trays brought in piled high with delicacies—kebabs, pastries, fruits, sweetmeats and treats of every kind. Later, several of the girls danced charmingly and towards the end of the evening, they rolled back the carpet and played a rousing game, something like alquerques, using the checkered tiled floor as a make-do board, and themselves as living pieces. The Sheik, whom the girls had carefully blindfolded, called out moves, and one by one, amid much cheating and laughing, girls eliminated themselves from the game whenever they were moved onto a forbidden square, until only one girl remained. With a flourish, she untied his blindfold and her choli, and dropped them to the floor, revealing jeweled tassels dangling from pierced nipples. She finished with a short dance of victory, beguilingly pulled a veil across her face, and left the ensemble, her sassy bejeweled breasts proudly bobbing up and down with the motion of her steps. She had won the Master's *calling*.

I reasoned that the repressive culture of *purdah* that keeps women shrouded from the eyes and notice of men, releases from within these same women an intense eroticism—when behind closed doors and harem walls. Perhaps this display of eroticism was a private rebellion against purdah, and the scene I witnessed could be a testament to this, for I had never seen or fully imagined such a seductive and suggestive occasion. Certainly, the women were slave concubines, and, as my mother said, "Had no choice in the matter," nevertheless, I did not sense reluctance or coercion. All I saw was subtle enthusiasm, a willingness to please, a release of repressed womanly urges and desires that rose to the surface, peculiarly brought forward and intensified by the pervading presence of the sheik's immense masculinity.

LESSONS

A eunuch is often portrayed as a well put together ebony skinned man, bared to the waist, bulging arms folded across a glistening oiled chest rippling with muscles, a whip thrust through his belt to enforce his will on the women of the harem—his shortcomings concealed by baggy trousers.

Those sharing this image would be sorely disappointed in Mustafa. Indeed, he was bared to the waist, wore the requisite trousers, and had a whip at hand, but instead of the barreled chest and rippling muscles here was a podgy middle-aged man with a broad roll of fat where his youthful waist once resided—the soft fleshy build of a leisured man accustomed to good living. His appearance would improve in the eyes of many if he wore an all-concealing djellaba.

Eunuchs, throughout the ages, have garnered well-earned reputations for treating harem slave women severely and cruelly. I reasoned that revenge moved them in that direction. They would see the women under their care as the reason for their own mutilation. A mutilation inflicted upon them that rendered them forever impotent and unable to release their needs, needs that the women of the harem would unconsciously arouse while the eunuchs watched over them and readied them for another man's enjoyment.

I felt that Mustafa was not of this vein—but I did not trust Talil. I would be careful.

"Remove your clothes," and mindful of the whip at his side, I hurriedly obeyed his abrupt order without protest.

He sorted through my clothes with the handle of his whip, offhandedly flipping to one side my undergarments. "Put them away. You will not wear any of those while you are here. Now come, set your mark here," he said, holding out a dipped pen and pointing to the end of a column of names and signs in a book he held open—a calendar by the look of it.

After slight hesitation, I wrote my new name—Sapphira.

"Oh, you can write can you? So you are one of those clever girls, are you?" he said, sarcastically.

"I can only write my name," I replied, not wishing to build on his obvious sense of inferiority in this matter of writing.

"Before we start I will let you know that I keep this roster, a record of menses and callings to the Master's bedchamber. I have great influence over when and whom he chooses for company. When might I expect your bleeding?"

"It should be two weeks hence, Sir, but I cannot be certain. My menses are not regular."

He wrote a strange symbol in a column opposite my name in his roster and said; "You will have nights with the Master before then."

"Correct me if I am mistaken, but having come from Ahmad you could not be a virgin—he is too shrewd to swap a virgin for our well deflowered Nadya—and I assume that he used his marvelous balm on you," he said, kneeling down on one knee and slipping his fat fingers deeply between my thighs. Naturally, I leaned forward, pulled back slightly and squeezed my thighs against his hand, but apart from a questioning upward glance from him, he ignored my unintentional protest and continued unperturbed. "I feel a thorough denuding. Often when less knowledgeable slavers prepare women for sale they forget that a woman has ravines as well as hills and lay bare just the mons, but Ahmad knows better, there is nothing further for me to do here—you are as smooth as a rose petal."

He moved behind me. "Give me one of your feet."

Kneading my foot, he announced, "You have hard skin on the back of your heels. With young lively girls like you there is no telling where they may end up," he said, smiling. "I will give you a pumice stone and some oil to take back to your room. Smooth away the rough skin; I want your heels to feel as smooth as the rest of you.

"Now tell me, are you aware of the night ways of a harem slave girl, did he teach you?"

"No sir," I replied, offering as explanation for my ignorance of the night ways one of my well rehearsed answers that fitted the story of my enslavement. "I had been married for only two months before I was captured. The corsairs killed my husband." I paused briefly here, and tried to look somewhat unfortunate and sad. "They took me straight away to the slave market in Jeddah, and sold me to Sheik Ahmad. He had no time for me because of his travels and trading. I have had no instruction in the night ways of a harem."

"How old are you?" he asked, suspiciously.

"Eighteen, Sir," I answered, realizing too late that my untruthful answer—twenty-three was closer to the truth—had opened a chink in my story.

He pulled away, to take a full look at me. "Hmm, you look older than eighteen. You came to marriage late.

"However, it's not important. Let us proceed. And call me Mustafa, not sir, for I, too, am a slave, here to serve in ways not of my choosing."

Greatly relieved that he dropped the question of my age, I relaxed somewhat as he continued with my introduction to the ways.

"Consider yourself fortunate that Sheik Ahmad had little time for you. His teaching methods are crude and severe. He is too eager to use the whip to encourage learning. You will find my ways more skillful and sophisticated and more to your liking, but we will have to start from the beginning because two months of marriage is too short a time to learn the ways of the marriage bed, never mind that of the harem. Here the ways of the bed are different and more varied.

"Sheik Ali has ordered me to acquaint your mind and body with these ways and has permitted also for this whip to be put to you should you cause trouble or are less than diligent in learning. Fortunately for you, I am a patient man, unlike Ahmad, and not over-eager to chastise you," he said, slapping the whip handle sharply into his palm, the smacking sound and dancing thongs emphasizing the possibility that if I overwhelmed his patience, the thongs would not be dancing in the air.

"Now, it is not intended that you always enjoy or wish for what is demanded of you—that is the lot of a slave—even so, you will be ordered to do only what is possible for a willing girl to do, although you may at first find some of them unusual, awkward, and distasteful. However, you will obey his orders no matter what. The laws of the land do not reach through the walls of the harem; here there are no laws against his wishes, you yield to them or take the consequences. If you do not yield to him, I will take it to mean deliberate obstinance on your behalf and treat you to a good whipping, and if that is not sufficient to correct your ways, then other more painful persuasions will be used to remind you of your obstinacy and encourage change in your ways."

Following this short threatening tirade I allowed a moment of thoughtful silence to pass, time enough to make a face as though about to shed tears. "It frightens me when I think that the Master could disapprove of me, and order those things done to me," I said pleadingly, in an attempt to put myself in his guardianship, make him father me, and win his sympathy.

"That is why I am here with my skills and knowledge; to show girls how to please the Master. You have nothing to worry about; you have well formed womanly virtues that will override innocence and inexperience. You will please him."

In my mind I was not sure, whether "you will please him" was a softly spoken order or an opinion.

"And now I will continue where Ahmad left off, but before we start, I will tell you that you are a beguiling girl and our Master is quite overjoyed at his good fortune in having you here. You will be a frequent visitor to his bedchamber. My roster and the Master's desire to see more of you will ensure that, but do not be concerned if he does not call you for a few days—he will not want to show to others his great eagerness for you.

"Now let us start. It is time for your afternoon bathing; I shall show you how we do it here.

"When you were bathed shortly after you arrived it was sufficient only to remove the dust of your journey for your showing. What I will show you now is the more thorough cleansing required of all harem females in the Master's service. Remember, a woman spoils quickly after bathing; she can be sour again in less than an hour, and that is why I insist on your frequent bathing and why the Master has provided these luxurious baths for your use. Make full use of them, a woman cannot bathe too often."

I stood naked in the shallow water of the small soaping bath while he scooped up several pitchers of water and poured them over me before soaping me down from head to toe. He washed my hair, probed my openings, my every cranny and cleavage, and followed up with a cursory rinsing.

Was my new master watching from behind the screen as Ahmad had said he did from time to time? I did not ask, or look in that direction, although I did notice the screened-off room.

"Now rinse off thoroughly in there," he said, pointing to the larger and deeper bath. "While relaxing here, after afternoon bathing, many of the girls draw on the hookah. It is lit for your enjoyment on these occasions; one of the servants will pass it around.

"What I have shown you, you are to do yourself every afternoon, no less, whether you are on my calling roster or not. Is that understood?"

"Yes, Mustafa."

"Dry yourself and come back to my room and I will put on your mehndi."

I dried myself and left for his room, dressed in nothing more than a towel over my arm. "Had he been a whole man I would be going to his room for more than mehndi," I thought, having sensed that he found it arousing bathing me the way he did.

"Brush your hair till it shines and flows free," he said, handing me a brush and a brass comb.

I went to work on my hair. It was badly tangled and knotted from the journey and washing, although I soon had it separated, shiny, and smooth.

"For this evening I will mehndi you, however, this is something you will do yourself, or have one of the servants do. Try different things. It is an art—there are no rules," he said, as he approached with a tray of bottles and jars in hand.

I was surprised to learn from Mustafa that we had servants to attend us. Among the women were two black slaves who were there to assist in our bathing, grooming and dressing, should we so desire.

He applied liberal amounts of black *kohl* and malachite green to my eyes, rouge to my cheeks, painted my lips with *cochineal*, and smoothed rough edges from my nails. Not wanting to offend, I told him how pleased I was with my appearance when he held a mirror up to me, while thinking to myself that I looked garish and painted, and could do better on my own.

"Now,"—he often started his sentences with this word—"you will learn how to use oil and fragrance. Always use oil sparingly so your clothes will not stick to you. The purpose is to burnish and polish your skin, not hold your clothes in place," he said, smiling. "It is particularly attractive on breasts and buttocks, but I also want to see it used in other places where it can help catch the Master's eye and attract his scrutiny.

"Can you think of other places?'

"My face?"

"Yes, your face of course, and your legs and feet. And don't forget why your mons was smoothed. Do that place too. Now, lie over my knees."

He oiled my shoulders, back and buttocks and down the back of my legs, rubbing vigorously with long strokes followed by small circular ones, as though polishing a piece of fine furniture.

"Now, your breasts. Kneel here, between my legs," he said, pointing to the floor between his parted legs.

Mustafa took what I thought was an overly long time oiling my breasts and applying rouge to my nipples; I was sure he was taking advantage of me for his own enjoyment.

"Your breasts still have the look and feel of youthfulness about them, deliciously firm and not overly bountiful. Add to this the interesting beauty that comes from your mixed blood and I must venture that you will indeed be an intriguing gift for our Master to open," his choice of the word open, deliberate or otherwise, not passing me by unnoticed.

Flattering afternoon sunlight reflecting upwards from the polished marble floor outlined my breasts, and I thought they looked enticing and without doubt "irresistibly alluring" to a man. I was pleased with what I saw—my nipples proudly erect on glistening mounds.

"I see that your nipples have not been pierced," he said, pinching a nipple and stretching it away from the breast while twisting it painfully back and forth. "I will wait to see how well they hold jewelry before I do anything, but from the way they stand I doubt they will need a visit from my silver needle, however, they are somewhat pale in color.

"Smelling and tasting sweet at all times is important and something I insist upon from Sheik Ali's girls," he said, bringing to mind my mother's advice about helping nature with fragrances, "but remember, never put perfume in your openings or on your nipples, it tastes bitter. It is more than sufficient to put small dabs around them, and on your neck, hands and thighs.

"Now come forward for a little secret of mine—part your legs." He dipped his finger into a small jar and offered it to my lips to taste. The sweetness of honey and the coolness of menthol spread through my mouth. Again, he dipped his finger into the jar, and with his other hand parting me, he placed a dab of the sticky mixture on that most sensitive part of a woman. "Just a little," he advised, "just a hint of sweetness is all that is required, no stickiness. I have also cassia, *ylang-ylang* and oil of jasmine; all of them taste sweet and can be used there should you prefer."

I knew of the intriguing aphrodisiac powers ascribed to ylang-ylang, and I decided that if I had to be "flavored"—and not wanting to taste like a mint *bonbon*—then the nectar of ylang-ylang would be my choice.

He walked around me, lifted and fondled my breasts, supposedly to inspect my rouging, but more thoroughly and lingering than necessary for that purpose. He ran his fingers through my hair. "You are now ready to please your Master," he announced, "but I have more to show you, and that is how to present yourself in the Master's bedchamber.

"We do not conceal his possessions from his eyes. I arrange carefully his fine furniture and put valuable artifacts and vases on display. I hang his precious carpets on walls and spread them over the floors, and I show him his girls with the same care. Not that I intend to hang you on the wall or spread you on the floor, although I could," he said, with a chuckle as his hand reached out and rested on my knee, "however, you must show yourself to best effect. That is why we color your lips, rouge your breasts, remove your hair from certain parts, and teach you to present yourself so that he may see clearly the opportunities and make wise choices for his pleasures."

He led me to the center of the room and pointed to a small rug.

"Kneel before me as though I am your Master.

"Good.

"Now, spread your knees apart while keeping your feet together, and place your hands on the floor beside your feet. Lean backwards a little. Now throw your head back and shake your shoulders to free your hair and jostle your breasts. Raise your hips. Keep them high and push them forward."

He paused in his instructions for a moment as I held my pose. "Encouraging…for an inexperienced girl.

"Now I will show you a variation of that position. Raise your arms over your head and lie back till your head touches the floor."

I started to lean backwards and suddenly lost balance and toppled onto my back, my knees lifting up from the floor. For a moment, I cringed and closed my eyes, expecting to feel the sting of the whip. Instead, he laughed at my awkward predicament and helped me back onto my knees. I laughed with him.

"Try again. Spread your knees apart, toes touching. This time first sit back on your feet; that will stop you from toppling over. Raise your arms high over your head and hook your thumbs together. Lean backwards, slowly, until your head and hands touch the floor behind you. Now, raise your hips and chest to make a smooth arch from your knees to your hands, letting your hands slide back along the floor as you raise yourself. Your breasts should be uppermost, at the top of the arch. We call this 'making the bow'," he said, as the handle of his whip traced the curved path from the front of my thighs, over my hips and breasts, and down my neck. "You show well in this position, use it often.

"And there is no need to abandon modesty when you present yourself—jewelry and clothes may be worn. In fact, I think it often enhances your presentation if you wear some. In the harem wardrobe, we have fascinating clothes and adornments that enhance a woman's natural allure, and have no concerns; if they obstruct his course, he will remove them.

"There is one more position to show you today. Kneel again, and turn around, face away from me.

"Now, raise your hands straight above your head as before but this time roll forward until your hands touch the floor in front of you. Raise your buttocks, and arch your back downwards so your breasts just touch the floor. Keep your forehead and hands flat on the floor in front of you, and your knees and feet apart enough to invite the Master to kneel between them," he said, tapping my feet farther apart with his foot.

"We call this 'offering the peach'.

"Excellent, a beautiful and promising beginning," he declared.

"Stand up, and tell me about your conversion to Islam," he asked, with a smirk that hinted at his disbelief. "Your faith could cause a lamentable waste of your beauty."

"It was Ahmad's idea," I replied. "He taught me from the Qur'an." I then recited the first verse.

> "Praise is to God, Lord of the two Worlds.
>
> The most merciful and most forgiving.
>
> Lord of the Day of Judgment.
>
> It is you who we adore and in whom we seek help.
>
> Guide us along the straight path.
>
> The Path of those who are righteous.
>
> Not that of those who suffer your wrath.
>
> Or of those who stray."

Mustafa raised his eyebrows, obviously surprised, and asked questions about my new faith. I answered them easily as my upbringing in Tunisia made me far from ignorant about the teachings of Mohammed.

"It is unlike Ahmad to encourage a girl's conversion; he values infidels highly since they fetch higher prices and their enslavement is condoned. I thought for a moment that maybe your conversion was a matter of convenience, or even a false claim, to avoid the bedchamber obligations of a nonbeliever. Your answers to my questions were complete and show knowledge of the Holy Book. I apologize for my doubts.

"Come here, turn around."

He kneaded my buttocks in the same way that he had done earlier with my breasts. "You are so nicely rounded. Such is the pity, because laid over the Damascus bolster you would look enticing enough for a king."

I felt vulnerable as a woman assuming these positions before a man, naked as I was. Nevertheless, the knowledge that what I was doing was a secret held within the walls of this harem—and would remain there forever unless I chose otherwise—buoyed my spirits. Gradually, as the lessons progressed, I forgot about my nakedness, and felt free, uninhibited, and not at all ashamed or humiliated. Further emboldened by the absence of anyone I knew, or anyone who would ever know or meet my family, I grew proud and confident in what I was showing.

"That is all for today. In your room, you must make these positions every day and practice rising from them slowly and gracefully. That is difficult to do, it requires strength and agility, but you have the strength and suppleness of a young girl and will master the art." With a comforting smile on his face he added, "And no more toppling over!"

"Have you ever *pleasured* a man?" he asked quickly, in a casual way.

"Pleasured?" I asked, in an effort to add to the aura of innocence and helplessness I was trying to create.

"Then that must be your next lesson. Ali always enjoys a woman that way," he advised.

I felt a small sadness for Mustafa. A man in an unfortunate situation and condition not of his choosing, acting out the part without conviction. "Harmless," I thought—though I was not ready to test the possibility—I would obey him.

SANGARA

Although I had become conscientious and even enthusiastic in learning and practicing my lessons—I rather enjoyed them—I was not looking forward to this morning session, knowing what it was about.

After he had casually lifted high the hem of my modest morning *abaya*—his perfunctory check for forbidden undergarments—we sat on the floor in the middle of the room opposite each other, Mustafa having earlier placed several items there: a bowl of eggs, two ivory phalluses—one with the bulbous *glans* missing—and a lighted candle.

He began. "Pleasuring is the art of using your mouth and tongue to excite a man."

"I kissed my husband in that way," I anxiously interrupted, knowing very well what he meant.

He laughed. "You have kissed a man. That is not pleasuring in the Arab way. To pleasure your Master you must take his manhood into your mouth, play your tongue and lips over it, and draw him back and forth, as you would with your hips if you were astride him, until he is relieved of his lust. That is our way of pleasuring," he said, in his best patient voice.

"As I told you yesterday, this is one of Sheik Ali's favorite ways of enjoying a woman, one he is particularly fond of, and unquestionably he will expect to delight in the embrace of your willing mouth. So, under my tutelage you will learn to do it well.

"Before we start I will show how you will clean your mouth and teeth beforehand," he said, showing me a small bowl filled with reddish-brown fiber, "using palm fiber mixed with crushed leaves from the sidr tree."

Rolling up a small wad of fiber from the bowl, he rubbed my teeth and gums with the coarse damp fiber and afterwards probed between each tooth with a sharp splinter of wood. "A quick rinse and you are ready," he said, offering me the beaker of clean water. "Do this every morning and afternoon and whenever you are called to the bedchamber.

"Now,"—there was that word again—"your Master is smooth and easily scratched, so you must never let your teeth touch him unless done delicately such as in *parshvatoddashta*."

"Parsh...va...tasha...that is a mouthful. What does it mean?"

"A witty choice of words," he replied, with a hearty laugh, "but save them for later when I get to *sangara*[1]."

I smiled back at him, a puzzled blank smile, because I did not know what sangara meant either, and I was not inclined to ask and reveal that my humor came from ignorance.

"However, to answer your question," he continued, still smiling at my accidental humor. "Parshvatoddashta is when you gently grasp the head of his manhood in your hand, and then clamp your lips tightly about the shaft, first on one side then the other, taking great care that your teeth do not hurt him. That is parshvatoddashta (Biting at the Sides).

"Now, lean over towards me and open your mouth."

He ran a finger over my teeth.

"You have some sharp edges in the wrong places. We don't want to scratch the Master's tender skin and offend the tantric teachings, do we?" he said, mockingly.

"No, Sir."

"And it's Mustafa, not Sir," he reminded me.

"Then, I am sure you will not object if I attend to them. Come closer. Open your mouth," he said, at the same time reaching for a small narrow stone.

A loud scratching sound filled my head with each stroke of the stone as he ground away the offending edges of my teeth. Grit stuck to my tongue as though I had eaten dry sand, sharp twinges shot through my mouth, while tears waited but did not run. This unpleasant business continued until his finger found nothing but satisfying smoothness.

"That is all; I have finished. Rinse your mouth," he said, handing back the beaker of water.

---

1. From Ahmad's Tantra instructions: When you sense that his orgasm is imminent, you swallow up the whole penis, sucking and working upon it with lips and tongue until he spends. This is "Sangara" (Swallowed Whole).

My parched mouth welcomed the slaking, but my teeth panged from the assault of the cold water, while my inquiring tongue explored my new smoothness.

"Now we will proceed with the sangara lesson that you have so patiently waited for. Remove your clothes. I want to see your breasts while you learn this."

I unbuttoned the top of my abaya, and pulled my arms free. To his satisfaction, it fell loose and gathered around my waist.

He reached for the ivory phallus and handed it to me. It lay cold and lifeless in my hand, disgustingly large and ugly.

"Wet it down the sides and along its whole length with your tongue and lips and then take the end into your mouth."

"Well…" he inquired, impatient with my hesitation. "Just take it in…far enough for your lips to settle comfortably behind the head."

"That's better. We call that narrow part the 'neck of the bed-snake'. The underside there is the most pleasurable part to a man. Always find that place with your tongue, then, move your tongue slowly around and back and forth.

"Do not forget what I have just told you. It is precious knowledge I share, which will serve you well.

"Now, kneel up and bend forwards towards the floor. Hold the flat end of the ivory against the floor and let your lips find the neck again."

I felt the handle of his whip pressing into the center of my back, sufficiently firmly that I could not rise from my position had I wanted to.

"Good. Now, move your head up and down in short strokes taking in about half its length before you pull back. Never allow it to slip from your mouth. Asian girls who have studied the tantric ways call this *amrachushita*[2] (sucking clean a mango-stone). Never suck too eagerly, that will cause your Master discomfort and spoil his pleasure. Draw on him gently, just enough to keep him from leaving your lips.

"Now, when your Master is ready to give you his issue, take him further into your mouth, and when he erupts, swallow his seed. It's as simple as that.

"How do you tell when he is about to release? It is a matter of judgment and experience, but others have told me that Ali gives a slight shudder and a taste

---

2. From Ahmad's Tantra instructions. And now, fired by passion, you take his penis deep into your mouth, pulling upon it and sucking vigorously, as though you are stripping clean a mango-stone. This is "Amrachushita" (Sucking a Mango).

of what is to come when he is close to issue. That is the moment when you lean into him and take in his whole length, until your lips touch his bush, and then give him deep strokes until he releases. Some call it burying the sword, I call it a girl growing a moustache," he said, laughing and then sobering quickly. "Burying is not easy to do at first, but the skill will come to you little by little in your eagerness to please."

I did not share his pretentious assumption of eagerness to please, for I had never voiced such a desire. I resolved to do only what was necessary to stay out of trouble, avoid the whip and find words for my journal—nothing more, nothing less. An eagerness to please was not my motivation. However, I did quote from Sheik Ahmad's letter saying, "Do not confuse my lack of skill with a reluctance to please." He nodded back his understanding.

"I shall mention that to the Master.

"Look at your nipples; they are as hard as pebbles. Just as I thought, you will also get pleasure from this; you are well suited for it."

It was the chill in the air.

"Now we will proceed with the next part of your sangara lesson, and this may be the last thing for you to master before going to his bed."

He reached for an egg from the basket and with his other hand the phallus without the head. He instructed me to drip hot candle wax onto the scooped out end of the phallus, and then he quickly planted the egg in the pool of hot wax and allowed it to harden and hold the egg in place, making the phallus seem whole again. With an awl, he made a hole in the end of the shell, and using a short hollow stem sucked out the yellow yolk, spitting it into an empty bowl, leaving the white of the egg in the shell. I needed no explanation.

"This is one of my little inventions. It is incredibly realistic, and this makes it more so," he said, guiding a tiny pinch of salt through the hole in the shell and stirring it in with a short twig.

"You will now learn to suck out and swallow the white of the egg without breaking the shell.

"Close your eyes—lessons are better learned with the eyes closed—and imagine that I am the Master," he said, taking his invention in hand and holding it down and out from himself.

"Now, draw your mouth gently over the egg and close your lips around the shaft. Keep your teeth away from the egg and suck gently. The idea is to drain the egg without breaking the shell."

I started to gag.

"No, no, no. Take small swallows, not one large one. Don't save it in your mouth," he advised.

"When you can do this without breaking the egg I will consider you fit to pleasure him," he said, as he went about draining the yolk from another egg.

I broke one egg and drained two others, gagging each time as the egg white ran to the back of my throat. I choked on pieces of broken shell as well, however, my partially successful efforts seemed to satisfy Mustafa as to my potential proficiency, and no further lessons were called for.

To court his favor I congratulated him on the cleverness of his invention.

"I have other inventions," he proudly told me, pointing to a closed wooden box, "that I would be willing to share with you, if you were not a believer," he said, rather ruefully.

"That is all for today—back to your room for your rest, and don't forget to work on those heels of yours."

Kneeling at his side, I cautiously placed a hand on his knee, and thanked him profusely for taking the time to share his valuable knowledge with me. He shook his head in acknowledgment and smiled back at me distantly, perhaps thinking of how he would have taught me these things had he been a whole man.

Mustafa escorted me back to my room and I sat down alone on the padded bench feeling sick to the stomach from the choking and gagging. Furthermore, I found the words "bury" and "swallow" extremely troubling—I had to take Sheik Ali further along than I had ever taken Jamaal.

And in what other ways did Sheik Ali "enjoy a woman"? Would I be further demeaned and degraded to nothing more than an alluring vessel for his seed?

Unnerved by the realization that I had to know a man this way—a man I scarcely knew—made me want nothing more than to go back to Jeddah and sleep safely away from these things in my own bed.

HENNAED

Next afternoon, after siesta, Mustafa sent one of the servants to bring me to his quarters.

He pointed to a long narrow table, narrow enough to be a bench if it were not so high. "Undo your choli and lie down here, on your back."

The servant disappeared and returned with a small pot cradled in a thick towel. I recognized the smell as soon as she entered the room—hot beeswax. What more was there to do to me?

Mustafa pulled up a stool, sat himself down beside me, and pulled aside my loosened choli.

"Ahmad has prepared you well, but I have a small improvement to make."

Using a small brush dipped in the hot wax, he painted circles around my nipples, carefully leaving the areolas and the nipples unpainted and exposed.

At the snap of his fingers, the servant took away the wax and brought to him another, smaller porcelain pot. "Henna," he offered by way of explanation. "The dark brown color that comes from this Persian Black will look well against your skin. It will improve the allure of your breasts when you are not rouged. Our Master will favor them darkened."

Using a wood spatula, he spread the greenish-black paste over my unwaxed areolas and nipples. "It will take some time to give a good rich color."

The servant stayed with me, occasionally squeezing drops of lemon juice onto the drying henna and smearing the revived paste around with her finger.

An hour or so later, Mustafa returned and in his usual abrupt manner ordered me to sit up.

Holding a cloth under my breasts, he shook off the curled flakes of dried henna. "Wash them," he ordered the servant, and with a bowl of cold water and a damp cloth, she removed the last traces of henna, the cold water arousing my nipples nicely. Mustafa peeled off the thin translucent wax masks and lifted my breasts.

"Pretty, very pretty. The color suits you much better than rouge. When they have faded too much I will henna them again." The servant nodded her approval while giving me a gentle smile.

"Tonight in the great hall show them peeping over your choli, our Master will be pleased with my work."

Before leaving the room, he instructed the servant. "Show her how to roll down and fold back her choli for tonight."

THE BEDCHAMBER

This afternoon Mustafa took me to the bedchamber to continue my introduction to the ways. He came to my room smiling and in good humor telling me that I was to take the place of Hortensia on his roster for tonight. "He asked about you, I am certain you will be called. You will offer him more than food tonight," he smiled. "But before that, we must go to the bedchamber to finish your instruction. Follow me."

Mustafa pushed open the heavy bronze doors to Sheik Ali's bedchamber, the heart of a harem girl's existence. Ahead of me, behind a large intricately carved mashrabiya screen, laid an intimidatingly opulent room resplendent with painted archways and ceilings, spiraled columns and marble floors, and brilliantly colored silks and damasks. And against walls and between columns colorful rugs draped down, their patterns mirrored in a shallow reflecting pool carved into the marble floor.

From behind the entrance screen led a narrow walkway, marked in the floor by lines of contrasting marble mosaic, between which ran a long carpet. Where the narrow carpet ended the lines of mosaic tiles opened out into a large circle before the bed, clear except for a small round carpet at its center.

The Master's bed, square and easily large enough to sleep three or four, stood on a raised dais. Four wooden pillars at each corner supported an ornately carved and painted canopy and to one side hung many ropes each ending in a large colorful tassel. On the bed lay a polished silk cover, the color of rubies and wine, stitched with gold thread into a pattern of squares. Sewn to the center of each square was an iridescent teardrop pearl—"perhaps the tears of captive girls who had laid there", I imagined. From a ring set high in the ceiling a white silk canopy swooped down over the bed and in my mind I saw myself on the bed with the white canopy draw closed around it, surrounding me in a misty cloud of seclusion, a lover by my side intent on seduction.

Cushions, plump rolls, and puffy pillows at the head of the bed promised sumptuous comfort, in stark contrast to the promise held by a coiled whip that hung on a corner post, its leather handle tooled into the form of an erect phallus.

For light, perforated brass lanterns hung by chains from the ceiling, and there were candleholders set on floor and tables. As well, there were several windows, cut through the thick stone walls, but high enough to keep prying eyes from breaching the privacy of the bedchamber. Tightly shuttered, they kept out the cold and the *khamsin* dust, opened they allowed in cooling breezes, depending on needs called for by the season.

On one side of the walkway, a huge carpet held a scattering of silk cushions and a large bolster. On the opposite side, despite the Holy Qur'an forbidding illustration of the human form, carved bas-reliefs depicted nude women posed in suggestive ways. These bas-reliefs formed the backdrop to a small sunken bath in which a submerged marble shelf served as a seat. Cakes of soap, sponges and vials of oils and perfumes in ornate bottles, arranged around the edge, were in easy reach of the bathers. Wisps of mist floated over the surface of the water and I later learned that burning charcoal cleverly heated the bath from below, which explained this mist.

If you are from a more temperate country, you may be surprised to learn of a heated bath in a hot desert climate, but here days could be stifling hot, and after sundown, a determined chill could set in, often accompanied by a cool sea breeze. A private bath, never mind a heated bath, was the epitome of luxury. I had never before seen so much water in a household, reflecting pools and private baths were uncommon, and by any measure an expression of extreme wealth.

A small wooden door, set in the stone wall, opened to the toilet, which was outside in a high-walled room open to the skies. A second similar door opened to a hallway leading to the rear of the wives apartments, so a wife could come and go to the bedchamber without chance of anyone in the main courtyard seeing her. An open arched entranceway led to the Master's wardrobe and dressing room, another to a storage room for cottons, candles and lamp oil, and yet another opened to a dark passageway leading to the base of one of the gilded towers. There at the end of the darkness, was the most feared room in the entire complex—the *erga*.

ERGASTULA

Mustafa's smirk and forbidding tone of voice gave a sinister introduction to the horrors of the erga as he informed me that "Here is where the Master or his eunuchs chastise errant slave girls for breaking the rules of the harem, or for not serving him to his satisfaction. Please enter."

Carved into the stone wall in large flowing script, were the eight rules of the harem. Mustafa told me forcefully, even with glee, that he would bring me back here if I broke any of the rules. I clearly recall unquestioned obedience and submission, always accommodate him, never spill his seed, and bestow undivided pleasure. In my previous years of marriage, it seemed that I had broken most of the rules at one time or other and I thought some of the rules, such as not passing wind or yawning in his presence, were petty and easily broken, and others vague. And what was his measure of undivided pleasure? Was I not permitted to share or show pleasure while giving it to him, or did it mean something else? And could it be that some of the rules were deliberately vague so that slight or imagined causes could see a girl brought to the erga?

Deeper inside the cool chamber, caught in shafts of light streaming through the high windows, was a disturbing display of silk whips, some rattan canes, loose cords of various lengths arranged neatly in a row, and a narrow metal collar with rings attached to it. A branding iron, tipped with finely worked silver lay across a small wrought iron brazier filled with black unburned charcoal.

"We call that one the scorpion," he said, pointing proudly to a sturdy whip that had a single braided thong. "It was a favorite of Ali's father; we kept the name in his honor. It has a nasty sting to its tail. And this one," he said, picking up one that burst to several thinner thongs, "is for here."

A tingling quiver followed the whip as he traced it over my bosom.

A pair of the infamous Turkish breast cups hung from a wooden post, their tightening chains dangling loose. "Exceptionally painful," was Mustafa's callous remark, delivered with a smile, as he pushed the polished metal cups to one side with the whip, making them ring like bells when they swung back together. I took some small comfort from the shower of dust that slid off the polished metal—they had not seen use for a long time.

Satisfied with his introduction, he put the whip back in its place.

Embedded iron rings protruded from two white alabaster restraining columns, and other rings and hooks were set in the walls at various heights. Leather wrist bindings dangled from two of them and beneath one, lying on the floor, an iron bar with shackles at each end. He saw me staring at it. "To spread the legs," he casually advised.

Mustafa opened the dust-covered lid of a partitioned wooden box without explanation, and revealed its contents: carved ivory phalluses arranged in order of increasing size, and other items whose uses were left to my vivid imagination, now in turmoil with disturbing thoughts of painful and thoroughly indecent torment.

"You no doubt realize by now that I am most important to you," he said, taking a deep breath and puffing out his chest like a strutting pigeon before picking up a cane. Waving it at the list of rules and flexing it between his hands threateningly, he said, "Chief eunuchs are entrusted to decide with what, and how, you will be disciplined. Eunuch Talil and I make sure that a visit here is not quickly or easily forgotten."

I had always enjoyed the company of the men I had known, few though they were, and I was disheartened and disillusioned by the realization that Satan-minded men had callously and purposely crafted such heinous instruments and devices of chastisement especially for use on women. I noticed that in the presence of these devices Mustafa's temperament stiffened and became dominating and cruel towards me. How was it possible that men, who turn to us in our beds with love and affection and make us revered mothers of their children, seem at other times disposed to mistreat us and hold us in such low regard? Was this a hidden dark side of Arab men—one that I would come to know?

"Now that you have seen all and are undoubtedly inspired to please, we will complete your instructions." He led me back to the huge bedchamber doors.

"We have traditions and customs to follow when a slave girl is serving her master in the bedchamber. The origins of many have been lost over time, but their purpose will be clear to you. We can thank the Turks and Persians for most of these traditions for they were keepers of great harems. We will start today with some simple requirements.

"When you enter through these doors you disrobe down to your night garments behind this screen," he began, pointing to the tall mashrabiya screen intricately carved from acacia wood, "and then walk around to here," he said, pointing to the start of the carpet, "and drop to your knees. Then you will crawl on your hands and knees along this carpet until you reach the round kneeling mat at the foot of the bed. There you will present yourself in any of the ways I have shown you, and await your Master's commands. If he summons you to bed, you enter at the foot-end, lifting the covers over you and crawling up towards him. Never enter from the side; that is only for a wife to do. If you are here before your Master, then you kneel at the foot of the bed, facing it. When he enters the bedchamber, do not turn around to greet him; wait for his commands. If he orders you to leave the bedchamber, then walk backwards to the door. Never turn your back on him when leaving.

"Stay here," he ordered, as he strode to the bed and took the whip from the post and returned to my side.

"Remove all your clothes and proceed as though your Master is waiting for you."

I did his bidding and started my crawl as he walked alongside me calling out correcting instructions. "Keep your head down; look only at the carpet. Keep your knees and feet apart," he added as he poked the cold phallused handle of the whip between my thighs to encourage their parting—the touch and intrusion of the tooled leather handle in such an intimate place being acutely intimidating.

"At the mat make 'the bow'. Present yourself."

My thoughts flashed back to the time when I first tried on my harem clothes in my bedroom in Jeddah, pretending to be a haseki before a Sultan. How amazingly accurate had I imagined and portrayed the real thing.

"Now, one more time, starting from the screen, but this time when you reach the bed 'present your peach.'"

I completed his instructions and held my pose as he played the thongs of the whip over my raised buttocks, not saying a word. I understood his message.

"On that table there is always a bowl of perfumed water, sponges and towels," he said pointing to an alabaster and silver table. "Use it to wash your musk off him and yourself if he chooses not to bathe. If you are with another girl and he has chosen her for his pleasures, then you stand at the side of the bed, with your eyes to the floor while he is with her, and then sponge them off when a moment opens. If you are the last one called to the bed, put out all the candles and lamps except that one," he said pointing to a large bulbous lamp of polished brass. "That one always stays lit."

"Now, walk backwards to the door and put on your clothes."

He escorted me back to my room and left with the words, "I have told Yasmeen to help you dress. I wish you the most excellent for tonight."

What a thoroughly unnerving situation I had gotten myself into. On one hand, I looked forward to knowing these things, yet on the other, I was aghast at the way I had to show myself to the Master and the distasteful things I might have to do to please him. It thoroughly unnerved me to realize that I must know a man in these ways—a man I scarcely knew."

FIRST NIGHT

As you can well believe, my first calling that evening was an unsettling experience, for although I had been forewarned and had learned much about what could be required of me, I was worried. I had no idea of what this stranger, my new Master, had planned to take from me for his pleasure that night. I nervously left the hall in the company of another chosen one, a black Nubian slave with the harem name of Black Pearl.

I followed her lead in readying myself, glancing at her from time to time to make sure I was not missing or forgetting anything.

"Did Mustafa show you how the Master has us show ourselves?"

"Do you mean how to crawl to his bed and make the bow and present your peach?"

"Yes. So tonight let's show him our bums—he hasn't seen mine for a while," she giggled, irreverently, while standing with her hands behind her back, oiling her buttocks and the back of her thighs. "Are you a believer?" she inquired, but before I could answer she said, "I'm not."

I joined her in preparation, oiling only my shoulders and chest.

"You will see that there is bare marble floor around the kneeling mat. Kneel close to the edge and bend over low enough to let your breasts brush the marble; its cold touch hardens and raises the nipples. It makes him think he has inspired desire in you, even if he has not." She grinned, adding, "Tonight he inspires me. I don't have to pretend."

She rang a small hand bell. "Mustafa's moment," she said. "We stand here with our legs wide apart for this," pointing to a spot on the floor. Mustafa appeared with a small bowl. "Pessaries," she whispered. Mustafa inserted a small sea sponge soaked with pomegranate juice into us. "Here, wipe off the dribbles, he always makes them too wet," Black Pearl said, handing me a small cloth.

"Will you be using any of those?" she asked, casually pointing to the jars and bottles clustered on the table.

"Yes, I use ylang-ylang," I replied, confidently.

"I use nothing there, I'm sweet enough for him," she said, followed by another of her girlish giggles.

Yasmeen quietly appeared with a bundle of clothes and body jewelry.

"I have chosen these for you, Sapphira." She handed me a pair of diaphanous black chalwars, silver embroidered slippers, and a handful of silver chain. I held the chain up and let it unravel. It fell into a lovely chain breast bridle[1].

"It is important that the upper garment is not too tight on you. Unlike cloth, it has no give; it leaves no room for your breathing. Too tight and it will snap if you take a deep breath. Wear it loose."

She cupped me in to it. It did nothing for me. My breasts looked like two dead fish in a net. "Too loose," I thought, and after she had left, I tightened the clasp at the front by two catches, and tied a small loop in the shoulder links to shorten them. The fish came to life.

Peeking through the screen, I saw him waiting for us, sitting up on the bed, leaning back comfortably against a pile of cushions, without any discernable expression on his face.

While crawling towards him, my breast bridle broke at the back—as Yasmeen had warned it would do if drawn too tight. My breasts dropped free, the silver mesh slithered down my arms, gathered about my hands and then scrunched under my knees as I passed over it. I didn't look at her, I was too intent on keeping my head down and staying on the carpet, but I know I heard a giggle from Black Pearl.

As we had planned, we knelt on the small mat in the center of the mosaic circle and prostrated ourselves before him, taking advantage of the cold marble floor. Still kneeling we turned around—it was all naughtily exciting to me.

He clapped his hands once to tell us that he was ready for us, and patted the bed on each side of him to show where he wanted us. I followed Black Pearl's lead, kicked off my slippers, stepped onto the raised dais, and clambered onto the bed, contrary to what Mustafa had told me about crawling up from the end.

---

1. A literal translation of her Arabic words. At this time, the bra as we know it today had not been "invented" by Western civilization.

In turn, we passed him back and forth between us. Unsure and uncomfortable about what to do, I followed Black Pearl's lead, coming over him on hands and knees, and dropping down on him to pay attention to his startling erection with my lips and hands, but without her enthusiasm and confidence. Clearly, our deliberations brought him to a peak of excitement and anticipation—and somewhat satisfied my curiosity—before I was motioned off the bed, leaving Black Pearl entangled about him.

Deftly, he untied Black Pearl's chalwars, pulled them off to bare her offering, and determinedly stroked her legs apart. With powerful impressive authority, he sowed his seed, while I stood in the shadows ready to sponge away the musk and love juices with perfumed water and moist towels. However, my afterwards attention was not required. They withdrew to the bath leaving me standing at the side of the bed, giving time for my thoughts to cool and subside.

Later, a quick flicker of Black Pearl's eyes and a slight tilt of her head told me to join them in bed. I put out the candles and lamps, slipped out of my pants and slid into bed, on the other side of the Master.

I awoke to a room painted by the watery light of a breaking dawn. For a moment, I was unsure of where I lay, as I looked up at the unfamiliar underside of the elaborately carved and painted bed canopy.

Shortly, when I felt him stirring, I pushed down the coverlet to my waist to uncover my breasts, thought better of it, pulled it back up, and lay on my back pretending to sleep—waiting for the expected. Even so, it gave me quite a start to feel the touch of his hand on my breasts, the everywhere sign of what a man's thoughts are leading to. Lazily, I turned towards him, to give him better access to his interests, and pretended to awake. My eyes opened to the warm smile of an invigorated and rested Master, gazing upon a shy and apprehensive slave girl about to receive her first bedchamber command.

How should I respond to his touching? Just lie in listless indifference and let him have his way with me, or acknowledge his touch with mine? He answered my unspoken question. With gentle firmness, he took my arm by the wrist and guided my hand down to his member, which I duly encircled with my fingers, at the same time being startled by its rigid abundance. It seemed even harder and larger than I remembered from the evening before when I attended to it and saw him thrust it into Black Pearl.

"Pleasure me, my pretty one, I am eager to savor one of your talents," he whispered, as though trying not to awaken sleeping Black Pearl, the firm press of his hands on my shoulders leaving no question as to which talent he expected to savor. Fortunately, and not to mention Mustafa's lessons, I had done this on occasion to my husband, although more in teasing play and never all the way, so I was knowledgeable, and surprisingly willing even in the absence of affection. I slid down under the silky bed coverlet to face my task, eye to eye, so to speak. "No need to fan the fire of desire, just put out the flames," I thought, before taking him into my mouth.

Caressing hands and fingers on my ready breasts urged me on with a slowly rising tempo. I stroked back and forth as though moving to the quickening beat of a drum, before slowing to match the pace of his lustful rhythm. His thrusts deepened, sounds of fulfillment were uttered, and his issue came.

Disregarding Mustafa's instructions, I discreetly spat out his seed and rubbed it into the bedclothes. There was no swallowing or burying of anything.

Despite these possible shortcomings, ignored or not noticed by Sheik Ali, he was pleased saying, "For a girl of little experience you were delightful in your ways, not at all hesitant, and that makes for a good companion. You are well suited to serve me. Tonight you will be with me again. There are more ways for a slave girl to delight her master."

Supposedly, it was forbidden to talk amongst ourselves about what took place in the bedchamber between the Master and his night companions. Fortunately, the girls ignored this rule, and my journal writing benefited greatly from these morning discussions. They often discussed and compared the most intimate details of encounters and it took me a while to grasp the meaning of words used to describe various goings on. Phrases such as, *lady position*, moist embrace, making the sword dance, and lazy man. Each had a special meaning and were new to me.

At first I thought the girls were exaggerating and embellishing their stories with wild imagination, but I have learned that this was not so. The Master was most inventive and varied in his ways with women, and so were the girls with their Master.

Many who are opposed to slavery will have to forgive me for writing this, though some, no doubt, will understand. To many, I know it will sound trite and condescending, but it was the truth. Although the women were his slaves and lived daily under his whim, they understood and accommodated, even enjoyed, this relationship with him and lived contently with it, rarely lamenting their position or openly wishing for something else. Even those indifferent at times to his advances served graciously. I saw emotions that swept through love and respect, boredom and enthusiasm, but never through fear and hatred.

In their small world, defined by the four walls of the harem and Sheik Ali's callings, this was what life had to offer, and they grasped it gladly. They saw nothing extraordinary in their presence and purpose in a slave harem—it was their vocation, their duty and their purpose—just as I understood the terms of my commitment and held no complaint.

This softly spoken sentiment of Yasmeen may be an exception to generality: "I have one regret in my life—that Sheik Ali has not taken me as his wife, for I have loved him from the beginning. However, that silliness, I know, does not entitle me to be a wife, and besides, I am too old to be seeking the affection of a young man. He has never taken a wife," she said, sadly.

SETTLING IN

Today is a landmark occasion for me. My past has caught up with the present, as far as my journal writing is concerned. You know now how I got myself into this situation and how it came to be that on this hot sunny afternoon I am sitting at this table, writing. From now on, I will write in my journal only when new events unfold. I will do this during the afternoon siesta while things are still fresh in my mind.

I have become quite familiar with the routine and workings of the harem, the roles of the various people, and the goings on. However, before I start I must tell you about the toilets. They are well worth writing about. They are marvelous. You sit over a porcelain bowl set inside a painted wooden box and when you have finished you pull a handle back and forth and water washes away your doings. So much better than a hole in the ground with a wooden plank over it—and they do not reek, even on the hottest days.

At night, a wooden bar is lowered to lock closed the doors to the harem courtyard and two armed guards sit against them throughout the night, their guarding duties taken over by Mustafa and Talil in the daylight hours after the doors are unbarred. We are also required at night to bolt our room doors closed from the inside as a final precaution against intruders.

The two servant women assist us in our toiletries and look after the washing of our clothes and bed cottons. Twice a week two gardeners, an elderly man and his young apprentice, tend to the trees, plants and pools while our afternoon siesta conveniently confines us to our rooms. This is the extent of male presence in the harem, except for the Master, whose entry is always announced by the sounding of a large brass gong.

I find the antics of the slave girl Hortensia and the gardener's young assistant amusing. He is an attractive youth—an opinion obviously shared by Hortensia—and a quiet courtship of sorts goes on between the young gardener and the sloe eyed Hortensia, for when he works in the garden in front of her room she tactfully opens the shutters, or stands back from the open doorway, and teases him wickedly by showing him what only a husband or master should see. He responds in kind—to the extent possible without raising suspicion—by working discreetly bare chested whenever he is within her view. Her room is opposite mine and I have watched them. In front of her room lies the best-tended garden!

Sheik Ali and his harem gather each evening in the great hall for dining and entertainment. In the center of the large room is a square sunken area bordered by two steps leading up to a surrounding mezzanine. The lower sunken part is where we eat, and later it is the place for story telling, singing, dancing, and board games such as chess and backgammon, and other entertainment. Ali often reclines on a large upholstered divan set in the center of a huge carpet scattered with an array of cushions, taking pleasure from the attention of three or four serving girls. Mustafa selects the serving girls after consulting the written record he keeps of our menses and visits to the Master's bedchamber. Others lie or stand along the sides of the room, often indifferent to the goings on at the center.

I must mention one of the amusements of this place, a favorite game of the girls—possibly not of the Master. They blindfold him before each one in turn presents part of her anatomy for his feeling, such as the buttocks, leg or thighs—the girls claim breasts are too easy and are not offered. Cloth draped over the proffered part makes his task more difficult. The game is to see how many girls he can identify correctly. Those guessed wrongly accompany him to the bedchamber that night to refresh his memory.

They also try to upset Mustafa's carefully planned roster by encouraging Ali to choose a girl not on his list for the evening. Success in this small amusement delights all…except Mustafa.

A bright oil lamp placed some distance behind a large cotton sheet forms the screen for a Magic Lantern. Between the sheet and lamp, girls act out scenes and stage poses, sometimes with props, many lewd and naughty, which tell stories from their wild imaginations. They depict in moving shadows, trees, birds, animals, and aroused men pursuing unwilling women, bringing to life stories for the audience.

Eunuchs are both blessed and damned. Blessed to serve in comfort from a position of importance—damned by castration[1] and the constant stimulation of their latent desires, desires that they can no longer relieve by lying with a woman. Mustafa, the chief eunuch, is fortunate. His slaver had cut off only his sac; he is a *semivir* eunuch. The still intact member above is useful for emptying his bladder but for nothing else. Nevertheless, I notice on occasion, when he is ministering to a girl, preparing her for her master's enjoyment, that he often shows a slight stirring and bulge beneath his trousers. Talil, the second eunuch, is less fortunate. His captors cut off all his manliness; he is a *sandali* eunuch. Both sport beards and deep voices, signs that they met the knife as men, because castrated boys do not grow beards or have their voices deepen.

Castration is a terrible fate, particularly for a grown man. In all likelihood, he had experienced the pleasures of manhood before they were cruelly and permanently denied him. Emasculation left memories intact and no means of relief for any desires or urgings that lingered on.

Sheik Ali bin Shareef al-Saalih is a beneficiary of the discovery of copper and gold in Buraydah, in the province of Qassim, a desperately dry, impoverished kingdom populated largely by nomadic warring tribes. This newfound wealth sustained an extremely wealthy class of ruling sheiks, and the building of a new and luxurious palace on the shore of the Red Sea in the market town of Makram. Slave concubines, their supervising eunuchs, household servants and staff moved by camel train from the old palace in Buraydah, protected by

---

1. "The operation is performed in this manner: white ligatures or bandages are bound tightly around the lower part of the belly and the upper parts of the thighs, to prevent too much hemorrhage. The parts about to be operated on are then bathed three times with hot pepper-water, the intended eunuch being in a reclining position. When the parts have been sufficiently bathed, the whole—both testicles and penis—is cut off as closely as possible with a small curved knife, something in the shape of a sickle. The emasculating being effected, a pewter needle or spigot is carefully thrust into the main orifice at the root of the penis—the wound is then covered with paper saturated in cold water and is carefully bound up. After the wound is dressed, the patient is made to walk about the room, supported by two "knifers", for two or three hours, and then he is allowed to lie down. The patient is not allowed to drink anything for three days, during which time he often suffers great agony, not only from thirst, but also from intense pain, and from the impossibility of relieving nature during that period. At the end of three days the bandage is taken off, the spigot is pulled out, and the sufferer obtains relief in the copious flow of urine, which spurts out like a fountain. If this takes place satisfactorily, the patient is considered out of danger, but if the unfortunate wretch cannot make water he is doomed to a death of agony, for the passages have become swollen and nothing can save him."

armed Bedouin mercenaries. Traveling from oasis to oasis, the journey took over thirty days to complete, so hostile is this country. This southward migration took place seven years before I arrived, spurred forward no doubt by the outbreak of fighting in the north and east and the increasing likelihood of invading Turks attacking and plundering the Buraydah palace.

Most of the statuary, bas-relief plaques, elaborately carved alabaster and stone pieces, came from the old palace. The builders incorporated them into the new one, adding both warmth and a feeling of history. Of course, many of these pieces would remind some of the old palace, its master, his ways, likes and dislikes, many of which were not pleasant to recall.

Ali's father, Sheik Shareef, a ruthless dominating man with a taste for cruelty, was reputed to be the largest slave owner in Arabia. Male African slaves worked his gold and copper mines in Buraydah, and for his carnal pleasures, he owned an extensive harem. He thought nothing of flogging male slaves for failing to produce their quotas of gold nuggets and flakes, and in the same spirit, taking his harem slave women to his erga to punish them cruelly for real or imagined offenses.

A few years before his death, after he had amassed a huge fortune in gold, he abandoned the worked out mines. Luckily, only his fortune, and not his cruel tendencies, flowed down the bloodline, and though strong willed and demanding, Ali is fair and forgiving. Few mourned the death of his father, and the frequent beatings.

All the girls confide in Yasmeen, sharing their problems with her and seeking her advice. I have many opportunities to talk to her about life in the earlier days in his father's harem, and she gives me wonderful first-hand accounts of how it was then—a very different scene from the one I am now part of.

Yasmeen told me about life with Ali when he was younger. Under her tutorship, he acquired a fine appreciation and healthy appetite for the pleasures a woman can bring to a man's bed, and on each birthday his mother presented him with a new slave girl. This birthday tradition ended with the death of his mother when he was twenty years old and his harem held seven beautiful women.

Four years later his father died, and Sheik Ali inherited his fortune, the palace, lands, household, and of course, his father's extensive harem. Ali sold off the women to eager buyers except for three younger girls whom he selected to keep for himself, swelling his harem to ten exceptionally beautiful nubile females all well versed in the arts of pleasing a man.

Fewer possessions and less wealth flowed to his younger half-brother Hussein. Since he is the second son and born to a lesser wife, he inherited little, as is the common practice under the laws of the land. Hussein depends on the benevolence of his older brother, which is generously forthcoming and speaks of how extraordinarily attached and devoted they are to each other. He willingly left the palace at Buraydah, taking three slave girls with him, and took up residence in the small port city of Al-Lith, a short distance south of Jeddah. He lives a life of importance and comfort on an annual stipend provided from the family fortune.

As a boy grows into a man, preferences and attractions emerge for particular parts of the female body. Young Sheik Ali has a fondness for breasts, and to lesser extent buttocks, not to suggest that his interests stop there. Our legs, and surprisingly to me, the small of our backs, call to his eyes and hands. My Master is never tired or jaded by the sight and feel of shapely breasts, and they are on hand to him in every shape, size and color ranging from white through shades of Asian brown to Nubian black. His girls have noticed this and take care to cater to his likes. Many girls pattern their breasts with henna and bejewel them to enhance their appeal.

Sheik Ali is in every sense of the word a strong individual, but behind this hard veneer is a man about thirty years old, a man at his peak of virility—I can not imagine there ever being a higher peak—and a man susceptible to the charms of women. He immerses himself in their carnal attentions but also enjoys conversation and board games with them. Outside his bedchamber, we address him as "Sheik Ali"[2] or "Sire", an English word I did not know the meaning of at first. I later learned that the English slave Paeonia first used it, and in her language, it has the same meaning as sheik.

Inside his bedchamber, "Master", uttered with deference, is the proper word to use. There he becomes a man of purpose, a man of fewer words, who relies more on gestures than words to bring us to a place and position to his liking. He leaves no doubt as to who is the Master and who is the slave—he expects and receives unquestioned attention and submission.

Zahra, one of the two Iberian sisters he took in from his father's harem, sports a *tugra* below the nipple of her left breast. This is the old Turkish sign of having pleased the Sultan many times, and in a Turkish harem, it is a prized sign of having won the Sultan's approval and much sought after. I pondered about the perceived shortcomings of Noszahra[3], the other sister, in view of her

---

2. Ali, Arabic name meaning, "Exalted one".

equal beauty and poise, and wondered how anyone could see the pain of branding as a coveted prize.

Where were the children?—a mystery of this harem that has piqued my curiosity since I arrived. This is puzzling and odd, because in Arab culture, the number of children a man sires is a measure of his standing amongst his peers, and certainly, there is no lack of opportunity, surrounded as he is by a multitude of women, primed and yearning for much talked of motherhood. And by age and wealth, he is well eligible for fatherhood.

"In the Saalih household, slaves are unsuitable beings for bearing the Master's children," Mustafa explained, a woman-belittling notion I suspect he has carefully nurtured. "Childbearing is reserved for wives," he said, "and *pronging* for careless slaves."

The threat of pronging, the excruciatingly pitiless fate for slaves who unwontedly conceive, instills the diligent use of pessaries—sea sponges rinsed in pomegranate juice—to prevent pregnancies. Mustafa always inserts them to ensure there is no cheating—humiliating, nevertheless, much preferable to pronging.

---

3. The prefix nos can mean half of.

RING FOR SERVICE

One afternoon during siesta I was lying on my bed and lazily discovered that if I pulled on the rope that hung by the side of my bed, it pulled back as though attached to a thin branch, and I could make it jump up and down and ring the bell. Small amusement for a small mind on a sultry afternoon.

"What are you doing?" Ali inquired loudly, sounding somewhat annoyed, as he stood in the open doorway.

"Nothing, Master," I replied, as tension filled the space between us.

"Well, I know what you were doing; Katana's bell-pull near my bed was dancing like a dervish."

"I was touching the rope, Master," I admitted.

"Yes, I thought so. It is amazing. After all these years this one is still working. Then again, it never saw much use. May god bless Katana."

"How does it work, Master?"

"Come, I will show you."

I followed him to the bedchamber, greatly relieved by his now pleasant manner.

"You see those ropes hanging down at the head of the bed. When building this palace the stonemasons cut grooves in the stone blocks as they raised the walls, and ran rope to each of the girl's rooms. I could summon a girl by pulling on a rope and ringing the bell in her room. Clever of them, don't you think? However, they overlooked some finer points. The ropes frayed against the rough-hewn stone and rodents gnawed through others. Because they buried them in the walls, there is no way to repair them, so they fell into disuse. I had the pull-tassels left by the bed as a pleasant reminder of past times, and they make pleasing decoration. Regardless, it seems yours has survived the ravages of time and still works. I shall use it to summon you. Whenever you hear your bell ring, come to the bedchamber."

"Yes, Master."

True to his word my bell chimed at dawn next day, and I hurried, almost ran, to the bedchamber, but not before I found Mustafa who was surprised to see me so early in the day, and pleased that I had remembered to have myself pessaried.

I pushed open the heavy doors to the bedchamber and walked to the side of the bed. Yasmeen, draped in a loose diaphanous gown, was kneeling at his side. She managed a small smile.

"There, what did I tell you, Yasmeen? It still works."

He turned to me. "What took you so long?"

"I went to see Mustafa, Master."

"Good girl. But haven't you forgotten something else?" he said, frowning at me.

Nothing came to mind and I remained silent. He continued as his gaze changed from fierce surprise to a gentle smile. "You're supposed to take your clothes off at the door. Those are the rules," he said, resignedly, as he turned to share his despair with Yasmeen.

"I thought you had called to talk to me," I blurted out, to his further amusement.

"And that's why you went to Mustafa? To have a tongue put in?"

"No, Master."

"Anyway, it is just as well you did because I can assure you I would never ring a girl to the bedchamber at dawn for conversation," a statement followed by that boyish grin of his.

I turned around to head back to the door, to take off my clothes and correct my error.

"Stop," he called out, and before I could muster a reply, he continued. "A slave must never turn her back on her...."

"Ali, stop making fun of her, she is nervous and it is making her forgetful. Remember she is new to our ways—and you told us all to have patience with her," interrupted Yasmeen, in a manner closest to a rebuke that I had yet heard, and coming from one of his slaves!

"Come here and join us on the bed, Sapphira," she said, in a kindly manner while patting a place for me by the side of Ali.

"You are right, but now that she is here I will put her to good use."

Drawing me before him, he turned me around and set me on my knees and elbows, flipped my night garment over my raised hips and down my back, and invaded and banged against me—like an animal that had no understanding.

I was not interested in, nor did I enjoy, his rushed and rocking invasion—a woman always needs time for a little romance and seduction beforehand and he knew that. Detached from his doings, I rested my head comfortably on my forearms while he went about his urgent business. Glancing up briefly, peering through the fringe of my eyebrows, I saw Yasmeen leaving the bedchamber with her back towards him.

She had reprimanded him, called him "Ali" in the bedchamber, and turned her back on him. She was somehow special to him.

A few days later, a loud crashing sound awoke me from my afternoon sleep. I found my bedside bell lying on the floor where it had fallen, the rope silently eviscerating itself from the hole in the ceiling, coiling into a neat pile on the floor, while a choking cloud of gritty dust and plaster showered down, engulfing me in a white powdery cloud.

As I was shaking and brushing off the dust and flecks of white plaster that had rained down on me, Ali appeared at the door. His hand held a pull-tassel with a length of frayed rope trailing out behind it, and his face held a mischievous smile. "I was calling you. The rope broke," he explained.

"However, I had good intentions in mind; we will not waste this moment. Come with me, I will wash the dust off you in the bedchamber bath," he said, beckoning me to follow him.

BEJEWELED DANCERS

No harem evening was complete without the swirl and sway of nubile bejeweled dancers. It was a highly admired and valued part of late-day hours in a harem, a part that a young girl's graceful and supple body, and deep inborn nature, was supremely suited for. I found that I, too, had this innate desire to dance before a man—even removing my clothes, piece by piece—to show myself, and arouse his lust for me. I wanted to be part of this spectacle, fulfill my fantasy, and not stand aside when the music started.

On the other hand, I knew my skills in this art were inadequate—in fact nonexistent.

I confided in Yasmeen, explaining that I had no experience or lessons in dance, and was concerned that it would exclude me from the evening entertainment. She took me under her care and for an hour or more each morning she instructed me in the art of dancing for a man's pleasure.

"It is a simple matter," she explained. "Men are seduced through the eyes and nose. His eyes follow the movement of a woman's body just as a hawk's eyes follow the undulations of a slithering snake. For that reason, we undulate and slither like snakes climbing a tree; and like beautiful fragrant flowers in a gentle breeze, we sway and bend and spread our fragrance. And surely, you have noticed when you first come to the eyes of a man he looks at your face, then your chest, and then the rest of you. So, we show him our face and feet when we dance, and," she laughed, "everything in between."

To the accompaniment of music played by our servant, Yasmeen taught and trained me. "Never let your arms hang at your side," she admonished. "You must always put them to graceful use, raised over your head in the Turkish arm pose, or outstretched, but never down at your side. And your knees are to be slightly bent—always."

It took me three weeks to gain any proficiency whatsoever in the many moves such as the shoulder shimmy, the layback, the leg lift-and-sweep, hip circles and thrust, and the alluring finger to toe body wave, at the same time playing my finger *zills* in time with my movements and the music.

Mostly, dances were improvised to suit the moment, but some were played out to well-known stories or songs, with a short story or verse of song leading to the dance. Other than that, few words were spoken—body movements spoke for themselves. You could dance while standing or even lying on the floor. At first, I preferred to be on the floor, as it required less grace of movement, and mistakes and stumbles were less noticeable, but I quickly learned the standing positions. Either way, the purpose was to show your womanly charms slowly and enticingly to the Master while never touching him. Clothes and veils were encouraged to fall and you ended your performance in a seductive pose, but not completely naked, as protocol demanded that at least one piece of clothing remain, whether it be nothing more than a small veil or sparse wrap.

I enjoyed performing, particularly when alone with Ali in the privacy of his bedchamber. With him reclining on cushions on the floor, I became adventurous and inventive with increasingly tantalizing moves. I learned to present my charms closely and in ways that encouraged his touching and survey, and at the same time never ceasing to surprise myself as to how bold I had become. I wondered how my marriage would have faired had I behaved this way in front of my husband. I expect for the better, at least for him.

To a man, a pretty face and a curvaceous body seductively shown were powerful aphrodisiacs and tirelessly sought after. And I think I speak for other women as well, when I say that a well-dressed, kindly authoritative man of wealth, with a strong sense of humor and a warm and caring disposition, spoke to me in the same way—not that a handsome face and build was unappreciated or went unnoticed.

Ali's girls always wore body jewelry whether called for dancing or not; its slinky glitter embellished natural feminine charms and caught the eye. It was a predictable part of harem evening dress.

Nipple dangles and delicate silver chains with a matching silver collar made up one of my favorite ensembles. I wore the chains attached to the collar and looped down to each nipple, or simply looped across from nipple to nipple. Under a diaphanous choli they looked stunningly sensual, and never failed to pique the interest of the Master, although he must have seen them on others many times before.

Hip belts ranged from a simple chain to elaborate assemblies of chain fringes, coins and medallions. I often wore one with fringes of overlapping loops of chain that barely covered my hips. Two long silk veils tied through a loop or tucked under the chain, one at the back and one at the front, transformed the hip belt into a most becoming and intriguing garment—and a more modest one. As the loops swayed from side to side, they gave off a metallic swishing sound and rustled the silks between my thighs, adding to the glamour. Also favored was a chain fall of many fine links that cascaded from a neckband down over the breasts, and then parted just above the waist to go under the arms and back up to the neckband at the back. Worn under or over thin silk, or alone, it was most alluring—the chains moved and separated in such inviting ways.

"Master and Slaves" was the name for wrist bracelets that had finger rings attached to them by short chains. First, you slipped the rings over your finger and then fastened the bracelet around your wrist so that the chains ran along the back of the hand. Arm bangles, ankle chains, earrings, headbands and tikkis, nipple shields, tassels, belly brilliants, belled bracelets and various breast supports made for a fine set of exciting and alluring accessories to choose from.

My nipples proved full enough that by teasing them through a small ring, I, too, could wear breast jewelry without help from Mustafa's needle. Piercing held breast jewelry in place for the less fortunate with small or short nipples, and if deemed necessary, a painful needling from Mustafa had to be accepted.

A dab of spirit gum held belly brilliants in place or small jewels to the forehead. Glittering bindi appliqués were also gummed in place—often in places unimagined by me even in my wildest young girl fantasies.

Women of the harem were not the only ones to adorn themselves with body jewelry. Often the Master sported a heavy gold or silver chain necklace about his neck and large jewel-encrusted rings on his fingers, or jewelry on his member, my favorite being the "Circlets and Chain" in which two rings circled his member, one at the base the other near the head, with a short chain strung between them. Early in his arousal, the short strand of smooth chain looped loosely down between the two rings, but as his excitement and hardness grew the linking chain pulled tight, enabling it to stimulate exquisitely the most sensitive spot of a woman as he moved back and forth.

SHEIK ALI

By now, I expect you will be interested in learning more about my Master's hidden assets.

I had limited comparisons to make, as the only mature men I had seen naked were my husband and this man—I remember nothing of Ahmad. From the outset it was obvious that my Master was well endowed compared to my husband, being somewhat longer and of much greater girth. As measure, his length exceeded the span of my outstretched thumb and middle finger and I could just close my thumb and first finger around him. I know this is correct; my hand took careful measure of him last night—he did not notice. That he was larger than my husband was most evident when I pleasured him, for if prolonged, my jaw would ache for some time thereafter. I surmise that his plentiful size was due to lavish use since early manhood—his youthful excesses not held in check by the inconvenience of availability and consent—and his slave girls surely caused him frequent arousal with their alluring dress, stolen glances and provocative posturing.

Usually, he took two girls each day, starting his day with one in the morning and ending it with one at night before going to sleep. Often, he took his pleasure during afternoon siesta in our rooms, and occasionally something happened between him and the girl attending him during his afternoon bath.

But, he too, had his cycle, not as regular or predictable as that of a woman, but noticeable nevertheless. At its peak, he had a voracious, almost insatiable appetite, on occasion taking as many as four girls in the course of a day. When he was at the valley of his cycle, he took only one, occasionally none. It was at this ebb that we wore our most alluring dress and danced the most provocative dances. For our part, it was a point of honor for the one who overcame his apathy and found his favor—that was the purpose of our being.

He was generous in his attentions, but on occasion he took me abruptly—gentle rape best describes it. It was a master's right of assertion, but I found it not unpleasant. I saw him in these moments as a splendid animal, a finely honed animal in its prime, whose strength and domination compelled me to complete acceptance.

While I considered myself an eager and passionate woman,—just like my mother, I think—and sought often the press of him against me, I needed a little help, the play of fingers or his tongue on me, to move me to release. A penis alone was not enough, no matter how skillfully wielded, and I was not alone amongst his girls in this respect—we had talked about it. Our careful freshening and flavoring had a purpose and Ali always obliged without mention—he knew women.

Harem rules forbade a girl to be with another girl in her room. Happily, this rule was not enforced, and we freely visited each other's rooms. I believe this was allowed because Mustafa's roster ensured that the Master's attention was rotated to all girls, and since all were kept sufficiently satisfied, the common harem-girl to harem-girl relationships—which were strictly forbidden, since they were seen as an affront to a master's masculinity—never developed, and *bijoux indiscrets* were not called for. Nevertheless, we were not above touching ourselves in the privacy of our rooms if unsatisfied by the Master, although the supposed punishment, if caught in the act, was cruel and painful chastisement of the parts intruded upon and amputation of a finger.

As mentioned before, bathing was a large part of harem life, almost a ritual, and four times a day was normal. It was refreshing, and as Mustafa had been careful to point out to me, it ensured a girl's readiness at any time should the Master call for her. While not bathing as lavishly as his girls, Yasmeen had impressed upon him from when he was a young boy that personal cleanliness was of utmost importance if he wanted his girls to be willingly adventurous in their lovemaking. For our part, after lovemaking we accompanied him to his private bath, or sponged away our musk with perfumed water.

It was required under the laws of Islam, and common practice in this part of the world, to circumcise all males within three days of birth, and there had been no exception here. Unlike his female slaves, he kept his hairy bush, which was black, thick and tightly curled. While taking his late afternoon bath he would on occasion call for Yasmeen to trim his beard and check the lower area and keep it also trimmed and neatly shaped. His thighs and chest sported a modest fleece of short curly hair, and I thoroughly enjoyed running my fingers through it and brushing my breasts against it.

To my eyes, a penis was not a pretty sight when flaccid. Not ugly or revolting by any measure, but not as attractive with its loose skin and lopsided embellishments as, say, a woman's smooth breasts or the firm buttocks of a man. To my mind, it's not something to look at. It was created for a purpose other than to draw a woman's eye, unlike a woman's body, which was fashioned to attract a man, to arouse him, and invite his loving caresses and penetration.

Nevertheless, I admit that on occasion outside of the bedchamber, when the opportunity presents itself, I try to catch a glimpse of Ali's manhood or perhaps imagine what the clothing of a stranger concealed—such was its primal allure. In no way was I ashamed of this; after all, men—and the French boys at the Embassy School—tried to look down our dresses, something Jacqueline teasingly encouraged, but not me.

However, I favored holding it possessively in my hand, feeling its pulse, caressing and stroking it, encouraging its transformation from innocence, then marveling at the forceful dichotomy of hardness and softness. And I admit, particularly when he knelt or stood over me, with his member standing out full and hard, that he was a remarkable sight, one that excited my womanly feelings, buried my inhibitions and compelled me by some unknown force to surrender to his urgings and guide him into me. Mustafa's ivory carvings made no exaggeration of his manhood.

TANTRA

Ali was often away for a few days leaving us to our own devises, and today was one of those occasions. I would take advantage of his absence and entertain the girls by reading to them. I had sworn them to secrecy. I wanted to keep the fact that I could read a close secret.

I sent Yasmeen to the erga for an ivory phallus, a prop for my readings, for I would read from Sheik Ahmad's tantra instructions and the girls would try new things.

Ahmad had divided his paper into six sections; Lying Down Positions—Samputa Group; Positions from The Medieval Texts; Sitting Positions; From Behind Positions; Standing Positions; and Mouth Pleasures.

We would study one section each day and take turns showing each other the teachings.

It was with lighthearted enthusiasm that we engaged in this effort; we marveled at the ingenuity of the positions and the acrobatic maneuvers required to do them. It seemed many were impossible to achieve without extreme discomfort or tying ourselves into impossible knots.

When Ali returned, we had surprises for him.

PLEASURING

Many think of this as an unnatural thing to do. To me though, it came comfortably and easily as part of lovemaking, albeit with earnest encouragement from my husband. In those first eager months of marriage, I was so curious about the workings and parts of a man, and anxious to excite and please him, that I never questioned it or refused to do it. It was one of my girlish fantasies brought to life.

Some of the harem girls believed that it was possible to conceive this way and those who were fortunate enough to do so would give birth to a boy and not be pronged. Why enlighten them to the truth and remove a hope that may make it more palatable for those disinclined to do it willingly, I reasoned. But most slave girls, including myself, welcomed an order to pleasure the Master, as it gave her delightful power and control over his satisfaction. Manipulated lips and tongue easily excited him, and she was able to shorten or prolong his pleasure at will—influence and control that were rare and welcomed happenings in the life of a slave.

In the harem, pleasuring was given the admiration and respect of high art, and frequently practiced. I had done it many times with my husband to tease and arouse him, but we always finished in the way God intended. Sometimes I suspected he wanted it otherwise—there were "accidents"; I found out how seed tasted—but I didn't volunteer to go further and he never asked. Ali, also never asked—he presumed and took for granted that I would bring him to completion in my mouth. When less experienced this seemingly simple requirement of the harem gave me difficulty. I would often gag as the contents of his sac pulsed into my mouth[1], however, after much practice, I was able to

---

1. If any reader has doubts, try this. Place a finger far to the back of your mouth, hold down your tongue, and try to swallow.

embrace the etiquette that required a slave girl—but not a wife—to render this service, and swallow the sometimes-salty tasting fluid.

Let me now tell you how Ali first instructed me in his likings. I remember the incident clearly—it was also the first time he had taken exception to my breaking of a harem rule.

One morning, when kneeling between my Master's legs, his member slipped from my mouth when he unexpectedly made vigorous finishing thrusts. Milky white seed spluttered over his belly as his freed member pulsed about in its final throes, its tiny mouth opening and closing as though gasping for air.

He strode to the bath, wiped himself off with a towel and returned to the side of the bed, and I remember thinking that he would reach out for the whip on the bedpost, he looked that annoyed, but he passed it by.

Instead, he snatched away the bedclothes that I clutched tightly to myself—my illusory protection—and gazed down on my nakedness.

"Go to your room and wait for me," he commanded, in a threatening voice that was new to me.

I picked up my clothes and hurriedly backed out of the bedchamber.

If he was looking for reason to have me whipped, he had found one. Spilling his seed, although a simple thing of little consequence to him, was nevertheless an offense according to the rules of the harem, so indelibly carved into the erga wall to remind all. Would Talil soon be readying his whip, feeling its heft, and gauging his stroke against a pillar in anticipation of my bared back?

My heart surely missed a beat with the knock on my door. I should have known it was not Ali—he never knocks. It was Yasmeen looking for me, as I had missed the first meal of the day. I told her my woes. "Will he hurt me?"

"No, it's nothing," she said.

"Nothing?"

"It's not the first time for him and likely not the last. He always reacts angrily to a veiled insult."

"Veiled insult?"

"Yes. It comes from the belief that only weak-minded men and naughty boys spill their seed. You insulted his manliness, which is all the harm you have done. It's not precious or wasted, there is plenty more where it came from," she chuckled. "Now, do not worry anymore, he will not hurt you. I will talk to him as soon as he returns. He has gone along for the ride with a hunt and will be back before noon. I will bring you some food and then wait near the pool for him."

I heard the sound of the gong resonate over the gentle splashing sounds of the fountains and followed his footsteps, briefly halted while Yasmeen spoke to him, then resuming and growing louder as he made his way to my room. For a moment, he stood in the open doorway, silhouetted against the light, dressed in riding breeches, a long thin riding crop in hand. Fear passed a tingling hand over my body and my heart pounded fiercely as he continued towards me without speaking a word.

Abruptly sitting down on the padded bench, he placed the leather-covered crop by his side, within easy reach, and removed his riding boots and unbuttoned his shirt while at the same time giving me what I saw as a slightly roguish smile.

"Stand up and turn around, face away from me," he ordered. Reaching around me, he unbuttoned my choli and pulled it off my shoulders and down my arms, the short sleeves gathering about my wrists, entangling my arms behind me. My breasts protruded, exposed and vulnerable. I hunched over to diminish them, to shield from his eyes the obvious, causing my bared back to tense in readiness for the prescribed strokes—nine for spilling his seed read the decree.

"Master, this morning, it was an accident, I was careless in my enthusiasm to please you," I said, pleadingly.

"That is what Yasmeen said and that is my thinking also. You did not lose me by intent or with disrespect—it was an accident. As I have told you before, you are a delight to have in my bed; however, you have shown a small shortcoming since you arrived here, a small forgetfulness on your part that revealed itself again this morning. I thought you might learn on your own, but seeing that that has not happened I will take this opportunity to give you a short lesson. That is all I am here to do."

A flood of relief washed over me with the lessening of earlier fears, fears that saw him putting the crop to me or ordering me to the erga. My body and mind softened as the stiffness of fright left me, helped by the gentle manner with which he pulled me close so my back rested comfortably against his fleecy chest, his hands closing over my breasts.

"I can feel your heart, it trembles and flutters like a captive bird. There is no need to be afraid when you are with me; no need whatsoever to be fearful of me."

Encouraged by his kind words, I shook the loosened choli free from my wrists, raised my arms above my head and clasped my hands behind his neck. I settled my back against him as he leaned forward over my shoulder, his head beside mine in a loving manner.

Palming my breasts, he lifted them upwards as though measuring their weight or assessing their firmness, circling the nipples with his fingers, teasing them to awareness. His searching hands traced downwards, sweeping over the swell of my hips to find the side slits of my harem pants. There they slowly burrowed under the silk, seeking my bare thighs and smoothed mons before retracing their way back to my waiting breasts where my nipples again awakened to his caressing touch, tightening and tingling deliciously, as I relaxed and luxuriated in his attention.

Firmly, he turned me around to face him, and with his broad musky hands on my shoulders, gently pressed me down onto my knees.

"Close your eyes," he commanded, though kindly. "Sangara is better learned with the eyes closed. Do nothing until I tell you."

I disobeyed. I cracked my eyes open ever so slightly, unsure, even after his kind words, whether he would reach for the riding crop. But all I saw was the blurred shape of his hands as they worked their way down the buttons of his riding breeches, the silence broken by the sound of dropping clothes and his belt buckle hitting the floor.

His soft warmth pressed lightly against my lips, my face flushed as though in reply.

"Take me in, slave girl Sapphira. Give your Master full pleasure."

This I did while kneeling before him in bare breasted submission. His hand held lightly and firmly behind my head gave me no choice but to swallow his seed when he came in my mouth. And when he came, he came quickly, with abundant enthusiasm, which told me that during the morning he too had been writing this chapter of my life in his mind—with an ending different from the one I had imagined—and one that I was more than thankful to be acting out.

"Tonight I will test your learning," he said, while dressing.

He left quietly, leaving me on my knees with my thoughts. Although he had always sated his lust with nothing more than the coolness of indifference, I felt a warming towards him. He had not come with crop in hand to punish me, but with understanding and forgiveness even if for only a trivial offence. I stayed on my knees for a while, thankful and pleased for the opportunity to redeem myself, then I lay down on my back, stretched out my legs, and thought of unattainable romantic things, and the night to come when, if I had my way, he would do more with me than just test my learning.

Swallowing his seed was neither an unpleasant nor a gratifying experience. It certainly satisfied his inclination to excessive indulgence, so I would oblige him in the future.

Were Mustafa's eggs "incredibly realistic"? No. A man is not that bountiful.

Yasmeen told me that had my morning insult taken place in his father's harem I would surely have spent time between the columns in his erga while he witnessed his cruel eunuchs laying whips to my bared back.

Many considered the art of pleasuring a man to be at its peak when a girl completely swallows his member so her lips briefly touched his bush. Four of his girls could bury the sword—Paeonia called it "bobbing for apples"—but I was not one them, and not driven to join them, as I felt it added little to the experience for either lover, although I had tried to do it on occasion and failed. It made me gag.

Once I watched in fascination and awe as Briar Rose pleasured the Master. She was decidedly skilled in her movements, always faithful to his changing rhythms. With her hands behind her back, thumbs hooked under her waist chain, she dipped down on him as he thrust upwards, and drew away as he fell back. As his pace mounted towards the moment of release, she buried the sword, her tight black hair springing down and splashing over his belly and thighs.

Paeonia and even tiny Yasmeen were the other girls I knew who were remarkably adept in this way.

I was told, and now believe, that receiving pleasure by the mouth is the highest form of erotic pleasure for men, and it must never be interrupted or denied to masters—or husbands and lovers if you like.

ENSLAVED CAPTIVES

The palace at Makram was guarded around the clock. Armed guards manned the only entrance, and kept the huge doors closed and bolted, and opened only to allow known and authorized personnel to pass. At all hours, other guards patrolled atop the high perimeter walls. While making escape from the harem impossible it had another purpose—to keep out unwanted intruders and thieves.

Many years ago, during a mild sandstorm, bandits had scaled the walls of the old palace at Buraydah stealing precious jewelry and many slave girls. The ensuing sandstorm covered the abductor's tracks and neither the jewelry nor the girls were recovered. After this loss, Ali's father enforced the Turkish practice of marking by branding, to identify abducted or escaped slave girls should they be offered for sale in local markets or put to work in one of the well frequented brothels. All of Ali's girls bore a mark—his, or that of a previous owner.

How valuable were slave girls that they were worth the risk of stealing? Blond haired European virgins less than sixteen years old were the most valuable and could be worth the price of twenty camels or more to those buyers who found them exceptionally attractive. A budding younger virgin, who showed good promise of things to come, could fetch the price of ten camels, her owner then putting her to work as a harem servant girl until her showings were full and regular. Girls who had lost their virginity varied widely in value depending on their age, color of skin and hair, and the fullness and firmness of that part of the female anatomy that most appealed to the buyer. Prices varied widely but were never less than the equivalent of three camels.

Warring between nations and tribes had always been the main source of slaves throughout history. Spoils flowed to the victors, the vanquished taken as slaves, and sold along with their seized possessions. Tribal war and rivalries yielded black African men and women slaves who arrived in Arabia ports by ship[1] and boat, and in the Far East, gold purchased Asian girls who came back overland along with silks and other goods in one of the many trade caravans traveling the great Silk Road.

Ali owned one Asian girl, Briar Rose, indentured by her poor family, supposedly for household service in a wealthy man's home, as was common practice with female offspring in India and the Far East. Briar Rose, taken westwards and sold to Arab slavers, never saw household service.

Pirate bounty was a large source of European girls. Raids mounted from pirate lairs dotted along the coast of the Barbary States, on ships passing through the narrow Straits of Gibraltar or becalmed in quiet waters yielded many captives. Those captured who were of noble birth, or wealthy, commanded ransoms in gold, but the fate of the poor was slavery.

It was common for a raiding party to return with a hundred or more captives after looting undefended towns along the coasts of the Iberian Peninsula, Ireland and Scandinavia. Captains of pirate vessels were wealthy and respected citizens in their homeports and as such, were beyond reproach. There they dallied with impunity with the choicest of their captives before delivering them for ransom, or selling them on to eager buyers.

Now is perhaps a good time to write about two of Ali's girls: Yasmeen and Paeonia. They have most interesting stories to tell.

Yasmeen, a Visayan girl from the Far East, was a prisoner of pirates who had raided and looted her coastal fishing village. In the slave market in Al-Aqaba, a corrupt official bought her to give to the Grand Vizier of Baghdad as a bribe to curry favor and protection. The Grand Vizier took her into his harem as one of his bed-slaves.

All came to an abrupt and unexpected ending. Convicted of embezzling taxes collected on behalf of the Caliph of Baghdad, the Grand Vizier and his sons were put to death and his household goods and chattels sold. His wives

---

1. Parker, in *Life in Abyssinia*, detailed the importation of 1600 slaves through the port of Jeddah alone in 1853:
Galla slaves, female, from Massawa. 130 valued at 3 ½ ounces of gold each.
Galla slaves, male, from Massawa. 270 valued at 2 ¼ ounces of gold each.
Slaves from Abyssinia. 200 valued at 2 ¾ ounces of gold each.
Negro slaves from Suwakin. 500 valued at 1 ¾ ounces of gold each.
Negro slaves from Zanzibar. 500 valued at 1 ½ ounces of gold each.

and daughters were enslaved and exiled beyond the far corners of the Caliph's empire where they were sold along with the vizier's harem girls and eunuchs. That is how Yasmeen found herself aboard a boat taking her back to the slave market at Al-Aqaba. Here in her own words is an account of what took place there after her arrival.

"The slave trader washed and groomed me and gave me a loose fitting white cotton gown to wear, before he brought me before a seated well-fleshed woman of high rank. Her attending eunuch stood at her side. The slave trader opened the front of the gown to reveal my breasts and then peeled it back from my shoulders and let it fall to the floor about my feet. Both the woman and the eunuch asked many questions about my previous duties and knowledge and then the eunuch took me aside. With my hands behind my head, he poked and parted me, sharply slapped and pinched my breasts, buttocks and thighs, and opened my mouth to examine my teeth. An ivory rod, inserted deep into me and then withdrawn, tested the sweetness of my musk.

"A price was negotiated; I was bound tightly to a camel and taken to the old palace at Buraydah. There, after further instruction and enhancement, Ali received me as a present to mark his fourteenth birthday. I was his first slave."

Paeonia was born unwanted and unloved, the illegitimate child of a prostitute, a "Lady of the Night" who worked the dock-lands of the British port of Bristol. Her mother sold Paeonia's virginity to a sailor, "To make good for my board and keep, and the other troubles I had caused her—I stole things and told lies." In the squalor and dirt of her mother's hovel, Paeonia surrendered her virginity, while her mother looked on through a drunken gin-induced haze, encouraging him to, "Give it to her good, Mister."

Following this ordeal Paeonia cropped her hair short, dressed herself in boys' clothes, and ran away from her mother. She signed on as a cabin boy on a coastal freighter, joining two other adolescent boys in the crew.

Paeonia told me how Ali came to own her.

"One evening we were ashore spending our hard-earned wages on tankards of tavern ale when the town hall clock struck eleven. We ran down the dockside dodging and jumping over sprawling bodies and stacked cargo and up the gangplank, beating the curfew by two minutes—the first mate always pulled the plank at exactly five minutes past eleven. On the boat, the elder boy, feeling a strong need to relieve himself, challenged us to a pissing contest to see who could pee farthest over the rail and into the sea, a challenge accepted by the other boy. "Belly up to the railing," was his rallying call. I, of course, being ill equipped for the contest, declined the challenge. We traded derogatory names and a scuffle started during which one of the boys tried to grab me between my legs. He found nothing to grab onto! They pulled off my trousers to reveal my secret and those dreadful boys kept my trousers while they relieved themselves over the railing and then, for their amusement, made me squat on the deck and do the same. Under threat of exposure, the older boy took advantage of me, but the younger boy, probably a virgin, failed to perform when his turn came, and the older boy and I made fun of his inadequacy. He told my secret to the captain.

"The outcome was unexpected. I was 'promoted' from cabin boy to cabin bed-wench and when we sailed I had the pleasure of waving goodbye from the rail to the two boys who were left squabbling on the dockside, laying blame on each other for their predicament.

"During voyages I 'made good' the captain, and whenever the boat was in port he locked me below deck for safekeeping.

"I was quite content to be away at sea and far from my mother and bad memories, but a year or so later he tired of me, or more likely needed money. In Dublin, Ireland, he handed me over to another captain who stowed me down below in a cattle pen along with three Irish peasant girls, a young boy, and hundreds of bleating and stinky sheep.

"In the cattle pens we were watched over by a youth who had designs on me, but I soon cooled his ambitions. I let him undo the first buttons of my shirt and then kneed him sharply between his legs sending him yelping away like a beaten dog. He didn't bother us again, except to tell us horrible tales about what awaited us in the next port where the boy would have his balls cut off and the girls would be displayed naked and sold in the market place. I told him he was a liar, not realizing the truth in his words.

"We sailed to Alexandria and there, under cover of night, I was sold to an Arab slave trader and taken overland to the slave market in Al-Aqaba where Ali's mother bought me. She gave me to Ali for his nineteenth birthday."

Of all the girls, she was the most vivacious and friendly, always cheerful and smiling. I would say with certainty that she was happy living her life as a harem slave. I could understand why, given her unpleasant taste of life in her minor years. She had known no master other than Ali.

All the girls adopted her word Sire when addressing Ali, an English word that I know now means "lord" or "man of high rank".

Paeonia's harem name comes from a flower that grows wild in the Atlas Mountains of Tunisia and Algeria. I know it well. It has beautiful bowl shaped blooms flushed with pink—just like her breasts. She is the most buxom of Ali's girls, and refers to them in that fun way of hers as "England's gift to the Arabs".

Her eyes, catchingly framed by her abundant hair, do not go unnoticed. They are an exquisite green, a color I had never seen in such intensity in eyes before. Hair the color of apricots—"my ginger tresses," she called it—falls in waves down her back like ripples on water, and freckles on the bridge of her nose spill over her cheeks and shoulders. She hates them—the freckles that is—and she has the whitest skin. She keeps to the shade, for the heat of the sun turns her skin from the purest white to a pink as deep as tamarisk blossoms.

To the eyes of Arab men, she is a rare and exotic beauty.

THE DARK ART

I wanted to find out more about life in older harems, those that existed before my time, as I had heard frightening but fascinating rumors of diabolical practices in those days. I recruited the services of Yasmeen who was knowledgeable in these things.

One morning, when we were certain that the Master would not return early we sneaked into his bedchamber and then down the dark passageway to the erga. There, Yasmeen gave a full account of the items on display, and an explanation of the consequences if harem rules were broken.

"Out of respect for the softness of a woman's skin," she recounted, "whips for women are made from light braided silk, a fiendish Persian construction that causes pain without breaking the skin. Men have to endure the lash of heavy leather, because scarring and roughness is not something that spoils their quality, as it would a woman's, and the marks serve as a lasting reminder to others."

Two whips were laid out, one for use on the breasts and front, the other for the back and buttocks. The silk breast whip, about as thick as the little finger, unraveled into eight thinner cords half way down its length. "It leaves a lacework of fine stinging welts but does not have enough lash to damage the nipples. Your breasts are tender and sore for days after a whipping. In my mind, this is the worst of punishments, to me worse than my branding," said Yasmeen, speaking from experience.

"Eunuchs or the master give a whipping or caning after tying you between columns or hanging you by your wrists," she said, first pointing to the two alabaster restraining columns and then to an iron hook set in a wooden ceiling rafter, "or you could be made to lie over the 'horse' or the edge of a bed."

The second whip, Ali's father's infamous scorpion, was similar in length but thicker and did not burst into thinner thongs. "For this one, they wrote the name of your offence on your back or buttocks," she advised matter-of-factly, "and lay down as many as nine lines through the writing."

Saying nothing, I pointed to the charcoal filled brazier and she told me that branding was a common punishment, less so now than in the past. Then, prisoners were willfully tortured by branding to extract information and confessions, and after a prisoner confessed it was turned against them as proof that further branding was justified that gained nothing more than a thrill for the crowd and cruel executioner before the criminals and traitors found relief in execution. But not in Ali's erga. Here, the branding tool, skillfully crafted from fine silver, mercifully left a small clear impression that soon healed, unlike the deep scar seared by the crude heavy irons used on men and animals. Bed-slaves wore their mark on their breast, buttock or thigh; work slaves carried them on their upper arm or shoulder.

Yasmeen recounted her early experiences in the Grand Vizier's harem, the harem of a cruel man indifferent to the sufferings of others. She was a young innocent virgin when given to the Vizier, and shortly thereafter, he marked her with a hot iron on one of her buttock cheeks, and made her a lowly *joy-girl*. Such were his ways. Although taken to his bed often, it was almost a year later, when some new arrivals took his attention, that one of the Vizier's sons deflowered her.

On occasion she, too, had received the punishments prescribed for not accommodating him and for drawing his blood.

"The Vizier was taking me from behind when he stumbled and unexpectedly thrust painfully deep. My head and shoulders reared upwards and the back of my head banged into his face, abruptly ending his pleasure with a splash of blood from his nose, and a spilling of his seed. For that, he ordered me whipped and caned across my breasts and buttocks.

"In the erga, before the other slave girls of the harem—they were commanded to watch all punishments—I knelt on the hard stone floor with my skirt raised around my waist exposing my buttocks to the cane. The Vizier gave me five strokes, after which his first wife, a jealous and spiteful woman, dispensed the remaining measured strokes. After ripping away my upper garments she made me lay back over a low padded footstool and four girls held firm my outstretched arms and legs. Nine times she brought a whip down across my uplifted breasts, while the Vizier watched from the comfort of a chair, with a girl between his legs. For him inflicting pain was a source of arousing entertainment."

Such a small body to take such merciless punishment—I could feel her pain—and felt sickened by the whole business of ergas and punishment. "Let's go back to the courtyard," I told Yasmeen, "and leave the rest for another day."

Yasmeen recalled that when Ali was a young boy his father forced him to watch as he whipped a slave girl, a young girl who in earlier years had been an innocent childhood playmate of Ali, and for whom he held great fondness. His father told him that all new slaves should taste the whip, even if they had done no wrong, saying "it makes them better slaves if they know what awaits them should they displease their master".

"The experience sickened Ali, and I believe it was then that his mind was made up never to do it. Speak to Hortensia; she will tell you about it."

Yasmeen continued. "When I first went to Ali's bed he asked me if he had to whip me first. I told him that I already knew the whip well, and that it made a slave girl hate her master. I said a girl would not serve him well if he whipped her, and his slave girls would conspire against him and find ways to poison his food. As far as I know, he has never put a whip to a girl or ordered one to be whipped.

"He was so naïve then. A boy of fourteen is not ready for a woman. I had to put his hands on me to show him things—it does not come naturally at that age. I think a boy has to be eighteen before he is a man. Girls are different; we become women as soon as our menses start. I thought a lot about touching long before I was fourteen."

"If our Master is loath to use these instruments of punishment and torture, why has he built an erga? Mustafa didn't tell me those diabolical things were never used."

Yasmeen laughed. "No, of course, he wouldn't. Mustafa is always threatening us and trying to swell his importance. That is the reason he carries a whip around with him. Ali's father was responsible for the architecture of the new palace. He started the construction, but died just before its completion. Besides, it is a matter of pride amongst wealthy harem owners, and a topic of conversation, as to who has the best ways to discipline their slaves. Without an erga, other men would see it as a sign of weakness, a masculine shortcoming; just as granting mercy is seen as weakness and cruelty as strength. A man of status must have an erga.

"I can tell you, none of us have been brought here, except for marking and piercing, yet we have all, at one time or other, committed wrongdoings and given offence."

I was enormously relieved.

We passed from the cold of the erga to the comforting warmth of the bedchamber.

"I remember from my time in Buraydah, the girl who posed for the carvings here," she said, pointing to the bas-relief panels behind the bedchamber bath.

"An artisan slave from Africa carved them, and after they were finished, Ali's father had him put to death for supposedly having touched the girl. He also punished the girl, and sold her on before we could ask her for the truth. No doubt, the real reason the black artisan carver saw death was that no whole man other than the master could have knowledge of the harem, although rumors persisted that jealousy had a part in it because of talk amongst the women about how generously endowed the was."

"How was it done? Putting a man to death."

"A male slave who touches one of the master's women is cut and staked; a free man is strangled from behind with a cord around his neck. They drown slave girls in the harem bath."

"What does it mean 'cut and staked'?"

"They mutilate the slave and stake him out in the desert to die slowly under the sun."

I wished I hadn't asked.

Yasmeen thought that torture and hurting punishments were uncalled for. "A carefully instructed girl, one treated fairly and kindly, is more than willing to accept and meet her master's demands. It comes naturally without coercion," she said.

I hurriedly agreed, thinking that ergas were despicable props needed only by weak and insecure men. A strong and confident man can easily convince an enslaved girl to yield to his ways without threat of the erga, and all the more so if he was young, kind and handsome like Ali! Even if she was not fortunate in having a handsome master, I believe that strength of character and confidence were all a man needed.

Snapping out of my daydream, I asked, "I have Katana's room; was she drowned?"

"Oh, no, no. Much worse than that, drowning would have been a mercy. It was horrible. She took so long to die, and of all people, she didn't deserve to. It all started with something in her foot, a sharp splinter or thorn. At first, she couldn't speak or swallow food, and then her body started to rack with spasms and convulsions[1]. She had the best of care, but died two weeks later, shortly after we moved here. The doctor said that the poisons came from that tiny prick in her foot. How could that be so? It was Satan's foul work."

---

1. Symptoms of tetanus (lockjaw) infection.

WRITINGS DISCOVERED

It was early afternoon—I was sitting at the small table near the window catching up on my journal entries.

Without warning, the Master appeared at my side and leaned over me to see what I was writing. He gave me a start—I had left the door open and even then had not heard his approaching footsteps on the hard courtyard path, or the gong. Or, was this an intended surprise visit? Fortunately, I always wrote details of my intimate encounters in French, a language my Master neither read nor understood.

"I didn't know you could write. Ahmad never mentioned it. It is most rare indeed to find a girl who can read and write. It is something for you to be very proud of.

"And what have you written in your strange language?" he asked.

Pretending to read from my journal, I replied, "It is a beautiful day today in Makram, a breezy coolness floats in from mountain and sea, birds flutter and twitter in the trees, and flowers bloom with vibrant color." I lied, obviously convincingly—I had acted in many school plays—for he said he was flattered that I would write such pleasant words about my stay and hoped one day I would write for him a copy in Arabic so that he might also recall these days.

Sitting down on the divan, he untied his caftan and leaned back against the backrest, beckoning me to lay down naked beside him and cradle my face in his lap. Arousal flickered within me, and encouraged by his gentle words and caressing, I eagerly brought about what he sought.

As he turned to leave, he encouraged me to continue my writings and left with welcomed words. "I will call you tonight."

Over the next week or so, I noticed my Master asking for my company more and more, rather than commanding or ordering it. He began treating me less and less as a slave and more as his willing lover. I believe that had I objected to any of his unusual requests he would not have insisted, nevertheless, I wanted to carry out all and every one of his wishes. I was beginning to enjoy being in his possession and giving him his pleasures.

BETWEEN DIGNITY AND DESIRE

Shortly after my menses, Mustafa placed my name on his roster of serving girls for the evening. With that thought doggedly in my mind, a restless agitation stirred within me for the rest of the afternoon. I felt overwhelmingly romantic. I had lusty yearnings and strong desires, or as my mother would say, "your womb is craving his seed". I desperately wanted the company of a man, with an intensity not felt since my early marriage years.

Between the English girl Paeonia and me, a comfortable easiness had grown as though we had known each other for a long time, and I felt relaxed and at ease discussing even my most private thoughts with her and asking for advice. She was also worldly and funny—she knew about winking, and called her night callings to the bedchamber "going to worship in the church of the holy sword".

"I have had the thoughts of a needy woman since I woke up this morning. I want to go to church tonight," I confided, jokingly, with a smile to hide my acute inner restlessness. "What can I do to make sure the doors are opened for me?"

For the last few nights, the Master had succumbed to the seductions of Hortensia, the buxom dark beauty, and we thought that she was my most likely rival for his attention this evening. But what to do?—her breasts were truly magnificent, large, proud and firm and the rest of her was splendid. We decided to draw his eyes to my legs and the areas below my waist, which, we agreed, were at least as pretty as hers—and it was the source of my restlessness and where I wanted his attentions.

"Come along. Cheer up. We will get you to church tonight by giving his eyes a treat," Paeonia laughed, beckoning me to follow her to the wardrobe room where she rummaged through chests and emerged with an unusual pair of harem pants, bright indigo blue, with matching top, ones she said she had made and kept tucked away for "desperate situations". I excitedly tried them on.

With no tie ribbons running up the side of the legs, the sides were fully open from ankle to hip; they were different and eye catching, able to show a shapely thigh and leg to good effect. The waistband dipped low in the front—so low that had I not been denuded hair would surely have spilled over—and it dipped low enough at the back to bare the small of the back and the start of the divide. And the top was delightfully unusual; the front panel had two open slits running up to the nipples. Worn loosely draped over the breasts the nipples could be coaxed to peek out enticingly where the slits ended, and the rest made for a short silk valance from beneath which my bobbling under-swells enticingly appeared and disappeared as I walked. "Perfect," I thought.

Unfortunately, my breasts were too small and bouncy to keep my nipples peeking out as I walked, so Paeonia crocheted small loops at the end of the slits to capture them, and further adjusted the fit. Then my breasts and top moved together and my nipples stayed peeking out.

As further inducement I spread *ultramarine* eye color around my nipples, covering what Mustafa had so carefully darkened. The blue of the ultramarine closely matched the color of the pants and choli. "Quite fetching," I thought, if I could induce Ali to remove my upper garment so that my artwork and more was exposed. "Yes Mustafa, I am eager to please," I murmured, undoing my earlier resolve to do no more than necessary to stay out of trouble and find content for my journal.

After dinner that evening, Hortensia soon had her choli off, exposing her oiled breasts and proud nipples. Dismayed and dejected, I thought I had lost, but when I noticed that his eyes were following me as I handed around the dishes of food a little of my hopeful brightness returned. Encouraged, I made sure when I leaned over to offer him food, I offered him more than food—a view of my charms, as much as my costume would allow. As I served him the last course—figs preserved in honey—he told me to put the dish aside and stand before him.

I did not wait for him to discover my colored circles. I proudly opened my top and pulled it aside, the crocheted loops tugging at my nipples before they freed themselves and my breasts fell free. His curious eyes drifted over my breasts, followed by his fingers as he reached up to touch me gently, taking care not to smear the blue mehndi. He lifted my feet one at a time, undid the cuffs that gathered my harem pants about my ankles, and reached for the drawstring that closed the waistband, a prelude to nakedness that sent a shudder of excitement through me.

With my arms above my head, my hands back to back in the "Turkish arm pose", I started to swirl and circle my hips as Yasmeen had taught me, swinging the drawstring back and forth so he could not catch it. I maintained this tease for a while, amid low giggles from the other girls, before slowing my swirling sufficiently to allow him to catch the ends of the drawstring and pull me closer. I pulled back in pretend resistance, the drawstring tightened and then loosened as the knot unraveled. My pants shimmied to the floor in a cloud of blue silk. Stepping out of them, I nonchalantly kicked them to one side, and continued my hip circles, turning around slowly several times to present both the front and back of me to his gaze. Our eyes met briefly. He smiled, somewhat amusedly, and slipped his silk under my silver armband—he had called me to bed.

Upon reflection, I believe my lustful behavior tilted that delicate balance between dignity and desire—in favor of desire. I had come to know little or no shame—within the four walls of the harem—and ignored my mother's advice to seduce with grace and discretion, wanting more for others to see me as one of the girls.

Mustafa, while checking my readiness, told me that I would be the only girl in the Master's bedchamber that evening.

I caught a glimpse of him drying himself after bathing as I crawled towards the bedchamber kneeling mat.

Abruptly, two feet appeared, one on each side of my outstretched hands, blocking my progress. "Show me your pretty face," he said, gently cupping his fingers under my chin to lift my face. I raised myself, sat back on my heels and opened my eyes.

I was startled to find him standing so close, with his bathrobe draping open from top to bottom, and startled again to see his member, bejeweled with silver circlets and chain, slowly rising from between the bathrobe folds and protruding towards me in a softly swelling arc.

"You dressed yourself excitingly this evening, indeed a novel use for eye mehndi," he said, smiling down at me. "As you can see, thoughts of it find favor with me. Come, Sapphira—excite me some more with your interesting ways."

Without further encouragement, I bunched his robe at the back of his waist.

Freshly bathed sweetness contrasted sharply with the metallic taste of the rings and chain, while my playing tongue and lips stiffened and straightened his member, swelling it against the rings and tightening the chain until it was no longer slack and looping down. He led me to the side of the bed, but not before turning the rings so that the chain lay on top of his member—he was not planning to take me from behind. Flitting away my remaining garments, he placed me face down on the bed, near the edge—not forcefully, but with firm determination—and I feared I had been wrong about the turning of the rings and forbidden things were about to be done.

From head to toe, he caressed and kneaded my whole body as I lay luxuriating in his attention, unable and unwilling to turn over onto my back to return his favor. My breathing grew heavy, love juices flowed, and my breasts tightened in their longing to be touched. He turned me over, parted my legs and knelt on the floor between them, and slowly pleasured me, almost to the brink, before I eased him away. I did not want his tongue—I wanted him in me, all of his rigid desire.

I slithered backwards over the silky bed sheets to the middle of the bed, drawing him with me, where, with well-practiced skill he entered me, no guiding hand needed, no hair to part. I convulsed in true ecstasy, wrapping my legs and arms tightly around him. His chain stirred exquisite sensations within me as it brushed back and forth against my bud and I relished the press of his body on mine, while deep within I felt his hard manliness stroking me to rapture. Caressing hands rewarded my pleading breasts; my probing tongue tasted my ylang-ylang on his wet lips, while he fervently plunged me to engulfing completion—but not himself.

He took me with him as he rolled onto his back, my red dappled chest attesting to the sincerity of my passion. Erect nipples called for his hands once more, and I knew as soon as he touched them and I started to ride, that I would again join him in ecstasy. He palmed my breasts, toyed with my nipples, the chain played my bud, and I contracted about him. His generous release pulsed into me, and I cried out loudly in my mind, "I love you…I love you Ali…I love you"—before collapsing onto his chest, my passion truly spent.

We lay side by side on the bed flushed of face, hearts beating strongly. Ali turned to me, curled an arm about me, and smoothed my hair back. As he slowly ran his fingers through it, he told me in a quiet voice how pleasingly I had peaked him, and I thanked him for calling me, and told him how much I enjoyed his company and the feel of his jewelry inside me.

"You are some woman, Sapphira. I enjoy having a woman respond passionately to my touch."

It was the first time he had called me a woman, and I felt that it was the first time he had really made love to me, rather than simply using me for his own gratification.

"Let us bathe before we sleep," he said, leading me to the bath where we submerged ourselves in the warm water and washed away our musks.

"You kissed me in a new way tonight—tell me, did you learn it from another man?"

"Oh no, Master. I learned it from a childhood friend of mine, a French girl. She told me it is the way a French girl kisses her lover when she wants him to bed her. The tongue and lips suggest those parts of a man and woman that she wants brought together. You are the first man I have kissed this way," I answered, in part untruthfully.

"Come closer," he said.

Our tongues played together. "I could come again with ease," I thought, but Ali must rest and replenish.

"Are you going to mark me?" I asked, to his and my own amazement. Ali looked at me, surprised.

"I would willingly put my mark on you and claim you as mine, but as you are not mine to keep, I must return you to Sheik Ahmad just as you came to me, unmarked."

Inwardly, I gave a slight shudder of relief, and to this day I do not understand why those words flowed from my mind to my lips, for branding was, of course, not something to encourage or speak of lightly.

"Why has Ahmad not put his tugra on you?" he inquired. "He always marks his goods."

Quickly, I made up a lie. "After I return to Al-Ta'if, Sheik Ahmad is going to take me to Jeddah and sell me to raise money for another trade caravan to India. He thinks that unmarked I will fetch a higher price."

Ali smiled and nodded knowingly. "Yes, that is true; no mark is seen and valued as a sign of freshness in the markets of Jeddah, however, I was thinking that maybe I will save Ahmad the trouble of a journey to Jeddah and travel back with you to his place, negotiate a favorable price for you, and bring you back here. Then I would mark you as my own," he whispered, his mouth tickling my ear.

"I would like to stay here," I whispered back.

He turned to face me, placed an arm over me, and drew me close. I felt loved and loving.

I awoke at the break of a cool dawn to find him sitting in the warm bath, deep in thought. I slipped off the bed and joined him, slowly descending the steps into the bath, the warm water circling around the swell of my hips. He was sitting on the submerged ledge, arms outstretched along the edge, the shallow ripples my descent had caused gently lapping against his hairy chest.

He stood up and leaned back against the edge of the bath, a splendid morning arousal breaking the surface of the water.

"Kneel," he abruptly ordered, "and pleasure me…slave," he commanded, an impersonal command that ended my dreamy thoughts.

I had expected words more endearing than slave. I wanted and expected a continuation of the evening before when he had shown me nothing but tenderness, caring and understanding. Possibly love. Of course, I obeyed his command, and with my breasts floating and bobbing enticingly, received a copious amount of his seed and nothing more for my care and trouble.

Dejected and hugely disappointed with the thought that only a few hours ago I was his lover and now nothing more than one of his pleasure slaves, I asked myself unanswerable questions. Where had I gone wrong? Had he had second thoughts about the way the evening before had unfolded? Was he trying to take back an unspoken message or conceal his true feelings?

TRAVELING COMPANION

I was delighted when Ali informed me that I would accompany him on a twelve-day visit to the oasis town of Ranyah where he would indulge in his favorite sports—camel and horse racing.

A retinue of eighteen people would attend. Fourteen, including Talil, would travel ahead and set up camp, and Ali, me, and two armed guards would arrive later, bringing with us two race camels. Ali would be riding his black stallion, I would be on one of the camels, but for the return journey, Ali said I could choose to ride either a camel or one of the racehorses. I would choose the horse—a more comfortable passage—and be grateful for the opportunity to practice my riding skills.

I looked forward to this glimpse into another side of an Arab sheik's life—a rare experience for a woman, as in the main, men attended public events alone while their women stayed home. My excitement was obviously showing and Ali had to remind me of my position in his household, advising me to bring traveling clothes for daytime and slave dress, jewelry, and mehndi for evenings.

"This is the first time I have taken a girl with me; it is something we agreed to do last year. You are someone I can be proud of when I show you to others. Bring along the clothes Ahmad sent with you; he has a fine taste for clothes…and women. I have chosen you to come with me because it will cause the least amount of discontent amongst the girls left behind, and Mustafa tells me you travel well and are not afraid of horses and camels."

Was he making fun of me or was he perfectly in earnest? I had felt special at first—and then perhaps a little let down when I thought it possible that he chose me only because I was not afraid of horses and camels.

Yasmeen—she was so thoughtful—gave me pessaries and a vial of medicine to take with me. She prescribed: "Five drops on the tongue each morning will hold back your menses until you return, but I warn you, when you stop you will flow with a vengeance."

"I know when I am due, and this will be most helpful—I thank you for your foresight." She only told me later that the medicine was made from the urine of pregnant camels!

At the meet there would be all kinds of goods to purchase, brought there by traders from afar. It was a most important event and a time to acquire goods from other parts of the world. Yasmeen had me write out a list of items to buy for the harem: kohl, henna, rouge, ambergris, vermilion, blue ultramarine and green malachite for our eyelids, oil of attar, and oil of sandalwood for our hair. She asked me to search hard to find the little paper tubes of bright red lip color from Europe. This mehndi was new and brighter than the mixture of rouge, ambergris and powdered vermilion we were using on our lips and it was very easy to put on. Ali had brought one stick back with him last year, and the girls had used it up in short order. This time Yasmeen wanted twenty sticks. Also on the list were silk and cotton thread, buttons, two bolts of chiffon silk or fine gossamer cotton, and one bolt of sturdy cotton, in my choice of color and pattern. And pomegranates to be bought on the way back.

Ali perused the list and nodded his approval, commenting on the overly extravagant use of oil of attar by his girls—this being an expensive ingredient of perfume, but one I knew Ali favored, and used for other purposes as well.

At the break of dawn we left on our journey, following in the footsteps and tracks of the rest of the entourage who had left a few days earlier to set up camp in readiness for our arrival. We journeyed for two days, taking rest overnight close to the water of a small wadi.

In late afternoon of the second day, our destination came into welcomed view as we crossed over the brow of the last of many tiresome dunes. Spread before us was the town of Ranyah, shimmering in the heat. It was surprisingly green and lush, with at first clusters of fine houses and buildings, which gradually gave way to smaller well worn ones at the center. I saw people moving about, passing in and out of the cool dark shadows cast by the colorful awnings of the souk and market square.

Beyond the town, away from the far side of it, was a large encampment of tents of all sizes and colors, swarming with men, camels and horses. Ali pointed out our encampment, a large colorful tent surrounded by several smaller black ones. It was set higher on the flat crest of the hill, separated from the rest.

We rode down the dusty main street, gathering a following of barking stray dogs and shouting children as we went past the usual amenities of an important town: the souk, market square, a large inn, the adjacent brothel, and a large outdoor meeting area set under a canopy of low scrubby trees. We continued onward up the hill to the encampment, shedding our uninvited followers as the town receded behind us, but not before Ali halted and cast a handful of coins into a small sea of outstretched hands. "Share them equally between you," he said.

Ali's tent was ready and waiting. A Saalih emblem flag fluttered from a short pole set at the center of the royal blue roof and the white sides billowed and heaved with every slight breath of wind. A tented canopy, decorated with a jagged blue fringe along each side, led to the entrance to the tent. In an unusual gesture—for an Arab man—Ali drew aside the silk entrance curtains, bowed slightly, and allowed me to enter ahead of him.

What a startling revelation greeted my eyes. The heavy canvas sides of the tent had been rolled and tied up, opening to the sunlight white muslin curtains that draped all around from eave to floor. Soft airy light filtered through the muslin, giving life to the rich colors and patterns of the interior. A huge carpet from the orient covered the center of the floor and brightly colored cushions piled on the carpet, low stools, a chair and table, a canvas hipbath, and polished brass lanterns hanging from each of the nine supporting poles finished the pleasing decoration. A large pad in one corner made do as a bed and I noticed a small kneeling rug on the ground in front of it. A comfortable home away from home, with no detail overlooked.

Seven smaller tents housed the rest of his entourage, and the camels and horses were nearby in a fenced enclosure where four boys, who attended the animals, had made themselves a crude shelter out of sticks and a piece of old cloth.

SOHRAB

By mid afternoon we had settled in, and Ali told me that in the evening we were to attend a large celebration at the home of a wealthy merchant to mark the opening of the meet. "All the sheiks and important traders will be there along with attending slave girls. I will be taking you," he said. "You will wear Ahmad's blue chiffon."

I was apprehensive and worried as we walked into town just as the sun was setting. Ali had said that others would see me as part of some special entertainment for the guests, and before leaving, he inspected me thoroughly, checking my freshness, my mehndi and my body jewelry. In doing so, he tightened the rings around my nipples so much that they swelled to the size of small red cherries and hurt from the chafe of my choli as my breasts bounced with my step. Was this to be part of the entertainment?

Ali noticed my discomfort as I hunched over to relieve the touch of the cloth and mercifully, he pulled me into a darkened doorway, untied the laces holding my choli closed, and carefully opened the rings and took them off my distended nipples, touching my tenderness gently. "Too tight," he muttered, "Talil knows better how to fit these things." He pulled me closer, planted a soft kiss on the top of my head and I settled myself back into my choli and retied the laces.

The door of the merchant's house was almost a hole in a crumbling wall and even I had to stoop down to pass through it. The doorkeeper led us down a narrow corridor around a sharp bend that served to shield the interior from the inquisitive eyes of passersby in the street, and into a beautiful well-tended garden courtyard. From there we walked across a central tiled court, flanked by tiled columns and curved arches, to the *beit al diafa* (guest parlor), where the men sat on large curved divans arranged around a low round table. A high ceiling of cedar wood painted in red and gold, lent warmth to the room as well as beauty.

Never be misled by the poor outward appearance of the many windowless dwellings lining the streets of Arab towns, for many were purposely built that way. Many Arabs consider it poor taste to show wealth ostentatiously, and this home was a fine example of that teaching. A modest exterior may well enclose an extremely luxurious home.

Ali took his place on a divan and I joined other girls standing in line to take turns serving the table. I returned to the guest parlor with a silver samovar from which I served mint tea to the seated men as they nonchalantly chatted and passed the hookah. All except one largely ignored me; although I was dressed revealingly in a way I knew found favor with men and had to lean low to pour.

Talented slave girls from the host's harem danced, sang, and played musical instruments to entertain the guests, and time passed quickly and pleasantly, until the host moved to the center of the room and held up his hand for silence.

"I welcome you all to my humble home this evening," he began "and may Allah grant many such visits.

"Last year, we agreed to add some variety to our gathering—some more attractive company than ourselves—and I thank those who were able to answer this call and bring with them a choice member from their harem. And I will add that I have never before seen so much talent and beauty under one roof; you have all surely brought your prettiest slaves. Alas, there are fewer of them than us, so," he clapped his hands, followed by a loud call for "Baseema," and an older slave woman immediately brought a large volume of the Qur'an and lay it before the sheik. "And so," he continued, "we will draw lots for the pleasure of their company."

I was taken aback somewhat, to put it lightly. I had not anticipated this! It made me realize, with an acute rush of feeling in the pit of my stomach, exactly what I had done. I had contracted for this. I had to do as commanded of me, without question, for I had bargained to be a slave girl at the call of men.

"Let us commence," said our host with a broad toothy smile on his face. "Help the girls display their virtues, Baseema, so that my guests may choose knowingly."

She set out a row of candles on the floor before the guests and, one by one, we were ushered forward to stand behind the lit candles, where Baseema, with great ceremony removed our clothes. Our host made pointed and sometimes lewd comments while we faced the scrutinizing and lustful eyes of the men, and after our showing we moved to one side, clutching our flimsy garments in our hands, where we formed a disorderly line.

The host held high the Qur'an, revealing white strips of paper that protruded from between its pages. "Some of these are long, some short. Those lucky enough to draw a long strip will have their choice of companion for the night."

"A blasphemous use of the Holy book," I thought.

Ali had the honor of first draw, and the host, after a drawn out inspection and much head shaking and feigned concern, conceded that Ali's strip of paper was indeed one of the long ones. Predictably, knowing his predilections and his desire to pay credit to the host's taste in women, he chose as his night companion a striking black Nubian girl belonging to our host of the evening.

I was sorely disappointed with the man who chose me—a small rakish merchant of unknown nationality—and even more disappointed that I was the seventh one chosen. Was it true that I was only seventh in rank of desirability!

Two unlucky and impatient men, after talking to the host, escorted Baseema—who, while older was still an attractive and generously proportioned slave—in the direction of an empty room, loosening her garments as they went, so eager were they to apportion her services. And how would she be apportioned to their lusts, how would she accommodate them, I puzzled to myself—both at the same time? Two men and one woman yield several possibilities. A *ménage a trois*.

A few men chose to bide their time and wait for the privacy of their own tent or house to spend time with their prize. Less patient ones took their choice into one of many side rooms for more immediate gratification—a gesture appreciated by the unlucky ones, as the girl could afterwards be bathed and again given over to someone.

Behind me, voices rose above the din of the room. "I hear that Sheik Ali Saalih is here. Who was the lucky one to get him?" My head turned sharply around at the mention of his name to see two girls talking to each other.

"That black Nubian," I said, pointing out his choice as I moved towards them to join in their conversation. "Why is she lucky?" I asked, curious as to their thoughts about him.

"You haven't heard about him?"

"Some—but what do you know?"

"He is wealthy beyond compare and lives in a huge palace and has a harem of over one hundred women," bubbled one of the girls, "and he takes as many as ten before he goes to sleep at night."

"It is said that he is so big and heavy that under his djellaba he wears a solid gold pouch to hold it," said the other.

"I wager the Nubian won't be walking with that proud stride after he has finished with her," said the first. "And I wager she won't be hungry," parried the other, crudely, amidst laughter.

"Who told you this about Sheik Ali?" I asked.

"Our keeper. She was with his father's harem, but she looks after us now because our eunuch died. She told us that on his fourteenth birthday he was given fourteen virgins and that on every birthday he gets again the same number as his years."

As I turned to walk away, I said, to their amazement, "What you say is true, he is a remarkable man. I know, because I am his haseki."

My eyes sought Ali amongst the crowd of men across the room. They found him, and held him, and within that short moment, something passed between us…and I saw clearly in the dim light that I loved him. I knew that there was no other explanation for my feelings, nor did I want one. I longed for him frantically and unquestionably and wanted nothing more than to end this ungodly separation and go back to the tent with him, to tend his needs, belong to him—and let go of my secrets. Brave thoughts soon swept aside by a rising flood of despair. Love had recklessly drawn me into the unrest and hopelessness of an impossible romance, one I new I could not possibly reconcile—I was a married woman.

It was well into the night when the merchant decided to leave for his own tent. As I hurriedly followed behind him, an unfamiliar and unpleasant odor wafted back over me. He and a small group of friends had been drawing heavily from a hookah all evening, and now his footsteps were unsure with an occasional stagger and stumble.

Darkness and stale air laced with a sour stench greeted me when he pushed me forward into his tent. There were no windows or openings of any kind to let in fresh breezes—or a splash of moonlight—as there were in Ali's tent. He lit a lamp and I saw the source of the terrible odor—numerous falcons dozing on perches in one corner of the tent—clumps of white guano mottling the ground beneath them.

A loose bundle of rattan and an untidy collection of empty and partly made birdcages littered one side of the tent, and a small rug and sleeping pad lay on the sandy floor not far away. Two sturdy wood poles supported the canvas roof, and ominously, hammered high into one of them was a black iron ring. A chain with gaping open wrist shackles riveted to each end dangled from the ring. A key hung from a small nail.

He first spoke to me in Farsi or Urdu, I thought, languages I did not understand, and realizing this he spoke again, this time in poor Arabic with a heavy accent. But words were not required, his intentions were obvious and no surprise to me. Without pleasant formalities, he thoroughly eyed me from head to toe, thought for a moment, and reached for a knife in his belt. He approached threateningly, testing the blade of the knife with his thumb, before he slid the cold curved tip of steel between my breasts and brought it up sharply; cutting through the ladder of laces that held my choli closed—thrrrr…up. He flipped the parted cloth aside and threw the knife down.

He pressed closer to me, staring into my eyes and then at my uncovered charms, while the smell of his stale clothing assaulted my nostrils. His small rough hands—resplendent with uncut dirty nails—explored my body and for one horrible long minute, I endured those grimy fingers on my skin—poking, stroking, pinching and squeezing my breasts and stomach until I thought I could stand no more. His breath was close and foul in my face before his eager mouth found my breast, and pain and revulsion so severe swept through me, that without thinking, I swept my arms upwards, hitting him sharply under the jaw and sending him sprawling backwards into the pile of empty birdcages.

"You, you will pay for that! I punish you," he spluttered, as he stumbled to his feet, pushing cages aside and brushing sand off himself.

Viciously he grabbed my hair and slammed me against the tent pole. Stunned and winded, I could not resist as he snapped the shackles around my wrists, pushed my chest against the pole, and hoisted my hands above my head. For a dazed moment, my bewildered mind called back with childlike simplicity to the peace and tranquility of the palace courtyard back in Makram. "Yasmeen will be annoyed with me," my mind was telling me. "She will tell me to be more careful with my clothes—and then mend them for me."

When I heard it, a swell of rising panic swamped these calming thoughts. It was the unmistakable swish and thwack, that frightening sound of something smacking into an open palm, something being tested for its heft and flex.

He tore away my beautiful pants, leaving them where they fell on the dirty ground, and started to shuffle back and forth behind me, tapping my bottom lightly now and again with something that was not his finger.

A white-hot sting flared across my buttocks. It extinguished in one bright flash of my mind, any thoughts I had. The swish, thwack, and sting were one; nothing separated them when he brought his instrument of chastisement down sharply across my bared buttocks. In my shock, I did not cry out. I would not give him that satisfaction. A resolve that was swiftly undone.

I danced like a marionette on strings when the second stroke hit home, and I shrieked out in the vain unrealized hope that my cries would summon help—that Ali would somehow hear me and come to my rescue. It was a loud and piercing cry that echoed through the camp, more than making up for my earlier silence.

"My name Sohrab, I rich and strong man, you a slave woman. I hit you till noise you make no more. People sleep," his slurred voice dictated. For his pleasure, I must suffer in silence or be beaten into unconsciousness so others may sleep. I clenched my teeth and held my breath in fearful anticipation, as he bade his time.

His further judgment came down heavily, three or four more strokes, laid down in brisk succession followed by a loud snap and something flying against the tent side that startled his captive birds into a frenzy of flapping wings. My body arched and collapsed, my knees buckled under me, leaving me hanging by my wrists while my feet thrashed around trying to find footing in the loose sand. The iron shackles cut deeply, and my outraged shoulders burned under the separating weight of my dangling body.

"My stick break. You lucky this time," he sneered.

To my utter surprise, he keyed open one of the shackles, freeing one hand, leaving me still tethered by the other. The chain, now out of balance, pulled and rattled through the eye of the small ring—the opened shackle rode up the pole, and the one still closed around my wrist rode down, along with it my tethered arm and slumping body. An abrupt and noisy clang signaled the end of travel and jolted me to a stop, leaving me hanging awkwardly by one arm, with the rest of me sprawled in the sand at the foot of the pole. I found my knees and knelt up high to slacken the chain and relieve the cut of the shackle, while my free hand soothed my burning bottom that throbbed painfully with every beat of my pounding heart.

On his sleeping pad, a mere rug spread out on the bumpy sand, he undressed, and amid cursing and fumbling, set up a hookah, and squatted behind it. After several shaky attempts, he lit a small bed of fiber, the center of which cradled a small black ball. For several minutes, he slowly inhaled and exhaled the dense white smoke, until the little ball melted, shrank away, and flared up and died out. Strings of acrid, pungent smoke, floated in layers in the stagnant air of the tent and my nostrils filled with the same unforgettable smell that had wafted over me when I had earlier walked behind him. Unseen and unheard, I vomited onto the ground and brushed sand over the splatter with my foot.

Although covered by my torn pants it caught my eye. I could see it shining through the delicate blue chiffon. His knife. My mind sank to new levels. I would stab him when he came close to me again—kill him! "He deserved nothing better than to die," I thought.

But could I do the deed when the time came? The curved blade of the knife was more suited to ceremonial dress and cutting through strings than stabbing through human flesh. Besides, would my wrenched arm possess the strength to plunge it into him? I flexed my free hand; it closed weakly.

If I only wounded him, it would serve no purpose. It would only enrage the vicious beast within him, and his vengeance would be swift and thorough. Still shackled and chained to the pole by one arm I would be utterly at his mercy. Likewise, if I killed him, I could not escape. Others would find me still chained to the pole, with the bloodied weapon at my feet, and drag me to the town prison. There, no doubt, a brutal jailor would unmercifully scourge me, as he would any common murderer, and after he had done, he would take me to the public square for "beheading by the sword". There, face down on a long wooden table with my ankles clamped in heavy wooden blocks, head hanging over the end, my head would be severed—my exposed neck, taut and pale, giving deadly aim to the sweep of the scimitar sword.

I took a deep shuddering breath and thought better of my plan to kill him.

When he next stumbled towards me, I was relieved to see he held nothing in his hands, other than the key to the shackles. At least he did not intend to beat me further; instead, he fumbled with the iron shackle around my wrist springing it open. My aching arm dropped like deadweight, my twisting shoulder protesting its release with a burst of pain. Grasping the back of my neck, he pitched me towards his sleeping pad where I stumbled and sprawled out, half on the pad, half in the sand, the flying sand dusting and clinging to my damp limbs and sweat-beaded chest.

He tottered back to the pad, lay down on his back, reached out and pulled in a saddlebag for a pillow.

I could only guess at what he had smoked with his hookah, opium maybe. Whatever it was, it was truly intoxicating him. His eyes flickered and rolled up into his head, leaving the sockets filled with grotesque jaundiced balls—a toppled heathen idol. His loosely parted lips exposed teeth that looked like a row of broken brown almonds.

Taking himself in his hand, he stroked for a few moments, then seized me with his other hand and forced me to kneel between his spread legs and replace his hand with mine.

His penis was thin, short and uncircumcised, and as I pulled down the foreskin to free the head a smell of stale urine and unwashed skin revolted my senses. He had not bathed for days, perhaps never in his life. With my hand, I brought his sticky appendage to full hardness, and hurriedly clambered on top of him. Nevertheless, I did not slip him into me. I kept my hand on him and stroked him while I moved my body, pretending, for his benefit, that he was in me. His breathing quickened and deepened to short gasps as he released his issue, and in his drowsy intoxicated state, it went unnoticed that I had used my hand.

I had no qualms about doing it to Jamaal or my Master. I enjoyed pleasing them that way; they were always clean, sweet tasting, and appreciative. This man, however, disgusted and sickened me so much that I decided that if he did not chain me back to the post for the night I would sneak out after he fell asleep and return to my Master's tent. I would face the consequences of leaving my night companion. Nothing could be worse than pleasuring him.

When his breathing deepened in true oblivion, I picked up his curved knife and my clothes from the floor, bundled them about me to stave off the cold, and left his wretched tent.

Moonlight reflecting on the water of the oasis gave me direction, and I headed downhill to the water's edge weaving my way between tents, daintily stepping high over ropes and pegs so as not to trip over them and rouse sleeping occupants.

At the edge of the water, I knelt down and washed my hands thoroughly using wet sand to scour away the lingering residue from my filthy encounter. Splashing water over my face and body, I waded out until the water was about my waist and waited for the cool water to douse the fire of my buttocks. Then I flung his knife into the depths and returned to the shore, dressed as well as I could in my torn clothes, and picked up the path that led back to Ali's tent.

A guard intercepted me, recognized my face, and after discreetly glancing at my partially clothed body, allowed me to pass. I curled up outside the tent under a piece of canvas and spent the rest of the night's cold hours in fitful sleep.

At dawn, I awoke to the sound of muffled voices coming from inside the tent, sounds of laughter and lovemaking—and the sight of a small turbaned man crouched on the ground not far away staring straight at me, with a look of bewilderment on his face. I froze and lay motionless beneath the canvas, intensely aware of my furiously pounding heart, but I was of no interest to him, other than to his curiosity.

Shortly thereafter, the Nubian girl appeared in the entrance to the tent, completely oblivious to my presence, and extended her arm in the direction of the turbaned man. He rose, tied a rope around her wrist, and led her away.

Scampering from my hiding place, I entered the tent to find my Master reclined on his sleeping pad, obviously relishing the afterglow of a pleasant experience.

"Sapphira! You are back earlier than I—what is that red mark on the side of your face?"

"I bumped into a tent pole, Master, it is nothing," I replied calmly.

"Look at your clothes!" he said, jumping to his feet.

He took me by the shoulders and held me in front of him, frowning, and then lowered my tattered clothes that I had crudely tied about me. Inspecting his goods for damage, his eyes traveled slowly from my head to my toes. He saw the bite mark on my breast, made a muffled sound, and then turned me around and found the angry red welts on my bottom.

"Who did this to you? Who were you with?"

"I don't know. He told me his name was Sohrab, I think—or something like that," I managed to say, before my composure collapsed and I burst into tears.

"That doesn't tell me much; what did he beat you with?" he demanded, after my tears had subsided.

"He was behind me when he beat me. I think it was with a stick."

"It wasn't a stick. The lines are too thin to be the work of a stick; it was a cane. One, two…three, four, five…six strokes. He's a swine. And look at your wrist. He shackled you. Where is his tent?"

"Up on the side of the hill, Master," I sobbed.

"That doesn't tell me much either. Could you find it again?"

"I don't think so, Master, it was dark when I was taken there, and dark when I fled."

"Allah help us all! This is not the way it is supposed to be. God gave women to men, but not the right to beat them, no matter that she is a slave. He will pay for this abuse of God's gifts," he said, muttering a few choice curses that I will not repeat.

"He is an animal. An ignorant foreigner no doubt. He does not deserve to be a man. This treatment of you is outrageous. I will avenge it; I can assure you of that. Next time, if there is a next time, you will go with someone I know. And, as for him, when I find him, and I will, he is finished as a man.

"May the curse of God settle on him."

Turning away, he strode to the entrance and called sharply to someone beyond, ordering something brought bring to the tent, the name of which I did not catch. Shortly, to my immediate concern, Talil appeared…with a vial of ointment in hand.

"Sapphira was caned last night. See to it that she is cared for properly. Bathe her and spread the ointment where she has been hurt. Be gentle with her and let her rest afterwards."

"Yes, Master," replied Talil.

Ali dressed, Talil walked behind him to the opening in the sidewall of the tent, and saw him out and on his way for the day.

Talil turned to me. "What happened? What did you do that inflamed the Master to this?" he asked angrily.

"It was not the Master. I was with another man last night. He did it to me. I knocked him over. It was an accident, but he still beat me."

"Ah, now I understand, because Ali does not permit anyone to be caned or whipped since we moved to Makram. Please turn around. Let me see the place of your torment.

"Oh, may Allah comfort you. This is a terrible. This is the work of an uncivilized animal with no talent or understanding. A girl has to feel her master's anger, of course, but never this severely for an accident or small offence. A smack with the hand would be enough. Small wonder the Master is furious. Your tormentor should have known better than to damage the jewel of the harem."

"Jewel of the harem? Who calls me that?" I asked, stirred by pride and the thought that it might be Ali.

"Mustafa and I do, because since you arrived there is a new sparkle about the palace that comes from you."

"It comes from the name Sapphira," I countered, with a smile full of false modesty.

"It is more than just your name. We notice that Ali is settled now and more thoughtful and passionate about life. You have refreshed his being and we want to keep it that way. It is good for everybody.

"Come let me bathe you, and make you well again."

His gentle caring was a complete surprise so far removed from my first impression of him—my chilling encounter with him at my first showing. He bathed me gently and continued his polite chatter.

"When you first came to the harem I imagined you would cause trouble with the other girls, because at your first showing you stood proudly and looked defiantly at the Master, almost with disrespect. But you are not the kind of girl I thought you were. We are all delighted to have you with us."

"And you are not the kind of person I though you were," I replied, carefully avoiding the word man.

"What was your name before you were enslaved?"

"Mariyah," I replied.

"You have two enchanting names. If I was to have a daughter I would want to call her Mariyah."

Talil bathed away any unpleasant thoughts from my night encounter, and after he applied the ointment, he left me to rest. I lay on my front, with my head on my arms, thinking of my Master and the concern he had shown for me. Pleased with my painful achievement, I allowed myself to wear a secret smile of satisfaction and dozed the morning away.

Ali returned shortly after noon and, after my assurances that I felt much better, told me that he would take me for a leisurely walk into town and buy our mid-day meal from one of the many street vendors.

"They do it in Europe you know."

"Do what Master?" I asked.

"Take their women out with them."

"It's a lovely custom, you're very modern in your ways, Sire," I said, in subtle flattery that he accepted with a nod and proud smile.

"Before we go, let me see your welts. How are they? Are you well enough to walk about?" He raised the hem of my skirt; I wiggled my bottom imperceptibly—I thought.

"I see you are feeling better," he chuckled, as he gently felt the ridges before letting the hem fall back. "And so you should. That ointment is expensive, we use it on our best horses when they have been cropped too strenuously," he added, bursting into laughter.

Horse medicine! Now, what do I make of that?

A SMALL GIFT

I dressed in a *burqa*, covered from head to toe, because I did not want my awful night companion to recognize me should our paths cross. It would only cause a disturbance between him and my Master and would spoil our outing. Ali, I knew, would handle Sohrab in his own way, at his own time.

We walked to the center of the old town and browsed the displays of the souk looking for items that pleased the eye. I felt safe; nevertheless, I stayed as close to Ali as convention allowed for a man's woman—two paces behind—even so, better than the usual place for a slave—ten paces behind—and at least I wasn't tethered to him like an animal.

We paused in front of a jeweler's shop, the display of precious merchandise spilling over into the street, under the owner's watchful eye. At the rear of the place was the workshop where two craftsmen hammered gold and silver into beautifully crafted items, and set jewels and precious stones.

I saw him from the corner of my eye, across the narrow street, sitting under a canopy in the shade, surrounded by his wares—hunting falcons gyred to wooden perches—my hated merchant from the night before, and he seemed to be staring straight at me. Ali and the proprietor entered the workshop and I followed hastily, my weak legs trembling so much that I tripped on a well-worn floorboard and had to grasp Ali's thobe to catch my fall, but greatly thankful to be out of sight of the merchant.

Radiating enthusiasm about the high quality and value of his wares, the shop owner proudly presented a tray of jewelry. Ali selected three items and took me into a small room at the rear. He asked me to raise the front of my burqa while he knelt down and tried to put the jewelry pieces, one at a time, in my navel. They were belly brilliants.

He was having difficulty; they kept popping out, and he suggested calling in the jeweler for help, "Maybe the tips need to be made a little longer." At this time, with my burqa raised, I did not want a stranger to see me, so I bent down and whispered to Ali that he should first wet my navel.

Still kneeling before me, he unexpectedly nuzzled his face into me before moving up to my navel. "You're tempting and pretty down here," he said, looking up at me with a boyish grin, a grin that did not hide from me his later intentions.

The brilliant slipped in easily and felt almost comfortable, and I told him that if a girl could not enfold it, then a dab of spirit gum would hold it in place.

He offered me my choice of any one of the three. I deliberated for a while imagining how I would look with each one, and which of my outfits would be enhanced. I chose one with a blue crystal at its center, to match the color of my harem name and Paeonia's blue harem outfit that I had used so successfully two weeks before and intended to use again. He nodded his approval. "It's for you to keep as your own, to take back with you when you leave my service. A small token of…."

"Of…? Of what? Of his love for me? Please finish your sentence," my mind pleaded, but nothing more was said.

Was the precious gift a sign of love, or was it just given out of kindness, with nothing more attached or hinted at?

Where did I stand in his affections? Did I have a standing at all? I desperately wanted to know.

As we left the jewelers shop, I caught a glimpse of the *qanass* merchant as he hurried down the street in the direction of the market square, leaving a young boy to take care of his birds.

SLAVE MARKET

From the moment I saw the black braid hanging down her back I knew she was one of Ahmad's "pearls" standing on a raised platform, with her back to us, naked—hands and feet bound. A slave for sale.

On our return I would try to steer Ali back in this direction, to walk in front of her and try to catch a glimpse of her face when we came by. Of course, I could do nothing to comfort her, or even smile at her; my burqa precluded that. Still, I wanted to know for certain what had become of her. I was curious.

In the next few minutes I saw many sights—all far removed from what I was accustomed to—one particular one stayed with me—a harried turbaned man yanking along a girl by a chain around her wrists. The girl, a slave no doubt, tugged back, resisting. Growing increasingly angry with her, her owner snatched a crop from a passing man leading a donkey and gave her three vicious lashes across her back. She fell to the ground. He handed the crop back to its surprised owner, impatiently jerked his slave to her feet and went on his way—dragging along a less rebellious girl.

"She will likely be put up for sale later this afternoon," Ali muttered. "We will go and watch; perhaps I shall learn today's price for slave girls so I can be sure to make an offer to Sheik Ahmad that does not offend…or delight him." Again, that grin, and again I wasn't certain if he was serious or joking.

The sound of a crowd drew us to a small courtyard off the main square. Vetted by two burly eunuchs we walked down a narrow passageway that opened into it, and here, out of view to the casual passerby—and the authorities—a sale of humans in bondage was taking place.

By the time we arrived the auction had been in progress for some time and bids for the last two males, fine looking light skinned youths still in their teens, had been called. Both were kneeling upright at the edge of a raised wooden platform in a position of subservience, legs apart, hands held behind the head.

"So, they do it to male slaves as well," I thought, answering a question I had long harbored in my mind, for it was the first time I had seen a depilated man. I found it unattractive. "Grotesquely overgrown boys," came to mind. I readily decided that if Ali were my slave I would not have him shaved down there, just trimmed and groomed—so manly that way, in keeping with the rest of him.

Penises were in full view, limp between their legs, but only one had testicles, the other without had been castrated in the Christian style.[1]

"Those three bidders with *kaffiyehs* pulled across their faces," Ali whispered, pointing to a group of shrouded figures standing close to the platform, "are women. I know two of them. The tallest one is a wealthy young widow, the Turks killed her husband last year in a skirmish, and the shorter one by her side is the brothel owner. They could be buying men for their own use."

Hearing this made it clear why they displayed youths in this manner. It was for the women who were buying on the pretense of needing a house servant, and the auctioneer played along with their deception by referring to the youths as strong servants, eager for work, with stamina and other pleasing skills and urges.

I asked Ali, "If they are truly women, and interested in a man that way, why would they be buying a man who has been castrated? He cannot perform his duties."

"The one you refer to, the gelded one, has been prepared for a man, nevertheless, he could also be bought by a woman if she is looking for a servant or bath attendant. They can still bring pleasure to a woman."

Women, by law, were forbidden to own bed-slaves—something I thought most unfair in the light of my situation—but man-to-man coitus was also against the law and punished by "beheading by the sword". These laws, however, did not concern the organizers of the sale, other than perhaps prompting the prudent move of the auction out of the main square and into this side courtyard.

We were in time to watch the next part of the auction, the sale of women. In front of a platform, a roped off area was reserved for qualified buyers—men either known to the trader, or men who had shown sufficient gold to make a

---

1. White eunuchs were bought from slave dealers in Christian Europe and Circassia. (Vienne in France was the main center of 'eunuch production', because laws of Islam forbid castration at the hands of a Muslim). Their emasculation was not as complete as a black eunuch's was.

purchase. Behind this section, a large crowd of voyeurs whiled away their time, including ourselves.

Under the watchful eye of the slave trader seven women were brought forth from a small tent and encouraged, by sight of the short whip in his hand, to mount the steps leading up to the platform. Hesitatingly, they lined up in a row at the rear of the platform, in the shade of a canvas canopy, with their backs to the crowd. A bell sounded. One by one, the auctioneer worked his way along the row of captive women, pulling their garments off their shoulders and down to their waists. Three crimson welts on her back identified one as the girl we had seen earlier in the souk. At the snap of his whip against the platform and a shouted command, the women turned to face the crowd, bared breasts catching the sunlight and the lustful gaze of the crowd. With shouted encouragement from those watching, he walked behind them, teasingly lowering their garments to their feet until they all stood naked before the buyers.

Four of the women still sported their fleece, a true measure of hair color to the eyes of Arabs. It was something Arab men attached great importance to—and then removed!—and always favored the fair, unfortunately for me, for although my skin was light in color, my hair was almost kohl black. As Ali said, "You have French skin and Berber hair"—but he did say he found the contrast fetchingly attractive. I was satisfied with that.

In turn, the auctioneer had each naked girl parade herself back and forth along the length of the platform until halted at the center by his out held whip, where, with exaggerated ritual and show, he forcefully pushed her to her knees close to the edge of the platform. Prospective buyers stepped forward to inspect her mouth and feel for the qualities they sought, before the auctioneer shuffled her around and bent her over to expose her for a more intimate inspection, by probing fingers and parting hands, by men peering into places no man had the right to peer into.

Ali noticed my unease and embarrassment. "It is something new for me, too, to see this done before a crowd, but remember, they are slaves, not wives or daughters deserving respect. They lost that status," he explained.

"They were and will always be someone's wives and daughters. Slave traders stole and buried their precious status and freedom. They did not lose it!"

A serious look from Ali did not deter me and I continued.

"It is a sin against God to enslave his creations and I despise those men who draw from this evil offense," I replied angrily, then regretting that I had used the word despise with such force. "They should be set free, not sold like animals, and a man of your status and influence should stand up and do something about it!"

He looked at me again, as much surprised as I was by my nerve, and then, somewhat subdued, continued without comment.

"As I was saying, usually, buyers appraise women beforehand out of sight in a holding tent, but let me explain to you why this scrutiny is necessary. In any business, there are unscrupulous purveyors and slave traders are no exception. With the shortage of goods, they have resorted to cheating; there is no honor amongst slavers these days. Nowadays they are not to be trusted. Hair is bleached with alum and lemon, and skilled surgeons are hired to restore the vestiges of virginity to well-used girls with a few well placed stitches, or she could be sachetted."

"What is sachetted, Master?" I asked.

"It's an old trick used by brothel owners to sell a girl's virginity many time over to unsuspecting strangers and now used by slave traders. They insert a sachet, a small bag of thin goat or sheep membrane tightly filled with blood, into her. When the man thrusts into her the sachet bursts and the unsuspecting master believes he has deflowered a virgin; he thinks that the burst sachet is her torn curtain and the blood the 'blood of the first night'. Clever deceit, don't you agree?" He continued, without waiting to hear my opinion. "Black girls from North Africa, in particular, have to be looked over thoroughly as the practice of female circumcision is spreading rapidly, a practice that in the minds of many Arab men diminishes the desirability of a woman. She is unable to reply naturally to her master's passion, and many harem masters take pride in taking a girl to her peak of excitement and hearing her cry out."

I would remember that—outbursts were easy to make.

"This mutilation of women is a hideous practice. I prefer my girl's petals uncut," he said casually, adding, "How good it is that Black Pearl and Hortensia are as God made them."

With the pre-bidding inspections over, the women again formed a line at the back of the platform in the dark shade of the canopy. When their turn came, they stepped forward into the full glaring sunlight and bidding commenced. The slave trader read out her qualifications, age, and origin, pointed out attributes that might have escaped the eye of the bidders, such as the small Christian cross one of the girls wore around her neck, and closed his remarks with an opening price. The older, less attractive and least expensive women were first put up for sale, while the younger girls were held back to last.

Bidding was lively and raucous, with the crowd yelling remarks over the shouts of the auctioneer as he called out the latest bids. The fifth girl, a small but pretty captive from Syria, was sold to Sohrab—that sordid filthy qanass merchant—of my previous encounter. He signaled his delight with his winning bid by raising both hands in the air, revealing a shiny new item tucked through his belt. That horrible, pig-eating coward had bought a whip, conjuring in my mind visions of his new purchase shackled to the wooden pole of his tent awaiting his barbarous pleasures.

"Did you see who bought that Syrian girl?" I whispered, pointing to Sohrab. "That man is the man who beat me. He doesn't deserve a woman, never mind such a young innocent girl. I know he will be cruel to her, poor thing. Look how young she is, and look at that whip in his belt." These thoughts sickened and saddened me, and I urged Ali to take me back to the encampment, claiming that the heat of the sun bearing down on my black burqa was about to overwhelm me.

"So, that is the man. He is the one who sells falcons in the souk. And yes, we will leave, but did you notice that he paid nearly four thousand *qirsh* for the girl? She is a lesser beauty than you are. She has smaller breasts, and her narrow hips promise less vigor than yours do. You are worth more, but should I pay Ahmad your price?" he asked, suggesting that he could afford the price but perhaps I was not worth it. Was he making fun of me again or was he serious? I dared not ask for the answer.

Ali continued to bemoan the shortage of new slave girls that was driving prices up. For hundreds of years, he explained, Arabs had brought black girls north to stock their harems, but now black kings, chiefs and nobles were buying white girls and taking them south. The flow of human cargo had reversed direction. A further exacerbation was the scarcity of new slaves from Europe and the East now that wars were being waged in Europe, and piracy policed by the navies of the European states. He reflected that well over half the girls of his father's harem had been black, and he went on to tell me that black girls, particularly Christians from *Nubia* or *Abyssinia*, "are highly prized for their pert breasts and generous buttocks."

As we walked back, Ali reminisced about the times when he first came to these meets with his father. "At that time, on slavers day, the entire main square was filled with slavers showing their wares," he said. "Some set up tents or rented buildings facing the square, while others erected wooden platforms from which they conducted their business. It was exciting for a young boy awakening to the charms of girls and women, to see them exposed naked like that," he chuckled.

I thought about the casual and matter-of-fact manner in which Ali discussed the most intimate details of women. Did he see his girls and women as mere possessions without emotions and feelings of their own? Possessions displayed like fine furniture or valuable carpets, used to add comfort and variety to his life, to relieve him of his lust, and lend to his friends at will. Was having many women at his call the same to him as owning many camels or having many servants in service? And if so, why would he feel any different about me?

Yet, on the other hand, he had shown encouraging compassion and concern for my misfortunes at the hands of the merchant, which gave room for hope that my first thoughts were wrong.

ENGLISHMAN

Afternoon walks to the souk had become almost routine, something I looked forward to every day, but never took for granted. I was one of the few women seen in the souk, which spoke well for Ali. He was quite modern in his customs.

On this day, during our walk, Ali met with an attractive man who, I later found out, was an English arms dealer. It was obvious that he and Ali knew each other well. They spent time in hushed conversation interspersed with occasional raucous laughter while I stood to one side, out of earshot. Nevertheless, it gave me excellent opportunity to scrutinize this interesting man. Dressed in the European style of loose fitting shirt, breeches, and high leather boots, he cut a dashingly handsome figure to my eye.

Suddenly he turned to me and caught me looking at him in a more than casual way. His eyes did not turn away. I pulled my *hijab* across my face, hoping he would not notice my rising blush, and clearly returned his searching glance. They continued to look at me, that unfair prerogative allowed of men, while they obviously discussed my qualities.

We returned to our tent.

"This evening a small reception is being held where I will inspect some of the latest European rifles and pistols. Just six men and their companions will be there, and you are coming with me. It will not be a repeat of the other night; I can assure you of that. However, my good friend, the one you saw this afternoon, has hinted of a favor of me, and I noticed how he looked at you. I thought it would be nice for him to have you for a night—he has been away from home for a long time. What are your feelings about that? Think about it for a while," Ali said, with a slight hesitation.

I was taken aback for a moment, not as much by the nature of his suggestion as by the fact he had almost asked for my permission. Nevertheless, it did not take me long to make up my mind. I had a motive—maybe it would make Ali a little jealous, appreciate me more—and his friend was an intriguing and appealing man.

After a suitable pause to hide my enthusiasm, I said, "Master, your words are my command. I am your slave; I will go with him."

"Yes, you belong to me, and don't forget it," he said, hooking his foot under a low stool and pulling it away from a pole. "Now come here, stand on the stool and reach forward, hold the pole with your hands."

It was not thanks I received, and I thought, "If he thinks that taking me abruptly in this manner will somehow impress me and cool my ardor for tonight's liaison, he is sorely mistaken."

In strained silence, we set off for the reception.

It seemed the Englishman had rented this room in the inn for the occasion, to display his wares to interested buyers. I helped to pour mint tea and pass around sweetmeats, which gave me excellent opportunity to scrutinize the company more closely. The Englishman looked dashing and tempting in a way that disturbed me, and to my surprise and liking, his companion was no raving beauty. She looked much older than he did, with a rather drawn face, imperfect teeth, short hair and a thin body without eye-catching form. She was an unexpected choice indeed for a handsome man of substance. This was my first impression of the Englishman's companion. I flattered myself—no wonder he wanted some time with me.

After refreshments, the men got down to business. Prospective buyers admired and handled the guns, leveling and aiming them at imaginary foe, while the English man and his companion pointed out various aspects of their manufacture and quality.

As the business concluded, Ali leaned over and whispered in the ear of the Englishman. Agreement seemed to be made, and again his eyes fell on me, making me uncomfortably aware of his appeal. He raised his hand and pointed to his empty cup and as I poured yet another of many cups of tea, the Englishman slipped his handkerchief under my slave bangle. My Master's white silk, surprisingly, appeared shortly thereafter tied around the wrist of his female companion, the one I was not too complimentary about in my mind. Did this mean that Ali would sleep with her? I suppose he might, if just to be polite.

After the reception, the Englishman escorted me to his tent. I wore a burqa to shield me from peeping eyes as I was scantily dressed underneath, wearing only the beautiful white gossamer silk pants and choli I had brought with me from Jeddah. They were revealingly sheer and diaphanous, and having the concealing burqa over them added to the sense of alluring mystery I was basking in.

"Ouch! What are you doing?" I asked indignantly.

"Pinching your delicious bum."

"How do you know it is delicious?"

"My dear, I took a good look at it at the reception, those enticingly sheer pants you are wearing left little to my imagination and even less when you bent over to pour. Even here in the twilight I can see your curves outlined by your burqa."

"I think you are not quite a gentleman, Sir" I replied, trying to find words that would convey modest indignation yet not insult.

"I know, people have told me that many times," he laughed, giving me a firm pat on my bottom. "And call me Barry, and by what name do I call you?"

"Sapphira," I replied.

We arrived at his tent, a nondescript abode, square, with four corner poles and one in the center—not luxuriously appointed and colorful like Ali's, but rather plain. He had rented a serviceable shelter from an outfitter in town, as did many others who were not able to travel with such heavy and bulky supplies.

He took off his boots and I lifted my stifling burqa off over my head.

"Those clothes you're wearing are enchantingly flimsy, they look as though they could be blown off by a slight gust of wind," he laughed. "There could be a good breeze where we are going. Here, put on this dress of Anne's and you will look as if you are my mistress. Save the gossamer for later," he said, in a perky tone of voice as he handed me a light cotton dress.

The dress, buttoned down the front, was tight on me—my bosom pushed out in sympathy as I drew in my stomach to close the buttons.

"I have to wee-wee," he said, with a grin.

"You have too what?" I asked.

"Pass water, piddle, piss—whatever you call it—use the latrines. You plied me with too much mint tea. How could I refuse? You smelled so lovely and looked so beautiful and gracious—I kept drinking beyond need, just to have you pour more."

"Thank you for that lovely compliment," I replied, feeling very flattered.

"My pleasure," he responded. "Now we will go to the waters to bathe. I know a quiet tranquil pool high up under a rocky ledge near the source of the waters where no camels have left their dung. It will be refreshing and cooling."

"That sounds inviting—I too, shall make use of both the latrines and the bathing, for nature has a habit of calling at all the wrong times, have you noticed that?"

"Indeed. Let's go," he chuckled, as he snatched a block of soap and towels from a small washstand.

At this time, my mind was full of unanswered questions. As we walk, should I walk at his side in the European manner of a French mistress, or follow several steps behind as required of an Arabian slave? Should I keep my clothes on while I bathe, and should I help bathe him, as Ali had me do on occasion? After all, Ali had loaned him my service just as Ahmad had loaned it to Ali. He was my master for the night, and I his slave.

He answered my first concern for me, for we had no sooner left the tent than he cocked his arm and invited me to link mine through his. We promenaded arm in arm, man and mistress, to the odorous latrines.

On our way to the "source of the waters", we passed many tents. "That is an interesting lantern show," he said, pointing to a large white one, and there, splashed on the side of the tent in moving shadows was the shape of a man and a woman in the final throes of lovemaking. "He should be more careful where he places the lamp! Then again, maybe he could charge admission—this is just as good as a Montmartre[1] show," he laughed.

A romantic interlude at the waters quickly displaced these discomfiting yet amusing diversions from my mind.

We made our way up and over rocks to his chosen place, where he promptly stripped, soaped himself down, and plunged into the cooling water, inviting me to follow suit, my remaining questions answered.

I thought he might make advances, perhaps touch me in a groping way, however, nothing of that sort happened. We just swam and splashed around in the moonlight, throwing the slippery block of soap back and forth between us, laughing when one of us missed the catch and had to fish the dark waters for the missing soap.

Two children at play, my carefree childhood revisited.

I slipped my borrowed dress over my head and we headed back to his tent.

"Barry, is Anne your slave?" I inquired.

"Surely you jest. Anne, my slave? A trader would have to give me money to take her away!" he laughed.

He sobered quickly.

---

1. A "red-light" district of Paris

"That is just a joke. She is a wonderful woman; she is my business partner. I have known her for many years. It is convenient for both of us to travel together; a woman traveling alone attracts certain difficulties so we pose as man and wife, in name only. We both love to travel and see new and exotic places such as your Arabia. We are both unmarried, and I, alas, am one of those pitiful men who have to buy, beg or borrow a woman's favors."

"With your handsome looks I wager you don't have to do much begging," I consoled.

"And with those beautiful deep brown eyes of yours and your other enticements, I wager many men have begged for your favors," he added.

My heart started to beat strongly as we approached his tent, not out of fear of what he may do, but more out of concerns of my own making. Would I be able to please him, meet his expectations? He was obviously well experienced.

Would he find me irresistibly desirable? I wanted it to be that way, not out of sense of duty to him or Ali, but for myself. Ali's cautious affection of late had raised doubts in my mind. I needed confirmation that I could be attractive to a man. Here was a chance for me to frolic in my femininity, flaunt my charms before a stranger, and see his reaction. After all, I would never see him again after tonight; he would be just a memory for me to take back to Jeddah.

However, apart from a few compliments, he seemed in no rush to seduce me. There had been plenty of opportunity—and masters had no need to win or seek permission. This only added to my concerns, and piqued my curiosity.

"Would you care for some wine?" he asked.

"Yes I would, thank you very much. I enjoy a good wine."

"Unfortunately this is Algerian, a little rough," he apologized, as he poured two cups.

"The French make the best wines. I am part French you know. My mother is French," I added, with pride.

"I agree with you about the wine, and I would also add beautiful women to your claim, but what I cannot understand is why the religion here forbids wine, something I am pleased to see you have chosen to ignore."

We drank a toast to the wine makers and women of France, followed by another disrespectful one to all the Ayatollahs and Mullahs of Arabia, accompanied by mischievous chuckles from my evening companion.

"Anyway, enough of this talk of wine; let us speak of something for which Arabia is famous—its harem girls. Tell me, how did a French girl like you become one?"

I told him a short version of my fictitious life in which Algerian corsairs captured me and sold me to Sheik Ahmad who then loaned me to Ali.

He popped open another bottle.

"What will Ahmad do with you when you are taken back?"

"I expect he will sell me—auction me off to the highest bidder. He is a slave trader."

"If I could be at the auction I would buy you," he said, seriously. "You are particularly beautiful as a woman and attractive in many other ways; a view obviously shared by Sheik Ali. He has mentioned you to me on several occasions, and tonight he was unusually concerned and insistent that I do not lay a hand on you or hurt you in any way. I was surprised that he mentioned it, because I would never treat a woman that way, and he knows that. He is very protective of you."

"Maybe he said that because I have some painful bruises on my bottom. I had a nasty fall off a horse." I said, secretly wanting to believe Ali had other reasons.

"I'm sorry to hear that, I shall be more careful. I sincerely hope my pinching didn't hurt you. If it did, I apologize, and will drink a toast to your bruises, your beauty and," he added, raising high the cup that made do as a wineglass, "to Sheik Ali's fine choice in women."

At this point, he changed, almost imperceptibly, but I noticed it. He looked me straight in the eye—a most penetrating look—and said slowly, "I hear that Arabian harem girls are taught well to please their masters. Do for me what you do for your master."

"Yes, Master," I replied, leading him to my understanding of his rank for the night.

Before I started, I carefully moved the oil lamp to a higher hook on the pole to cast our shadows only on the rug and bed pad. I did not want to project a Montmartre lantern show on the sides of our tent for any wandering insomniac to see. I carefully placed it not too far away though, because I knew a man liked to watch a woman as she touched and aroused him and see his member penetrating her, confirming to him his virility and dominance.

At this moment, I had no particular thoughts about my mother, even so, her words "irresistible and alluring" came to mind when I said to him, "Free my breasts, Master, and take pleasure from them." I leaned forward to allow him to pop them over the décolleté of the dress, having quietly undone the top three buttons to ease their passage to his hands.

I felt his arousal strengthening beneath me as I sat astride his thighs, close to him, rising now and then to brush my breasts across his face, inviting his hands and lips to touch them. I unbuttoned his shirt, uncovering an expanse of chest under broad shoulders. Slithering to his feet, I unbuttoned his fly and enjoyed his wiggling as I slowly pulled down his breeches and cast them aside, giving him release from his growing discomfort. Moving up to kneel astride him I brushed my smoothness against him once more before standing up to start my dance of seduction.

I unbuttoned the bodice of my dress and let it ripple down to my feet to show him what was his for the night. This, and my short improvised dance that followed was obviously sufficient for the purpose; he was hard and erect. I finished my dance with a leg sweep, landing my thigh on his shoulder and my leg hooked down his back. Standing over him like this, I rested for a moment, my smoothed mons close to his face—men like that I had learned—before lying down at his side.

"Arab masters certainly know how to give girls a haircut," he said, with a smile.

"You are nicely trimmed yourself, sir," I replied, lifting his circumcised member with my hand.

We both burst into laughter.

"Did you know you are bent over to one side?" I said, wanting to continue the amusing conversation.

He grinned, raising one eyebrow at the same time. "I am told that it is caused by too much hand play. That is the unsavory lot of a traveling salesman you know—lonely nights."

"Well I will do my best to straighten it tonight," I laughed back in reply.

After we had calmed I told him in a more serious voice that I would show him some of the ways that an Arabian slave girl pleases her Arab master.

"I shall come to you from the entranceway and present myself. Clap twice to dismiss me, should I displease you or do something in an unsatisfactory manner."

He said nothing, but nodded—a look of eager anticipation on his face.

Before I walked to the entrance, I propped a roll of blankets and pillows behind his back and shoulders, gently parted his legs, and noticed the lamplight fluttering delightfully across his bared chest in concert with his deep breathing. "Relaxed and vulnerable to my charms and quite appealing," I thought.

I went through my well-practiced preamble and crawled naked towards him, emphasizing the side-to-side sway of my breasts, and then I bent over backwards to make "the bow" before him, jostling my raised breasts as Mustafa had instructed weeks before.

A considerable pause elapsed—my back started to ache a little—before he moved closer and roamed his hands over my taut body. They firmly brushed my waist and hips, caressed my thighs and smoothed pubis, and explored the smooth skin between my legs. Gently uncurling me, he brought me to his chest, and my lips to his. This man was an experienced lover; he knew about women.

If he had guided me onto his member, and taken me there and then, I would not have objected, but he gave time for me to continue my play. I crawled down between his splayed legs, put a mischievously sultry smile on my face, held his eyes with my gaze, and settled my mouth on him.

I quickly became eager and hungry for his invasion, more than ready, and I lithely moved on top of him and guided him into me. Slowly I sank down and rode him at a leisurely pace, holding back our greater pleasure. I knew I could bring him on hastily if I needed to, on the other hand, here was a man I could play with and enjoy, tease a little, and that I did.

Compelled by my inviting play he rolled me over onto my back, never leaving me, and with vigorous enjoyable thrusts and playing fingers, he took command and finished us both. As Paeonia would say, "With thrust and heave we came together."

"Did I please you, Master?" I inquired.

"Marvelously so, the best lay with a woman I have ever had. I shall fondly remember this Arabian night, my pretty Sapphira."

I went to the washbasin, a hammered brass bowl on crossed wooden legs, and brought back with me a towel and a wet cloth to wash away our musks. I slipped into "those enticingly sheer pants" and this single token of clothing, although concealing little, made me feel more comfortable, more alluring and desirable, and renewed lustful thoughts within me.

It was obvious what he had on his mind too, a definite stirring was showing. He was indeed a virile man—or one very ready for a woman after a long abstinence—but I knew that this faint recovery would peter out and amount to nothing. However, I decided to encourage him.

"Master, are you ready to call for another slave girl from your harem. Shall I have one bathed and fragranced for you?"

"And why would I want a different girl? You were fabulous in your ways. I want the slave Sapphira, again."

"Thank you, Master," I replied.

"This time fellate me, slave," he commanded, with a brusqueness of voice that told me he had entered fully into the spirit of my play.

"I do not understand your command, Master."

"It is a foreign word to me also, an Italian word. It means use your mouth on me. I loved the feeling you gave me when you captured me with your lips and worked on me that way."

"Yes, Master. Here we call that pleasuring, but I think you are a little too ambitious. You're too floppy after your spending. You're broken," I said, with a facetious laugh.

"We have all night," he replied, smiling back at me. "Things will mend themselves. Pleasure me later, but then all the way till I…."

"Yes, Master, we call that sangara," I interrupted, "but first you must rest and take some sleep."

Wives and observant sisters know that men and boys sport an involuntary erection in the early hours of the morning before awakening; it comes to them in the night without a woman's help or encouragement. When first married, I took advantage of this, sometimes awakening my husband with gentle pleasuring. I had never done this with Ali because I thought it was too boldly precocious for a new slave girl to awaken her master in that way, but with the Englishman it would not matter, as it was unlikely I would ever see him again.

I awoke to find him still sleeping and I snuggled closer and nudged him onto his back. Then, slowly and carefully so as not to wake him I moved into the "lady position". With one knee on each side of his head, I lifted myself off my heels and leaned forward onto my arms and hands, and lowered myself to position well my breasts and head. My nuzzling mouth and teasing tongue scooped up his swollen and excited shaft from its hairy bed. He awakened to a close view of my "Arab haircut", which he caressed and explored with his fingers and tongue while I gave him sangara.

As I left to return to my Master, I gave the Englishman a backwards glance and a generous smile, hoping that the smile, hidden by my burqa, would show in my eyes. I had enjoyed my foray. It was a night by which I would judge all others.

"Wait a moment, I will walk you to the bottom of the hill and watch that you get back safely."

Everything was still and eerily quiet as we walked through the encampment. Wisps of smoke rose from newly lit fires. Other than that, the only movement came from hijabed women going about their morning chores, and the occasional man escorting a night slave back to her owner.

At the crest of the hill I turned to look back, we waved, and he walked away and out of my life.

I entered my Master's tent to find him standing with his caftan loosely draped about him—waiting for me.

"How was the evening?" he inquired.

"All went well. I thoroughly enjoyed myself."

"It's not for a slave to enjoy herself. That was not the purpose," he abruptly informed me. "You were sent there to look after a good friend of mine. Did he enjoy your company?"

"Yes, he did, Master. I obeyed his every request. He was well served and pleased with me."

"That is good to hear; because that is the last time you will be with another man. Hmm, Ahmad would not want that, would he?" he said, with a tinge and hesitation to his voice that I was more than willing to ascribe to jealously.

"Now you will please me in my every request. Come, lie down with me."

I soon learnt that he had not had a woman that night, celibacy had been his lot, and proof came quickly and abundantly.

Strangely, his aggressive and abrupt manner dwindled—although I was still miffed and confused by his attitude. With his abruptness now replaced by calmness, he told me what I already knew. He said that the English woman "is not a slave. She is the arms dealer's business partner—a woman of wealth and standing in her own country, and associated with the Enfield family, the arms manufacturers famous worldwide for the Lee-Enfield rifle. Furthermore she is of that sex that has no carnal interest in men—she thinks as a man in those matters and prefers the company of women."

All had been prearranged. He said he had asked the Englishman to treat me well; he wanted to avoid a repeat of my unsavory experience with the merchant. His concern and thoughtfulness gave me considerable comfort—then again, if he felt the same way about me as I felt about him he would not lend me to strangers and friends. He would want to keep me for himself.

With the passing hours of the day, our minds healed, and dark thoughts and words that had earlier assumed gigantic and awkward proportions now shrank to forgettable insignificance. That evening I took Ali to the guelta, the "source of the waters". We bathed and sat together on the flat rocks, which were still warm from the heat of the day, our pleasant reverie interrupted by brief and pleasant conversation—to me nothing more than that—until Ali turned and looked at me intently. "Something unseen is drawing me to your company. I feel lightened and without concerns when I am with you," he whispered, as he turned and lifted my face to his.

I closed my eyes in confident expectation.

"I think I am in…in…the mood to take you back to the tent and continue this evening in my bed."

"You can say it Ali. It is not an admission of guilt. It is not a sin to love a woman and tell her so," I thought to myself, and wanted to tell him, but didn't.

As we walked "home" another incident sparked a small hope within me—Ali pulled me closer to walk by his side and "not back there like a slave."

"But I am your slave, Master, and you told me never to forget it."

"Well, when we are out walking together I deem you are not my slave—and you can forget what I told you. It's different now."

"Thank you, Sire," I replied, deliberately dropping the word master but not daring to probe deeper and ask in what way it was different now.

A man, I believe, may be content with passion without love, but not a woman.

I desperately wanted him to know me, to love me, and tell me that he loved me.

AT THE RACES

It had been my observation that men gamble with their lives and money at the slightest provocation, and this was fully demonstrated by their irresponsible youthful behavior at the races.

These contests lasted a good part of the day, starting in the morning with camel races, followed late in the afternoon by horse races after the heat of the sun had subsided. Wagering on outcomes was frenzied, and bags of coins changed hands at a brisk pace. Ali wagered that his horses and camels would win and was always looking for someone who thought otherwise.

Riders—bent on suicide it seemed—collided, spilled, and bantered insults back and forth. Dust kicked up by pounding hooves swirled and drifted off the course in long lazy clouds tumbled along by the waft of a light breeze, and during the quiet after each race, grooms led the foaming horses and camels to the oasis for a cooling splash and rub down.

"It is cruel to tie those jockeys to the camels; they are mere boys. Look how they are thrown about—their bones could break," I told Ali.

"I assure you it is a much sought after honor amongst the boys to ride for owners. We tie them on to stop them from falling off, otherwise they could not go so fast and they would fall and break bones. There is purpose in these things."

A choking cloud of dust swelled towards us and just as I pulled my hijab across my face to shield myself I saw him from the corner of my eye emerging from within the cloud and shuffling towards us—Sohrab, the filthy qanass merchant! I thanked Allah that I was wearing concealing clothes, and even so, after the dust had passed, I kept my hijab across my face.

Against my silent wishes, Ali talked to him and started wagering with him. I caught a quick glance from Ali that told me that he knew with whom he was dealing, and a strange confident smile, almost a smirk, passed over his face.

It went badly for Ali; he lost his wagers on the first two camel races and handed over two bags of coins, which he reached for from a small strongbox at his feet. Eager for more winnings, the merchant confidently increased the size of his bets, which Ali matched and lost each time. Seemingly unperturbed, Ali bent down to reach for another bag of coins, and as he did so, he turned his head ever so slightly towards me, and gave me the slowest, most deliberate smile I had ever seen.

When the horse races started, Sohrab's good fortune ended abruptly. Ali, winning more often than not, recovered his earlier losses and more. For the second from last race of the day, in a sorry effort to recoup his losses, Sohrab desperately waged his remaining money.

Boxed in by a clutch of slower horses Ali's horse gave the merchant a brief moment of optimism. He was noticeably excited and grinning at the prospect of an easy win. It was short lived. The grin faded when Ali's horse broke free from the slower ones and pounded ahead to take a narrow win. Dejected and impoverished, the merchant turned to leave. Ali beckoned him closer.

Amid much gesturing and bargaining Ali held out four bags of coins and pointed to a disheveled figure crouched on the ground a short distance behind the merchant. A female in servitude no doubt, clutching about her form a dust covered cloth that draped over her from head to toe. Frightened and bewildered eyes peered from a small oval slot torn out of the cloth, and I saw that the slot made do as the only relief from the stifling heat trapped within. From beneath the hem of this suffocating shroud of black poked a slight forearm and hand about which was knotted tightly a short length of rope—the other end equally well secured to an iron stake firmly driven into the ground.

"Take four bags of coins and put them along the top of that railing," Ali whispered, pointing to the wooden railing that separated the course from the spectators. Still holding my hijab across my face, I lined up the bags of coins on the railing, one by one. It was a considerable amount of money, enough for Sohrab to recover his day's losses should he win, and a great temptation to undo and better his earlier misfortunes.

Sohrab was hesitant.

Ali gave me a fifth bag to add to the row. Then a sixth.

Sohrab eyed the enhanced wager, paused for a moment, took the bait, and sealed his bet with a handshake. A greedy smile prevailed, until covered over by a look of horror and disbelief when I drew aside my hijab.

Ali confidently whispered to me that he had saved his best horse and rider for the final race of the day. "I bought the horse recently. This is her first big race but she is feisty and eager, and well trained. Some think she is an ugly horse, she doesn't have the bloodline and gracefully curved neck of an Arabian mare, but wait until you see her deep well-muscled chest; she is built for speed. I honor her beauty. Bought her for a good price because she has a white mark on her forehead and the superstitious fools around here think that will bring bad luck. Well, it is going to bring someone bad luck today," he said, casting a glance at Sohrab. "My wager will please you, if I win," he added, this time with less confidence about on whom the bad luck would fall—it was, after all, the horse's first big race.

Ali's horse swiftly answered any question, or doubt, as to who would win the bet. She burst to the forefront and never relinquished her claim to the lead, even for a moment, as she pounded around the course. The crowd erupted, winners collected their spoils and Sohrab stalked off, teeth clenched with fury, his head shaking in stunned disbelief. As he hurried away, he cast a last evil glance at me and his shrouded wager still huddled on the ground. She turned her head to watch him disappear into the crowd and then settled her beseeching eyes on me.

I knew her well, her unusual dishing gait and the white star on her forehead. "Etoile" was the name I had given her. She was a high-spirited Akhal-Teke from the steppes of Asia, north of Afghanistan, rarely if ever seen in these parts, yet a breed renowned for their stamina and adaptation to the desert. Jamaal had sold her only a few months ago after I had trained her to the saddle.

To my utter shock, her eyes settled on me and her pace quickened to a trot. She came straight towards me, pulling the walking rider along with her, swishing her tail from side to side, and nodding her head in excitement. She nuzzled my hands looking for her reward, and, finding none, she bared her teeth in disappointment, snuffled loudly, whinnied, and turned to Ali, who rewarded her with a piece of honey-dipped kneifah.

"That's strange," he said. "I feed and groom her, yet she comes to you first. I think she knows you."

My heart quickened to a fierce pound.

"That is impossible; she has mistaken me for someone else. We all look alike in abayas and hijabs," I replied, trying not to sound anxious and guilty.

"What you say may be true, you do look alike, however, there are no women at my stables. She must have known one before I bought her," he replied. "I bought her from Jamaal al-Jubier of Jeddah, a man who truly knows his horses. His family has been in the horse business for many generations. She must have known a woman at his stables."

Startled beyond control, I felt my throat tighten and choke. It was all I could do to swallow down small gulps of air. My face froze and started to spill my story. My time had come—thanks to a horse.

Why God saved me I do not know, but the hand of God it surely was that pushed the impatient youthful rider between us, interrupting our conversation and Ali's dreadful line of reasoning. With pride and bubbling enthusiasm rider and owner noisily congratulated each other for the win and ignored me. I was saved—pulled out of the inquisitor's fire by an ill-mannered boy.

With my guilt relieved, I calmly leaned forward to stroke her long nose—a horse's nose always reminded me of a man—hard and long, and ending in unexpected softness. I had ridden her often during her training, and could claim some credit for her win, but of course, it would have to stay inside me, I could say nothing.

Etoile and her rider left for the cool water of the oasis, and Ali turned his attention to the pitiful heap he had won. With one smooth draw, he pulled the iron stake from the ground and dropped it down on the sand. "Bring my prize back to the tent," he instructed, as he picked up his overflowing strong box and a winner's proud smile.

The dragging stake, still roped to her wrist, gouged a ridged trail in the sand amidst our footprints as we followed Ali. "His winnings" and I hurried several paces behind, struggling to keep up with his eager stride, the short rope tied between her ankles that hobbled her progress going unnoticed.

Inside the tent, after our eyes had adjusted to the dimness, Ali cut the rope from her wrist and stepped behind the quavering figure. With proud determination, he lifted and snatched the concealing cloth from her grip, and dashed it to the floor. She collapsed in a curled heap, overcome with fear, her delicate arms and legs flaying the air as she tried to shield her naked body from imaginary blows.

She was the young Syrian girl we had seen sold at the auction. I ran to Ali and promptly burst into tears, and thanked him and thanked him, until he had to put his finger on my lips to silence me.

"I took risk and played the game for you, knowing how ill you felt about the fate awaiting the merchant's new slave. She is mine now, and I put her under your care," he said, proudly.

He looked down at his new girl. "And you will do without question what Sapphira tells you. Is that understood?"

"Yes Sir—Master."

I turned my attention to Ali's girl, a fact of ownership he had made quite clear. I helped the poor girl—who was still shaking from fear—to her feet. Her eyes kept darting to the crack of light between the two curtains closing off the entrance to the tent, no doubt wondering about escape. She winced as I held her firmly with my arms around her.

It was a long time since I had seen a girl with fleece, and it took a moment for me to divert my eyes from that dark curly patch to the hobbling rope tied to each ankle, which I quickly untied. I noticed sharp red marks around her wrists and knew that he had kept her shackled.

Ali started to turn her around to examine his winnings more carefully, only to stop abruptly when her back came into view. Weals from the stroke of a whip crisscrossed her skin.

Gently feeling her back he announced, "Her skin is not broken, only bruised. Fortunately, she is not lacerated and will heal without a mark. Nevertheless, these strokes were much too hard for a young girl to have to bear.

"The whip he used on you. Did you see it? Was it made from leather?" he asked, his voice rising steadily with anger.

"Yes. He made me pick it up and bring it to him. It was leather," she whimpered.

"A camel whip! He is ignorant; he knows nothing. When did this happen?"

"This morning, before the races."

"A cruel man. My father—and he was a hard man known for his harsh use of the whip—even he put silk to the backs of his slave women.

"And look at your wrists, he kept you in iron. You are a slave, not a criminal—we do not use iron to fetter slave girls, do we," he said, turning to me.

I nodded back my agreement. "He uses leather gyres to tether his falcons to their perches, but not to tether his slave," I enjoined, with newly inspired indignation. "He treats captive birds better than captive girls. He should be severely punished."

"I agree with you, and a man of my standing can see to it. He will pay dearly for his abuse of our Arabian customs and his disrespect for our traditions and women. It only adds fuel to the fires of unfavorable foreign opinion we are receiving about our slave harems, and we can do without that," he spluttered. "I know only too well men of his kind. Look how he treated you, Sapphira. You were fortunate that you were with him for only a few hours."

Thoroughly angered by her condition Ali continued to examine her wrists and back. I heard him say aloud—loud enough for all to hear but to no one in particular—"This is a sin. It cannot be God's will."

I hurried to find her some of my clothes to wear. They were too large but they covered her nakedness. I held her close, a careful hug from a caring woman, and the stiffness of fear left her frail and damaged body.

"Ali! Send someone into town to buy a soothing ointment for her back and wrists," I said, realizing after I had spoken that I had called him Ali and given him an order instead of calling him Master and pleading for a small favor. It went unnoticed, lost in the urgency of my tone. Emboldened I called out—"Not horse medicine."

He sent me a smile. "I will go myself. I'll take a horse, that will be quicker," were his departing words before he disappeared through the entranceway and out into the dying heat of the day.

I heard his horse gallop away and I started to sob again. I cry more often from unexpected kindness, than from pain or hurt. She was puzzled. We cried together.

On his way to the souk, he had been thinking about the girl, and planning his next course of action, for when he returned with ointment he promptly announced, "She will take the name Topaz, the same name as the filly who won her.

"Now I must go and congratulate my grooms and riders and join in their celebration. This has been a good day. I may be gone for several hours, as Talil and I have also other business to attend to. I will have food and drink sent to you and post four guards around the tent; there is no need to keep her tethered or bound, just keep her in the tent.

"Now, give me one of your rings," he demanded, and without question, I went to my jewelry casket, retrieved two rings and offered him a choice "Gold is too good for him. Don't you have a silver one or better yet, brass."

"These are all I brought with me."

He took one ring, rose to his feet, and with three bags of coins and the ring in hand he disappeared into the fading afternoon sunlight saying as he left, "The money I won from the merchant will be put to good use tonight in a way he will not forget."

I turned my attention to my charge.

After the heat and dust of the afternoon, we needed to bathe, and we helped each other to master the awkward hipbath.

It was my turn to be stared at, for Topaz had never seen a depilated woman and was full of questions and apprehensions about who did it to you, why, and how. "Did it hurt? Does it grow back again? Will the Master do it to me?"

I answered her questions briefly without elaboration, knowing that as Ali's slave girl she would no doubt soon experience all for herself.

"You have marks on your bottom and a bruise on your face. When he beats you does he do it hard?" she asked, cautiously.

"They were put there by the same man who whipped you, not by your new master."

"How did it happen?" she asked, surprised at my answer.

"I was sent to be with him—I shall tell you all about it later, but now I will attend to your back. Turn around." I carefully applied the soothing ointment to her back and wrists.

"Will I be sent back to the man?"

"Not if I have anything to do with it." I said, with boldness and authority not befitting my lowly position in Ali's household.

After we had eaten—she ravenously devouring most of the food—we spent the rest of the evening talking about ourselves, and events that had brought us together.

Her father had died when she was eleven years old, and an uncle took her, her mother, and two younger brothers into his household, an expensive obligation of tradition her uncle begrudgingly assumed.

At a tender age, an older cousin raped her, threatened her into silence, and forced the liaisons to continue until her uncle discovered them together one night. Her cousin claimed that she had come to his bed and he had awakened to find her astride him, a blatant lie taken as true without question by her uncle. Since, in her uncle's eyes, she had brought dishonor to the family, he had a convenient excuse to banish her and gain relief from some of his expensive obligation. He took her to the distant port city of Latakia where, he advised his family, he would find a position for her in household service.

"I stayed in a small room in the inn while my uncle went into the town to seek out my future employer. To stop me from leaving he locked the door and took all my clothes with him, leaving me naked and alone. He returned later with a well-dressed man of wealth, and I stood before him while he walked around me gazing on me and touching my body. I could not understand why this was necessary before employing a servant girl, and my worries grew when the man handed gold coins to my uncle.

My uncle threw my clothes at my feet and told me to get dressed and go with the man. In surprising kindness before leaving, he sorted through the gold coins in his hand and handed one back to the man, with the words, 'Do not blind her.'[1] I knew then that he had sold me as a slave. That was the last time I saw my uncle or anyone from my family.

"I was taken aboard a moored boat and pushed into a small cabin with several women and a shackled man. From there we sailed to Alexandria where my owner sold me to an Arab slaver who brought me here to be sold again."

I placed two lit candles on each side of the small mirror I had brought with me from Makram and started to mehndi my face, under the watchful eye of Topaz. After I had finished my face, I pinned a maanga tikki to my hair, the jeweled medallion resting on my forehead.

"What is that stuff in those bottles?" asked Topaz.

"Rose oil and ylang-ylang," I replied. "Rose oil makes you smell sweet and ylang-ylang makes you taste sweet."

"What do you do with them?"

"You dab the rose oil on your neck, wrists and thighs and the ylang-ylang on your nipples…and lips,"—which was true, in a way.

"I will show you." I coated my nipples with ylang-ylang and eased them through the loop of my nipple dangles and dabbed myself with fragrant rose oil.

"Will you let him see you bare like that?" she asked.

"Most likely," I replied.

"You look so pretty. Will you show me how to make myself pretty?"

"Yes, I will someday. Now you must go to bed. You have had a grueling day," I told her, not wanting her around any longer.

By the time Ali returned, Topaz was at peace and deeply asleep on a small rug. I had invitingly turned back Ali's bed pad before taking up position at the tent entrance where I breathed in the cool night air, while watching for his return.

As soon as I saw him striding towards the tent I scurried to the small mat at the foot of the sleeping pad and knelt submissively, head demurely bowed, breasts enticingly bared and bejeweled. I wanted to thank him.

"You look lovely. What a welcoming sight," he whispered, while glancing over briefly at sleeping Topaz.

---

1. No doubt a reference to the Syrian practice of scarring, or even blinding, the eyes of work slaves "so that the slaves may not see clearly the beauty around them and grow discontented and rebel".

After I had undressed him and folded his clothes, he recounted the earlier part of his evening when he treated his men to a night on the town and arranged for their visit to the brothel.

Disrespectfully, I did not pay good attention to what he was saying, being more interested in touching him in disturbing ways and wafting my fragrance over him than listening, until he said, "Your friend the merchant will have visitors tonight. I hired four mercenaries and a surgeon and they will not be buying falcons from him. Instead, they will give him your ring as a gift from me for mistreating you and Topaz. By tomorrow morning, he will have lost more than his urge to hurt a girl; he will be a eunuch. Your jewelry will be put to good use."

"A eunuch, wearing my jewelry? That ring is for a woman to wear."

"It's very simple," he said. "First his testicles will be removed and the empty pouch threaded through your ring, after which it will be crimped tightly in place to stem the bleeding. A quick slice with a sharp knife will cut off the empty pouch below your ring. He will be a semivir eunuch—his falcons will feed well on the evidence."

My eyes widened as I heard the words and pictured the ordeal the merchant would face and I felt queasy thinking about hungry falcons squabbling over and tearing to pieces his severed parts.

"He will wear your ring for the rest of his life. If he removes it, the wound will open up and cause fatal bleeding. In a grown man, that part does not heal well.

"We Arabians know how to punish a man," Ali reflected, sounding pleased with himself.

"What will happen to him?" I asked.

"He will fatten and lose desire for a woman, that's all," he said, rather casually. "The wild beast within him will be tamed. He will no longer be a man."

Was the punishment excessive for the crime? I loathed the man, nevertheless, I had thought that perhaps a severe public flogging with a cane would suffice, preferably administered by Ali. However, I kept my thoughts to myself. I wanted to end the conversation; I had other things on my mind.

The next day Ali arranged for Talil and an armed guard to escort Topaz and me into Ranyah to buy clothes for her and to shop for the items on Yasmeen's list.

"Here, wear this," he said, looping off over his head a light chain necklace threaded through a small gold pendant. "It was my mother's; it is the seal of the House of Saalih. Wear it whenever you leave my company. And you may buy clothes for yourself as well as for Topaz. Some of yours are a little tattered," he laughed, and smiled a warm smile at me. A loving smile?

"Thank you, Sire."

Buying these items took most of the day. Shopkeepers treated me as a woman of great importance; the pendant, my armed guard, my well-filled money pouch, ensured this, and I thoroughly enjoyed the respect it garnered. I did feel, however, that on seeing the pendant the shopkeepers were less inclined to bargain down their prices. "A small price to pay for my new-found status," I thought. And what a great treat it was to shop freely for luxuries with little concern for their cost. We chose to buy luxuriously colorful salwar-kameezes from an Indian cloth merchant and his wife who kept a small shop in the heart of the souk. She would have them sewn up in two days.

We were tired when we returned to the tent and pleased to learn that the three of us would stay there that evening.

Three uneventful days passed for us. Ali and his friends kept busy trading, talking, and riding, while Topaz and I kept busy as best we could by finding small chores to do. Nevertheless, confined to a small tent for most of the day with this girl was too much for me. Topaz yielded up a tiring stream of questions and chatter like a tedious child. Only by reminding myself of her frightful past, and her tender innocence, was I was able to maintain a semblance of civility and decorum. Ali's morning departure was dreaded—his afternoon return was a delight.

There was another kind of tension. I moved her sleeping rug to the far corner of the tent. I suspected she eavesdropped on my conversations with Ali, and spied on us as well.

On occasion, she made me feel shameful, whether deliberately or otherwise I did not know.

"Do you like me?" she asked, her doleful eyes playing my face. "I like you. You are kind to me like my father was before he died."

I replied with a half-truth and a question. "Of course I do. Who couldn't but love a girl such as you?"

She thanked me and hugged me—pressing guilt into me—and told me that I was a kind person.

And the next moment she told me that I reminded her of her mother, and later of her older sister. "She was strict with me, too, but I loved her. My sister has a new baby," she said.

Acutely, I recognized well the symptoms, and only time could lessen them. She was desperately homesick. To distract her mind I played pick-up-stones and other games with her—anything to keep her mind busy. I taught her to play backgammon and to mehndi her face. I showed her how to make the bow, which she did with alarming acrobatic ease—and, I suspect, with a clear sense of its purpose and effect.

The angry red welts on her back faded to less noticeable yellow-blue bruises, and I sensed she was as happy as she could be considering her circumstances.

It was a pleasant diversion for me, not so pleasant for Topaz. Ali had arranged for Topaz's smoothing. "You will accompany her into town today. I have called for Talil and made morning appointments. A room has been reserved at the hammam where both of you can rest and bathe afterwards."

Ali told me to make sure the barber followed his instructions. "I want a thorough smoothing for her. You know all the places where a woman wears unwanted hair. Make sure none is missed."

"Yes, Master."

"Topaz is to have a full smoothing, her arms and everywhere below her waist must be polished."

He took off his gold pendant necklace, looped it over my head, gave me some coins to give to Talil to buy refreshments with, and handed me a piece of paper for Tamil with directions to the barber's shop and the hammam written on it. I was unfamiliar with the term "polishing", when it came to denuding, but before I thought to ask what it meant, Ali had left.

Topaz sensed something, and I explained as gently as I could what Ali had ordered for her. Drawing on my recently acquired knowledge, and what my mother had told me, I explained in a matronly manner. "A woman is not a 'bowl of roses' down there. The hair takes on the odors of a woman just the same as a man's hair takes on the odor of the hookah and washing will not dispel it. Furthermore, a man finds that part of a woman pleasing and pretty to the eye, and more so when it is bare and not concealed behind a bush. After all, God did not put hair on a woman's face or on her chest for that reason. We have all been done this way," I added, for her comfort.

"Does Master Ali look at you, there?"

"Yes," I answered casually.

"Really?"

"Hmm, hmm."

"How many women does he have?"

"He owns nine girls."

"Are they pretty? Will I be one of his slaves?"

"Yes, you are already his slave; that is why he has ordered your smoothing. All pretty harem slave girls are smoothed, he prefers us groomed that way."

"In the harem how will I know what to do?"

"There are rules to follow. His eunuchs will show you the ways."

"What is a eunuch?"

"He is a man who looks after the harem. He has had his manliness cut off. Talil is one. He will be coming with us to supervise your smoothing."

"Why do they do that to a man?"

"So he is deprived of both the means and the desire to dally with his master's property. We are for the Master's use and enjoyment only."

"It must have hurt him."

"I'm sure it did—in more ways than one. Are you a believer?" I inquired, changing the subject.

"I have denounced the faith; it is unfairly in favor of men and against women. It is because of these beliefs that my uncle was able to punish me. I despise the teachings of Mohammed."

She was quite vocal and adamant in her position, it would be fruitless to advise her to reconsider, and besides, I was not inclined to try.

Although apprehensive, she was not fearful as we set out for town accompanied by Talil and an armed guard who fell in step behind us as we left the tent.

Talil pointed to a sun-bleached door behind a scattering of empty chairs and tables. At some time past, a *halaaq* sign must have hung from the wooden bar that poked out from over the door. A notice pinned on the door read: Closed—Open after noon.

"This is the place, take her inside."

A man just inside the doorway and the sweet cloying smell of confectionery greeted me. "Is this a barbershop?" I asked.

"Yes it is madam. You are in the right place. Those rascally town boys have taken to stealing my sign ever since I caught them spying through a window in my workshop. They have learned to read the notices and know when the auctions are and what I often do afterwards for bought girls. But I tell you, if I catch them they will learn more than about girls, they will learn about the shame of a shaved head."

I noticed the barber chair and realized that my asking if this was a barber's place was needless. Somewhat flustered, I said smiling, "it smells sweet, I thought for a moment I was in a confectioner's shop."

"You smell the honeysugar. I boiled it down earlier today. I was expecting you. Everything is ready."

"Do you want her in the chair?"

"No," he said. "Please follow me. Bring her with you."

We passed through a bead curtain into a smaller room illuminated by a shaft of bright sunlight beaming through a high-latticed window. Lower down I saw the boys' boarded over window. "I find it easier when they lie flat on here," he said, pointing to a crudely made wooden table that looked more like a roughly hewn work bench that a piece of furniture. "Please take off her clothes and have her lie down on her back."

The barber, a jovial fellow, chatted as he went about his work dripping and working the hot sticky sugar into her hair, while Topaz lay on his table, her thighs spread widely. "What is going on in Ranyah? You are the third girl I have done in as many days," adding for her benefit, "and the prettiest one."

"Owners of slave girls are fortunate men; they don't need permission from their girls. I wanted to do my wife in this way, but she would have nothing to do with it. Can you imagine, a skilled professional barber denied practice by his own family? Such a pity, because I take pride in improving women this way," he laughed regretfully, as he went about his work, the sweet smell of boiled honeysugar and lemon juice being more pleasant than the wax and rosin they had used on me.

I pointed out a small oversight and interrupted his banter. "I want a thorough denuding for her. Not just her mons, a woman has ravines as well as hills," I said, "and polish her forearms and everywhere below her waist," hoping he knew what polishing was, and wouldn't ask me.

"Yes, madam," he replied, smartly. "I haven't forgotten. Your husband gave full instructions. When I have finished, there will not be a shadow on her. You will both be pleased with my work. But now, a short break from our labors while the sugar hardens."

A quick glance and nod of his head in my direction forewarned me.

"This may sting a little," he said casually, as he peeled away the thick layer of hardened honeysugar from between her legs—the sound reminding me of uprooting weeds from the garden. Topaz heaved and flinched and silent tears pooled in the corners of her eyes. After looking closely for missed hairs and finding none, and congratulating himself over his fine work, he turned her over and had her offer her peach, with knees drawn up and apart.

"Allah help her! Look at her back; she has had a good whipping. How could such a pretty and well-made girl not please a man?"

"It was done by her former owner for insolence in the bedchamber."

"Well, at least she has learned a lesson, this must have hurt. On the other hand, new girls are often defiant and have to be broken to the ways of the master."

"Yes, you're right, they are often defiant."

"I was not insolent or defiant. He whipped me because I wouldn't let him put his thing in my bottom," countered Topaz, her voice muffled by the towel she had buried her face in.

The barber and I exchanged knowing glances before he intently resumed his work, brushing the hot sugary mixture onto the small of her back, over and between her buttocks, and down the back of her legs to her feet, squishing in and smoothing over strips of muslin as he went. A mummified Egyptian came to mind. After the honeysugar had cooled, he stripped away the sugar bound muslin and I saw immediately how the term polishing came about—her buttocks and everywhere were shiny and silky smooth to the touch. He turned her again onto her back and added her forearms, underarms, lower legs and ankles, and even the tops of her toes to his endeavors.

On my own initiative, I asked the barber to stone away any sharp edges from her teeth. Ali had not asked for this; I assumed it was an oversight, knowing his tastes. With a stick of fine sandstone in hand, the barber went about his work, a tiring and awkward procedure for Topaz.

"This is from Al-Ta'if," he said, holding up a familiar yellow striped jar of Ahmad's balm. "A trader brings it back from the orient—expensive you know—but it saves women a lot of trouble and discomfort. Cuts into my business though. In the old days girls had to be smoothed every month or so and I used to travel around regularly selling my services, but now with this remedy there is less call for my services. Your girl is lucky your husband can afford it. Unfortunately, it makes my hands tingle and smell of tomcat piss. Now when I go home the smell forewarns my wife about my day at the shop and she knows to lock me out of the bedroom if she wants a restful night," he laughed.

"And where does this lovely girl come from?"

"Syria," I replied. "She was bought six days ago at the auction," omitting the details of her changing ownership, as I did not want to prolong our stay with idle chatter.

"I have never before improved a Syrian girl; the Syrians are usually buyers, not sellers. For themselves, they favor Jewish and Hindu slave women. Jews make the best slaves, although the slender brown-skinned Hindus are prettier don't you think.

"Please inspect my work before I balm her," he said, while vigorously stirring the contents of the yellow jar with a wooden spatula, causing the foul odor to spill and waft about the place.

I called in Talil who gave her a thorough going over and finding nothing amiss he told the barber to start her balming. Talil, holding his nose closed, promptly left the stuffy room for a breath of fresh air.

"She must stand up for this, I have to do both sides," he said, somewhat apologetically.

I helped her off the table.

"Put your hands on your head and keep them there. There must be no touching while the balm does its work," he told her. With her standing this way, he smothered the reddened depilated areas with the foul-smelling cream, thoroughly rubbed it in, and turned the hourglass to start her hour of torment.

I saw her discomfort grow as the burning sensation smoldered its way across her skin. She danced lightly from foot to foot, fidgeted about, and winced and wiggled like a girl who had to relieve herself.

He washed his hands, lit a hookah, and we repaired to the chairs and tables through the sunlit doorway, with hookah and hourglass in hand. Talil sent the guard to buy refreshments for all of us, and on his return, the guard joined us and took a quiet smoke, turning his head occasionally from side to side, sniffing at the air that drifted through the open doorway.

After the hourglass had run its time, the barber scraped off the darkened and expired balm with an ivory scraper and wiped Topaz down. She dressed, I thanked him, and we hurriedly left for the hammam to relax and wash off the last traces of Ahmad's smelly concoction, the breeze we created in our haste drying the tears from her eyes and cooling her tormented skin.

"Are you Master Ali's wife?" Topaz asked, between mouthfuls of falafel that I had saved for her lunch. "The man called him your husband."

"That is what he would think when he saw Ali's necklace around my neck. It is most unusual for young slave girls to be in the souk together like this. Ali is very modern in his ways."

"Why did the man rub my teeth with that stone? He has made them feel smooth and slippery," asked Topaz, as we hurried on our way.

"You will find out later; it's better for your Master."

"Why?" she asked, innocently.

"You will find out in due course."

"How long does this stinging last for?"

"Not for long once we get to the hammam," I replied.

To avoid letting the staff know what our mission had been that morning, should they recognize the distinct odor of the balm and know its use, I had Topaz wait outside with Talil and our guard while I checked on the arrangements Ali had made.

In the hammam the staff treated me with great respect; they, too, thought I was Ali's wife. I did not enlighten them. I relished the notion of again being mistaken in this way.

In the room that had been reserved for our exclusive use, our attendants, two black women, were adding pitchers of heavily perfumed water to the hot bath. I asked them to bring in a large mirror; Topaz would surely be curious to see how she looked.

I went back to the street for Topaz and hurried her past the staff and into the room as quickly as possible. Topaz, not waiting for permission, slid beneath the soothing water.

Ali had ordered for us a massage, a face and body gommage, and a Lebanese dusting. After a long and luxurious soak, attendants soaped us down with gritty black Moroccan soap, scrubbed us vigorously with loofahs, rinsed off the last traces of soap, and left us to rest serenely in the hot steam of the hammam.

Our bodies, relaxed by the moist heat, offered no resistance when they returned to knead and massage us from head to toe with fragrant oils on their hands.

One of our attendants left the room and returned shortly with another woman I had not seen before. She looked somewhat aloof and I assumed she was the supervisor of the hammam. "This is for your slave, if you will permit," said the woman, holding up a small bottle in her hand. "Oil of hamamelis. I always recommend it for first-time girls. With your permission, the attendant will apply it to the smoothed places. It soothes and cools away the redness. There will be a small charge for the oil, five qirsh, but it is well worth it."

A Lebanese dusting was something unfamiliar to me, and explained why the attendants had not washed our hair. They sat us on stools, draped a cloth about our necks, and twice rubbed sandalwood dust and grain into our hair followed by a vigorous brushing that swept out the soiled grain, and along with it the sand and other natural debris that accumulate in hair. It left only the sweet smelling oils of the wood to glaze and perfume our hair. A dab of rouge, eyes lined with kohl, a smear of lip color and our thoroughly enjoyable indulgence was over.

Topaz slipped a fresh burqa over her head and bundled up her old clothes while I went outside to ask Talil to pay for the oil of hamamelis. After a small diversion to pickup our new clothes from the Indian cloth merchant's wife, we set out on the short walk back to the tent feeling relaxed, pampered and buoyant.

In my curious mind, I had a nagging question about Topaz that craved an answer. "When you refused to 'take in' your previous master and he whipped you, why did he not then bind you and take you by force, rape you? Or did he?" I asked.

"No, I was lucky. While he was whipping me he got excited and wasted himself all over the floor, then he was too soft to do anything. We left for the races and he told me he would teach me a lesson when we got back. Thanks to your wager that never happened."

My wager? She must have seen me putting the moneybags on the railing. I let it rest without comment.

We entered the tent to find Ali dozing in the hipbath, sprawled out in an undignified position that allowed Topaz to take interest in his fully exposed manliness. It floated up just below the surface of the water like a fish rising for a gulp of air. We silently backed away and entered again, noisily, so that Ali would awaken and be unaware that we had looked upon his nakedness while he dozed. He stepped out of the bath and threw on a caftan, while Topaz and I stowed our burqas in the far corner of the tent, and changed into our new silk salwar-kameezes.

Topaz whispered to me. "He is big; does it hurt when he puts you on it?"

I assured her, smiling slightly at her choice of words. "For the first few times he puts you on it you may find it a little uncomfortable, but he will not hurt you on purpose." At least Topaz had come to realize that her wagered rescue from the clutches of the merchant was not entirely an act of charitable kindness. Repayment was in order.

Ali lay back against the cushions on his sleeping pad, casually inquired about our day, and complimented us on our radiant appearance and beauty. I informed him that all had gone according to his instructions and proudly told him that I had taken initiative and had her teeth rounded.

"Most excellent," he said. "I forgot about that. Show me how she looks after the barber's good work."

Topaz stepped forward, a little too willingly for my mind, and I seductively undressed her, opening the front of her kameez and dropping it to her feet before sliding down her salwars.

She had an innocent fragile beauty about her, and I thought that with good food and rest and a little more maturity to fill her breasts and swell her hips, she would be gorgeous.

"You are a pretty girl. When we return to the palace, you will join the other pretty girls in my harem. You will be a worthy addition, I think. Turn around slowly a few times so that I may feast my eyes on the beauty that has been uncovered."

Without Ali seeing me, I signaled to Topaz to raise her arms above her head as she turned. She looked beguiling.

"Come kneel beside me," he said, taking Topaz's hand and slipping it under his caftan. "Feel how you already please your new master," he said, pulling his caftan open to reveal his hardening member encircled by her tiny hand.

"Do you know about pleasuring?" he asked.

"No, Master."

"Then Sapphira will show you how she pleasures me, and tonight I will take delight in showing you some ways of the harem.

"Pleasure me, Sapphira."

"Now, Master?" I replied, taken aback by his unexpected and uncaring command.

"Yes, now."

I felt enormously uncomfortable and unenthusiastic taking him over the brink, while the cause of his arousal watched wide-eyed in amazement.

"Will he show me how to do that?" Topaz inquired, later.

"Yes, he will; he is particularly fond of enjoying his women that way," I replied, echoing the words of Mustafa.

"Is that why the barber-man rubbed my teeth with that stone?"

"Yes."

"What did you do with his stuff?"

"That is *semence*, not stuff. What do you think I did with it? I swallowed it. It is part of harem etiquette," I brusquely informed her. "You never spill his seed."

"What does it taste like?"

"Slippery like raw egg and salty like tears," I replied, sharing recently acquired knowledge.

"I won't do it. I don't like the taste of raw eggs."

"Yes you will. You will do everything Mustafa tells you. You are a slave girl; and it is the custom. All I can tell you is that if you don't want to taste his issue when it comes, then take him to the back of your mouth and swallow quickly a few times and you won't taste much," I said, caught between reluctance to share one of my newly learned secrets and an underlying desire to help her.

"Who is Mustafa?"

"He is the chief eunuch at the palace. You will be placed in his care."

"I can look after myself!"

"I am sure you can. Nevertheless, you will start your learning under his care; you have much to learn about our ways."

"Will the Master whip me like that other man did if I don't do it right?"

I wanted to tell her yes. I thought a little fear would be good for her—it might slow down and temper her growing enthusiasm—as her line of questioning had started to annoy me. I felt my position threatened and usurped by this waif and almost regretted that I had spoken out at the auction and had been so particular with her "improvement" at the hands of the barber. I felt my pity turning to resentment, but in fairness to Ali, I replied, "No, he will give you time to learn."

"What are the other rules of the harem? Are they hard to do?"

"I'll tell you another time."

We bathed at the guelta that evening. On our return Ali told me to pessary her and to sleep on her rug, from where I unhappily eavesdropped and spied on them before falling asleep.

In the morning, I awoke to the disturbing rustle of bodies in rhythmic motion, a bobbing head, and the murmuring of Ali as he inspired and encouraged her in that way of the harem. While I slept he had given her his second command, and again his choice of succor did not rest comfortably with me. I regretted that I had asked the barber to refine and perfect her mouth for that particular task. I turned my back to them and covered my ears.

"He told me that for a girl of little experience I was delightful in my ways and that I am well suited to serve him," a jubilant Topaz informed me later, in more than vaguely familiar words. "I like lying with him, he is a kind man. I want him to keep me—I didn't spill his stuff."

"It's not stuff, it is *semence*, it's his seed," I replied, curtly.

I would not let her seduce him away from me. My thoughts ran to improbable reasons why this would not happen. She was too small for him. Her thin coltish legs, her less vigorous hips and her adolescent breasts would not appeal to Ali. He spoke of her beauty out of kindness just to soothe and comfort her at this trying time in her life.

In cold reality, none of these reasons carried any weight of conviction. She was plainly desirable, and I could not deny that my turn from pity to resentment was complete.

BAD NEWS

An exhausted messenger interrupted our morning dressing—he had come to tell us that Ali's half-brother was seriously ill with the typhus. Our stay at the oasis was over, we would leave post-haste as soon as overnight supplies were packed and horses saddled. Topaz and I would share one horse, and Ali and two guards would ride their own mounts with one packhorse in tow.

The sight of my saddled horse thrilled me—I would be riding part of my secret past—it was the mare Topaz. I had to be careful not to show too much enthusiasm or call her "Etoile"—but to me she would always be my Etoile.

We left for Al-Lith around mid-morning, five riders with four riding horses and one packhorse in single file, heading out into the sun-drenched desert. Our pace was a brisk measured trot, for although it was mid-morning we were riding against the growing heat of the day and the next oasis was three hours away.

Topaz, the mare, was tiring and we decided to ease her load by rotating Topaz, the girl, to other riders. We had to keep moving, for if the pace was broken or stopped it would be difficult or impossible to convince the flagging horses to resume. Topaz jumped down from my still moving horse and ran quickly over the hot sand to one of the guard's horses. With one smooth sweep of his arm, he scooped her up from the desert floor and plopped her onto his saddle, facing him. She swung her legs over to face into the breeze, nestled her back against his chest and pulled his arm around her waist.

This overt show of her acrobatic abilities and knack for seductive teasing didn't help my leaning! It only added to my disquiet following her earlier show of willing deftness at making the bow and her growing and obvious enthusiasm for Ali.

Ali pulled up alongside me.

"From the way you ride I would say you were born on a horse; you handle her uncannily well."

"If that is your measure, Sire, then I would say you were born on a woman."

I urged my horse to a gentle gallop with Ali in pursuit, enveloped in a cloud of dust kicked up by my steed. I allowed him to catch up and pull alongside me.

His eyes jumped from the desert ahead to me at his side. "You seem to have forgotten that you are my slave. I should have you whipped for impertinence. Fortunately for you, I take your comment as a compliment, and will spare you a good lashing," he said, with a shake of his head and a huge resigned smile. "You have a stimulating and attractive way with words; I like it when you speak your mind, but Allah, you are full of surprises."

His eyes settled on mine. "I command you to always speak your mind whenever we are alone—it is truly refreshing and highly agreeable. My other girls have been slaves for too long and do not speak their true thoughts, they only tell me good things or untruths. Do not speak your mind before the other girls, I mean this only for when we are alone."

"I will do that, Sire," I replied. It was all I could do to keep from smiling outwardly, as I thought of his pride; he still wanted to maintain his masterful presence in front of the harem.

"And challenge me in other ways. Win at chess and backgammon—if you can!" he said, with a narrow-eyed glint on his face.

A small oasis came into view. We would take time there for a short rest and refreshment before continuing our journey. With 'challenge me in other ways' fresh in my mind I called out, "If I beat you to the water, Sire, I win you as my bed-slave for a night." I urged my horse forward with Ali in hot pursuit. I pulled back to allow him to pass for I had no intention of winning the wager even if I could, but Etoile smelled the water, and with feral eyes and flared nostrils she galloped forward out of my control, ignoring my commands. Only at the edge of the water, with rigid legs thrust forward and sand spraying from digging hooves, did she come to an abrupt stop. I, however, did not. I continued on my journey over her head and splashed face down in the clear water.

My wet, clinging clothes, did not go unnoticed by the laughing riders who had gathered around as I struggled to paddle out of the shallow water with an air of dignity. I doubted my success, but at least the scrutiny I attracted was pleasing—a small compensation for my misfortune and ridicule.

"You win Sapphira, you will have your night," he said, still bent double with laughter.

"Sire, I did not intend to win. My horse smelt the water and I could not hold her back."

"Then the horse has more sense than you have," he said, grinning. "You won, I will make good on your wager, although of course, it was unfairly in your favor."

"Thank you Sire, I look forward to that night."

I would get my revenge on him for twice choosing Topaz over me—he would get little sleep that night!

I took my refreshment in seclusion while sitting naked in the shade of a spreading doum (palm), my clothes spread out on rocks to dry in the sun.

Our journey continued without other notable events. With time to think, I pondered possibilities for my future. I was already halfway through my stay with Ali and the thought of returning to my husband's house to live under the thumb of his hostile mother and aloof wife depressed me immeasurably. I sneaked long looks at Ali. He was dashingly handsome and evocatively attractive with his white *djellaba* and *ghutrah* streaming behind him, billowing and twisting in the sunlight. I saw in imagination spending the rest of my life with him.

I had never been in love before, in passionate love that is. Certainly, I loved my family, my mother and father and brothers, but this was different. I noticed new sensations and thoughts sweeping through me: flutterings in my stomach, a trembling heart when I kissed him, the wish to make myself pretty for him. When alone, I thought only of him, and was always overjoyed seeing his face when he came back from wherever he had been. His attention to Topaz bothered me—I wanted to be the one to care for him, to breathe in the scent of his clothes, to feel them, to be near him, and to please him in every way. I had no appetite, for food.

These feelings were surely the trappings of passionate love, were they not? This had to be love that was consuming me, love that at times made me happy, and at other times unhappy with desperation.

"Why do you hide from love, Ali?" I murmured to myself.

HUSSEIN

I cannot write much about Hussein, however deserving he may have been to be remembered in that way. He had departed this world as we rode across the desert and was dead before we arrived.

Although I had never known him, I was saddened, perhaps unknowingly feeling Ali's sorrow within me.

Ali went to be alone with his stilled brother, leaving Topaz and me with Hussein's three slave concubines. He, like Ali, had never seen the need to marry. The three women were wailing and sobbing, perhaps with false grief, I could not tell. "What shall become of us now? We are nothing without Hussein, we have no one," they cried. I tried to console them, but had nothing to offer except sympathy.

Ali returned with reddened eyes and a dour face, and settled to the embrace of the concubines, for they knew him well and wished to comfort him. "Too well for my liking" I thought, feeling a bit ashamed at my less than pure thoughts at this time of grieving.

"What shall become of us, Ali?" they sobbed.

"For many years you served my brother well; you gave him happiness and comfort in his brief life. You were his wives in truth, if not in name. I will not sell you along with his chattels. You will come with me to Makram and enter the House of Saalih., not as my slaves, but as free women," he said, glancing briefly at me.

They could not contain their joy in their relief, his offer of a safe haven and release from slavery. It burst through the pall of grief, spilling over all of us and lightening our thoughts.

Ali stood vigil through the night at his brother's side, his five women sleeping together in another room, taking rest from the rigors of the previous days. I lay there staring into the blackness, pondering the thought, "Would Ali bed these three women?" They too had their needs and desires, and I believe they possessed great fondness for Ali, not just because of the events of today, but from experience of him from previous visits. I had again the thoughts of a jealous woman.

Before sunset of the second day, as required of the faithful, a donkey cart arrived to take Hussein's shroud-wrapped body for burial "What an ignominious end to such a short life, to be carried out of this world on a donkey cart," I thought, as the cart trundled down the road and out of sight, followed by four figures in black.

Word of Ali's bereavement spread through the town. Many who hoped to profit from his grief came to the house and offered to sell him special foods and sacred goods to intone the blessing of Allah and to lessen his grief. Two slave traders offered to buy the three women sight unseen—it being well known about town that Hussein owned beautiful women. "They are his wives," they were told, "and are not for sale. Be on your way."

Ali hired a band of mercenary guards and two horse-drawn carts for Topaz and the three women, and the meager belongings they had selected to bring with them as a remembrance of their life with Hussein. Many of these were simply tokens of no great value or necessity, but memoirs of happier times: clothes, jewelry, pieces of furniture, carpets, beds, cooking utensils and a large potted plant from the courtyard that one of the women had tended to over the years.

Ali designated me to lead the assemblage back to Makram, an assignment I accepted with astonishment and pride.

"Write a letter for me, it is for the captain of the palace guard and for Mustafa and Yasmeen," he said, thrusting pen and ink into my hand, snapping me out of my daydream.

He dictated:

> *The woman who carries this letter to you and wears my seal about her neck is my emissary; she speaks for me in all matters. Do as she commands as though her words are mine.*
>
> *My brother has passed away, taken by the fever—may the peace and blessings of Allah be upon him.*
>
> *I will remain in Al-Lith to settle his estate and will return to Makram within ten days.*

I have taken his three wives into our household. They will share one of the wives apartments, the one farthest from the bedchamber.

There is a new slave girl for the harem, prepare also a room in the courtyard for her.

Signed and sealed,

Ali bin Shareef al-Saalih.

I was to pay the hired help upon arrival at Makram and Ali wrote out for me a schedule of payments. "You may increase these payments by one fourth for those who give you exceptional service, and when you arrive they are to be provisioned for their return journey," he instructed. "You should know that although the letter is also addressed to Mustafa and Yasmeen, they cannot read. In kindness, read it out aloud to them in a manner that does not betray your knowledge of their inadequacy in this matter."

We departed the next morning with me proudly leading the way with my newfound sense of importance, until I suddenly snapped back to reality. I did not know the way! I summoned the guard, the one who had scooped Topaz from the desert floor, and asked him to lead for a while, saying, "I will drop back and console the three women at this trying time in their lives." I tied my horse to their cart and jumped onto the bouncing wooden deck to join them for the first part of the journey—concealing my ignorance of the way and demonstrating compassion for the women. "Rather clever of me" I thought, smiling inwardly.

RETURN TO KASRE EL NOUZHA

The captain of the guard emerged from a small door set into one corner of the massive main gates, rifle in hand, to investigate this motley bunch of bruised, tired, and dusty travelers who had unexpectedly arrived from the desert. He took one brief look, and then fired a startling shot into the air, and dark heads and burnished gun barrels quickly dotted the high rampart walls.

He looked for the man in charge and was surprised when I instead thrust Ali's letter before him. Hardly giving him time to read the letter, I issued my orders: swing open the gates, tether and water the horses, help set up camp for the hirelings, re-provision them, and find Yasmeen and Mustafa and bring them here. He protested that Yasmeen was not allowed to leave the harem courtyard except in the company of Ali. I fingered the seal necklace about my neck and reminded him to read the first lines of the letter again, and then to bring Yasmeen. He reluctantly obeyed.

The confusing scene before them—horses and carts everywhere, tents being erected, and strange men milling about—took Yasmeen and Mustafa by surprise. Sitting high on my horse, with a manner of importance about me, I told the captain to read aloud Ali's letter to them. Then I kindly asked Yasmeen to take the three women and Topaz under her care, and a miffed Mustafa to organize beds for them, and then unload and sort their belongings.

A payment table was set up. I piled the copper and silver coins Ali had brought back from the races in rows by denomination. An eager queue formed. Working from the list of agreed payments, I paid them off, adding two extra silver coins to all—Ali later said I was too generous, a sign of weakness. In the most stern and commanding voice I could muster, I instructed them to give the extra coins to their wives or mothers for them to buy something for themselves. And if I found out that this did not happen and they kept the extra for themselves, they would have to answer to Ali, who would carry out my most severe instructions. I was confident that they would not test my determination. They had no way of knowing that I was his slave.

When I returned to the harem courtyard, all four women were in the bath, grateful to relieve their aches and pains. I noticed red marks and bruises from sitting and bouncing on the carts. The two servants were waiting nearby, ready to apply soothing emollients and balms. After soaping and rinsing off, I joined the others in the water, happy to find relief for my own saddle soreness. Although I had ridden horses for pleasure on numerous occasions, three days in the saddle with the saddle-skirt against my thighs was too much for me. I would be stiff, sore, and aching for days to come, preferring to stand up rather than sit down.

Ali returned quietly at night five days later—earlier than expected—and we were surprised and pleased to see him the next morning.

He spent most afternoons with a visiting cleric. Previously, these were hours he had often spent with one of us in our room, now he read from the Qur'an, receiving instruction and taking time for prayers.

On a few occasions, I walked with him quietly, hand in hand. He took me out of the harem courtyard, through the great hall, and into the surrounding gardens—they were beautiful. He had never before walked hand in hand with a woman in an affectionate way. It was a simple affection, yet something new and comforting I had shown him.

For twenty-nine days he was in mourning and celibate, and quiet in his manner.

Yesterday, the official mourning ended. There had been much discussion amongst his irreverent girls about his return to the carnal world. Who would be the one lucky enough to relieve him of his pent up passion and seed?

Ali had informed me earlier in the day that he had chosen me to be his companion that night, a commitment the other girls were unaware of as they preened and glossed themselves. This was a welcomed opportunity to nurture further a place in his affections, and when I learned that I would be alone with him, thrill and excitement grew within me. I readied myself thoroughly and carefully, for I was eager to lie in his arms again and lose myself in his eyes.

I had planned in my mind how the evening in his bedchamber would unfold. I would dance close to him, and curve myself into him to let him taste and breathe the sweet smelling ylang-ylang I would spread in secret places. Purposely, I would spill something down my front and go into the bath to wash it off. He would follow. Our hands would disturb each other, and he would dry me off and carry me to bed. There I would lay on my back with a pillow under my hips to raise myself to him, to let him know clearly how I wanted to give myself to him.

Mustafa swung open the heavy doors to the bedchamber. I stepped forward, disrobed down to my night garments, and dropped to my knees, crawled around the screen and started down the carpet towards the kneeling mat. Behind me, the doors thudded shut.

"Stop there, Sapphira. Stand up," Ali commanded.

Something was different, slightly unsettling.

"Come, walk to me."

With hands behind my back and breasts thrust forward, I obeyed his command. Although confident and buoyed by his calling, I was somewhat nervous. I cast my eyes downward, and walked toward him beguilingly, faintly emphasizing the swing of my hips. I silently counted my steps and as his feet came into view, I dropped to my knees and prostrated myself before him.

"Stand up," he ordered, again, "and come with me."

He took my hand in his and we walked to the carpet, arranged cushions to our liking, and made ourselves comfortable. He poured me a large goblet of wine saying that I looked pale and in need of wine to ward off oncoming illnesses, while he drew sweet smelling smoke from the hookah.

"Barry, the Englishman, gave me this bottle of wine for you. It's Algerian. A little rough," he said.

I smiled at his borrowed knowledge and thanked him.

"It was too heavy for him to take back with him; that is why he gave it to you."

I accepted this explanation outwardly, but noted another with inward pleasure.

"From now on," Ali continued, "when you enter my bedchamber, you will walk to me, and you will enter the bed from the side, no longer from the foot end in the manner of a slave—but only when we are alone. If you are with another girl, except Yasmeen, you will remember the old traditions and come to me on hands and knees as before."

"Yes, Sire," I replied, knowing well that "Master" was the right word to use in the bedchamber.

"Yes, Sapphira, you may also call me Sire," he said through a sigh, looking at me with eyes that told me he was aware of my discreet audacity and found it amusing. "You and Yasmeen are the only girls given these privileges," he added.

"These may be small gestures on his behalf," I thought, nevertheless, they were ones I enormously appreciated. I was elated by these small things.

Ali thanked me for all I had done to help him through these last difficult weeks. "I hear you were particularly hard on the captain of the palace guard—he was complaining about having to take orders from a woman. Tomorrow I will send for him and we will reconcile over tea. However, you have managed everything so well there is no need for me to do anything further," he claimed.

Formalities were soon over. He was "tenting" his caftan; urgently ready. I stood up to start my planned dance of seduction, but he stood up too, and what little clothing I had on found its way to the floor. "Come, bathe me," he said, shrugging off his caftan to reveal his stiff member assertively jutting forward, shamelessly alert and bouncing up and down with his stride as he walked me to the bath, the sac underneath tight and round.

Kneeling deeply in the water, my buoyant breasts floated and bobbed delightfully, while he stood against the side, leaning back, making his member jut out over the water, delightfully. Knowing it was not bathing he craved at this moment, I settled my lips comfortably around the neck that nature had conveniently provided—can you see any other reason for it?—gently holding his glans, his "purple plum" as they speak of it in Eastern writings, in my mouth while I played my tongue over the vulnerable underside. I pushed forward, the swell of his shaft further parting my lips, until he pressed against the back of my mouth, and then drew back until he again rested securely in the embrace of my rounded lips. But as soon as I started to play my tongue and repeat my ministrations I tasted a little of him, and felt his telltale shudder. There was no turning back, his course was set and my plan of seduction had collapsed. I plunged onto him three or four times, no more, before he erupted into me—a flood of salty slipperiness. The little tricks and techniques of the harem I had learned were useless—he was too plentiful for me to cope with. His seed bubbled from my mouth and ran down my chin, dripping onto the water and floating away like a splatter of stracciatelle.

There was no cause to be embarrassed, but I was. I looked upwards. He was still relishing the moment with his head thrown back and his eyes closed, and I took advantage of his blind rapture to splash water over my face and swish away the floating seed. Two more surges and he relaxed completely, spent and satisfied. I calmed him with gentle strokes until he softened, and drew him off with my lips. His urgent lust had ambushed my carefully thought out plan of seduction, nevertheless, he did carry me to bed and made me a woman, then, and again later.

I knew the girls would be inquiring in the morning, but I wanted to keep this episode for Ali and myself alone to relish, for he too spoke of his supreme enjoyment. I answered their questions with only a knowing smile and a coyish tilt of my head.

In the days following, Ali clearly reasserted his position as master of the harem. All were bedded, even Hussein's women.

They commandeered the kitchen that day and prepared a meal to give thanks to their rescuer, and for the rest of us to enjoy: yellow lentil soup, Greek style roasted lamb encrusted with herbs and honeyed lemon served on a bed of couscous with carefully arranged garnishes of colorful vegetables, mint tabbouleh and exotic condiments. To sweeten our mouths they had made sweetmeats of rose-flavored Turkish delight, honey soaked kneifah and sesame seed halvah. Hovering over Ali they lovingly helped him savor the choicest morsels and small delicacies they had made with their own hands that morning.

We were told to dress modestly for they had asked Yasmeen for permission to take special care of him for one day and a night, all three of them together, to thank him with kindness and their sweetness.

They entertained us that evening with dances depicting stories and places from their homelands. One was from the Black Sea region, and the two black girls were "Red Oromo" from Ethiopia. Amongst slave traders and harem masters Oromo girls from the Omo Valley were renowned and valued for their unquestioned beauty and willing sexual temperament, and everything I saw that night bore out that assessment.

They had brought clothes with them for occasions such as this, and they were different from those in our wardrobe. Although I knew about them, this was the first time I had seen metal breast bridles worn. Against the black Oromo skin, they were most alluring. One of the girls, her pert and firm breasts requiring no support, wore only many arm bangles, ankle bracelets, and a large broach on the back of her flimsy skirt that drew the eye to the graceful curve of her back and what lay below.

We left the hall early, leaving Ali with his three admirers sprawled at his feet. Later I heard their chatter and laughter as they passed by my room on their way to the bedchamber. I was pleased for them and buried my envy.

Ali looked well and was as frisky as a colt. We were happy to have him back in our lives.

CHANGE OF POSSESSION

Ali suggested that I collect my wager from him, the one I had unfairly won on the journey from Ranyah to Al-Lith. I agreed, but had reservations. I was unsure of the courage or disposition to give him orders, and I did not know what to order him to do. I spent the afternoon thinking about possibilities and settled my mind on a short play, some theater, to make him see harem slavery from a girl's viewpoint—a reversal of roles, at least as much as anatomy would permit. I thought for a moment that I might take a phallus from the erga and violate him with it, but in truth, the small details of that part of a man's anatomy did not enamor me, its outlines and burly feel more than satisfied me, and I didn't like going into the erga. I dismissed the thought.

He called me that evening and after we entered the bedchamber and the doors closed behind us, he knelt down. "How may I serve my mistress, what is my mistress' pleasure tonight," he asked.

"We will act out a little play I have thought up."

"Yes, Mistress."

I had him stand on a small low table—my imaginary auction block—and I slowly took off every piece of clothing he had on. Then I walked around him, slowly, eyeing him up and down from every angle. I took the whip from the bedpost and came behind him, tracing his buttocks with it before moving in front of him and thrusting the phallused handle between his legs. Bringing it upwards, I jostled his sac, perhaps a little too sharply as I saw him wince slightly. Walking around him I stroked and pinched his thighs, buttocks and chest—as Yasmeen told me they had done to her—jostling his manhood, feeling its heft, assessing its condition and suitability for my purpose. "I will buy him—ten thousand qirsh," I said, to the imaginary slaver. Then turning to Ali, I told him, "You are now my slave. If you fail to please me, I will give you a good lashing with this whip, and if you continue to displease me I will deem you an inept and useless man, and have you knifed and sold on as a eunuch. Is that understood?"

"Yes, Mistress."

"Now you will bathe me and when that is done you will ready yourself and crawl to my bed."

As he stepped off the table, I reached down and firmly squeezed his bunch, at the same time offering my lips for his kisses, which were forthcoming.

He bathed me, dried me off, and followed me to the bed, turning back the coverlet for me. I slipped in between the silky cottons. He returned to the bath, bathed himself, and crawled to the side of the bed naked.

"Stand up," I ordered, before I reached out and thoroughly kneaded him once more. More than a definite firming was in progress. "Enter my bed, slave," I demanded, "from the end. You will crawl up to your Mistress."

My spread legs stopped his progress.

"Pleasure me," I ordered.

His tongue and lips slowly brought me to a thrilling peak, while I writhed with ecstasy and exaggerated my movements to make it difficult for him to keep his mouth on me. Nevertheless, with my hand behind his head to discourage his leaving, he managed to stay with me amidst the heaving. Certainly, he had pleasured me on other occasions, but never so skillfully or so completely. Now I knew why men wanted pleasuring so often—the mouth and tongue could be sensual tormenters.

After urging him upward to kneel at my side, I used my hand to stroke him to release, catching his milky issue in the other. His ejaculation surprised me. I expected it to jet out with force and shoot a great distance—considering the time and effort required to bring it about—but instead it just weakly squirted and dribbled into my hand. So little, for so much work.

"It is not to be spilled. Swallow it," I ordered, holding my hand to his lips. He hesitatingly obeyed, followed by a grimace of distaste—would he be less demanding and more lenient with his girls after this? Perhaps.

Later, as we lay side by side, a thoughtful Ali broke the silence. "You must be a descendent of Queen Kahina[1]," he mused. "You make a fearsome mistress. It's your Berber blood no doubt."

"Who was Queen Kahina?"

"She was Chief of the Berbers in Northern Africa. In one account it is said she ruled over a mighty harem of men who were servile and willing to accommodate her every wish."

"I think one, maybe two men, are all I can handle," I replied. "But I have not finished with you yet."

In the morning, to tell him again that I, too, enjoyed that way, I had him pleasure me. However, after he satisfied me, I did not urge him up and relieve him. I unlovingly left him hard and full of seed, hoping he would languish in unfulfilled urges and be driven to break one of the harem rules, as his girls were inclined to do when his attentions are too hurriedly and selfishly given. My hope was not fulfilled. Shortly after leaving the bedchamber, I saw him escorting a surprised looking Paeonia into her room, she worriedly glancing back at him, trying to read from his face his intentions as he ushered her forward.

I often reflect on that night as a mistress, but I do not want it again. My nature was such that I wanted to be submissive to a man. I wanted to allure him, to turn his eye, to make him desire me, then yield to him, and give myself to him. That was the natural and right order, when you are in love.

Paeonia is pregnant, for which I take credit, because Ali's mid-morning urgency of lust had left no time for a pessary.

Our Peony is in full bloom.

No one has told Ali. Paeonia is too frightened and Mustafa is mute. Praise be to Allah that she confided in me. With help from the other girls we have planned to be called together and then Paeonia will tell Ali. I will be there to speak my mind forcefully if necessary, for I cannot allow her to be taken for pronging—even if it is the last thing I ever say to him or do before I leave.

---

1. Queen Kahina of the Berbers (c. 650-702)—400 husbands.
    Chief of the Berbers in Northern Africa, Kahina relied on her cunning and indomitable will to withstand the Arab invasions of her homeland. This enigmatic figure was not especially attractive—later Arab historians describe her as "fleshy"—but was such an intriguing figure that centuries after her passing she was still romanticized in French literature. Kahina was the name Arabs gave her; it means witch. Her real name was Dahia.

MY JOURNEY ENDS—in the month of Safar

With mounting sadness, I watch my noonday shadow shrink as the sun rises higher in the sky with each new day—and with each passing day, I am reminded that my stay here is growing to a close. When my noonday shadow falls only on myself,[1] I will know that it is time to say goodbye.

I cannot imagine it, nor do I want it—a life without him. I wish I could be more grateful, more thankful, for the time I have spent in his Kasre el Nouzha. I should not be ungrateful and saddened. After all, I have spent part of my life with a man I loved and it has been an exciting adventure. But in truth, I have withdrawn quietly into myself and mope over the prospect of leaving Ali and having nothing more than memories to hold. And driven by nothing but my envy, I picked a huge argument with Paeonia, which ended in tears for both.

On our last night together Ali was in a quiet mood, I think he, too, was thinking about what the future held for him. He took my hand in his as we walked to the bedchamber. At that moment I was not his slave girl going to the bedchamber for his pleasure, I was his lover.

We made gentle love, nothing elaborate, and talked of the time we had spent together. We recalled happy moments: the visit to Ranyah, the time the horse threw me and I splashed into the oasis waters, my triumphant return to

---

1. On the summer solstice (June 22nd), the longest day of summer, anyone standing on the Tropic of Cancer will see the sun directly overhead at noon. Makram is slightly south of the Tropic of Cancer, about the same latitude of Havana, and just before the solstice, the noonday sun would pass directly overhead, hence her phrase "When my noonday shadow falls only on myself."

Makram with Topaz and Hussein's women, and the commotion that it caused throughout the palace. Ali told me how anxious he had been to come home and be near me again. "I missed seeing your face," he explained. Five words, not overly romantic ones to the ears of a woman utterly in love, yet to my mind precious words thoughtfully spoken. They spoke the same to me as the three words I had wanted to say and hear. They told me what I wanted to know—that he loved me—although he had never said the words. I had wanted to tell him that I loved him, but it was now too late and pointless. He never heard the words "I love you," and I would leave with the words I never said. I regretted that a fear of foolishness had wasted all fitting occasions, and felt that this regret would carry forward into the rest of my life. Why had I found it impossible to risk foolishness and say simply, "I love you"? The thought that my silence had left him with nothing disheartened me, until I realized that it was not true. I would be leaving him something—my love—whether I had spoken of it or not. Love lives on, even when faces have gone, and my leaving didn't mean I loved him any less.

Ali deflated my vision of a triumphant return to Al-Ta'if riding on the back of Topaz. "We will travel by camel, it is too hot this time of the year for horses," he said, rightly. "We will take the white camels and travel by night and rest during the heat of the day."

My journey would end as it had begun, on the hump of a pungent, bad tempered camel.

I bid a tearful goodbye to the girls I had come to know so well and love, Ali's slaves and Hussein's women. When I reflected on my experience, I realized it was an amazing episode in my life, and one that gave me extraordinary understanding of the theme for my book. I decided that when I was home in Jeddah, I would rewrite and expand upon my notes and complete the illustrations. I had thought of titles—*Arabian Slave Girl*, or *Tales from an Arabian Harem*, or perhaps just *Harem Girl*.

I carried the clothes I came with, Sheik Ahmad's pages of tantra translations, my journal notes and the belly brilliant Ali bought for me in the souk at Ranyah. I vowed I would never wear the jewel for anyone else. No other man would ever gaze upon its inviting glitter. I would keep it secret for the rest of my life, a hidden keepsake, brought to light and mind only in those nostalgic moments I was certain to have when alone.

Our entourage traveled with a spare camel. It confirmed Ali's intention to buy me and bring me back to Makram together with his other girl. Could I let it happen? By rights I should, and would, return to my husband and his unfriendly household, a prospect that saddened me. In spite of this resolve to return to my husband, my mind would not release me from confusing thoughts about the alternative. Hour after hour, I mulled over in my mind how it might be if I did not go back to Jamaal. Realistically though, even considering my love for Ali, being a slave confined to his harem courtyard for the rest of my life did not inspire me. But being with Ali did, particularly as his wife. Then I could make a home, manage the household purse, settle in, and go to him and not wait for his calling. However, the likelihood of him ever marrying me seemed remote—there were many other eligible women available for him to choose from, should he ever decide to take a wife. And why would he marry? He enjoyed in abundance the carnal pleasures that come with marriage, without the objections, difficulties, and aversions that wives present from time to time.

Reluctantly, I resolved that as soon as we arrived in Al-Ta'if, I would tell Ahmad to refuse all offers from Ali—even to lie, and tell him another master in Jeddah had already bought me. Returning to my husband was the proper thing to do, after all, I was married to the man, but I was miserable and downhearted at the thought.

How to explain my smoothing to Jamaal took over my mind. He would find out eventually, so I would tell him first. I caught myself smiling as I made up various stories for Jamaal's ear, such as it just wilted and died away on its own, or I fell into the hands of a band of wandering barbers. Of course, I knew he would never believe any of this, so I settled on a more plausible and suggestive explanation—"I asked the sheik's wife to do it for me for my homecoming. I thought you would like me groomed that way."

When I got home, I intended to bathe deliberately in sight of his younger wife whose second child, I hoped and prayed, had wrought devastation on her shape and charms. If she asked, I would tell her I did it for Jamaal, and flaunt myself as a threatening *femme fatale*.

We arrived two hours before mid-day in Al-Ta'if. Sheik Ahmad greeted us with obvious anxiety, punctuated by his pointed baboushes slapping noisily against the hard tiles as he paced the floor. He was agitated and uneasy. His eyes went everywhere but to me.

After the usual formalities, a servant escorted Ali and his entourage to their quarters and Ahmad hurried to my side.

"I have perilously bad news for you—may the peace and blessings of Allah be upon you," he said, in a nervously quavering voice. "I will tell you about it in your room. Please follow me." A nasty feeling settled in my stomach, but he ignored the room key hanging in its place at the entrance to the courtyard as we passed through.

"Please sit down," he said, gesturing towards the bed.

"A disturbing message was delivered a few days ago. Your husband's second wife has declared you an adulterer. In Jeddah, the Mullahs have issued a fatwa against you and posted public notices. When found, they will punish you according to the censures of Islam. You return at your own peril—great peril I may add. To seal the fatwa his second wife placed a reward of five hundred qirsh on your head. People will be looking for you, to bring you in for the reward," he said, wringing his hands, trying to show concern; to me unconvincingly, for I felt he was almost gloating.

"A messenger delivered the letter; I couldn't talk to your husband, there was nothing I could do. I feel responsible for allowing you to get into this situation. Stay here as my guest for as long as you wish, it is the least I can offer. Take good time and think well on what you will do."

What would I do? What would I face in Jeddah? Islamic Shariah law prescribes severe punishment for adulterers, often given to the woman without restraint, as tradition had always made her the temptress who lured the man from his righteous ways. Unfair, despicable, hostile—call it what you may, that was what I faced. I was an adulterer, undeniably so, and would have to face the consequences.

And in reality how could I possibly expect Jamaal to help me. Ahmad and I had callously tricked him. French tutor indeed! And another, more compelling reason existed. He would not corroborate my testimony, and turn away from his second wife, because the law turns against those who bear false witness. If a woman falsely accused another woman of adultery—and it was often done out of jealously or to settle a family feud—then the woman who bore this false witness faced the same severe punishment, something my husband would never allow to be inflicted on the nursing mother of his second child. "Justice requires Marie's back, not hers," would be his rightful thinking.

Even if Jamaal sided with me, saying that he condoned my conduct and helped with the arrangements, it would hold no water in the eyes of the law. Adultery was *haraam*; it was blasphemous, against the law, with or without consent.

Depending on the deemed severity of the adultery one of three sentences was handed down. For a minor deviation: public flogging and banishment. For a major deviation: ride "the wooden donkey" from sunrise to sunset, followed by branding and banishment. Worse yet, she could be buried up to her waist or neck, immobilized at the bottom of a shallow pit scooped into the sand, and stoned to death by the women of the town. The pit, when filled, leveled, and obliterated, became the blasphemer's ungodly and forgotten grave.

I had seen the cruelty I would meet. Early in our marriage Jamaal had taken me to witness two thieves, a father and son, have their right hands cleaved off and an adulteress receive her "wooden donkey and branding" sentence. A pleasant way to spend the day! He may have seen this as an essential part of my education, even as a warning. Who knows?

That morning, after the bloody and sickening spectacle of the amputations, we found the unfortunate adulteress in a tent chained to a post and straddling a sharp wooden beam. She was still there when we returned that evening to watch a hooded Mullah brand her. I still remember my husband's cryptic remark as she screamed out—"That will be a lasting reminder for her to keep her legs together except for her husband."

In the short time I had had to think about my present predicament, I became convinced that there were only two possible outcomes. I would end up either a slave, or dead, whether I went back to Jeddah or not.

The perils I faced were stunningly clear. If I were to leave Ahmad's protection and wander out in search of a living—even if I could survive in the desert—the Bedouins would find me, if not by intent then by accident. Then, no doubt, they would take me to their *friq* (encampment) and splay me for raping—they answer to no one—before taking me to a slave market. Moreover, if I tried to live in Al-Ta'if—if I had money for shelter and food, which I did not—I was sure to be soon recognized as the wanted stranger, captured, taken back to Jeddah for the reward, and brought before my accusers. And if by some miracle I was not sentenced to death by stoning, and was instead flogged and banished, in banishment I would face those same perils that haunt any unprotected foreign woman—abduction and enslavement.

Furthermore, I had misgivings about Ahmad; I could not put my life in his hands and stay with him. I didn't trust him. Money would speak to him. He would turn me in for the reward or more likely sell me at the first opportunity that came along—all promises forgotten. That I was sure of.

Not having the protection of a man, family or ancestral tribe, I had no safe refuge from death or enslavement; I could draw no other conclusion. Of these dismal prospects, death held no delight. And if enslavement was to be my lot, I could not do better than to be one of Ali's slaves, rather than serve in a Turkish brothel, be sold to a new master and submit to his unknown penchants, or be taken as the white slave of a black tribal chief to somewhere in darkest Africa.

I could not stay in my collapsed life, exposed and vulnerable. I had to find safety. I had to go on with what was left of my life, even though at that moment it seemed unbearable. There were no good ways to end my wretched plight, only bad ones, and I chose the least bad—enslavement to Ali. At this time, for me, it was the best that life had to offer.

I dressed and walked to the entrance of the courtyard where I would wait for the bell summoning us to the evening meal, and pocket my room key. But Ahmad had beaten me to it—the key was gone.

Shortly he appeared, with my room key hanging conspicuously from his belt, and rang the bell sharply.

As we walked together to the main room, I took him aside and whispered in his ear. "You must sell me to Ali. I will not go back to Jeddah." He stopped walking and looked at me inquiringly, head tilted slightly to one side, and I answered his unspoken question. "Yes, sell me—you must. This is my clear choice. Ali wants to buy me; he has told me so. Sell me tonight so that he can take me to Makram when he leaves tomorrow afternoon. If you sell me, keep the money. I will have no need of it a harem."

The prospect of immediate money noticeably perked up his interest in my request, no doubt displacing any enthusiasm he may have had for turning me in for the reward, or for the other lucrative choice I had unwittingly alluded to, of keeping me captive and selling me later to someone else.

He pursed his lips and nodded his head in fatherly approval as he would to a child who had made a shrewd and wise decision. "That makes sense," he confirmed, as though I was ten years old.

Towards the end of the evening, Ahmad dismissed his servants and I stood up to depart for my room, to leave the two men alone to bargain over my fate, thinking, "When the evening is over who will come into my room, Ahmad or Ali." But Ahmad commanded me to refresh the hookah and pass it around, and to draw on it—a welcomed calming for my ragged nerves. He then motioned me to sit down on a padded bench opposite himself and Ali, yet still within earshot.

Ahmad casually opened the conversation. "Did you find Sapphira to your liking? You must agree she is tantalizingly innocent girl and a fair exchange."

"Yes, indeed, a fair exchange, pleasant enough company, but I doubt whether she will ever learn to do some things properly."

"You can expect that with new girls, but you don't have to put up with intransigence—our forefather's ways to encourage a girl's behavior still work well today," he advised, casting an insidious smile in my direction, reminding me of what I knew awaited me if Ali left me in the hands of Ahmad.

"However, your other girls, have you tired of any of them? I always have buyers willing to pay a good price and sellers with attractive replacements if you are thinking of refreshing your harem."

"No, I am content with what I have," Ali replied, firmly, "except a careless one is with child. She was one of my favorites, but you know how it is after a woman has birthed, they are not the same."

"That is true, they are less enjoyable, so have her pronged or give her the medicines that I have for that condition," advised Ahmad.

"It is too late. I have let her go too long. Besides, at my age a few sons would rest well with me," Ali replied, with a little chuckle. "I could be interested, however, in one, or both, of your Pearls of Allah. Show them to me."

"Ali! I did not receive a reply to my offer I sent with Sapphira," protested Ahmad. "They are gone."

"That is most unfortunate," Ali said, before thoughtfully pausing. "I suppose I could settle for less, and buy Sapphira from you?"

"She is not any less, and she is not for sale, unless you can convince me otherwise. I find her fetching, more so than either of the two Pearls of Allah, and I am thinking to keep her for myself." replied Ahmad.

My heart sank. Ahmad could indeed keep me and do what he wanted with me. No one would know; no one could intervene. This country had no registry of births, marriages or deaths, no *gendarmerie* or Foreign Legion to investigate these matters. Only four or five people knew of my circumstance—he could deny my very existence. I was utterly at his mercy, which I had come to believe was not easily given.

"Perhaps I could persuade you with three thousand qirsh."

"Ten thousand," was the instant reply from Ahmad.

"Ahmad, old friend, you have taken too much hookah—may the blessings of Allah be upon you. I can buy three or four beautiful well breasted girls from Salim the Turk for that price," said Ali, feigning shock at Ahmad's asking price.

"He is an unscrupulous scoundrel, his girls are only fit for Turkish brothels, not for your harem; they have sores," replied Ahmad.

"Yes, that may be so, but look at Sapphira's breasts. They are already softening and on their way down, and her stomach sags like a mare's," countered Ali.

"And she is so slow to learn. She will be an old woman long before she bends to the ways."

"There are ways to hurry along a slave's bending, however, let me show you something you seem to have forgotten.

"Sapphira, unbutton your choli, show him your bosom," commanded Ahmad. "Show Sheik Ali what I am offering him. Lower your chalwars; I believe his memory needs to be refreshed.

"Now Ali, be honest to yourself, is that not an offering worthy of a place in your harem? Would she not lie well on your bed?" said Ahmad, gesturing in my direction with a wave of his arm. "This is your only opportunity to buy her. If I don't keep her for myself, I have others interested and willing to pay a good price. Sweeten your miserable offer, Ali, and come to your senses. A white girl with her form would fetch twenty thousand if I sold her in the market in Zanzibar, in gold no less—sagging breasts and all."

"Those African chiefs are fools with too much gold. Accept my offer and you will not have to sail down the treacherous east coast of Africa to Zanzibar and risk boarding by pirates or foreign navies, and having Sapphira and even your life stolen from you." replied Ali, followed quickly by a renewed offer of four thousand.

"Six thousand," countered Ahmad.

"Four thousand and five hundred," countered Ali. "I will go no further. Even that amount is too much for a believer."

"Ah, this is not a time for pious thoughts, good friend. What goes on behind the closed doors of your bedchamber is between you and the four walls. No one knows, and in God's eyes, a slave girl is nothing but a veil and a tomb[2]. Do not allow your faith to spoil this opportunity for you to acquire something beautiful."

"Her veil has long since been torn away, and her tomb well plundered. She is far from a virgin; although by the price you are asking it is plainly something you have forgotten. Nevertheless, I will sweeten my offer, but this is my final offer. Five thousand," Ali said, gloomily.

"Others will appreciate her more. I can do better than that," replied Ahmad, followed by a long silence.

---

2. An old Arabian proverb—"A girl possesses nothing but a veil and a tomb".

"I have *kif* from Morocco, why don't we draw on some for a while and talk. Perhaps wisdom will return and join old friends," Ahmad announced brightly, signaling the end of business. "Sapphira, leave us. Go to your room."

I pulled up my chalwars, buttoned closed my choli, and hurried from the room and then ran the rest of the way to my room in the courtyard, leaving the two men to coldheartedly continue with their uninterrupted lives.

I collapsed on the bed, staring into blackness. Ahmad had heard in his head the clink of five thousand qirsh and wanted more. Sold to the highest bidder regardless, would be my fate. Ali could have paid with ease Ahmad's price. Only one thousand qirsh kept them apart. For one thousand miserable qirsh, Ali had condemned me to a life of wretched servitude and obscurity. How could he value so lightly the love I thought he had for me. And why, oh why, hadn't I told him when I had the chance, that I loved him and would stay with him.

Frantically, I started to plan my escape from this dreadful place. When Ahmad had finished with me and all was quiet, I planned to sneak out and ask the night guard to take me to the camels. There I would steal some money from Ali's saddlebag and ride to Jeddah and board a boat to Tunis—if I could convince the guards that I was a free woman and not an escaping slave—if the saddlebags were there with money still inside them—if Ahmad didn't lock me in for the night.

If he locked me in, I would....Ahmad swung open the door, startling me. I pulled back to the corner of the bed expecting worse.

"Get up. Come with me," he demanded, sounding impatient. He escorted me briskly back to the room from which I had earlier fled.

The room was empty except for the sweet smell of kif, and Ali who sat with his head lowered, looking tired and dejected. He turned his head slightly to one side, and greeted me with eyes that told me nothing, and a thin smile that could not interpreted as either a look of guilt or mischief.

"Come here, slave," commanded Ahmad, curling a finger at me. He took firm hold of my arm and with the blade of a knife pried apart the soft lead rivet that held closed his silver slave bangle around my arm.

"In a generous concession and gesture of friendship, I have decided to accept Sheik Ali's last offer. Slave Sapphira, kneel before Sheik Ali bin Shareef al-Saalih, your new master. Kiss his feet."

I enthusiastically bent to my task, with colorful visions of a joyful return to Makram swirling through my head distancing my mind from the ridiculous enthusiasm I was showing for his feet.

A clap of hands interrupted my fervor. I raised my head from Ali's feet and caught his clever smile, and the hurried appearance of a young boy. Ali sent him to bring in the leather satchels I had seen slung over his camel, and me to sit on the far cushioned bench. From there I watched carefully counted money change my life. I became a stranger to my past, as though it had been erased, made invisible, and irrelevant. My enslavement had set me free. I would start life over with a clean slate still to be written on, and again look to the future with its encouraging possibilities and somber uncertainties.

"There are two more things I need to buy from you Ahmad, a small amount of burnt umber—a spoon-full will be enough—and four measures of your famous elixir." Ali dropped a pinch of coins into Ahmad's extended palm.

"You are a considerate man, Ali. Your slave will be grateful."

Late the next afternoon, when we were mounted and about to leave on our return journey, a gangling boy in a colorful turban ran up to Ali. "Your medicines and burnt umber, Sir," he said, handing a small package to Ali.

Ali thanked him and nudged his camel forward.

Once on the way back to Makram, Ali let fall his formal business-like airs. He laughed, and confided that he was delighted with his purchase and had gotten a true bargain—to the point of having cheated Ahmad. Conversely, I was sure, Ahmad was equally delighted with his windfall—I had visions of him squatting on the floor counting and gloating over his ill-gotten money—and I thought, "How easily money transcends friendship."

"Although I won't be able forget that you cost me over five thousand qirsh, I will tell you again that my purchase pleases me. Having you return to Makram delights me."

"Thank you Master, I will do my best not to disappoint you."

In a friendly manner, I took Ali to task for the less than flattering description of me he had given Ahmad. "My breasts do not sag, my tummy is as flat as a mill stone, and I am not slow to learn!" I protested, "and I won't be able to forget that you played a game with my life to get your blessed bargain!"

"I know," he replied, with a sly grin, "but it is not as though you were in peril or faced death, and I know you understand that you can never praise the goods you are buying—you must always find fault with them or pretend no further interest and walk away. Slave traders are no different from other merchants, you have to bargain with them in this manner or you will pay too much. Besides, you should thank me, for without my intervention and generosity you could be on your way to Zanzibar instead of Makram."

"You will get your thanks," I replied, cheekily.

"Master, what is that burnt umber and elixir you bought from Ahmad? What are they used for, that I should be grateful?" I asked.

"Umber is a dark brown earth, a special mehndi, and the elixir is to dull pain when you are hurt," he replied, with hesitation and a faint distant smile on his handsome face. He pulled ahead to break off the conversation, leaving me alone with little more understanding than I had had before.

Our journey back to the palace gave time for talk with the girl whose place I had taken earlier, Ali's slave Nadya[3]. It was awkward making conversation while we both swayed about on piles of sheep skins high on the backs of our camels. To others, we must have looked like two chirping birds in wind-blown nests far above the ground. We persevered, however, and it gave welcomed relief from boredom, for we had time on our hands and it speeded along our journey.

She was a lovely girl from Northern Europe, as fair as they come, with rare blue eyes—I could see the attraction, and I was not pleased about it. She hated her stay at Ahmad's house—a stay with a new master, no doubt, was rarely anything to be happy about—for shortly after she had arrived he left on a trading voyage down the coast of Sudan, leaving her alone. On his return, he used her to show the two new Indian girls what would be required of them in a harem—without defiling their precious virginity. "They were always there, made to watch," she said, frowning, "as Ahmad took me in his Asian ways and made me do what is more comfortably done without voyeurs looking on. And he had me help him as he showed them how to pleasure him and take him in from behind. He is a horrible man—ruthless and without compassion, giving no second thought about hurting someone for his own end," she said, giving me confirmation, as if I needed any, that I had made the right decision not to trust Ahmad.

"I know exactly what you mean about feeling uncomfortable," I replied, and I described the incident in Ali's tent when he had me pleasure him in front of Topaz.

She was of course surprised to learn about Topaz. I recounted in brimming detail the whole episode at Ranyah. It made for a long story as I included my adventures with the merchant, the Englishman, Ali's winning of Topaz, our afternoon at the hammam, Hussein's passing and chattels, and my return to Makram.

---

3. Nadya—'Moist with dew.'

MY JOURNEY ENDS—in the month of Safar

Sometimes ahead, sometimes behind, I purposely found quiet places amongst the others, small corners so to speak, where I could be alone with my thoughts—time alone for the reality of what I had done to take firm possession of my mind. On the journey back to Ahmad's, thoughts of how my venture would end had saddened me but now I was saddened not by the ending but by the beginning and how I had deceived and walked away from my family and Jamaal. I would never again see the house in Jeddah or Jamaal walking through the door. We had had many good years together and despite what he had allowed his wife to do to me, I found that many moments in the years we had spent together—even some that I had once despised and fretted over—were being reborn as fonder memories. Had I loved him and never known it? The thought that I would never see him again swelled to my heart and eyes, as did thoughts of my mother far away in Tunis. Who will tell her, and what will they say to her? What will she think of me?

A welcomed site, a glimpse of the familiar coastal mountains and sea, pushed all sadness aside. Someone shouted "Makram!" and we halted to take in the sweeping view from water to peaks—with the Kasre el Nouzha nestled between. I felt a rush of feeling in my heart and stomach—I was going back to a life in a beautiful palace amidst many I had come to regard as almost sisters—and back to Ali. My spirits soared.

A boisterous and noisy welcome greeted us. Ali's girls were surprised that I had returned for good. Nadya chatted, gossiped, and caught up on things. Usually, there was not much to catch up with in harem life, but this time there was Paeonia's barely rounding tummy, Hussein's three women, and the new girl Topaz.

And I? I quietly contemplated my future as a lowly slave, feeling terribly alone, although surrounded by many.

NADYA AND TOPAZ

Of all the harem girls Nadya was the quietest and least outgoing, often withdrawing into a private world of her own. I noticed when she was on Mustafa's list of serving girls that she never made a special effort to catch Ali's eye. Others, including me, were always discussing and planning various ways of dressing and behaving to make him notice us, and for the most part, hoping for a calling to his bed. She could not, however, easily hide or downplay her natural beauty and attractiveness, particularly her blue eyes and fair hair, and she was often a bedchamber companion.

I turned to Yasmeen for words for my journal, and she told me: "Nadya comes from a land far away that she calls Sverige (Sweden), where the winter is so cold the rain falls as white sand, water turns to rock and summers are wet with rain and green. There is no desert.

"She was the seventh and last girl to be bought by Ali's mother and was of great attraction to his lustful father. He claimed that she showed rebelliousness and a wild spirit that needed to be broken before she was ready for his son. Not wanting her to be subjected to his cruelties, I invented excuses as to why she could not be handed over to him, resorting at last to the lie that I had discovered that she was a virgin and that it was Ali's privilege to deflower her. He accepted this false excuse and ceased his course, but insisted that I give him her fleece after her smoothing, so that he could show this rarity to his friends and boast about how generous he was to buy such a rare and expensive gift for his son.

"Nadya took unkindly to Ali's father's demands. To preserve her fleece, he ordered me not to use wax or sugar. I had to *thread* and pluck her one by one, which was a tedious task that took me all of a morning and part of an afternoon, while she was held down because of her resisting." Yasmeen sighed, "He could have easily asked for a lock of her hair to vouch for her fairness.

"She was hostile towards me for what I did to her, for at that time she thought I held high rank and authority over her. She did not know that I was a lowly slave who was simply obeying orders. I could not explain, we did not speak each other's tongue, but after she learned of my position she forgave me and we have been friendly with each other ever since.

"Nadya was lured onto a boat by a soothsayer promising to turn the cards and tell her what her future held. While sitting across from the woman an accomplice attacked her from behind, bound her, and gave her over to another man in a boat who sailed her to Jeddah. She is lovesick for a young man to whom she was pledged to in marriage, which is why she is often sad. She told me she thinks of this man whenever Ali is over her.

"To this day I do not believe Ali has congressed her although she is a Christian and he has the right to make her present her peach. Even he is cowed by her coolness, which speaks the words 'I dare you.'"

If what Yasmeen spoke was true, and I had no reason to doubt that it was, then it spoke well of Ali, for many masters would take what they wanted from a slave girl regardless of her demeanor—the devices in an erga were exceedingly compelling in that respect.

Topaz became a source of great amusement to us all. Acrobatics came easily to her young supple body. She practices most days, walking on her hands, tumbling, doing back bends, handsprings, and cartwheels.

Topaz also took naturally to seducing the Master. She enjoyed this essence of femininity—the excitement a woman gets from engaging the lust of a man, and arousing his desire for her. No one had to teach her, but she lacked finesse. One of her favorite seductions was to wear a long loose-fitting abaya and do cartwheels across the floor. The speed of her turning flung the abaya outward, not allowing it to fall down, until she stopped before the Master, with her hands on the floor and legs in the air. The abaya then floated down and off over her head and arms, showing her all. Or she would stand with her back to Ali and bend over backwards until her hands touched the floor—pausing for him to survey her offerings—before flipping her legs over so that she stood on her hands with her feet resting against his shoulders. Her slowly spreading legs left no doubt in anyone's mind as to her desires. It was the tease of a young girl newly aware of the affect her body could have on a man, I recognized it, this realization all girls come to have. It was a rite of passage from girl to woman, but she was yet unaware of the subtleties required for seduction. I thought the spreading was lewd; it was too much—too overt. This part of a woman was better given to a man's eyes in short glimpses—a fluttering skirt briefly lifted, a robe carelessly parted, or revealed seductively by a slowly lowered waistband. Better shown through a haze of gossamer silk by gentle candlelight after his ardor had been aroused, not thrust before his eyes in a crowded room. Yes, Ali was entertained, amused and titillated, but not seduced.

Last night the Master called both Topaz and me to the bedchamber. Ali and I were taking the hookah, and Topaz was doing handsprings along the length of the carpet, stopping abruptly, and then springing into the air. She asked Ali to stand on the carpet at the foot of the bed and face the door. She paced out to the other end of the carpet and after a measured distance, turned around and began handspringing towards him. Landing on her feet just short of him, she sprang up, wrapped her legs around his waist, and pressed her breasts to his chest, while clinging to him with her arms around his neck. She knew what she was doing. Her childhood had ended. He carried her to bed.

I sat quietly drawing in the sweet smoke, and kept my hazy thoughts to myself—because some were not too charitable.

I learned from her. Although I could not handspring with any degree of finesse, I could jump onto him and tighten my thighs around his waist while pressing myself tightly against him, until he carried me to bed. Or, if he were ready, I would slip him into me and let him impale me against one of the spiraled marble pillars, to celebrate our passion standing up, not in bed. I believe I was the only one he took that way, as I never saw pillar marks on the backs of the other girls. I never did this in front of Topaz. I was too proud to admit I had learned something from the desert waif, and I did not want to show her another way that she could probably do better than me.

FORBIDDEN

Most husbands, I suspect, have propositioned their wives at one time or other for this kind of lovemaking. Most wives, I suspect, have refused. In slave harems, nonbelievers accepted this invasion—they could not refuse or question the propriety of it.

A few days ago, about an hour before sundown, we were bathing and splashing about in the harem bath while Ali sat on a stone bench, watching. As I climbed out of the bath, he called my name and beckoned me to his side. "Tonight you and Topaz will be my companions. It is time," he said, "to teach Topaz another way of the harem."

As soon as Ali had informed Yasmeen of his thoughts and had disappeared through the entrance to the courtyard, I hurried to her. "What has he planned for tonight?" I inquired.

"To share her peach."

"Why does he want me there? You are experienced in that way, not me."

"I do not know," Yasmeen replied. "All I know is that I have to make her ready."

"He is a big man for a small girl."

"If she is willing to be taken that way, Ali will be gentle."

"Does Topaz know of the Master's order?"

"No. I will tell her shortly," replied Yasmeen.

"How does it feel to share your peach?" I asked, and was somewhat surprised by her reply. "Some girls just endure it," she said, "but many others enjoy it and even reach fulfillment and entice the Master to take them that way."

Her answer satisfied me somewhat, nevertheless, I still felt uneasy about the whole subject.

I left to gather up my clothes, and by the time I returned to mehndi myself for the evening, Yasmeen was already talking to Topaz.

"When a master is between your thighs you tense your muscles to pull him in, to squeeze him. However, when he is between your buttocks, you use your muscles to try to push him out, but gently or you will lose him. In this way you will not close down on him," she advised.

Proudly, Topaz informed me. "The Master will be bending me over tonight. It is forbidden to take a girl that way, you know. He told me it was a beautiful part of me. He only does it with those who have the prettiest bottoms, the ones he is unable to resist."

"I know," I replied nonchalantly, "and I will be there to make sure you do it properly," I said, secretly hoping that my tone of voice would convey the lie that I, too, was irresistible. "This is certainly a change of heart for you. If I remember correctly your last encounter with this, you fought the man off and he whipped you for your trouble."

"Well, Hortensia does it that way all the time. She told me."

"Is that so?" I sniffed.

"Yes, that's so. And she says it doesn't hurt the way Ali does it. Anyway, it was different before; Ali and I love each other."

"How do you know that," I snapped back. "Has he told you?" realizing too late that my voice bristled with anxiety.

"No," she replied, calmly, "but I know he does, or he wouldn't be kind to me."

"He is kind to all of us, it has no special meaning." I added, detractingly, with less anxiety.

Nevertheless, I was hurt. Those simple words, "Ali and I love each other," echoed in my mind for the rest of the day, and somewhere within, a small part of me died.

It felt strange, even a little perverse. Topaz stood with her harem pants gathered at her feet, breasts covered, seductively swaying as she shifted her weight from foot to foot, while I had on my harem pants, but was naked to the waist. It was as though Ali was trying to create a perfect woman, out of two faultless halves.

Ali, sitting on a stool, took Topaz's hand, pulled her to his side, and collapsed her across his knees. I thought he might spank her, as I understood some men found pleasure in that. Instead, he just passed his hand over her oiled and polished buttocks as though relishing their purity and innocence for the last time, while his other hand played over her breasts.

"Let us bathe," he announced, taking Topaz's hand.

Topaz and Ali entered the bath—I knelt at the edge awaiting his commands.

Ali looked intently at the water rippling high around Topaz's waist. "She is short, bring me a large cushion, Sapphira, and place it here," he said, pointing to a place close to the edge of the bath, "and kneel behind it."

When all was in position, he lifted Topaz by her tiny waist and placed her on the soft cushion, belly down. She cradled her head between my thighs and hooked her arms around my waist. The cushion raised her bottom conveniently.

"Pass me the oil," he asked, and proceeded to anoint himself. I had never seen him this engorged, this inspired—he was more than ready for a woman.

Parting her cheeks, he pressed his head against her opening, poured a little oil at the meeting of the two, and urged his head to penetrate. Topaz's hands tightened around my waist. He pressed a little harder, paused for a moment, before sudden acceptance allowed his engorged head to disappear between her cheeks.

With each gentle stroke, he penetrated a little deeper; Topaz's nails dug into me at the start of each stroke, and then relaxed again at the end of each new advance. When he had buried himself to the hilt and could go no farther, Topaz raised herself on her arms and arched her back downwards, as our Master held her hips and slowly, with oiled smoothness, plunged back and forth. I stared incredulously as I watched his huge shaft disappear and then reappear as it violated her tiny opening, finally pulling free before the unbridled enthusiasm of completion took hold of him. A shallow ripple of a superior smile crossed her face—for my benefit alone no doubt—that I saw through and ignored.

"Did you find pleasure?"

"Yes, Master."

"You gave me rousing pleasure, too, and I have yet to savor my peak with you this way. You would make a worthy joy-girl, but that is not my intention. We will do this occasionally, when I am so inclined."

"Tomorrow, Master?"

"You will be told when. Now, my pretty slave, wash off the oil and kneel down in the water and please me some more. Take me to the end of my pleasure."

"Yes, Master."

In deep contemplation and lost in thoughts of my own, I watched the oil floating on the water, entranced as it swirled into spirals of iridescent colors.

Lying together in bed later that night, I thought about how much he had enjoyed taking Topaz that way, and how her oiled buttocks had enormously inspired him—even though he withdrew before completion. "If it would please you to congress me from behind in that way, make me your calling for tomorrow night," I whispered, so that Topaz could not hear—I would make sure she heard about it tomorrow, from others.

"I will do that," he replied, squeezing me tightly against his chest.

"I'm a virgin there, Sire."

"I will be gentle with you."

"I want to be alone with you when you do it."

"It will be so, my pretty one."

I spoke again with Yasmeen. Although I had heard her talking to Topaz, and I had inquired of her earlier as to how it felt, I still wanted confirmation and a little assurance.

"I can enjoy it that way," she said. "It is a different feeling, but pleasant enough. I think you will enjoy it and I know Ali will. Just remember to relax and be slow and gentle in your movement—try to push him out, though gently or you will lose him. But relaxing is by far the most important thing to remember."

"What is the best position?"

"For the first time you should kneel on the edge of the bed and have Ali stand on the floor behind you, in that way he has a firm footing and a better grasp, and is more consistent in his motions. And I tell you, that devil of a man has the bed set at just the right height."

"Will you help me get ready tonight?" I asked.

She agreed adding, "We will use fragrant oil on the sponge, and have no concern about the sponge, for although Ali will push it in deeply, you will pass it tomorrow and not know it."

I felt a little uneasy walking to the great hall that evening, three ways ready. I could feel the slippery squishy sponge, a sensation Yasmeen had warned me to expect.

I lay back on silk cushions, trying to hide a slight uneasiness by soothingly caressing him, while he casually spread open my upper garment and removed my slippers before pausing in his deliberations. An awkward silence followed. Was he having second thoughts or looking for confirmation that I wanted him to continue? I took the initiative from him and took hold of his hand, slipped the bottle of oil into the other, and led him to the bed.

Dressed only in my skirt and nipple dangles, I was feeling very naughty and daring as I clambered onto the bed. Turning to face him, I pleasured him a little, anointed his rigid member with fragrant oil of attar, and turned around to present my oiled peach. He flipped my skirt up about my waist, outlined the swell of my hips with his hands, and gently spread my cheeks.

I clearly felt him carefully positioning his hot manhood against me, and the cold oil running down to meet it. He pressed firmly, not harshly, yet unwaveringly, and when I remembered Yasmeen's advice and relaxed, he slid into me slowly and surely all the way until I felt his thighs bump against me. The feeling was exquisite—I had no idea. What a surprise—I thought that women just endured this to please their man.

With his hands molding and gripping my hips, he rocked me back and forth with powerful long smooth strokes while, in sympathy with his thrusting, my breasts swayed back and forth, causing my nipple dangles to dance about in random excitement, stimulating and awakening my nipples.

He paused. I thought he was going to withdraw as he had done with Topaz. I turned my head around to gaze into his face in the tantric svanaka[1] way. "Don't stop, Master," I said.

His fingers found my denied petals and bud, moist and expectant, and my body convulsed and contracted in answer to his playing touches and renewed thrusting. Moments later his seed fell on barren ground, well *tilthed*[2] ground.

Gripping me firmly, he waited for emotions to subside and then withdrew, causing me to gasp before falling flat on the bed.

Before retiring for the night, we sat in the warm water of the bath, drew on the hookah, and ate a few sweetmeats. We did not talk much about our tryst, other than agreeing that we would do it again.

---

1. From Ahmad's Tantra instructions. If he mounts you like a dog, gripping your waist, twist round to gaze into his face. Experts in the art of love say it is "Svanaka" (the Dog).
2. "Your wives are a tilth for you, so go to your tilth when or how you will...." from the Qur'an.

How was it? Did I find it pleasant? Yes. At least enough so as not to deny it to him—but then again not enough to encourage it either. In my future writings, if need arises, I will call this "sharing the peach" or the "forbidden way"[3].

Now he would have no reason to seek comfort with anyone else, no reason whatever to find me inadequate for his carnal desires. I had given him all of me in every sense of the word. I had no other feelings or part of me to give. However, I was pleased I had asked him, believing that I had removed an unspoken barrier, real or imagined, cleared the way for a deeper devotion—and outwitted Topaz.

---

3. Indeed, the Prophet said: "Whoever has intercourse with a woman in her rectum has disbelieved in what was revealed to Muhammad." Although there are many righteous and sensible women who refuse to do this, many husbands threaten their wives with divorce if they do not comply. Some husbands even deceive their wives who may be too shy to ask a scholar about this matter—they tell them that this is *halaal*, and they may even misquote the Qur'an to support their claim (interpretation of the meaning): "Your wives are a tilth for you, so go to your tilth when or how you will." [al-Baqarah 2:223]. But it is well known that the Sunnah explains the Qur'an, and the Prophet stated that it is permitted to have intercourse with one's wife in whatever way one wishes, approaching from the front or the back, so long as intercourse is in the place from which a child is born. It is also well known that this deed is *haraam* even if both parties consent to it—mutual consent to a haraam deed does not make it halaal.

MARKED

A goldsmith came to the palace yesterday, setting up his workbench outside the courtyard. We were unable to see him, of course, but we could hear him hammering and tapping away at the metal. Mustafa collected our broken jewelry for repair. I gave him the breast bridle I broke on the night of my first calling—given the chance, I would wear it again. He took measure around my bosom and around my upper arm with a piece of knotted string and disappeared through the archway, jewelry and the small silver tipped branding iron from the erga in hand. Returning later, he handed me the repaired jewelry and an insidious grin when I glanced down and noticed that his other hand held not one, but two branding irons, the second one a newly made copy of the first.

Later that day, Topaz and I were in the bedchamber after our calling, quietly enjoying the hookah. He had taken us both in quick succession, while we knelt on the carpet. An impressive show of virility and one I facetiously ascribed to the irresistible allure of his new women. I digress, however, from a more serious subject. Ali casually mentioned that the following evening, in a small ceremony, a family tradition of sorts, he would mark us to celebrate our induction into his harem. At sundown tomorrow, we had to go to the eunuchs' quarters where Yasmeen and Mustafa would make us ready.

"Why are we to be branded?" asked Topaz. "I have been a good girl since coming here. I have made no mischief and always do as he tells me. I have no thoughts in my head about running away."

"It is not that, Topaz. Slaves, both good and bad, are always marked; it has been that way for thousands of years. It is done to remind you of who you belong to, your position in the household, and should thieves steal you or should you escape, and are found, you can be returned to your rightful owner and dealt with."

"Perhaps he will put his mark on my ankle. I have seen slave marks there," she said, sounding optimistic.

We reported to Mustafa and Yasmeen at the prescribed hour. Yasmeen told me that she had earlier planned to discuss with Ali where to mark us—breasts, buttocks, and thighs were all places where I had seen girls carry their mark—and convince him to use the place that hurt the least—wherever that may be—but Ali was abrupt and not inclined to discuss anything. "I have decided; Sapphira is to be marked on her pubis and Topaz on her buttock."

Why this was to be we did not know, for Ali's mark resided on the inner thigh of those girls who came into his possession unmarked, girls he himself had branded—Paeonia, Nadya, Briar Rose, and Black Pearl. All others had arrived already marked as slaves in places chosen by their previous master or slaver.

"Ali has granted you two measures of an elixir, an oriental concoction of opium, honey and *kava* that he brought back from Al-Ta'if especially for you," Yasmeen said. "How fortunate you are; when the Grand Vizier branded me he gave me nothing to dull my pain."

After we swallowed our first measure of elixir, we went to the toilets to empty our bladders and bowels, "so that you will not soil yourselves, as often happens at the first touch of hot metal."

I felt dizzy from the effect of the elixir and lay down on my back, watching black dots swim before my eyes, which now and again joined into a wall of darkness. I became lackadaisical and self-assured, and not afraid. After all, my weakened mind reasoned, the other girls had been marked and they made no faltering mention of it, and mine was to be in a special place, one I absurdly fantasized in my hazy mind that Ali had been saving for a girl special to him.

Mustafa loomed towards me, a branding iron in hand. For a brief moment, I thought he intended to brand me there and then, but I realized that the iron was cold; there was no fire.

"The mark will be uneven and unclear if I do not make the iron conform to the curve of your mons," he explained, pulling my skirt up about my waist. He coated the iron with burnt umber, the same umber that Ali had bought from Ahmad in Al-Ta'if—he had planned for this!—and Mustafa lightly touched the cold metal to my pubis. I instinctively pulled away, nonetheless, it still left a dark umber print revealing where it had and had not touched. With finger and thumb, he bent the fine silver wire until, on the third print, the umber left a uniform mark. A drop of palm oil on a finger smeared the umber print into a dark brown spot to show clearly the place where the iron fitted. A short strip of cloth tied around the wooden handle claimed the iron as mine.

Mustafa turned to do the same for Topaz with the second iron, with her lying facedown, while Yasmeen explained.

"The burnt umber will be taken into your skin by the branding iron and it will emphasize and darken the mark—make it prettier. You will be tightly bound during marking, not because of any protest you may show, but because movement will spoil the mark. There is only one chance for a clear imprint." Perhaps as further consolation Yasmeen told us, "The silver tip will not be red hot, as it is when branding for punishment, but sufficient just to mark."

"A small comfort," I thought, nevertheless, I welcomed and appreciated it at that time.

Loose cotton gowns draped over our shoulders kept the chill away as we were led like lambs past a silent huddle of his other girls and women who had been summoned to witness the ceremony. We both needed help and support to walk the short distance to the erga—we were weak at the knees from the numbing effect of the elixir and from fear that had managed to break through the dreamlike shield raised by the kava.

Ali was standing calmly between two narrow wooden tables, their ends pushed closely against the cold stone wall. Gentle light from two oil lamps placed nearby cast a warm glow about the place and illuminated the bas-relief figures on the walls and the carved list of harem rules. Burning charcoal ominously sparked and glowed red in a small wrought iron brazier set to one side.

Our witnesses filed in and formed a line, backs to the wall, while Yasmeen folded heavy kilim rugs into thick pads and laid them over the hard tabletops. We lay down on them with our heads towards the wall. A pillow placed under my head provided some comfort and enabled me to see my outstretched body and the black iron ring mounted in the wall directly above my head. Yasmeen raised my head and gave me a second dose of elixir, much larger than the first one, and then secured my wrists to the ring above my head and parted my gown to my waist. Two leather girth straps buckled tightly around me, one across my hips and the other across my thighs, immobilized and flattened me against the kilim, forcing my pubis upwards into exposed prominence. A cord tied loosely around my ankles completed my restraint.

I watched, entranced, as the magnified ghost-like shadows of Ali, Mustafa, and Yasmeen floated silently over the walls and ceiling as they went about preparing for this barbaric medieval ordeal.

They made Topaz ready in the same way except that she lay facedown on her stomach, her outstretched arms tied tautly to a ring set low in the wall and her gown gathered up about her waist. Highlighted by the soft light that spilled from the lamps, her firm buttocks, unmercifully constrained and bulging from the tight leather saddle straps, gave grim meaning to the phrase "presenting the peach".

Mustafa handed my iron to Ali. I expected him to immerse it and stir it about in the red-hot coals. Instead, he held it just above the glowing bed of charcoal, carefully twirling it for several long minutes. Occasionally he tested its heat on a green palm leaf, closely examining the proof mark it left scorched into the leaf. When satisfied that he had good measure of its heat, he nodded, and Talil, standing somewhere in the shadows, recited the first five rules of the harem. Ali turned to me, hesitated slightly, and then pressed the hot silver to the darkened spot on my raised pubis.

A gush of hissing smoke burst forth as my moist skin quenched the heat from the silver, and my scream of agony from the bite of the hot metal shattered the quiet intensity of the moment. A puff of white smoke drifted slowly upwards towards the rafters. Mustafa grinned with satisfaction.

As quickly as it came the pain retreated, although Ali still held the iron to me to set the mark. Satisfied, he pulled it away and Yasmeen quickly dripped oil over the brand to smother the sting.

The rising puff of smoke hit the rafters, burst apart, and slowly spilled out to the walls as silence reclaimed the room, a silence interrupted only by the frightened sobbing of Topaz. Yasmeen leaned over her to comfort her, as Ali twirled and heated her iron over the glowing embers. Talil again recited the five rules.

I cannot clearly recall Topaz's branding. I saw her muscles tense as her tightly restrained body jerked against her bindings in answer to the touch of the iron. I heard her cry out in the far reaches of my mind, but the elixir was working, it had dulled my senses; I floated in the air and in and out of consciousness, and for the moment that was all I could remember.

Mustafa untied the cords from our wrists and ankles and loosened the leather straps. My hazy mind snapped to attention when he placed a porcelain dish upside down over my brand, its coldness contrasting sharply with the extreme heat felt earlier. It was placed there to prevent chaffing from the blanket that Yasmeen tucked down over me, for I was shivering with cold, although the erga was warm.

Talil dropped a piece of frankincense onto the dying charcoal embers, a wisp of perfumed smoke lazily twisted and swirled about clearing away the smell of burned flesh, and everyone left the erga. In the new silence, I reached out and slipped my hand into Topaz's hand and gently held and squeezed it to comfort her and reassure both of us as our minds faded into deep intoxicated sleep.

At dawn, we awoke to find shiny gold slave bangles tightly clasped around our upper arms—put there when, and by whom, I did not know.

Shortly thereafter Ali came to see us. He casually lifted the porcelain dishes to inspect his handiwork, expressed approval, and ordered the leather straps removed, and for us to be taken to my room. "They should be together while they heal," he directed.

Ali had hurt me, some might even say tortured me, with the hot iron, but I felt no ill will towards him, only a greater sense of belonging. My emotions surprised and overwhelmed my angry sense of being wronged. Tears welled and flowed.

"Don't cry, Sapphira, it is all over now," said Topaz.

For me it was not over, it was not an ending, it was a beginning. A bond had been confirmed that could never be erased, a covenant sealed. I was his, and I wanted it to be that way. I felt assured and settled, neither hating nor loving him more. In truth, I didn't want to give deep thought to what he had done to me, afraid of what I may find. Instead, in moments of shallow thinking, I found excuses, claiming that it was not his fault, that he was bound to follow family tradition no matter how much he loved me and didn't want to hurt me.

I looked closely at my brand. The shallow grooves where the silver had burned and sunk its way into my skin were brown and shiny and the surrounding area red and blistered. An ugly wicked sight, painfully delicate to the touch. After a few days, however, the abused surroundings dried and flaked off, leaving a clear dark imprint, and thankfully the tenderness receded. It took two weeks for the skin to heal and several more for the redness and ugliness to fade away.

Do not be surprised at the practice of branding. It was just one of many violent and painful customs still in common use in these times. Women and girls had their flesh pierced with impunity in the pursuit of beauty, baby boys circumcised in the name of God, eunuchs manufactured and slaves branded on the path to subjugation.

GIRL SOUP

Mustafa's bell summoned us to the bath for our late afternoon bathing, the last one of the day, and we scurried forth and went about our ritual, soaping ourselves down while standing in the side bath, rinsing off before entering the main one outside.

Ali entered the courtyard to the sound of the gong. He had come to walk around the bath and peruse his cache of girls, his "captive beauties" as Paeonia described us, to pick and choose from those on offer. We congregated in his view as he strolled along the edge of the bath eyeing our offerings. All present except for Topaz. Where was she?

Moments later, with a gleeful shout, Topaz came cartwheeling from her room. Ali turned to see what all the commotion was about just as she bumped into him and sent him flying backwards into the water with a giant splash, clothes briefly billowing and flying out before clinging with wetness. It was deliberate. I could tell.

We quickly scrambled out of the bath and silence fell over the gathering as Ali emerged soaking wet. With stoic determination and a matching scowl, he strode straight for Topaz, who stood motionless with a surprised innocent look splashed across her face.

With a firm grip on her arm, he led her to a stone bench, sat down, pulled her over his knees and raised her skirt to her waist, his large hand held threateningly high over her bared bottom. He halted its fast descent in midair, scooped her up, walked to the edge of the bath, and rolled her off his arms and splashed her into the water. Moments later, he joined her, with another huge splash, a wide mischievous smile on his face quickly chasing away thoughts that I may be a witness to a drowning.

Yasmeen was first to jump back in, then each of the others followed her lead one after the other, in no particular order, until the bath turned into frothy boiling water as they splashed at Ali and each other, relieved of concerns.

I stood at the side for a moment before joining them. "Girl soup," I thought, and it warmed my heart.

Life is made of small moments. I would not forget this one.

PIERCED

Topaz wanted her nipples pierced. Yasmeen said no, reasoning that she was too young and her nipples too small. Topaz complained, saying that was the reason she needed it done, so she could wear Hortensia's jewelry.

"Only Hortensia can wear jewelry the way she does. You don't have her shape."

"Far from it," I interjected.

"That doesn't bother me. I want to try it," said a defiant Topaz.

"You are too young, wait awhile," advised Yasmeen, kindly.

I agreed with Yasmeen—for a different reason. I thought to myself that she was already attracting more than her share of attention from Ali. He needed no more inducement.

She appealed to Ali; he succumbed to her wiles and agreed.

Angrily, Yasmeen told Topaz, "It will hurt immensely, and even if you complain after I have pierced one and change your mind, I will still do the other one. Both or nothing will be done."

"That rests well with me. A man once whipped me, and that didn't hurt."

"Then he was not much of a man," was Yasmeen's reply, and having seen the welts and bruises on Topaz's back, I knew her assertion, that it "did not hurt", had no truth to it.

"Girls are difficult at that age," Yasmeen mused, as Topaz went on her way.

I asked Yasmeen if I could watch, telling her that if it was not too painful, I, too, would have it done, but in truth, the real reason for my asking was to find content for my journal, as this procedure was very much a part of harem lore.

Yasmeen and Mustafa pierced Topaz's nipples the next day in the erga, while I watched from the shadows.

After removing her choli, Mustafa had sat her in a high-backed chair, and tied her arms tightly behind the chair back and her ankles loosely to the wooden legs. Several candles were alight and a small spirit lamp burned with a clear blue flame. Laid out on a small table nearby were sharply pointed silver wires, silver rings, and two thin brass disks with a small hole in the center. A wet cloth sat in a bowl of cold water.

Mustafa nodded and started to splash cold water over Topaz's breast while holding the bowl underneath to catch the dribbles. Yasmeen, pressing firmly one of the cold brass disks to Topaz's chilled breast, forced the nipple to protrude through the hole. Mustafa flicked the dark nipple back and forth, making sure that it was free and proud and not caught under the disc. When satisfied, he took a sharply pointed wire, positioned it close to the base of the erect nipple, and pushed it through stopping part way, leaving the wobbling wire poking out from each side.

Topaz did not flinch; she just squeezed her eyes closed and grimaced as a dark droplet of blood slowly beaded and ran down from her delicately skewered flesh. She did squeal out, however, like a wounded animal pricked by arrows when her other breast was attended to, her silent resolve defeated by the shocking pain. More was to come.

Mustafa held the blue flame of the spirit lamp to the protruding end of one of the wires, paused for a moment to allow the red heat to fade away, and swiftly pulled the wire through the pierced nipple. Topaz screamed out and thrashed about, the brass disc now free to fall off, fell away into her lap, and her head sagged to her chest. With the bleeding stanched, Mustafa threaded a silver ring through the newly made piercing. A satisfied smirk filled his face.

He turned to Yasmeen. She nodded.

Topaz never regained full consciousness while her other breast was cauterized in the same way. A fortunate blessing.

It is amazing what young girls, and women too for that matter, put themselves through to please a man.

"There must be something that could be given to Topaz to deaden the pain. Surely, a physician could prescribe something."

"Yes, there is something," replied Yasmeen, grimly, "The elixir you were given when Ali marked you, and there are other medicines too, but not for Topaz this time. She has to learn to listen to her elders first."

This was a side of Yasmeen I had not seen before—these were the words of an angry woman.

At dawn, I visited Topaz in her room. I could tell she was in pain, but she was too proud to admit it. Her nipples were red, swollen and weeping, angry at the abuse they had received. I left to speak with Mustafa and returned with a hookah, some tobacco, and five tiny balls of dark brown resin from the orient. "Place one ball on a bed of tobacco and have Topaz draw the smoke in deeply. Use it each time the pain becomes too much to bear," were Mustafa's instructions.

She drew in the smoke, relaxed, and smiled as lightness spread through her body, while I ran out into the courtyard and retched. I recognized the smell—it was the same pungent stench that had pervaded the air during my dreadful night at the hands of Sohrab.

After the smoke had dissipated, I returned to her room and bathed her breasts with salted water, washed away the dry crusting and carefully turned the rings to keep them free. I returned frequently during the next few days to continue these ministrations.

She was thankful for my caring.

Two months later Topaz proudly sported breast jewelry and, like an excited child with new toys, distracted Ali with them at every opportunity. "I did it for him because he likes them better that way," she told everyone.

That may have been true. Even so, I decided to accept that without piercing a nipple shield or tassel could fly off occasionally during a dance—I thought it rather saucy and bold, not something to avoid necessarily. I would forego this beautification custom. Smoothing and marking were more than enough for me.

BOREDOM

I gathered my courage and talked to him; after all, on our journey back from the races at Ranyah he had told me to speak my mind.

One afternoon he came to my room in an amorous mood and I pleased him, no doubt, for he told me he would call me that evening. When we were alone, I would make an opportunity to speak about what had been occupying my mind for many weeks, something that had been gnawing at me and weighing me down—the long hours of boredom here in the harem.

Hours were too long, days almost endless. We dressed and undressed, mehndied, bathed and ate and waited for him. That was the routine of the day. Without other things to occupy our minds, our thoughts always turned to the Master. No doubt, that was the intention of harem routine and our confinement within these walls, for I found that I thought about him most of the day.

Bathing filled some time but it was too frequent. It was a pointless ritual, more than was necessary. I could carefully bathe, mehndi, and dress myself in less than an hour should the need arise unexpectedly. Besides, if we were called, we always freshened ourselves before going to the bedchamber. We did plan our evenings during the day: what we would do that night, who was anxious for his calling and who would get preference—other than that, however, the days were empty. Without outside interests, conversation was narrow, tired, and repetitive. We were bored and tired of ourselves.

I had taken off my upper garment and was straddling his lap, offering my breasts, when I tried something that I thought might steer the conversation towards my concerns. I have to admit I stooped to a little playacting, to set the stage, so to speak. I acted withdrawn, labored, and silent in my obligations—there is nothing better than the silence of a woman to stir the conscience of a man.

"What is on your mind Sapphira? You are quiet and languish in spirit. Do you not favor my company or your place in my harem? You are a special girl to me, one of my favorites—you know that don't you?"

"Thank you for the compliment, Sire, and it is without question that I appreciate your provision and welcome your company. You provide well. We are well clothed and eat well, and the luxury of the harem courtyard and our rooms is beyond compare. You are a most generous master. But please, Sire, and I know I speak for all of us when I say, there is nothing for us to do during the day when you are away. We bathe, we dress, we mehndi, but this does not keep our minds alive. They are stilled and empty. We know nothing of new ideas, or for that matter, old ones either. How dull and uninteresting we must be to a man of the world such as you."

"So, what do you want?"

"Oh, Sire, our wants are simple. If you could permit us to learn the skills of the kitchen, if you could allow us to leave our own small space, to walk through the other parts of the palace and its gardens, beyond our *fondouq* (courtyard), and do things that other women do. We would be so much happier. It would broaden our minds and give us new things to talk and think about, and take pride in."

"Such as?"

"Well, I know that Hortensia has a talent with plants and flowers and would love to help tend to the gardens. Perhaps Yasmeen and Paeonia could study spices and learn to cook and prepare exotic foods, foods from lands far away—perhaps from their homelands. And maybe Topaz could make the candles. And Sire, I have no books to read."

"Sapphira, your requests are simple enough, but they go against long held convention. Confining slave girls to the inner quarters of a harem is for their own safety and well-being; there are reasons for these long held customs. Besides, I have people to tend the gardens and cook."

"Sire, look upon us this way. We are like beautiful birds in a gilded cage. Open the door, give us flight, and we will soar and see things in new ways, then each evening we will return to the gilded cage happily because it is such a beautiful and safe place to be. We will be refreshed and enthusiastic, and more grateful to our Master for what he provides...." I waxed on poetically, hopeful to catch his attention with my unfamiliar and overly dramatic words.

"I will think about it—now, come bathe me before I bed you," he said, avoiding commitment.

The next afternoon, he came to my room and we rested against each other, his arm about my shoulder, nothing more.

To my delight he had come to talk, to talk of my plight, about the thoughts that had poured out of me so dramatically last evening, for he said, "I don't want to see you saddened and unhappy. I willingly paid an extravagant price for you because I wanted your spirit and enterprise—not to mention your appealing demeanor and beauty. I do not want to crush these qualities and make you as others. Sapphira—you shall have your way. I will open the palace within the outer rampart walls to all of you and permit the teaching and learning of worldly things.

"All of you must cover your limbs and heads when you leave the harem courtyard; it is not good for others to gaze upon your charms. You do not have to wear full burqa, abayas and hijabs shall suffice. Each girl will sew one for herself—Paeonia will help. Do not tell them why. I want it to be a surprise for them."

"I understand, Sire, and I will ensure it is done according to your wishes," I replied, hardly able to contain myself.

"You have my permission to start this deviation in two days—time enough for the girls to finish their sewing. I will inform the guards and Mustafa and Talil." He glanced at me, with a mischievous smile—"They will be somewhat surprised, I imagine.

"I will also find books for you, but as you no doubt know, writing and reading anything other than the teachings of Mohammed is frowned upon in Arabia. It is not as simple as going into Makram or Jeddah to buy some. It will take me some time, but I have an idea where I might find what you asked for. Be patient."

"Oh, thank you Sire. I will make sure you never have cause to regret your decision."

I turned towards him and cooed in his ear. "There is one more thing I ask, Sire, before you leave."

"And what is that?" he asked, with a cautious smile.

"On the way back from Ranyah you commanded me to speak my mind when we are alone."

"Yes, I did, and so far," and again he grinned at me, "so far," he repeated, "I have no regrets."

"Then Master, come here, come to me," I whispered, as I slid down onto my back and raised my arms in an inviting manner, clasping my hands behind his neck, drawing him close.

With my skirt drawn up and my choli open, I guided him into me and placed his hand where I wanted to feel his play. I held him tightly, wrapping my legs around his back as unbridled urges swept through me. I came first as I smothered his face with kisses, and continued to cling to him and move until he collapsed—both our passions spent.

"I will call you tonight," he said, with a smile on his face as he stood up to leave. "In all my years as keeper of many women you are the first to ask for my favors. I have always taken, and never given."

My fervent ardor mystified Ali—he knew little about love.

SURPRISES FOR THE HAREM

Gloom descended over the harem; Talil had announced that the Master had bought a new girl. In the afternoon, at the sound of the gong, we were to gather in the courtyard where she would be unveiled.

Why would the Master take a new girl? Surely, we were enough for him, even too much, "and besides," I thought, "I could use his company a little more often," if he still had unfilled needs. Had we done something wrong—slacked off in our duties, not given him enough pleasure and comfort? No, it couldn't be. Perhaps he had won her in a wager, as he had Topaz, or taken her in payment for a debt. We were all looking for reasons—anything other than that she might be ravishingly beautiful and desirable, and had caught the Master's eye.

At the sound of the gong, we gathered near the fountain, a sullen group.

Mustafa and Talil proudly entered the courtyard carrying a litter between them with a large wooden crate on it partly covered with a silk cloth. They lowered it to the ground and stepped aside. Why was the girl imprisoned in this cramped box, was she so tempestuous?

Ali walked to the front of the litter and with a ceremonious tug, pulled the cloth away and opened one end of the wooden crate.

There was a long pause before she cautiously stepped out, looked from side to side, staring at us with large black eyes, blinking her long lashes against the bright sunlight. She was beautiful, lithe of limb—a juvenile, no doubt. We rushed to greet her and gathered around her, proclaiming her beauty, and cautiously extending our hands to stroke her soft hair.

Ali had bought us a present, a pet to care for—a cheetah.

He asked me to give her a name. Sasha it would be.

The Master called Sasha and I to the bedchamber that night, where Ali fed her tidbits, stroked her soft fur, and found her more interesting than me. Sasha slept on the bed, played with the pearls sewn on the coverlet, and pounced on our feet whenever we moved.

And this was not all. In the next few weeks, Ali gave us two more gifts to relieve our boredom and give us new things to do.

One morning we ventured out of our rooms to find that overnight a bicycle had mysteriously appeared in the courtyard.

We spent many days bruising and scraping our knees and elbows as we learnt to ride the infernal thing, but it gave us great joy. Topaz, of course, took to it right away. Wobbly at first, but even so, her balance and steering was better by far than everyone else's. She was able to ride at great speed, weaving back and forth between the flowerbeds and pools, even letting go of the handles and raising her hands above her head. Showing off…again!

After dusk last evening, we were all sitting outside in the courtyard enjoying the cool evening, our only light the twilight glow from the dying sun. Something tugged at Sasha's senses. Her ears pricked forward, her intent eyes piercing the gloom. Ali followed Sasha's gaze and saw her, high on the ramparts, silhouetted against the darkening sky—Topaz riding the bicycle and waving to us as she sped by, far above our heads.

Ali hurried to the empty guardhouse and blew hard on the garrison whistle that hung on a string near the door. Two guards ran into the courtyard. Ali pointed to the cycling figure and ordered them to bring her to him; he would wait in the great hall for them.

We were all highly amused, and tried to conceal our mirth from Ali, as it was obviously a serious situation to him. Moments later the lone cyclist came around again, this time pursued by a running guard who had no hope of catching up to her, however, the second guard came from the other direction, caught her arm and brought her to an abrupt stop. With one hand firmly about her arm and the other about the bicycle she was brusquely led away to the waiting Ali.

Although Ali had never given cause for us to think as we did, dark images from distant pasts went through many minds. Would he take her to the erga? Girls who had lived under cruel masters talked of severe punishment for silly mischievous things like this. But surely not Ali? Then again, Ali had ordered castration for Sohrab the merchant, a punishment I had thought excessive for his crime. Nevertheless, my mind cleared of these grave thoughts and I thought that maybe, at worst, he would spank her as he had threatened to do after she had toppled him into the bath a few weeks ago. There were limits to a man's patience, and a good spanking would hurt her ego more than anything else, and at the same time allow Ali's mastery to be asserted. Or would Ali rescind his permission for us to climb up to the ramparts? This would be a great disappointment to all of us, for we loved to walk around up there and watch the sun settle into the sea, or gaze over the town and wonder what kind of lives were being lived behind the walls and doors of the tiny houses lining the streets of Makram. It was part of our new freedom, one I valued, one I did not want to lose.

She came cartwheeling through the gateway and stopped abruptly before us, a large smile on her face, as if a schoolgirl just let out from class detention.

"What did he say? Will he punish you?"

"No. Ali just told me it was a silly thing to do, particularly in the dark. One spill and I could easily fall over the edge, he said, possibly to my death and he didn't want that to happen. And he told me I could not ride the bicycle again, until he gives his permission."

Ali came back into the courtyard, with an equally large smile on his face. Gentle applause and a few kisses on his cheek spoke our thanks.

"How, in the name of God, did you get that bicycle up those narrow, winding stairs? Even my guards had trouble getting it down."

Topaz looked down and said nothing.

"I helped her," offered Yasmeen, after suitable silence.

"Yasmeen! I do not believe it. What possessed you?"

"I don't know. I just wanted to do something mischievous."

"Well," he said, shrugging his shoulders in mystified defeat, "regardless of what got into you, you conspired, so I am obliged to give you the same punishment. Both of you are banned from riding the bicycle until further notice, and you will be my bedchamber companions tonight. I have more to say. Now go and make yourselves ready and think about what you have done.

"Yasmeen has found the young girl within that was stolen from her long ago," mused Ali, as they walked away giggling between themselves. "She never had the chance to tire of childhood."

No doubt, a male guest was expected. Mustafa told us to dress modestly, abayas with covered arms and legs, and assemble in the courtyard. Another surprise was waiting for us.

A domed box, with stylishly scribed words written on it in gold leaf, sat on a polished wooden table with black iron legs. What could it be? Paeonia and I struggled with it, and eventually, between my reading and her English we deciphered the label. "Singer—Made in America". But what was inside?

Paeonia told us that singer means "songster", a person who sang songs. Maybe it was some sort of birdcage for a singing bird. Gingerly we lifted the cover and peeked at what it concealed—a shiny black machine with polished silver parts and decorative gold lettering, scrolls and stylized birds. We waited for Ali—we had no idea what it was.

Ali joined us, bringing with him his "pleased with himself smile" and a small foreign man with a flushed face of pallid looking skin. Yasmeen was sent to find pieces of cotton cloth and thread.

We were amazed and flabbergasted. It was a machine to sew cloth, and how quickly the needle moved. The little man struggled with Arabic trying to explain how it worked, without much success, since most of the girls had never seen a machine of any description. Suddenly, in exasperation, he uttered words in English, and Paeonia leapt forward. A steady stream of English bubbled between them. The barrier of language was broken; we would learn the secrets of the new machine.

Ali was outdoing himself and we were thoroughly delighted.

Paeonia became an accomplished seamstress and mastered the "Singer" better than any of us. We asked her to sew the more difficult items, those with a complicated cut or fit and those made from delicate materials. Other members of the household also made use of her skills to repair and alter their clothes. She was always willing to help. There was often a pile of clothes quietly left just outside the courtyard for her to repair.

Ali was in a loving and happy mood. He had called Nadya, Paeonia and I together, and this often meant he wanted something special from us. To this end, I thought that each of us had been chosen for our different specialties—our perceived *forte*. No doubt, pleasuring would be my role while he fondled and toyed with Paeonia's generous breasts, before he took Nadya. He had at times an insatiable appetite for these pleasures.

This thought of mine turned out to be mistaken; he had another reason for our calling—an amazingly good thing to tell us.

Slowly and carefully, he undressed us one by one, and as I stood naked, I continued to speculate about what he had in mind for us, although he often just undressed his girls and gazed upon them; he loved the female form with its smoothness, curves, and flowing hair. He had often told me this.

He led us to the bath and sat down on the submerged shelf with Paeonia and Nadya on each side of him and me kneeling between his feet. He drew them closer and then reached forward to place my hand to his submerged member and Paeonia turned to offer him the feel of her breasts. Nadya, seeing

Paeonia's overwhelmingly bountiful offerings, wisely chose to gently massage his neck and shoulders while I stroked him slowly, resolving to only pause his speech, not bring forth his issue. Nadya would relieve him of that in bed later.

He told us how pleased he was these days with the ambience of his harem. "The girls seem…happier now with their new freedoms, there is more laughter and gaiety and all are more carefree. I have the most contented and cheerful harem in all of Arabia! Even my once reluctant Nadya," he continued, turning her face to his and moving it gently from side to side, "seems happy to be with me and gives herself most willingly. I have to thank you all, particularly you, Sapphira, for it was your idea and your assurance that it would turn out this way. Now…I want to continue with your ideas and try…more deviations from the traditional ways."

My hand was having affect. His speech was pausing now and then, and Paeonia's breasts increasingly took his earnest attention.

"Next week a traveling bazaar is coming to Makram…and a large market will be set up. Actors, acrobats, trained animals, men who eat fire, and vendors from afar will be there. Even moving pictures. It will last for three days, and there will be much to see. I will be going there every day and will take all my girls…with me. Mind you, only four at a time, that way no one will know the extent of my harem. Some things are best…best kept secret. Paeonia, you…will sew burqas…on the Singer for the occasion…."

In the excitement of the moment, I did not notice that the pauses had grown longer and had closed out all words.

I spilled him under the water. His seed erupted upwards and floated away. His announcement had distracted me from my earlier resolve, much to Paeonia and Nadya's consternation. He was unconcerned, however, leaning back against the bath, holding his words while he recovered his composure.

"Draw lots for who will accompany me each day. Do not include yourselves though. On the first day, Nadya will lead the group, on the second day Paeonia, and on the third day, Sapphira. You three are the worldliest and can assist me. A cobbler will come to fit everyone with leather sandals. The sands and pathways underfoot are too hot for the tender feet of coddled slave girls."

We dried ourselves and piled into bed.

It would be correct to wonder at this point if Yasmeen had fallen out of favor. After all, she was highest in rank and skilled in the bedchamber ways Ali loved, but she was not worldly. As a young girl, she lived a simple life with her family in an isolated coastal fishing village in what was now the Philippines. Since her capture and enslavement, she had never been outside the walls of a harem except to be taken from one owner to the next—first to the slave market in Al-Aqaba, then to the harem of the Grand Vizier of Baghdad, then to Buraydah and finally Makram. Many of the other girls had also never been outside of the walls of a harem, and for all of them this simple day-out would be a huge, exciting adventure.

I rode the bicycle to the gate to see the first group off; it was early morning before the heat of the day had set in. Five figures threading their way to Makram with two guards falling in line twenty paces behind. Four twittering black crows following a white thobe.

The first fledglings had flown the nest.

Faithful to his word, Ali delivered to me a large musty trunk. A treasure chest, because, to my absolute delight, I found that it contained books, magazines and old newspapers from France.

I became Scheherazade, reading aloud from the books and magazines to Ali and his girls whenever they wished me to do so.

I found it difficult to translate smoothly from French—which was after all my second language—into Arabic, and I took to preparing my translations during my afternoon rest by reading the chapters ahead of time, translating them in my mind, and making notes in the margins. This worked well, and I became an accomplished and oft-demanded storyteller—so much so that I wearied of the task, but Ali and his girls had an insatiable appetite for stories about people and events in other parts of the world and insisted I continue. Ali was always asking questions, about the great city of Tunis, about France and Europe, and other cities, lands, and peoples.

In deference to the girls' limited learning, I simplified many of the stories, and even read, much to their enjoyment, passages from children's books. Twice I read *La Vie et les Avantures Surprenantes de Robinson Crusoe*, *Les Trois Mousquetaires*, and *Le Tour du Monde en 80 Jours*. Ali was enthralled and particularly enjoyed Jules Verne's journey around the world. The fact that the journey was a wager between friends appealed immensely to him, and he was intrigued with the newfangled machines of the author's invention. He must find me a copy of *20,000 Leagues Under the Sea* to read—he would enjoy that tale.

My readings made me feel important and I enjoyed making this unique contribution to an evening's entertainment. No one else could do it.

The books were wonderful, yet it was the magazines and newspapers used to wrap them and line the musty chest that inadvertently provided even greater entertainment for the girls. There were a great many pictures showing the clothes the women of France were wearing, and these fascinated the girls to no end.

The brassiere was the subject of great ridicule. "Give yourself a boyish look,[1]" intoned the advertisements, and the girls were incredulous that women would want to flatten their chests to look like boys. "After all," they said, "if a French master favored a boy he could buy one," not fully grasping that slavery was not part of the French culture. Of course, here in the harem we drew cloth tightly under our bosoms, to push and coax them into being something more than they were, not flatten and diminish them.

Corsets and underwear incurred their share of ridicule. "Why would you bind yourself in such a way; how could you possibly dance wearing those clothes? Surely men found them unattractive," claimed Yasmeen, "and by the time a master had untied all the strings he would be limp!" This notion tickled our fancy so much that we all rolled in laughter. "Perhaps they come with a *jambiya* so they can be cut off quickly," was one practical suggestion from Capucine.

Our most vehement and raucous laughter, however, was saved for the ridiculous bathing costumes French women wore. Why would a girl get undressed and then dressed to bathe, concealing her charms from a master's view, and keeping the sweep of the water away from her body? They were ugly items, black and made of thick wool—and the pictures showed women descending from the back of strange horse-drawn carts standing in the shallow sea. What were they for? Even to me, it was a peculiar world, this faraway France.

But it gave me an idea. I made a sketch for Ali of what I wanted. Wooden posts supporting a canopy of palm fronds to cast shade, erected close to the waters edge. We would need towels, food and water packed in baskets. When I had first journeyed here, I had seen the ideal place—a small isolated cove opening onto the Red Sea. Ali was to send guards to sweep the area of possible voyeurs ahead of time, to set up the palm canopy and carry the baskets down the rocky slopes. We were to have a picnic, a day at the beach—and we would not be wearing woolen bathing suits!

I invited Ali for the day, but he said he could only "come by and stay for a short while." His visit was long enough for him to take refreshment and swim in the sea with us. We shouted and shrieked, threw sand and seaweed at each

---

1. At this time, the brassiere was a bandeau used to flatten the bust for the "flapper" look, but later its purpose evolved to enhancement and control.

other, and enticed him to chase us through the water. I dried him off and wanted more.

From the cove, we saw ships of many kinds: some huge ones leaving trails of black smoke over their wake, many small dhows, feluccas, and a full-sailed schooner heading north to the canal. What were they carrying in their holds? Exotic woods and teas from India, dates from Persia? Had some first ridden the monsoon winds up the coast of Africa from Zanzibar, with cargoes of cloves and slaves in their holds? I daydreamed that one day I would sail north and visit my family in Tunisia, although these thoughts always saddened me, knowing that this could never happen now that I belonged to Ali.

That evening in his bedchamber, Ali chuckled, and said that we were a remarkable sight to behold when he walked down the trail to the beach that afternoon. "Fourteen girls lying in a circle, heads together, laughing, gossiping, and happy. It made me feel happy too. A good master."

"Now, keep me in good humor—pleasure me, Sapphira. You must do it often," he commanded.

Pleasure him or go on picnics? I did not ask.

HORTENSIA

Her story is so compelling I feel I should tell it in full, though I have mentioned it earlier, somewhere in these pages. Hortensia was one of three girls chosen by Ali to enter his harem after the death of his father. In a way, we all owe her a debt of gratitude although at the time she did not know it nor was it her intention to incur our debt.

Hortensia had come to Ali's father as an infant daughter of one of his slave women. All she knew of her past was that she and her mother were Galla people and came from the farthest corner of Ethiopia. She had only her mother; she never knew her father or any other family members.

She, Ali, and Ali's younger brother were playmates. They had the common interests of children at play, and Ali perhaps replaced her father in her platonic affections, as she was by far the youngest of them all. Whatever the reasons, they became attached to each other—even inseparable at times—and the fact that he was the Master's son and she the daughter of a slave woman was of no consequence. Protocol does not cloud or color young innocent minds.

I wrote about Hortensia's cruel initiation into Sheik Shareef's harem in her own words, as nothing I could write about this ceremony would carry the same force of truth as these words of hers:

"The chief eunuch came for me in the morning. I remember his black oiled skin and his white teeth and grinning eyes. He told me I was no longer a servant girl, that the Master had chosen me to serve him from a higher rank, and that this was a favor given to me, for which I should feel honored and thankful.

"In the morning he supervised the other eunuchs as they plucked me bare and in late afternoon they washed me and wrote important rules of the harem on my back with henna.

"After dusk I was brought before the entire harem of slave girls and eunuchs in a dimly lit room still smoky and smelly from the hookahs of an earlier celebration. A wooden frame I had never seen before stood in the middle of the room. The eunuch took off my clothes and stood me facing the frame while my Master tied my ankles apart to a low rung and then bent me forward over the frame and tied my outstretched arms to a far-side rail. The chief eunuch read out the rules he had written on my back, and after each rule was read my Master asked 'Do you understand the rule', to which I replied 'Yes, Master', even if I didn't, because there were things I did not understand, but the eunuch told me to always say 'Yes, Master'. Even though I said yes, the eunuch brought down the whip each time.

"Ali and his younger brother Hussein were there by order of their father and made to stand forward from the others in front of me. I raised my head and looked at Ali throughout my ordeal, as he was the only one in the room other than my mother that I knew had compassion for me. He closed his eyes each time the whip came down across my back. After my whipping, my Master came behind me and took my virginity with thoughtless vigor. I called out for his mercy, but he gave me none.

"The first time he called me to his bed he made my mother stand by and watch as he took me—I don't know why he did this, it made my mother cry. Afterwards, he thanked my mother for bearing such an excellent gift, and next day took her to the slave market and sold her.

"I have never forgotten what he did to me and my mother, and even now after years have passed I have terrible dreams about it."

"I could not talk to Ali after that, for it was forbidden for a harem girl to talk to or even cast eyes upon another man without the Master's permission and I dared not seek it for fear he would think I had yearnings for Ali and have me whipped again."

Hortensia's suffering benefited us because the experience of seeing his childhood friend so cruelly treated and hurt for no reason left Ali with an aversion to such cruelties.

Hortensia understandably had a deep aversion to all men except Ali and his brother, as they were the only men in her life she could trust since all others had treated her depravedly and cruelly. It was no surprise that she was overjoyed when Ali's father died, and more so when his first son chose her to come with him and be one of his slaves. I think it was not so much out of love for Ali that she was overjoyed, but for the protection and companionship of a man she knew would treat her kindly—although she always appeared to be enthusiastically sensual when before him, and even had her nipples and other parts pierced to better entice and please him.

She repays Ali with her willingly given favors, and was thankful that he often sought her and appreciated the special effort she put into the gift of herself. And Ali learned a great lesson from Hortensia. A girl—a woman—could be more than a bed-slave and a bearer of sons; she could also bring to his life deep lasting friendship and companionship, and be cherished for these endearing qualities.

In those times, a woman, even a free woman, needed the protection and provision of a man, and a man needed the company of a woman. Unspoken but understood exchanges and favors were willing made between them.

Hortensia often sat at times alone and silent, sometimes rocking slightly, other times still, her dark grieving eyes staring ahead—a stare that betrayed her immense suffering. She did smile, but her eyes always told her story.

FIRST CHILD

Paeonia was the first of Ali's girls to be with child, and we all breathed a sigh of relief when Ali, following my unneeded urgings, readily agreed not to have her pronged, much to Mustafa's annoyance.

The changes her body was going through fascinated Ali, and he took her to his bedchamber throughout her pregnancy, "for my going over" she would say. She told us that Ali, aware of her tender breasts and swelling belly, made gentle love to her.

She had been with Ali that night and I was helping her with her morning bathing—one of us always helped her; the baths were slippery, and we never let her stand alone once she was in the water. She was being silly, assuming strange poses, wallowing about in the water. At first, she walked around on her hands and knees with her swelled breasts and belly drooping down, and then she lay on her side with the shallow water rippling around her tight tummy, her arms and legs thrashing about. "Stranded, stuck in the mud," she said, and then she turned onto her back with her legs drawn up, "Dead, washed up on the shore."

"What are you doing?" I asked.

"If I look like one, I may as well behave like one."

"One what?"

"A Nile River Cow (hippopotamus)," she laughed.

I started to wash her hair and asked her what pleased her so much this morning for she had such a radiance and smile about her.

"Ali says I can nurse my baby."

"Of course you will, what else did you expect?"

"Well yesterday Mustafa told me he will hire a wet-nurse because my breasts belong to the Master and must be kept for him. 'It's better for the breasts,' he said, which must be a man's point of view."

"Not an ordinary man. Those are the words of an unfortunate man who has never been and never will be a father," I countered.

"Anyway, I couldn't find words to say, so I cried instead—that always works—and told Ali what Mustafa had said, and he told me, 'That is nonsense. What is he thinking? Babies do not eat them, that I know. There will be no wet-nurse unless your milk does not come in.'"

"Your milk will come in; they are as big as two melons. Look at the size of them." We laughed.

"Sapphira, I am so excited," bubbled Paeonia. "Ali wants a boy, but I don't mind which it is, all I want is a healthy baby."

She gave birth to Constance. I attended the birthing for part of the time, and at the start of her labors I was pleased with myself about being barren—at the end, with my feelings torn, I dissolved into tears, envious and hurt.

One afternoon Paeonia handed Constance to me, a fussing, hungry and wet baby, to hold while she went for dry cloths.

I turned my back to the others, cradled her in my arms, and put her to my breast, holding her there to try to experience what God had denied me, to feel what it would be like to be a mother. She quieted for a moment then pushed me out with her tiny pink tongue and lips, disgusted with my dryness, and resumed her vocal protestations with renewed vigor.

Envy could not override my love for Paeonia and Constance, my love was too deep and sincere for that, but their dear presence always pushed my mind to despair.

After the aborted nursing incident, I retired to my room, lay on my bed and wept. Why had Allah made me barren? I was a sinner, but no worse a sinner than many others he had blessed.

And Ali always had me pessaried, snuffing out any chance of conceiving, however small or improbable that might be—dashing the faint hope that I still clung to—that it was possible for new life to begin within me. Sometimes, after being with Ali, I even took out the pessary and lay on my back, legs raised, propping my hips up on my hands, hoping that his seed would run down and seep into my womb. I grasped at small hopes.

It was a despairing situation, one that my mind was unable to accept or forget, for no matter how hard I tried to dismiss the emotion, it still haunted me most days—and with each passing month nature reminded me of my inadequacy.

In my room, after covering my hair with a hijab, I knelt down facing the qibla[1].

"Glory to You, O Allah, and Yours is the praise.

And blessed is Your Name, and exalted is Your Majesty.

And there is no deity to be worshipped but You.

Speak in your ways to Ali.

Counsel him not to impede my passage to motherhood.

And grant me, your faithful servant a child; that the child may worship you and the curse of Satan be vanquished.

Ali and his faithful slave Sapphira will rejoice in your name and benevolence.

I seek refuge in Allah from Satan, the accursed."

Kneeling at the side of the bed, I crossed myself and put my hands together in prayer.

"Hail Mary full of grace, the Lord is with thee; and blessed are thou among women.

And blessed is the fruit of thy womb Jesus.

Holy Mary Mother of God, pray for us sinners, now and at the hour of our death.

You know our union has not been blessed with a child and how much my Master and I desire this gift.

Please present my fervent pleas to the Creator of life from whom all parenthood proceeds and beseech Him to bless us with a child whom we may raise as His child and heir of heaven.

Amen."

Surprised? Do not be. My mother taught me that we were all children of the same God, and there were many good paths to the same God.

---

1. Direction of Mecca.

RELEASE

Yasmeen had noticed too, and we were worried and unsure of the cause. Ali had taken to quiet moments—not brooding, but taking time for thoughts—deep thoughts. He was cheerful with us after these moments, more than usual perhaps, so what was he thinking, what was he planning? He spent much time with the cleric, occasionally leafing through the Qur'an, but mostly in hushed conversation. I watched him, unseen from behind the screens of my room and tried to eavesdrop, without success.

I asked of him in a casual manner, "What are you thinking about, Master? What is on your mind? You are subdued at times."

"Nothing much," he said, but I knew better. Something was troubling him, and in turn, it troubled us.

Mustafa summoned all of us to the great hall at sundown; everyone was to attend without exception. There was to be an announcement.

Even though Mustafa had said all were to attend, I was surprised when I arrived at the hall to find not only the girls and Mustafa and Talil, but also the two black harem servants and a woman from the kitchen—who was openly shaking.

Two sharp handclaps from Ali, and the room collapsed into silence.

"Ever since inheriting the leadership of our family," he began, "I have met with many problems and made many decisions affecting our household. Some of these have been easy, some dangerous and difficult, but none, I believe, as important to you as the one I will make this evening. Please gather around.

"I have traveled widely and seen much of our country beyond our own gates, and I have heard of modern thoughts that are changing the world beyond the borders of our country. Many of these changes are for the better. Arabians must not let them pass by; we must embrace them. Tonight, I am bringing one of these modern ideas to our household."

What was coming? More than a few troubled glances passed between us.

"I am sure you are all aware that since the death of my dear brother I have sought explanation and enlightenment from the writings of Mohammed and his followers. I believe now that I am living my life in a manner not pleasing to Allah—one that is not in harmony with his wishes for mankind, or the teaching of the great Mohammed. Some old customs and traditions have tainted our ways, in a manner that does not find firm foundation in the enlightened teachings of the Great Prophet and his followers, and are unjust.

"Against your will, all of you have had your precious freewill and freedom stolen from you, and although some of the less enlightened say the teachings of the Qur'an allow a man to do this, I find the practice of slavery is not confirmed by deep inquiry, nor is it in keeping with these modern times or thoughts. I now believe that slavery is a sin against God and an offence against mankind. Therefore, it is upon me with extreme pleasure to make an important and joyful announcement. From this time forward you will not be my slaves."

What did he mean? Was he intending to sell us, or dispose of us in some way? Panic gripped me, heads turned and anxious faces spoke of separation, an auction, new masters. A grim silence descended.

Aware of our misunderstanding, Ali hastily continued. "Therefore, in the name of Allah…I give back to all of you your freedom. You are no longer slaves. I release you. You are free citizens of Arabia."

It was hard to believe so much sound could come from so few. It did not suddenly burst forth however—the event was too overwhelming for that—it grew slowly from the gentle sounds of disbelief, laughing and hugging.

He clapped his hands again; silence reclaimed the room once more.

"You may travel back to where you came from, or go to wherever you want—you are free to choose the company and course of your life. You may also stay here, if that is your wish.

"As a token of my appreciation," Ali continued, "for the years you have served me you will all be given a dowry and escorted to the place of your choice should you decide to leave. I will treat you as thought you are my brothers and sisters, and my children. I will not cast you out. You are free to stay here with me for as long as it pleases you; there is no urgency to these things."

The commotion resumed. Some rushed to Ali to press claim to him, kneeling and prostrating themselves before him, kissing his hands and feet, others stood hesitant in their freedom.

Ali luxuriated in the adoration, knowing he had done a great deed. Refreshment and celebration commenced to the high-pitched chatter and laughter of women, punctuated by the occasional silence of disbelief.

Surprised by his unexpected gesture, I was lost for meaningful words and the time to ponder clever phrases or prepare reasoned thanks. I did of course thank him, profusely and sincerely, because I was truly thankful. Still, in my mind I wondered briefly what difference this new freedom would make to my life. Whether his slave or not, I loved him. My affection did not need freedom to keep it alive.

Of course, in the days following, we talked about nothing other than our futures, and it does not need saying that I decided to stay. I desired no other company, and I was safe from those who sought to punish me for leaving my husband. For Yasmeen, too, it was an easy decision. All she knew of her childhood home was that it was a fishing village on an island—and there were thousands of islands in the Visayas (Philippines). It would be an impossible task to find the one from which pirates had snatched her, and besides, she was in love with him, so she would not leave. Paeonia also decided to stay. She had no desire to search for her mother, the only family member she knew, besides that, Ali was the father of her child, and Paeonia wanted her to have the special nurturing that only a loving father can give. She was happy.

For others, decisions would take more consideration and require more time, and as Ali had so graciously told us all, "There is no urgency to these things."

"More symbolic than necessary," I thought, but a new assuredness descended on the harem when stonemasons came. They sealed the entrance to the erga with stone blocks and imprisoned within its walls all of its unkind brutal contents, including the whip from the bedpost—gone, never used. Talil and Mustafa handed over their whips for entombment, together with Mustafa's "inventions". They chiseled away the rude bas-reliefs around the bath and covered them over with colorful tessellated tiles.

Gradually the girls tested new waters. Dipping timidly at first, they spoke their minds, saying things that they had never dared or thought to say, simple things such as "no", or "not now", and exercised their newfound freedom. "Today, I want to go down to Makram; Talil is going to teach me about money. Master, would you arrange for a guard to come with us?" The word master, so ingrained into their lives, took longer to fade away.

Ali had untied the bindings of slavery and released the seeds of freedom. They sprouted and blossomed within and around us.

AL-KHOUTBA—the Engagement

I looked forward to evenings when both Yasmeen and I were asked to his bedchamber. We were no longer "called". We shared good conversation and it was a time for me to dive into the deeper waters of the mind of the man I loved—he was still an enigma for me to solve.

Today Ali returned from a ten-day trip to places unknown to us, and I excitedly looked forward to eager lovemaking. As Paeonia would say with usual double meaning, "Abstinence makes him thick and plentiful."

Several small votive candles floated on large flat leaves in the reflecting pool carved into the floor of the bedchamber. Yasmeen had made them earlier that day. It looked so romantic, and that special sweet smoke of the hookah had gone to my head. I was ready for love.

I had undone the front buttons of my choli and encouraged it to fall open, as I had done so many times before. To my surprise, Ali leaned over and redid them without explanation. What he had found beguiling before was apparently distracting now. He looked extremely serious and thoughtful.

"During this latest journey I have had time to think further about my future and I want to make changes in the direction my life will take, the road I shall travel down.

"I have come to know well," Ali continued, "two women who have both attracted my eye and captured my mind." He was talking to no one in particular, just staring ahead, as though looking through things. "I believe they would make good wives and I have decided to marry, however, I cannot choose one over the other. I am hesitant to ask only one, for they are both equals in my mind. What is your advice?" he asked, as though reading from a well-rehearsed script.

My mind leapt. During his absences from here, he had been with other women, and this was the reason he had given us our freedom. These future wives objected to him having slave girls in service; that was the reason he let us go free, not out of any kindness or consideration for us. I was crushed and hugely disappointed. The gratitude I had felt towards him gave way to anger at his deceit. I wanted to hurt both him and those other women who had stolen from me my lover and shattered my dreams of the future.

I glanced over at Yasmeen. She looked tiny, abandoned and fragile. More broken than whole. Tears glistened her almond eyes.

Uncertain that I could find pleasant words to say amidst my surging anger, I waited for Yasmeen to reply.

A quiet moment passed, then halting words.

"One sees truly with the heart. Let it take you to where you want to go," she murmured, followed by a deeply drawn quavering sigh. "Let your heart and Allah guide you—will I still be able to live here?"

"You will always have a place here; nevertheless, I want it to be more than that for you. I want you to make it your home."

He took a deep breath, clearly heard in the strained silence. "Yasmeen, will you marry me, will you be my wife? Will you make this place your home and live with me as my wife?"

Her eyes widened in amazement, but she could not break the silence brought about by utter disbelief and the time needed to clear her mind of earlier despairing thoughts.

"Yasmeen, will you marry me?" Ali repeated.

"Oh yes, yes! Are you sure? Tell me that it's true." Disjointed words bubbled forth as she leapt back to life, throwing her slender arms around him. "I have wanted this for so long. I love you Ali; I want to marry you. I want to be your wife."

"Yes Yasmeen, I have thought about this for a long time too, it is right for both of us," replied Ali.

He turned towards me—I was expectant, hoping beyond reason, shaken out of my melancholy, my anger quelled.

"Sapphira, will you be my second wife and make this your home too?"

I managed a weak "Yes," and quickly realized that my bewildered reply sounded ungrateful and tepid. I clasped Ali's head between my hands and pecked kisses on his lips, and between each kiss, I said "Yes!" A clear and affirming "Yes," to seal his offer with enthusiasm before anything could change. Then I turned to Yasmeen and flung my arms around her, and we hugged and shared our joy.

"Does your husband-to-be get a hug and a kiss? You are not marrying each other!" interrupted Ali, in a laughing, inquiring voice.

We broke our embrace and lunged at Ali, toppling him over. We smothered him with kisses, stifling his words and barely allowing him to breathe. He struggled to sit up, wives-to-be entangled about him, clinging to him, weighing him down and hindering his efforts.

"Thank you for accepting, I know these unions will be blessed by Allah. It is right for us all, we will be happy and prosper and make a family."

The word "family" rested heavily with me. Nevertheless, I would not let my inadequacy spoil the moment. I refused to dwell on this thought for a moment longer.

"I propose our wedding for when the moon is again full. We have four weeks to prepare. Do you agree?

"Now, not a word to anyone until I announce our marriages tomorrow evening. All will be summoned to the great hall."

From within a large chest near the bed, Ali brought forth two beautifully carved boxes and two smaller leather cases. In each of the larger boxes nestled a splendid bridal headdress glistening with pearls from the East coast of Arabia. After our marriages, they would become family heirlooms, handed down from father to son.

From the leather cases, came marriage necklaces that he had bought in Riyadh in anticipation of our acceptance of his proposal. The necklaces were our *mahrs*—the customary gift from the groom to his bride-to-be—to keep. Both were intricately made of silver and set with lustrous pearls, mine finished with a blue sapphire from Ceylon, Yasmeen's with a red ruby from India.

We laughed, bubbled, and planned. We talked about the things we would do—and shared our past unspoken dreams, bringing them to life, into reality, and into our future.

"Now Sapphira," said Yasmeen, boldly and excitedly, "let us take our husband-to-be to bed."

And so, with a wife-to-be on each side of him, we took hold of his hands and led him to bed.

I did not stay. Quietly, I slipped out of bed, draped Ali's caftan about my shoulders and left the bedchamber, choosing to sit outside in the moonlight to reflect on this startling turn in my life, and I wanted Yasmeen to be first to be alone with our husband-to-be. She had earned and deserved this moment.

A moon in full splendor floated silently against the stars, pouring silvery light over the courtyard. Fountains sparkled in the moonlight, bushes and trees shimmered as though brushed with silver, and flowers blushed through in tempered color. A lone guard passed by on his rounds, walking atop the outer palace wall, his eyes cast outward over the town, oblivious to the solitary figure sitting in the inner courtyard, dazed with happiness, thinking about the unthinkable—marriage when the moon was again full. I thought, too, of my mother and my father and brothers. I thought of Jacqueline, and wished I could somehow share my joy with all of them.

And how would we share Ali? A man with many wives was common; how did the women manage? In my former marriage, there was another wife, but at that time, I had no call on, or great urging for, my husband's affection. However, this marriage would be different—we both loved the same man and he us. And there were the other girls and Hussein's women. Would they choose to stay, and if they did, would Ali take them to his bed or spurn their advances? I did know that the laws of Islam allowed for four wives, on the condition that the husband treat them with "scrupulous fairness", and that a wife could not be refused by her husband, but what about his concubines? Could they be refused? Does the law make provision for them, too? It was most confusing; my mind was struggling and finding no answers.

In the early hours of the morning, I returned to the bed and slipped in beside a sleeping Ali. Yasmeen's hand found mine, and squeezed and held it, and we spoke to each other in the silent language of understanding. We slept with our arms across Ali, as though protecting him and keeping him for ourselves. But sleep and dreams did not come easily to me. Tears came to my eyes and I sniffled as quietly as I could. I was thinking, "Ali does not know I am barren and inadequate as a woman, and wasteful of his attention." I feared time would reveal my damage and I would disappoint him.

When I awoke in the morning, Yasmeen was gone, and so had my gloomy thoughts of inadequacy. She was giving me my time with our husband. I pillowed my head on his tummy, carefully sought his morning hardness, and woke him in that special way. He stirred, gathered me in his arms, and satisfied me in his gentle caring way.

Lying side by side, basking in the afterglow of lovemaking, I brushed my fingers over his chest and caressed him in contentment, while his fingers twirled my hair. Ali quietly interrupted my thoughts. "May I greet the day now? I have a late start and have much to do."

"Of course you may, my little chou-chou."

"What does chou-chou mean?" he inquired, accustomed as he was by now to the occasional French word from me.

"It means my little cabbage," I replied, quickly adding before there could be misunderstanding, "It is a French term of great endearment." He nodded, pursing his lips and raising his brows as he continued towards the bath.

As he left the bedchamber, he remarked, with a smile on his face, "If last night was any measure, I doubt I can sustain my wives' demands without being ravaged to exhaustion."

Yasmeen joined me in bed and we lay there basking in our newfound happiness. We talked about our futures, our pasts and our ambitions.

"Ali was nervous last night. I have never ever seen him like that. He is always so sure of himself. Why is it with men that they cannot ask for a woman's hand in marriage without dissolving into nervous wrecks? We should have refused him or told him we would think about his proposal and give him our answer later, we were too eager, too easy on him." We laughed at the absurdity of this idea; we would never have done it.

"I am curious about one thing. Did you reach out for him again later in the night?"

"Yes, I did," replied Yasmeen, slightly defensively. "First wives can do that without asking anyone."

"That is true, and it explains his comment to me about being ravaged to exhaustion by his wives," I said, laughing and breaking the tension.

"When I am his wife I will not have to lie over the big Damascus bolster," offered Yasmeen.

"And I won't have to do those things Mustafa taught me," I enjoined, subtly reminding her that I also was worthy of high regard in matters of the harem bedchamber.

"It would be unfair to change," Yasmeen said, after time for reflection. "He loves us for how we were, for how he has grown to know us. Those are some of the things he must have found endearing. It would be deceitful to change now, and besides they are easy to give. Even in marriage, I will still be his bed-slave in bed if that pleases him."

I concurred. It would be unfair and deceitful to deny him these things in marriage. I would give him no cause for regret.

Once again, Mustafa told everyone to gather in the great hall at sundown, everyone was to be there, and as before, there would be no exceptions.

I shimmered in my silk harem pants and choli, the jade-green ones I had brought with me from Jeddah. Ali asked me to wear the same clothes for our wedding, together with the marriage necklace he had given me. Both it and the traditional beaded bridal headdress matched so well with my dress. I asked Paeonia to alter it for the occasion, make it more modest, although she had little material to work with. Perhaps a matching kameez to go over it would make it more fitting for the occasion. Paeonia would know what to do.

Yasmeen looked virginal. She wore a niqaab. I had not often seen her wearing a veil. Her kohled almond-shaped eyes peeked over it, making her look so seductive and innocent—for such a wise discerner of men.

With the entire household assembled in the great hall, Ali beckoned us to sit, one on each side of him.

He clapped his hands for silence.

"Today I have another joyful announcement to make.

"I have found two beautiful and charming women, and to my surprise and delight they have agreed to marry me.

"Please come forward and congratulate my wives-to-be, Yasmeen and Sapphira. We are to marry at the time of the full moon."

Such a slight speech to announce such an important occasion. But that was Ali. He was often faltering and short for words in emotional situations. To me this hesitation in him was a lovable sign of sincerity.

The other girls colluded and exercised their new prerogative as free women. They agreed that none would go to bed with Ali for a week before the wedding, and after the wedding only with the first wife's permission, as was the custom in a household of many wives and concubines.

HAFL AL ZIFAF—the Wedding Ceremony

None of the girls have family here. There are no mothers in the Kasre el Nouzha—except Paeonia, and she knew nothing about weddings. Who did, other than me?

A traditional Islamic wedding lasts many days although the rituals and ceremonies vary from town to town and from country to country. Here, I tell of one—mine to Jamaal.

On the first day, my family and I visited Jamaal's family who had traveled to Tunis for the wedding. On the second day, he and his family visited mine. On both occasions, my brothers carried candles, which they lit just before entering the house. After dinner, they sang songs that teased both of us.

On the evening of the third day, all the women congregated in my home—men were excluded—and I was placed on a small square table where they anointed me with fragrant oils, a holy cleansing provided by Jamaal's family. Revelry went into the night with singing and celebration, and the women danced for me. These "baladi" dances were not ones of show and allurement,—although men would see them that way if they had been present. These were dances to celebrate the belly as the cradle of life and fertility—they are the origin of the modern belly dance. Stories were told. Some about fumbling grooms—not too complimentary to absent husbands—others bawdy and not too holy—and a little frightening to the ears of a fragile virgin.

After this celebration, a married friend accompanied me everywhere and at all times. I could not wear jewelry or look upon the face of a man—the next man I saw must be my husband.

On the morning of the fourth day, the wedding day, the married women showered me with a dribbling of milk before I bathed and went to dress for my wedding. Meanwhile, Jamaal, dressed in the manner of a sultan in a turban with a *sehra* (short floral fringe) tied around his forehead, led a procession to my house where the ceremony was performed and he claimed his bride.

At the commencement of the wedding the bride and groom are in different rooms and cannot see each other. Guests, although separated by gender, are able to see each other.

The Wali Al-Amr called for the bride's representative—my father—and he came forward for the ceremony, bringing me with him. As required, I walked gazing down. He answered for me when the cleric questioned me. Jamaal represented himself, and joined the Wali Al-Amr and the officiator.

The Wali Al-Amr asks the bride if it is her wish to marry the man, and if this were her first marriage, her silence would indicate her acceptance. If she does not want to marry him, she must say "no". If the woman has been married before, the Wali Al-Amr remains silent and she must answer for herself, either yes or no.

By my silence I accepted the proposal and the agreed upon gift. The cleric then pronounced us man and wife, and Jamaal parted my veil.

Celebrations commenced, and men and women mingled and feasted. This part is the Walimah. In Berber ceremonies, the bride and groom would retire to consummate the marriage and only when they returned to the gathering and showed the bloodied bed cottons as evidence of virginity would the Walimah commence and the "bride price" be paid. My mother would have none of that!

The third day after the wedding was devoted to the "party of the third day of marriage"—Al Thaleth—and the fifth day for the bride and groom to dine at the house of the parents of the bride.

This was the ceremony of the wedding I had known.

Our circumstances called for changes to the traditional formalities. Just two days of celebration and ceremony were called for, as we had no families to visit.

The mother of the cleric offered to help organize the ceremony and make arrangements, and two widows and their daughters from the town, who had often catered our special occasions, were hired to help with the feast.

At dawn on the first day, Ali escorted us up to the east ramparts where carpenters had built a wooden platform against the outer parapet wall so that we could easily see over it.

Below us spread the encampment where guests had pitched their tents, and far away to the east, lined along the brow of a steep hill, I caught a glimpse of a long line of people on horseback—dark shapes set against the new morning sky.

A white flag hoisted by the captain of the guard signaled the start of a rumbling sound, like thunder rolling in over distant hills, which gradually built in intensity. A huge cloud of dust billowed against the azure sky as riders thundered and charged towards us with their colorful flags and pennants flapping and snapping in the wind they created.

I saw flashes of flame and puffs of smoke before my ears heard shots and the cries and hollering of men over the pounding of hooves. My eyes widened. War cries. We were under attack! I grasped Ali's arm tightly and the other girls cast worried glances in our direction. Ali smiled, assuringly. "They are firing old muzzle-loaders, ceremonial guns, as a sign of their loyalty and their promise to always protect you from harm."

The riders stopped abruptly, split into two formations, and then turned to face each other. With ferocity, blazing pistols, and fierce cries, they charged at each other only to emerge intact from the fray on opposite sides. Exchanging the guns for swords, they dipped the tips into flaming oil, turned and charged at each other again, back into the swirling brown dust and white smoke thrown up by their earlier clash, this time with flaming swords held high.

Quietly, two circles of horses formed, turning at greater and greater speed, black head plumes fluttered and danced in the swirl of sand and stones kicked up by thrashing hooves, while riders hung from the flanks of their steeds, their arms and heads brushing dangerously close to head smashing rocks and grazing sand. In the center of the circle, two small boys stood high on the backs of their prancing horses, balancing with nothing to hold onto except the air around them.

The circles uncurled into a long line, facing us. Riders reared their horses in careful sequence, sending a ripple of rising heads and beating forelegs from one end of the line to the other and back again, saluting us with their horsemanship.

We applauded our guests loudly and long.

Women and colorfully dressed children emerged from the tents and formed lines of family behind each rider. A long procession began, led by the men on horseback, their Arabian steeds now adorned with caparisons of richly woven and embroidered cloth. Men proudly held standards and flags, young boys beat drums, and girls and women shook and banged on tambourines. Narrow haunched Saluki dogs barked wildly as they deftly ran under the caparisoned horses, weaving back and forth, miraculously avoiding the horse's flaying hooves. They walked around the palace three times and each time they came around, the women and girls gathered into a chorus, pausing before us in their walk to sing verses from a traditional song sung before weddings—"A Song for the Bride". Again, we applauded their honoring of us while a flock of disturbed birds circled on high, screeching their noisy protest against our noisy presence.

Later that day, while we sat behind a muslin screen, the chiefs of the tribes presented us with their hunting kill, a brace of desert hare and two long-horned gazelles. Ali had earlier advised us to accept their gifts, but only after protesting, many times, that their generosity was too great and the gift too lavish, and then with equal insistence to give it back, with the provision that their bountiful gift be shared by all. Later they returned with platters of roasted gazelle meat and a large bowl of broth, from which stared the floating white eyes of the gazelles. Ali ate one with great relish. "A delicious Arabian delicacy," he proclaimed. We kindly declined his generous offer of a bite to taste.

That evening the women gathered in the great hall—they had evicted Ali to the encampment outside the gates to spend the night with the men and children—while we had our own celebration. There was baladi dancing and music and both lewd and loving stories told. We had our "layat al henna"—our hands and feet painted with henna in the traditional bridal patterns. To acknowledge my heritage I also had a circle of small motifs put on my breasts around the nipples—rectangular Berber style motifs that I had seen brides in Tunisia wear in silver about their necks.

Later into the night, when our tiredness had overcome our excitement, the cleric's mother escorted Yasmeen and me to her room, and the three of us slept there that night.

Next afternoon in the great hall, we were married.

For the splendor of the celebration, I wore my bright jade-green costume, with the sides of the trousers sewn closed, and a matching kameez over it that Paeonia had made. Yasmeen wore a creamy white abaya embroidered with gold thread. Secretly from his brides, Paeonia had sewed Ali a thobe and matching turban for this special occasion, in royal blue, stiff and heavy with gold and silver embroidery. She had it embroidered in Makram so we would not see its manufacture.

In a side room out of view, the cleric's mother pampered, dressed, and mehndied us, while the guests found their places in the great hall, men on one side, women and children on the other.

"Cast your eyes down. Your Wali Al-Amr is here for you," announced our chaperone, after she had opened the door to a knock. Of course, I could not look at him, but I knew who he was—the captain of the guard. Ali had told us.

We followed slowly in his footsteps until he told us to stop, while he stepped forward to join with the groom, a male witness, two female witnesses, Paeonia and Hortensia, and the cleric.

The cleric recited marriage verses from the Holy Qur'an before asking, "Yasmeen, do you accept Ali bin Shareef al-Saalih and the quantum of mahr?"

After a short pause to give her chance to say no, our Wali Al-Amr answered for her, "Yes."

"Ali bin Shareef al-Saalih do you accept this women, and the contract?"

"Yes," replied Ali.

The cleric then spoke to me. "Sapphira, do you accept Ali bin Shareef al-Saalih and the quantum of mahr?" and, having been married before, I answered for myself, "Yes."

"Ali bin Shareef al-Saalih do you accept this woman and the contract?"

"Yes," replied Ali.

"Bear you all witness that the mahrs and Ali have been accepted."

"Please raise your eyes."

"O Allah, create love and harmony between these three. Bless them and bestow upon them good children."

The women congratulated us, and the men congratulated Ali, as was the custom. And in a not strictly Islamic way, the men, women and children mingled and chatted while platters and pitchers were brought in for the elaborate feast that followed.

Many male eyes gazed upon the other girls of Ali's harem. So many, that the girls were overwhelmed and made shy by the huge male presence. Men gathered around them, nodding and whispering approving comments to their friends, while the younger, bolder ones took courage and spoke to the girls. It reminded me of a swarm of fuzzy black bumblebees buzzing around a colorful sprig of sweet-smelling honeysuckle.

WEDDING NIGHT

It was late into the evening before Yasmeen and I excused ourselves from Ali and the company. Brides have things to do at this time. He had seen and touched us before in every way and every light possible, but we wanted this night to be different, something to stand out in our memories, for all three of us. In secret, we had decided to forego the traditional wedding nightgown in favor of designs we had seen in the French magazines. They were different, and unlike their bathing clothes, delightfully becoming.

Paeonia made Yasmeen a Western style nightgown, copying the style from one of the magazines, drawn tight under the breasts—"Empire Line" they called it—with a ribbon at the front tied in a bow, all from diaphanous gossamer silk. There were no buttons—it had to come off over her head.

Paeonia sewed a peignoir buttoned down the front for me. I asked her to make it from the same red cotton cloth that Mustafa had draped about me when he first showed me to Ali in the great hall. Red was not my best color, blue or green looked better on me, but I felt the symbolic meaning of the cloth more than outweighed consideration of appearance. I hoped Ali would recognize my choice and admire my decision. Moreover, Yasmeen told me that in the country of her ancestors red was the color for brides and good luck.

We bathed, put mehndi on each other, perfumed ourselves, kissed and held each other in a long embrace of gratefulness, and retired to our new apartments.

Ceremonial drums broke the silence of the desert night with a rising double beat, a giant throbbing heartbeat that filled the palace from wall to wall with its sound. For one long minute the drums throbbed before the night again reigned in silence. My heart pounded on. The groom was coming to claim his brides.

I heard Ali enter the passage leading to our apartments. His gold tipped slippers clicking on the floor announced him. A hand-held oil lamp splashed light and long shadows down the walls, blackening them again as he went into Yasmeen's apartment, and lighting them as he emerged with his "prize". I peeked around the corner of the doorway and caught a glimpse of his gold embroidered caftan as they disappeared into the bedchamber. I was unreasonably envious, but she was his first wife and she had privileges. My turn would come.

In the morning, I would celebrate my love for him.

Yasmeen awakened me with a gentle touch—she was standing by the side of my bed with her nightgown draped over her arm, looking serene. She held a finger to her lips, "Ali is sleeping," she whispered.

It was still dark, but the sky was about to open to dawn. I brushed my hair to a gloss and gummed a jewel low on my forehead between my brows. I put on a little mehndi, just a hint, and slipped on my red peignoir and my marriage necklace. Yasmeen tied the strings of my niqaab veil behind my head and I tiptoed into the bedchamber.

I decided to stand to the east, away from the bed, so that the bright morning light spilling through the windows behind me would outline my figure through the light cotton peignoir. I could have had it made from sheer gossamer, but I wanted to look ethereal and enchanting, not alluring or seductive. I wanted Ali to come to me, Mariyah, with a free and clear mind, not enticed or lured by a flimsy dress or enticing pose. It was a small point, to which I attached great importance for reasons I did not know, therefore cannot tell.

I wished that I could give him my virginity at this time, but reality intervened. Nevertheless, I wanted him to take me gently and with thoughtful consideration, as though deflowering an innocent virgin at the start of her voyage into wedlock.

He opened his eyes slowly, bleary from sleep, and hesitated slightly before he swung his legs from the bed, put on the blue caftan from the night before, and walked towards me. Lifting my veil, he kissed my lips and whispered. "You are beautiful; a morning mirage of loveliness before my eyes. It is as if you floated here through the narrow windows, a houri descended from heaven to be with me. A cherished beginning to my new life, for I know it is my destiny to be with you, and love and care for you, for the rest of my years."

Stepping behind me, he leaned me against his chest, gently exploring and caressing my body with his hands; the coarse cotton weave between us causing arousing friction. He lifted my breasts, nuzzled my neck, and smelled my hair.

I had visions and thoughts of my father behind my mother in the kitchen in Tunis. Surely, this was how she had felt—wanted and loved. My nipples, alert and proud, craved his touch; my hands gently sought him behind my back.

My veil fluttered to the floor as he cradled me in his arms and carried me to bed, laid me down, unbuttoned my peignoir and spread it open. My marriage necklace lay on my chest—witness to my new standing. "I am your wife", it clearly proclaimed.

I laid my arms back on the pillow beside my head, my mind saying, "Show me the ways of the marriage bed, husband, for I am innocent of these things."

With his heart pressed close to mine, he melded me to him and made me his wife. We shared the joy of the moment and the promise of many more beautiful hours together.

I was Sapphira Mariyah Saalih.[1]

---

1. Muslim wives keep their maiden names. Sapphira obviously adopted the French custom of taking her husband's last name.

MATCH MAKING

Two of the young guards, brothers they were, had spoken to Ali about Hussein's women, inquiring if they were available for marriage. It had not gone unnoticed by us that these women spent much time walking near the guard barracks, their presence acknowledged by many. And Hortensia had asked Ali to tell the gardener's assistant that she was interested in him and was free of obligations.

Ali sent for Yasmeen and me and sat us down asking, "How is all this to be done?"

Women in his life had rarely been asked about their preferences, or given choice. Now he sensed something different was called for, but he was unsure of what to do. "Did one simply arrange their marriage, and have done with it?" he asked. "Or is a modern approach called for?"

"A marriage based on love is the strongest and best, where both the man and woman want each other," I said, "and for this to happen they must meet and get to know each other first."

"How do we do this? How are we to know? Perhaps it is easier to arrange it all for them."

"It may be easier, Ali, but not the best thing for your women."

"Then what are your suggestions?"

"Could you renew the girls' acquaintance with some of the young men who were at our wedding celebration?—there were attractions. Invite the men back under some pretense. For instance, you could open the palace gardens to the citizens after prayers on Holy Days and the girls could be guides. Or perhaps stage sports that will attract young men, such as horse races, or a target-shooting contest."

"Give us some time, Ali; we will think of many other ways," I said.

Now here was a challenge to test our ingenuity and to show Ali that our "other ways" were more than romantic daydreaming.

RETURN TO RANYAH

Ali often tries to surprise me and keep me in suspense, and today was no exception. He asked me to teach Nadya and the sisters, Zahra and Noszahra, to ride horses. He told me, rather proudly, that it was his, not the girls' idea, and that I had two months to accomplish the task. "They will be making a desert journey," he said.

The three of them were equally puzzled, but Ali insisted and I was happy to do his bidding—and it would allow me to spend more time at the stables.

A desert journey does not call for great riding skill; it is not a race or hunt, but more a test of endurance, and they learned quickly all that they needed to know. I soon reported to Ali that they were reasonably accomplished riders.

"Are they good enough for two days in the saddle?" he inquired.

I gave him a qualified, "Yes," as an answer, well aware and cautioning that long rides required long training, "They will be sore and aching after such a journey, but no doubt they could do it," I said.

"Good, then next month we are all riding to Ranyah for the meeting of the sheiks."

His reason for taking four of us, apart from the fact that it would be a pleasant occasion, eluded me and he offered no explanation.

The day before we left Ali arranged a special occasion for all with fine food and drinks. It was a celebration for Nadya and the sisters. Why the special occasion? Just because they had learned to ride, or because we were going to Ranyah? And why were all the girls crying and hugging each other? No one would tell me. They knew something I did not.

On our second day in Ranyah Ali asked me to organize an evening dinner for two important guests. He would not tell me who, although he did hint that I knew them.

Ali told us to dress in our finest costumes; he wanted to have an authentic Arabian ambience that evening. "Cholis and harem trousers will be in order," he said, adding, "with cotton underclothes."

Helped by the other three girls I went about making preparations. I discussed the menu with the cook, straightened carpets and curtains, arranged the seating, lounging cushions, low tables, and lamps. It was to be a sheik's tent in the desert. "A luxurious, exotic, and stunningly romantic setting," I thought, being quite pleased with myself.

I heard Ali coming towards the tent, talking loudly to the guests as I stood on one side of the entrance. As they came in, I bowed my head slightly to cast my eyes downward until introduced.

"I believe you have met my wife Sapphira on a previous occasion," Ali said, as a man stepped forward and kissed me lightly once on each cheek—the traditional European greeting and as such accepted by all without offense. I raised my head and was thrilled to see the man I could truly describe as the second love in my life, the rakish Englishman, Barry. He stood there looking as though only a day had passed since I had waved goodbye to him after our last encounter.

"I remember her well, although she had fewer clothes on then," chuckled Barry. He hadn't changed.

"You will also do well to remember that she is now married to me, and if you get too close, or even look at her in that way of yours, you will end up like the qanass merchant—a little lighter."

"Be reasonable Ali, any man with blood flowing through his veins cannot help looking at any of your girls. They are all beautiful—you always had impeccable taste."

"Thank you, but just remember they are no longer slave girls, and they are not available for the asking." He looked pleased with himself. I was pleased with him too.

"I understand, Ali. I will look, but I won't touch," he replied, with his characteristic easy smile.

Barry introduced his companion. "And this is Anne. I have often spoken of her, with complimentary words of course," he said.

Ali called Nadya and the sisters from the corner of the tent, where they had been watching us while busying themselves making tea, and introduced them. "A beautiful threesome you must agree," he concluded.

We had a delightful dinner. The three girls served us and then joined us for sweetmeats. The hookah was in great demand by all, and the Englishman and his companion brought wine with them and drank copiously. Many a flirting sideways glance and a veiled smile told me that he well remembered the other occasion when we drank wine together, and offered me many sips of it when Ali was distracted.

Nadya paid unusually thorough care to the needs of the Englishman, engaging him in conversation, making sure he lacked for neither food nor wine. I noticed that the top buttons of her choli had mysteriously come undone. The loosened corners tucked in against her breasts left little of her beckoning cleavage to the imagination, and made light of the cotton under garment Ali had insisted on. She ignored my gesturing telling her that her top was open and revealing.

"You owe me a favor, Barry," Ali said, to the surprised Englishman.

"How is that, what have I done to incur this debt?"

"Well, for all these years you have overcharged me for your arms and supplies and now I need redress," Ali said, assuming an exaggerated expression.

"Ali!" protested the Englishman in great surprise, "it is a time of high demand with the wars in Europe and North Africa. Prices have gone up, but you have always paid less than the going rate, I can assure you of that," he replied, defensively. "Is that not true, Anne?" he asked, directing the question to his lady friend, who we had met the previous year, and who had unknowingly lent me her dress.

"Yes, indeed it is true," she replied. "Absolutely. Your prices have always been most fair."

"Well I still want a favor from you," Ali said, hardly able to contain the grin that was breaking over his face.

"And what will that be, Ali?"

"That you take these three girls back with you when you return to Europe. Not for your own use, but to escort them to their homelands. Two are from Spain, and Nadya, the fair one, is from Sweden."

Silence fell over the gathering. With intently pleading eyes, the three girls looked at him, anxiously awaiting his reply. It was Barry's turn to hold us in suspense.

His generous smile broke the tension. "Of course I will do it. For old times sake, and for the girls' sake. However, I warn you now, my expenses will be high—I will have to recover the money I lost selling you guns at low prices."

"Do not worry, I will provide compensation in full," replied Ali. "Mind you, their company alone is worth a great deal. Hmm, maybe I should deduct something from your invoice to balance things out," he said, as he looked around with a broad grin on his face.

"You know, I have business dealings in Sweden with the Nobel Company, and I even speak a little Swedish," said Barry.

Turning to Nadya, he said. "*Hejsan, god morgon, talar ni Engelska?*"—Hello, good morning, do you speak English?

"No, no," insisted Nadya, wearing a smile from ear to ear. "It is *god afton*—good evening—now."

How clever he was, my Ali, to have thought up this whole scheme. The girls had been party to this plan from the start, which explained the celebration before departure and the large amount of baggage they had brought with them—the only unknown in the plan was whether the Englishman would be here and if he would agree to escort the girls.

Before the guests left our company, money changed hands and details discussed and settled.

"The Englishman was such a humorous and interesting man; I liked him," confided Nadya, as we recalled the events of the evening after the guests had departed.

"Yes, I noticed." I replied with a smile, as I reached forward to close the buttons of her choli.

"Is Anne his wife?" she inquired, seeming relieved when I told her she was only his business partner.

I shall never forget this evening. What a surprise. I was so proud of Ali. It was my turn to hug and kiss the girls goodbye, although they stayed with us until departure day.

I returned to Makram with mixed emotions. Thankful to Ali and jubilantly happy for the three girls who were going home, but all the same, I would miss them, and whenever I looked back at the string of riderless horses tethered behind, I was reminded of this.

RANYAH AGAIN

This is a short anecdote on my visit to Ranyah, the following year. This visit turned out to be just as exciting as previous ones.

Ali and I were out strolling along a sandy path, enjoying the early morning coolness when I saw three figures coming towards us. I knew immediately who they were, this man in Western dress with a woman on each arm. It had to be Barry, Anne, and the tall woman—Nadya!

"Nadya," I shouted, as I ran ahead of Ali to greet her.

"What are you doing here?" I asked.

"Same as you. Keeping an eye on my husband."

"Nadya, you married him!"

"Yes, I never got as far as Sverige (Sweden). We fell in love and are now married and living in London and Eastleigh."

Barry proudly explained what had happened the year before as we all gathered around.

"I took Zahra and Noszahra to a convent in Seville and the nuns there promised to return them to their coastal village and families. I have a note from the nuns acknowledging this and giving receipt for the donation I made to their cause.

"Nadya and I continued on to London, but Nadya worked her charms on me and I fell in love with her and asked her to marry me. I had a hard time convincing her; she is a plucky and choosy woman, but I prevailed and she accepted. We are now man and wife, and very happy, I must say. Please meet Mrs. Nadya Ingeborg Armstrong. I apologize for the mixture of Arabic, Swedish and English, but it is a name that truly reflects her provenance."

Nadya and I had a chance to talk to each other as we walked along arm-in-arm.

You have grown tall, Nadya; married life is treating you well."

"I haven't grown, it's the latest London fashion," she said, raising her skirt high to show a shapely leg and a pair of shoes with the highest heels I had ever seen.

"Here, try them on," she offered.

"They are lovely, but how can you walk in them?"

"You get used to them. They become comfortable—after awhile."

"Do you like them?"

"Oh yes," I said, enthusiastically.

"Then they are yours if you can fit into them."

"But…."

"Don't worry, I have others, and besides, I want something from you in exchange, if possible."

We dropped back behind the others and she whispered in my ear. "Do you have nipple jewelry with you, some dangles or shields?"

"Yes I do, luck is with you, and you're welcome to have them—I have two pair—the choice is yours. You may have both if you wish."

"Wonderful, I want to give Barry a little surprise one of these nights. I have shopped all over London, and they have never heard of them. The English women are so proper and prudish, I am surprised they ever conceive children," she said, shaking out her fair hair.

"When I left Makram, Ali said I could take an item of jewelry with me as a memento of my service. I chose my gold slave bangle. In London, I had a clasp fitted to replace the rivet so I can take it off. I wear it for Barry on occasion, and breast jewelry will add to the fantasy."

"Having your bangle clasped is a marvelous idea. I must have the goldsmith do mine in Makram when I return," I said.

"You know, Barry did not tell you the whole truth. It was me who had a hard time convincing him to marry, but Ali taught me well about those things men enjoy. I put them to good use and he succumbed. He is just a man after all, and too long a bachelor," she said, with a loving smile.

"And you will be pleased to know he is straighter now," she grinned.

"So he told you about our little tryst? That is not a gentlemanly thing to do—discuss with other women details of his private moments!"

"But he did, and you gave him much more than he needed or expected, you wanton woman—shame on you. Now he wants the same things and more from me."

"Serves you right," I said, laughing, as we walked to my tent to sort through jewelry.

That evening I paraded around the tent in my new shoes, staying on the carpet to keep the heels from sinking into the ground, swinging my legs this way and that, secretly admiring my newfound slenderness.

Ali was pleased. "They make your legs look long and elegant and raise you to just the right height. You don't need a stool."

I knew from the look on his face what he was imagining—taking me in the forbidden way while I stood high in my shoes. At this moment, however, I was too interested in my shoes to encourage him further, and gazed down entranced at my newly acquired treasures as I rocked my feet from side to side and back and forth, watching light from the candles dancing on the polished leather.

The cobbler in Makram told me the bad news—"Made from 'Bakelite'; they cannot be repaired."

I should have known better than to wear them in the courtyard on my way to the bedchamber, in the dark. I felt the soft earth give way beneath me as I lurched forward, but it was too late—the heel was firmly wedged in a crack in the flagstones. It snapped in half, my shoe was ruined, and my knee grazed and bleeding. The other girls were not pleased with me; we had all enjoyed sharing these Western fashions. They were different from our slippers, and so fetching.

UMM ISMA'IL

When I first became a woman my menses were never regular—often late or early, sometimes missed altogether—until I came here. It seemed that then my body somehow gradually caught the rhythm of the cycle from the other women. Now I was rarely late or early—and even then, by only a day or two. Why do I tell you this? Because I am excited—I am three weeks late!

Nature had played with me before, harshly tormenting me by teasing me and raising hope, only to cruelly wash it away in a crimson flood. However, this time I was confident I had caught. Why else would I be so late?

My excitement mounted with each passing day. I gazed down at my middle looking for any slight change, and checked the witness cloth between my legs—every hour it seemed. There was no showing. Nevertheless, before confiding to Yasmeen, I would wait for two full moons to pass. I avoided Ali, he might dislodge a precious life precariously held within me—I did not want him stirring me about down there. He was concerned and puzzled, and asked often about my health.

I confided my hopes and feelings to Yasmeen and Paeonia. They were certain. I felt unwell most mornings now, and even experienced yearnings for odd foods at odd times of the day or night. Inside of me, I wanted to wait for more confirming signs of coming motherhood, but I could not contain myself. I had to share my good news with my husband.

"Chou-chou, I am with child." To me these were the most wonderful and precious words I had ever spoken. They were the answer to my prayers and longings, and they healed my wounds. I was to become a fulfilled woman, joining the community of motherhood, and making us family.

Seven more moons to pass.

Things I clearly remember: Belly tight as a drum, breasts like melons. Senna pod tea, aching back, slippers too tight, silky hair and glowing cheeks.

Slight twinges in the small of my back growing quickly into engulfing spasms. Paeonia excitedly calling for Yasmeen. A mid-wife sent for. Mustafa standing watch at the doorway, bearing witness to the legitimacy of the child shortly to be presented.

Nature tightened her hands around me, pressed, squeezed and tore at me; my aching body pushed and heaved. Three fingers, four fingers; I breathed and pushed, pushed and breathed. I cursed Ali and all men for causing this pain within women. I vowed I would never go to his bed again.

I heard its cry, felt its wet warmth against my chest, smelled the odor of blood. Conception and birthing were messy chapters in the book of life that every woman should know. But my heart truly sang, new life was miraculous, and I could see all the way down to my toes!

Intensely weary, I fell into a blissful sleep.

Ali, kissing my forehead, hastened my awakening—a white bundle in his arms. "You have given me a son and heir, Sapphira."

I unwrapped the swaddling cloth. He was complete, undiminished, a tiny perfect being. His sweet-smelling fuzzy head pressed against my nose; a tiny hand grasped my finger. I held him to my breast—he was eager to sustain life.

God had healed me; I would name him Isma'il[1].

Cradled in my arms he fell asleep and I said a quiet prayer over him, asking God to protect him from those things that take children and to grant him the age of a vulture[2] and let him outlive me.

I felt one with god; I was Sapphira Mariyah *umm* Isma'il.

---

1. Isma'il—"God hears".
2. North Africans revere the vulture for its longevity.

TEARS—*a poem for Isma'il*

Men came and took you away, three days into your life.

I knew this had to be done.

Tradition—how I cursed tradition.

I joined you in your tears; comforted you with my breast.

Your tiny member, bandaged white.

حريم بنت

PART TWO
CLOSING THE CIRCLE

Time is too slow for those who wait
too swift for those who fear,
too long for those who grieve,
too short for those who rejoice,
but for those who love, time is eternity.

Henry Van Dyke

DERELICTION

I have been derelict in my duties as your journalist, for many years have passed since I last wrote in my journal. I have excuses—none of them persuasive. It is true that I have been busy, but in truth, I lost interest. Life and many happenings filled both my days and my mind to the brim, bringing me great happiness and contentment—I have come to a pleasant place in my life—but along the way, sorrow, deep sorrow, and terrible grief and despair found all of us.

It was quite a few years ago when Satan's Black Angel swooped over us, her evil wings trailing darkness and despair throughout the palace, and I believe by writing about it first I will, in some small way, show respect for Yasmeen.

Paeonia sounded the concern, and the doctor agreed with her. It would be a difficult birth; the baby was growing too large for Yasmeen's small body to yield up easily. At Paeonia's urging, Ali hired a doctor and his nurse for the event that was inexorably looming towards us, having them stay on hand in Makram, unknown to Yasmeen, who was blissfully ignorant of our concerns.

Yasmeen excitedly welcomed the first contractions and the breaking of her water, laughing and joking as we prepared the birthing bed that afternoon. At dusk, I quietly sent a rider to fetch the doctor and nurse.

Paeonia confidently assured all that everything was in order, proceeding, as it should, until shortly after midnight when confidence and changes ceased, except for Yasmeen's contractions, which grew stronger and more frequent.

All morning Yasmeen contracted and writhed while brutal agony sapped her strength and eventually, even her will to live. Her joyful optimism collapsed, crushed under the pain of the baby lodged in her unyielding pelvis, and I saw the shape of death patiently waiting in dark shadows and corners, ready to claim her and her unborn as his own.

Early that afternoon the doctor informed Ali that he had done all he could. The only remaining hope would be to cut into her womb and try to take the child alive from her. "One or both may live by this means," he said, "but if I do nothing both will die."

After brief prayers, Ali gave permission.

Yasmeen knew. I do not know how, but she knew, she just sensed it. She pleaded with me not to let them kill her baby if it were a girl, and made me promise to take care of her as if she were a boy and one of my own. Her mind had floated back to her youthful years in Persia, where it was customary to sacrifice a slave girl in difficult labor and take out the baby. If the child was a girl, they would sew her back into the womb, and both would be buried together—a small consolation. They saved baby boys. Such was the culture in those backward countries east of Arabia. I assured her that in Arabia all babies were cared for, and besides, she was Ali's first wife, not a slave. All and everything would be looked after, her included.

Amid tears, I renewed my promise to her.

Pretending to console her, I leaned over her to shield her eyes from the threatening instruments the doctor was unwrapping from enfolding cloth. They looked cruel and horrible to me but I knew he would wield them kindly and with good purpose. We were all told to wash our hands and arms with carbolic soap and rinse in chlorine water, then don tight cotton veils over our faces and mouths. The doctor told us that modern science had discovered that the poisons that caused childbed fever[1] were in our breath and on our hands.

And bless the new sciences, for the doctor produced a breathing cup to administer ether to Yasmeen. A sweet strange smell invaded the air when the doctor held the cup over her nose and mouth, her eyes closed and her frail body stilled and flopped to one side as though death had taken her.

When I saw this, I was sure the doctor had surreptitiously poisoned her—put her down like an injured animal on orders from Ali. I flung myself at Ali in my rage, with a ferocity that only a deceived woman could muster, pounding his chest with my fists, and flailing at his face with my hands. He picked me up bodily and removed me from the room, and calmed me while explaining the purpose of the ether.

---

1. Septicemia. Invariably fatal—a death sentence. Before the introduction of hand washing 30% of women whose uteruses were invaded during post-birth examination died from childbed fever.

Shame haunts me to this day that I could ever have thought such things of him.

Doctor and nurse went about their work confidently and quickly. Time was of the essence, and once I had been reassured and calmed by Ali, I returned to the room to help. I held a large mirror to reflect sunlight onto Yasmeen—the doctor forbade candles and flame while there was ether in the air—so that he could better see what had to be done. Ali left the room, pale and shaken.

Her body released the baby; it gushed into the world, slippery with *vernix* and blood. "A girl," announced the nurse, handing the baby to Paeonia, who hurried away to administer her new nursing skills. Smiles and glances flashed between us all when Paeonia summoned a cry of life from her charge, a welcomed cry of protest over its rough and bruising beginning. The doctor transformed to a tailor and quickly sewed to stem the loss of Yasmeen's lifeblood, and she slowly and hazily stirred back to life, weakened and pale, but released from the grip of death by the good doctor and his nurse.

We took turns sitting vigil, holding her baby girl and keeping her dry, quiet, and content, laying her by Yasmeen's side until she would be strong enough to do these simple things, and savor motherhood.

Ali, this man who in my eyes stands tallest amongst men, was remorseful and utterly humbled by this womanly event—one beyond his control and intervention, yet caused by his pursuit of pleasure. Guilt weighed heavily on him. Yasmeen freed him from his burden by telling him, at every chance she had, that it was what she had always wanted and that she was truly thankful and happy. It was a woman's birthright to bear children, she told him, and his duty as her husband to fulfill that right, and she would be angry with him forever if he had denied it to her, even in death.

Her recovery from the brutal invasion of her womb started quickly and was remarkably fast. She was able to sit and nurse and fuss over Yasmeenah as any new mother would, while unseen, Satan's vengeful angel watched and hovered about her, waiting patiently, undeterred by the cheating we had earlier dealt her. With cruel vengeance she sought and found revenge, swelling, twisting and poking Yasmeen under her angry red scar and setting a fiery fever raging through her body—yet leaving her hands and feet as cold as gray-stone. With warming hands I massaged her chilled feet, the doctor and nurse lanced and drained, while silently we conceding that the foul smelling vapor that seeped out from under her linseed poultice was the breath of death, and we knew that she was running quickly to the end and could not stay, that I must soon say goodbye.

Gently fluttering in and out of consciousness, she murmured softly in her childhood tongue[2], "*ako'y pagod na, nanay, oras ha para magsama tayo*" ("I am tired, mommy, it is time to go with you"). I understood her word for mommy—she had often used it when talking to the children, "ask your nanay", "your nanay is calling you"—although I couldn't understand the rest of what she said or see her mother, but I knew she was there, standing at the foot of the bed, waiting to show her daughter the way.

In tranquility, so tranquil that I could not tell exactly when life ended and death began, she passed over to the other side, leaving her baby and a huge void in our hearts.

To quell the smell of death that had clung to her damaged body—it had no place on her—we washed her well and anointed her with warm fragrant oil before dressing her in her wedding day abaya. So she could lie facing Mecca until the Day of Judgment we placed her on her right side on the wooden funeral pallet, and covered her with a plain white cloth.

Ali stood vigil by her side, in harmony with a long remembrance candle, a candle never to be blown out, but left to burn down and flicker out at the end of its life. He could have ceased his vigil at that time but chose to stay with her in the pitch of darkness until the sun declared a new day—perhaps wanting to be there for her should she come back.

Her burial was an unpretentious yet gracious affair beautifully befitting her shortened unassuming life. Next morning four guards carried her shoulder high to her final resting place outside the palace walls. Ali led the procession, and not bowing to the custom that women do not usually attend burials, asked Paeonia and I to follow closely with Yasmeenah snuggled in a wicker basket between us. Behind the four bearers walked Topaz and Hortensia, with our children clustered around them.

Perhaps startled by the sudden sound, perhaps compelled by divine intervention, Yasmeenah cried as the stony earth showered over her mother and clattered off her burial pallet. And the once silent stoic crowd of family, two of Hussein's women, our household, market people from the town and the purely curious who had gathered around, broke silence and joined her in a saddening under-song of wailing and keening.

---

2. Tagálog. A language of the Philippines

After her funeral, I went to the stables and found what I was looking for. Two small pieces of wood, one shorter than the other, both short enough to hide in my abaya. I locked myself in my room and with a small knife from the kitchen, and barely seeing through tears, carved the name Yasmeen, not in Arabic script, in French lettering, on the shorter piece and tied the two pieces together to make a cross. Hiding it in the sleeve of my abaya I went to visit her, and knelt at her side with the mound of soil and stones between me and my guard. I scooped out a small hollow in the sloping side of the mound, about where her hands would be if she were not so deep, and buried her cross. God will find her.

I did not do it to dishonor our beliefs but to honor her parents. They were Christians and would want the resting place of their child marked with a cross, whether it was buried or not[3].

We all held blame, and spent long hours searching our minds trying to think of ways we could have prevented this tragedy or how we may have caused it. Not finding any, we turned to wishing that we had behaved differently and not neglected to do some things when we had the chance. And simple things, frivolous and unimportant at the time, now haunted our minds. We could have been more helpful at times, or accepted less begrudgingly Yasmeen's first wife directions and not said unkind words behind her back about being a bossy queen bee.

Ali blamed himself. "It is my fault. None of this would have happened if I had kept her pessaried, it is obvious that a baby of mine would be too big for her; I should have seeded her when she was young and pliable; I should have had her pronged or taken her only in the ways that do not beget babies."

"Husband," I said. "Those are unkind and cruel things to do to a woman, never mind to a first wife. And Yasmeen would never, never, want to suffer those things, nor would you want her to. She was happy in her years spent with you, she told me so on many occasions, and I know she died a happy and fulfilled woman and will find peace in Jannah because of you."

No one wanted to ring the bell to summon us to evening meal, or make and serve the coffee, or light the hookah for Ali, things that Yasmeen had always

---

3. In Arabia, the graves of kings and sheiks, the common man and woman, rich and poor, are unmarked. Islam dictates that the only grave worthy of marking and remembering is that of the prophet Mohammed.

done. We stepped gingerly around the tasks and places that were once hers, not wanting to taunt her soul, or turn back our thoughts to how it was. But I often thought of how things were and could be if somehow she could return. She did come to me in my dreams and thoughts and sometimes I carried Yasmeenah to the top of the ramparts. There I told Yasmeen about the little things Yasmeenah had done that day, and held her up high so that Yasmeen could reach down and touch her. Love does not die with the body.

Yasmeen also reached down and touched me.

I often conjured up a vision of her in my mind and on the night of the twenty-ninth day, in my room, as I was drifting into sleep, she came to me in frightening clarity and spoke to me with the firm authority of first wife.

"Tonight is the last time I can come to you, the last chance I have to lead my family from grief, to lift you out of darkness into light and guide you to the next season of your lives, for tomorrow I must go on and join those who have gone before me.

"You have all held me with your tears for too long, take leave of them and find relief from heartache in these words of mine. Listen carefully, and in that clever way of yours write down what I have to say and read it out to the others when the moment is right."

With a light touch of her hand on my arm, she guided me to my desk. Keeping my eyes closed so as not to lose her, I patted my hand around the top of my desk to find pen and paper, and wrote out her carefully spoken words.

The following evening I rang the bell for dinner.

Sitting in a circle around the platters, I read out Yasmeen's magical message.

>Now that I have gone
>Cry for me a little.
>Think of me sometimes
>But not too much.
>
>It is not good for you
>Or our husband
>Or our children
>To allow your thoughts to dwell
>Too long on the dead.

> Think of me now and again
> As it was in life
> At some moment it is pleasant to recall.
>
> But not for long.
>
> Leave me in peace.
> And I shall leave you, too, in peace.
> While you live
> Let your thoughts be with the living.

After we had eaten, peacefully at ease, I poured the coffee, lit the hookah and announced that I would be with Ali that night, with a confidence that affirmed my position as first wife—although I only acted the part—there could be no other first wife, other than Yasmeen.

That Yasmeen's passing could ever become part of our yesterdays had seemed impossible to me, but miraculously, with the passing of time, fragments of our broken days came together, good days slowly outnumbered bad, and the mood of despair and disbelief retreated. Our thoughts returned to the living.

Two years after Isma'il was born, Allah blessed me with a daughter, Fatima. And the other girls have been busy. Constance has a brother and sister, and one more on the way. A large boisterous family has descended on Ali—but what should he expect from four women? He is holding up well. In fact, he relishes being a father and husband to so many, which raises the question of Topaz. She is of course, no longer his slave; she is his willing concubine, but we think Ali should make a respected woman of her. He should marry her—there is room for another wife. I know she would accept. Ali still insists she use pessaries and reminds me to remind Topaz of this. And of late Topaz has taken to holding the children on her knee and cradling them to her bosom, reminding me of the time I held Constance to my dry breast. Perhaps Ali wants to hold onto her luscious body for as long as possible, for luscious and slender it is, firm and lithe. That, however, is hardly reason enough to keep her as his plaything and deny her motherhood. We will talk to Ali and drop hints.

Mustafa, Talil and Black Pearl took their freedom to Constantinople, where, by last report, they had invested their "dowries" in a hugely popular nightclub called of all things "The French Harem". People from France in particular are their clients and take the overnight Orient Express train from Paris to Constantinople just to visit there.

Hortensia married the gardener's assistant and has children of her own, two at last count, and a small roundness tells me one more is on the way. She helps her husband tend to the palace gardens and is a frequent visitor, always bringing her children with her. While their parents go about their work, they play with our children, often in one of the many shallow pools.

I have visited her house in Makram on many occasions. It is a humble dwelling, far removed from the luxuries of the palace harem, but she has no regrets. She has made a life of her own much to her and her family's liking.

You know of course about Nadya and the two sisters. I see Nadya from time to time. Ali has joined in business with Barry, the Englishman and another man, a Professor of Geology from the London School of Mines. They are searching for oil in the eastern part of the country. Ali's skills of surviving and navigating the desert and dealing with local factions have proved invaluable. They are all away now exploring an area where Bedouin have told Ali of places where there is perpetual flame shooting up from cracks in the ground and oozings of *mumiyah* (bitumen) that burn like wood. The Professor is certain that this is oil and gas seeping to the surface from deep below.

Sasha is buried in the shade under the juniper tree, a place where she often lay to escape from the heat of the day. In life it was her lair from which to stalk us and paw at our ankles as we passed by, now, in death, her resting-place. She died of a broken heart—alone in this foreign country. Her passing saddened us all. She was kindred, and part of us went with her.

Ali asked Paeonia to marry him. She refused him. At the time, I thought his asking came more from of a sense of duty than an expression of love, but I was being too feline.

His proposal was not a surprise as we had discussed this between ourselves on occasion. She did pay visits to the bedchamber and he to her room, and they were together often enough to let each other know that they cared for each other. She refused him on the pretences that her place was as his slave—although this was no longer true—and that she was too low in station—a notion that had perhaps stayed with her ever since Mustafa had cruelly cowed her into believing she was unworthy and unsuitable for childbearing and should be pronged. Ali gave her a marriage necklace, and told her that if she ever wore it he would know she had changed her mind and had accepted the mahr and his proposal.

We were having tea one Friday afternoon, "Tea in the parlor" as Paeonia would announce, but of course, there was no parlor under the shade of the colonnade. Friday was a day of rest for Ali and he always spent it with us in the harem courtyard, a gesture we appreciated as much for his company as for the break from routine it provided.

As usual, the children were clambering over Ali. He seemed to attract them like ants to sugar, particularly the girls. He was infinitely patient with them, never chastising them no matter how unruly or noisy they were.

Constance was pressing gateau into Ali's already full mouth, force-feeding him. Crumbs fell and gathered in his beard and lap. Ali glanced my way, eyebrows raised, begging the question, "What is she feeding me?" I had made the cake from a recipe in one of the French magazines. I used sorghum flour. Apparently, it was a poor substitution, but who here, except me, knew how French gateau was supposed to taste. I smiled back at him—a long vacant smile of innocence.

Looking quizzically at his face, rocking her head from side to side in an adoring manner, Constance asked Ali. "Are you my papa?"

"Yes, little one, I am your papa and you are my pretty daughter," he replied, without hesitation.

Constance clambered down and ran to her mother.

"Mommy, he is my papa!"

"Yes darling…he is your papa," she replied, hesitantly.

Paeonia turned to face me, her eyes watering as she pressed her lips tightly together. A squeezed tear ran half way down her cheek. "I never told her. I don't know why," she said, and then turned away and quietly left our company.

I served dinner outside in the courtyard that evening, and Paeonia was late. Annoyed with her, I showed it by pacing about and picking at the food while we waited.

In the flattering pink light of a desert sunset, I saw her walking towards us down the long path, and was just about to call out and sarcastically deride her for keeping us waiting, when I noticed that she was beautifully dressed and mehndied more carefully than our simple *repas* justified. Around her neck, her mahr softly glistened in the warm glow of the evening light. I held my tongue. Ali walked towards her with outstretched arms, she ran between them, they embraced and kissed, and I cried my kohl down my cheeks.

Next day we gave her a *layat al henna*, her henna night. Hidden deep within the patterns on her hands I wrote Ali's name. Tradition says that if the groom can't find his name, then the bride would have more power in the marriage. I made sure he wouldn't find it.

Ali engaged a cleric, and four days later they were wed in a quiet ceremony in the great hall. Constance, carrying a basket of flowers picked that morning from the garden, attended her mother.

I am not slow to learn—I lined my eyes with kohl after the ceremony.

Our planned events, all contrived for the purpose of matchmaking, were highly successful in bringing the young men and women together. It took time; the women were choosy. There were many disappointed men and more than one with a broken heart. Two of Hussein's women married the brothers from the guard of their own free will, and Capucine, Briar Rose, and the third woman are married and living in Jeddah.

Ali has built a small hospital in Makram with six beds and a surgery. Paeonia and two young nurses manage it, and a learned doctor from Jeddah visits once every two weeks. Paeonia is studying to become a nurse's aide by correspondence. The teaching hospital in Cairo sends her books and materials. Eventually she intends to qualify as a nurse.

Ironically, Ali was one of the first patients of the Makram hospital. A mare, agitated while foaling, crushed his knee against the stall and stamped on his foot. The injury was serious enough to keep him palace bound for many weeks and leave him with a slight limp.

Last year we had a reunion here after our annual visit to Ranyah. Everyone came except the nightclub owners and the Spanish sisters, and the guests slept overnight in the rooms that once housed them as slaves. It was a nostalgic event, and Ali of course showered them with gifts.

After all these years, I have found out what Ali does in his time away from the palace. He sells guns and horses to the various warring factions in this part of the world. To both sides. A disgraceful profession I told him!

Ali and I go to school—that is what we called it—and we are learning to speak English. Our tutor is a horribly strict and mean teacher by the name of Paeonia. We have "English days" when we only speak English and although we are far from fluent Ali already has enough command that he can talk with his new Western business partners in their language and I can read and make sense of English books. I have taught Paeonia to read—a fair exchange.

My greatest joys are Ali, my children, and the horses, not necessarily always in that order. I have taken to spending most of my free time at the stables, and I usually take the children with me on those days. Topaz, the mare, has produced wonderful offspring and Ali rides one of her children whenever he ventures into the desert in search of his blessed oil, his black gold.

Yasmeenah is so sweet and loving, and just as petite and pretty as her mother. I have taken her under my wing, so to speak. Fully determined that she will have an education, I spend extra time and care with her in her lessons. Paeonia told me that a child of a difficult birth is sometimes slower to learn.

We have all embraced Islam. We have found our God and he is a good God. I promise to start writing again.

YEARS

It appears to me that the years are far kinder to men than to women.

We were all using the harem bath today; Ali is teaching the children to swim. It seems to be not that long ago when this bath brimmed with nubile slave girls bathing under the watchful eyes of Mustafa or Talil, or being eyed by the Master to see which one took his fancy—which one would be the apple of his eye for the night. I remember how I would strike casual poses with provocative undertones, such as lifting myself up over the edge of the bath, in full view of Ali, and pausing to let the water run over my curves and drip off me before asking him to dry my back, although, of course, I could easily do it myself. Or I would roll over onto my back as I swam away from him, my breasts parting the water, my legs and arms moving with an inviting rhythm.

With Ali, a slight limp from his accident with the horse, some gray hairs in his beard, and a few shallow wrinkles of his face are the only telltale signs of age I see. He has kept undiminished the virility, the eager bulge, and the narrow waist that comes with youth. He is still my splendid animal—when I want him to be—and he is eleven years older than I am.

Ali had once described me to Ahmad—when he was buying me and trying to talk down my price, I may add—as having "low breasts and a stomach that hangs like a mare's." Well, that time is approaching. Before Fatima was born, I still had a svelte figure, and used it much to my advantage and Ali's appreciation. It seemed then that I could do anything, assume any position before him, and nothing would be out of place. Now if I lie on my back to keep my tummy flat, my breasts settle down in sympathy and spread onto my chest. Paeonia doesn't help. She calls them fried eggs on a plate! And if I lean over him so that my breasts fall down to belie their lack of firmness, my tummy reveals the truth. Children do it to mothers; they make us droopy and loose. It is as though nature abandons us after two children when attractiveness to a man is no longer important, and sets us to nurturing instead of procreation. Our charms descend in favor of the young and childless.

Maybe I am too hard on myself, for Ali has never said anything to me to cause me to think this way. However, he often cups my breasts with his hands to rekindle their shape, molding them to their former prominence.

Why couldn't a woman's breasts be like a man and firm up, fill and rise, when the occasion demands?

In all fairness to Ali, he still beds me frequently. I am pleased and thankful, but at times, I would just as soon lie by his side. Then I hear my mother's voice: "Never deny your husband's needs, make yourself available to him, even when you are of different mind", and I heed her advice—most times.

I have denied him[1]. One time I was feeling nervous and ragged—that time of the month was coming—and Isma'il had behaved dreadfully all day, teasing his sister to tears amongst other things, and I did not feel inclined to go into Makram the next day. There were merchants' bills to be paid and the cook had asked for fresh fish, which I had planned to buy at the same time. Ali would be in Makram anyway, so I asked him to do these chores for me. He said resolutely, "Sheiks do not haggle with market women for fish; that is your business, you look after it!"

I shouted at him in that shrill voice of a slighted wife, "If you cannot do these small things for me then it shows you don't love me."

He took me to bed that night to try to cheer my mind, but I protested and shrugged him away and left him, and spent the night alone in my apartment.

Next morning, full of remorse, I went to the bedchamber to make amends, but he had gone and I had exaggerated thoughts throughout the day—he would divorce me, spurn me for the rest of my life, or perhaps never return.

I spoke to the cook and told her that we would have his favorite dish, lamb tajine, instead of fish, and I would help prepare it.

I waited at the door for him as inconspicuously as possible, as I did not want the other women to see me supplicate. He did come home, with a small smile on his face and a gentle side-to-side shake of his head when he saw me. I

---

1. *Abu* Hurayrah reported that the Prophet said: "If a man calls his wife to his bed, and she refuses, and he goes to sleep angry with her, the angels will curse her until morning."
A wife should hasten to her husband's call if he wants her, in obedience to the words of the Prophet. "If a man calls his wife to his bed, let her respond, even if she is riding on the back of a camel (i.e., very busy)."

put my arms around him, rested my head on his chest, and apologized for my outburst. I offered to be his bed-slave that night. "I have made you tajine, chou-chou," I added, thinking that these words would somehow invoke forgiveness from my mother for my naughty proposal.

I wore my old gold slave armband, "dancing swords" breast jewelry, a coin hip belt, and I called him Master. While I leaned over the edge of the bath on a cushion, he took me from behind in the forbidden way—and made the swords dance! He is not a good Muslim for taking me that way, although on Fridays he goes to the Mosque at dawn and again at sundown and prays three times in between.

For added peace of mind, I comforted him again in the morning and sent him on his way, his face glowing. I have never denied him since. If I am of different mind, I try to avoid his meaningful glances and wish his eye to others.

This is so different from the way I was in the months following Isma'il's birth when I would ambush him and almost drag him into my apartment—you have to seize the moment when there are other women around—or make him perform two or even three times a night. My fervor bewildered Ali. Paeonia called me "la nympho," whatever that is. But that boiling cauldron cooled with the years to a gentle simmer, particularly following Fatima's birth. I know now that the passionate, all consuming infatuation I had for Ali has run its course, not burned out, but replaced by the peace and serenity that comes with knowing you have a place in the life of someone you love. It is not a lesser love; it is the calmer, less consuming love that comes after the fire of new love has cooled.

I admit that when he is making love to me, I sometimes feign my ardor and gasp or cry out without cause. I do this to let Ali know I still enjoy being with him, that his masculinity still excites me, and to hide from him that the feeling is shallower now than when I was younger. But I mostly pleasure him; that way my looseness is no impediment and it assures his gratification. And there is another reason. Since Fatima was born, I have had miscarriages, the last one a bloody, draining affair that I barely survived. Advised not to risk another pregnancy, I pleasure him, and if I want Ali to take me in the way that begets babies—my womb still "craves his seed" from time to time—I pessary myself. Pleasuring is my forte and I get satisfaction from doing it. It allows me to show my love for him because he knows it is not God's way and that I do it just for him. It takes him a little longer to peak now and he no longer makes love three times a night—those days have passed for him—yet twice is still common. He rarely misses a night without the carnal company of one of his girls—yes, we still call ourselves his "girls"—although for two of us the end is closer than the beginning. I love him immensely, that has not cooled and that is why I do not refuse him. I know he loves me, he tells me so, and when he chooses to lie with me that also tells me so. There is a younger, less deteriorated and more alluring body on hand if that was all he wanted. He has choice, and he chooses me.

I am convinced of the truth of what I wrote earlier in my journal, "Even a free woman needs the protection and provision of a man, and a man needs the company of a woman—and unspoken but understood exchanges and favors are willingly made between them".

I am less eager now for Ali's company, however, Paeonia and Topaz are still virile and eager to have him any time they can get him. Behind his back Paeonia calls him the "Arabian stallion" and his girls his "stable of brood mares". Quite a fitting description.

I have concluded, at this point in my life, that there is wisdom in the law that allows a man to take four wives. One husband with four wives achieves just the right balance, in matters of the bedchamber. Do the arithmetic, taking into account a woman's "monthly rests". And I think the children would agree for another reason if they were aware, for whenever they have suffered misfortune at the hands of their siblings, or hurt themselves, they clamber onto the closest soft lap for refuge and consoling, without regard as to which one is their mother's.

You may well ask how four women share the love of one man and visa versa. I liken it to the love a mother has for her many children, it is undiminished by numbers, each one being loved equally and completely, and in turn the love they have for their mother is undiminished. Certainly, there are occasional delicate moments and conflicts, but these are nothing more than womanly rivalries, nothing that we cannot rise from later. I must admit that I start many of those that occur between Topaz and I. Her giddy hankering after Ali's company annoys me. In my mind, I imagine that he is mine alone—and always have difficulty sharing him with others—an unkind attitude derived from envy that I have not been able to shed over the years.

But I do believe I am his favorite, although I have never asked him and he has never told me so. He doesn't bed me as often as he does Topaz—if that is any measure of a man—but he entrusts me with keeping the household purse and has shown me the places where he keeps the family money and gold. And we share the husbandry of the horses and camels, all of which bring us together most days, and often we ride together. Sometimes, when it is stifling hot in the palace, when the other girls and children sleep under white muslin canopies atop the ramparts, Ali and I ride into the desert and wait for the sinking sun to float a dark canopy of stars over us—alone and away from the others.

Only one of us to his bed at a time is now the norm, except on special days, such as his birthday and other occasions of our invention,—such as when we are bored! Then we surprise him. We descend to his bed and overwhelm him, exhaust his stamina, and test if he is still "worthy" of us all. He is not.

Topaz has assumed the role of seductress. She has refined her earlier crude efforts and they are now exceedingly affective. Perhaps you will think it strange, but I enjoy watching her work her charms on Ali and see his face flush as she slowly and surely gets into his mind. I want Ali to live fully, to enjoy a man's life and never regret that he freed a harem of slave girls and gave back our freewill and lives. And it rests comfortable with me in another way. It gives me confidence that he will always be there to look after me.

He is always in good humor following a night with Topaz and we all benefit from that. Not that I suggest he is dour of spirit, but I am happy to have her assume the role of seductress, and she is just as happy to play it. "I have my babies now," is how I reason, unwilling to admit to age and lessened desire.

CONFESSION

This year, in the month of Rajab, my peaceful life came near to an end, buried under, blown over, as though nothing more than a foot print in drifting sand.

I was seated in the garden, sewing, when the sergeant at arms came striding purposefully towards me, his determined bearing denoting a matter of urgency. "Madam, there is a messenger at the gate with a letter addressed to a 'Marie'. I have told him that there is no one by that name here, but he insists. You most closely fit his description of this Marie—perhaps there is some confusion over the name. Please, will you come to the gate and talk to him?"

I felt the blood draining from my face as I followed in the sergeant's eager stride.

A scruffy, dusty man was brought before me, who immediately pointed an accusing finger and said triumphantly, "She is Marie." I maintained that there must be an error; nevertheless, I accepted the letter, as he was adamant that I was the intended recipient, and I wanted to avoid a confrontation during which things may be said that I would not want others to hear. Hiding the letter in the folds of my abaya, I walked back to my apartment, trying to conceal my anxiety with a casual and nonchalant stride, while the words "she is Marie", a name I had not heard spoken for many years, drifted in and out of my head.

Somehow, I knew that the letter heralded bad news. I could ignore it; pretend it had never arrived, and never open it. No one would know. No one of importance had seen me take the letter. To the sergeant at arms a letter delivery was a common occurrence attracting no special curiosity and requiring no comment or report.

I sat on the bed, drawn to the folded scrap of paper lying in my lap. Was it from my family? Perhaps my mother had found out where I was. Or it could be from Jacqueline. On the other hand, I had a dreadful sense of foreboding. I remembered the last time I had been in Jeddah with Ali, I had the feeling that someone was following us as we wove our way through the crowded souk. And on the way back to Makram, my horse was nervous and unsettled, and I kept glancing back over the path we had taken. It seemed to me that an elusive figure on horseback was following in our tracks, stalking us, dodging from rock to rock, hiding from view then reappearing for a fleeting second. Ali had dismissed it as my imagination playing tricks on me. "Women are prone to those things," he had said, belittling my notion. Now I had the anxious feeling that this incident and the letter were connected in some way.

I opened it and folded flat the paper.

Dear Marie:

You looked as beautiful as ever when I saw you in Jeddah. From the way you were dressed and the company you keep I would say you have done well for yourself over the years, better than I could have provided for.

It would be a shame for you to have to leave your life of luxury and face a charge of adultery.

Do you remember when I took you to see that adulteress receive her punishment? Would you like to be there soon riding the wooden donkey, awaiting the arrival of the Mullah for your final indignity? Or perhaps you will plead to be whipped 100 lashes and banished for one year, but I think stoning[1] will be their choice. The Wahhabi elders are being severe in their interpretations of the law nowadays and the women are anxious to play their part in punishing those of their kind who blaspheme against the good laws. My wife, the one who has stayed with me through these troubling times, has influence with the authorities; I know her views will prevail, and stoning will be her choice.

Money could persuade me to forego my satisfaction in seeing you punished for running away from me. It will take a large amount of money, although that should not be difficult for you. Your lover is wealthy. Fifty thousand qirsh, in gold, delivered to me within the month could stay my anger and silence my tongue.

---

1. And come not near to unlawful sexual intercourse. Verily it is a faahishah (a great sin) and an evil way (that leads to Hell unless Allah forgives)" [al-Israa' 17:32]. The married woman who commits adultery deserves the worst kind of punishment, which is stoning to death, so that she may taste the results of her deeds and so that every part of her body may suffer just as every part of her body enjoyed the illicit liaison.

My rider will return in seven days for your reply to this letter. Leave it outside the gates and he will pick it up and bring it to me. That is plenty of time. I am sure you have already decided to accept my generous offer. Of course, it will take time for you to make arrangements; all I need of you now is one thousand qirsh as confirmation of your acceptance so that I may postpone my visit to the authorities. Deliver the gold to me later, but within the month, and you will be spared.

Was that your daughter and son with you? So young to be without a mother.

Your loving husband, Jamaal.

Devastated and sickened, I threw myself on the bed and cried with unbearable worry. And when I thought I could bear no more, a new, overwhelming terror gripped me—I would see my children taken from me.

I was doomed no matter what. If I did nothing they would come and take me away from my children. If I confessed my deceit to Ali, he could lawfully open the palace gates and banish me, and keep the children with him. In truth, our marriage was void, illegal, and the children his. Where would I go, what could I do? Everything would be taken from me…except the end. The gates of the palace would close behind me one last time, severing me from my children, pushing me out into the unforgiving desert to die alone, in a place known only to God. My life would end in these awful, miserable, circumstances. Oh, how careless I had been to embark on this journal folly, without letting the truth be known. What an appalling mess I had gotten myself into. To me this was death in life—fatally wounded, yet unable to die.

Topaz found me crying on the bed. She came looking for me, since I had missed the evening meal. For a moment, Topaz panicked, thinking I was desperately ill, until she saw my tear-swollen eyes.

"What has happened? Why the tears?"

I thrust the letter into her hand, remembered that she couldn't read, and snatched it back and buried it under me.

"I will tell the others I have found you, I will be back," Topaz said, as she hurried from my apartment.

She returned and consoled me in her arms, not pressing me for an explanation. It was a long time before my sobbing subsided and I had the courage to read the letter to her, ending my reading with the words, "I am Marie."

I knew it was Ali by the forceful knock on the door.

"It is better if you do not come in, we have woman trouble; we can manage," was Topaz's reply.

Minutes later, Paeonia burst into the room, bringing towels and hot water. "Ali tells me you are miscarrying. Why didn't you call me earlier? I know what to…." She saw me, froze, and dropped the bowl. Water and shards splashed over the floor. "What in God's name has happened? You look deathly ill! This is beyond my learning; I will send for the doctor right away."

Topaz reached out, took her arm, and guided her to the bed. "Sit down Paeonia. Sapphira has received a troubling letter. May I tell her who it is from, Sapphira?"

"Yes," I murmured.

"It is from her husband."

"Why is Ali writing letters to his wife?"

"No Paeonia, it is not that, it's a letter from Sapphira's first husband. She is still married to him, and he is threatening to tell Ali and report her to the Mullahs if Sapphira fails to give him gold."

"Blackmail, extortion—Ali will not like this," was Paeonia's less than encouraging reply.

We talked for a long while and eventually agreed that no alternative existed—Ali must be told, and told soon. Paeonia went to fetch him; she would hint to him about the severity of the matter, to prepare him and soften his heart, while I tried to tidy up my face, which was a futile effort at this point, I may add.

As Ali entered my apartment, Topaz and Paeonia slipped out and left us alone.

"I have never seen you looking so upset. Tell me, what is this trouble that causes you so much distress?"

Silently, I handed him the letter. He moved closer to the lamp.

He read and re-read it, then turned to me, sat on the bed, and said, in that wounded voice of a loved one who has been deceived, "You told me your husband was killed when you were captured."

"It was untrue," I confessed, as a gulf of shame widened between us. "I lied to you—I'm sorry," I said, my voice barely scraping its way out of my throat before faltering to silence.

"This is serious. I do not need to tell you that this is an extremely serious matter. You have put us both in an awkward situation to say the least. Now, start from the beginning and this time tell me everything, and tell me the truth."

I knelt before him and told him my story, my ruse, about how things had gone wrong, and why I had not returned to my husband in Jeddah. I finished with the words, "I am Marie. In the eyes of the law, I am married to Jamaal—I never loved him."

Ali had listened, intent upon my words, his eyes not once leaving mine. When I had finished my sorry tale, he sat for barely seconds.

"Fetch the captain of the guard," he shouted down the apartment passage to Paeonia who was hovering outside the doorway. He was incensed. I had never seen him this enraged, this furious—angry was inadequate to describe his demeanor—and I thought, with good reason, that it was mostly because of me, not Jamaal.

"He will order the captain to inter me in the garrison prison cell," I thought. "I shall languish in his scorn and chains until they bind my hands behind me, set me on a camel, and hand me over. Cursed, cursed journal."

He stepped towards me. With head bowed in penitence to avoid his eyes I waited for his angry grip, my arms and hands limp at my sides shivering uncontrollably now and again. Tears ran down my cheeks, dripping onto my abaya where they bloomed into a dark wet stain.

A tender kiss on my head, my forehead, my nose, my lips, as he slowly lifted my face to his, and through blurry eyes I saw his eyes, and I knew that he still loved me and cared about me.

Taking me into his arms, wrapping me in quiet comfort, he said, "How this predicament ends is in the hands of others. I will do all I am able to do to persuade them to a favorable outcome, although you must understand that anything I do may not be enough."

Sheltered against his chest I answered with silence, for with Ali I share silence comfortably, and I knew that he had heard my unspoken plea for forgiveness.

Mired in shame, I sat meekly on the bed and made myself as small and inconspicuous as possible, not wanting my shame noticed, while starring at the flowing muscles of his broad back, barely hearing his words, as he instructed the captain.

"We shall be riding to Jeddah, leaving tonight, there is a good moon. I want to be there quickly, there is no time to lose. Double up the horses. Pick a third man to come with us, one who projects a menacing presence—one who may be seen as willing and able to impose on someone to change their mind. I will explain my reasons on the journey, and we will have plenty of time to plan a course of action. But in short, my family has received threats from a weak and cowardly man, threats of an extremely serious and distasteful nature that I shall redress."

Almost spluttering with rage, he continued. "A man who threatens to cut out the heart of my family has greatly underestimated me. I will not bow to a lesser man—the House of Saalih is not something to be trifled with."

The captain left with a satisfied smile, I could say an eager smile, and the words, "I have in mind just the man and tools you need, Sir."

Clinging to Ali, I buried my face against him and thanked him again and again, perhaps more for calling me the heart of his family than for his promise of help.

"I know your husband. I bought horses from him many years ago. I do not recall him being the kind of a man who would stoop this low. He was quite pleasant to deal with then. Nevertheless, write down the name by which the authorities knew you at that time, and refresh my memory with directions to your husband's house. Sketch me a map of his stables. Give me dates when all this happened."

"Paeonia," he called, struggling to free his arms from my clinging embrace, "Sapphira should have refreshment, maybe some hookah, some kif, to revive her humor."

Two nervous fretful days and delirious nights crawled by—days and nights I never want to relive. Days spent close to Fatima and Isma'il, keeping them in my sight, holding them close, sitting them on my knee for no other reason than closeness. And at night, I cried myself to sleep, into a world of dreams and restless turning that brought me no rest.

Bound and dragged to the stoning ground they buried me to my neck in a shallow pit scooped into the hot sand, readying me for execution. Stinging sand crusted my eyes and nose and dried my mouth as a circle of *keening* women closed around me, trilling their dirge, small piles of sharp rocks and rounded stones at their feet. Ali kneeling at the edge, his powerful arms outstretched towards me, pleading for me to grasp them. Desperately I struggled to free my arms from the binding sand and hold his saving hands, but to no avail. Isma'il and Fatima walked away, beckoned forward by a faceless apparition. I called out to them; my mouth moved, but all I uttered was a starved gasp; my desperate cries stayed trapped within me.

At first, my thoughts were in chaos, unable to tell where the dream ended and awakening began, order coming only when I thankfully realized where I was—in bed, tangled in bedclothes, my pillows scattered on the floor.

And when awake, thoughts consumed my mind. I relived every argument we had had, whishing each time that I had caused a different ending. I have been difficult, selfish, and unreasonable with him at times, and on occasion I have said foolish things that I felt badly about afterwards, yet was too self-righteously proud to apologize for.

Recently, less than a month ago, Ali sold a colt without my knowledge. I was furious with him, for I had trained and earmarked that lovely animal, in my mind, for Fatima—she was growing up so fast. This was a plan Ali was unaware of, a fact that I conveniently dismissed at the time, saying that as a matter of course, he should always consult me when it came to our horses. Such was my unreasonable reasoning. I stretched his ears with a piece of my mind—words of an angry woman—shouting out things I didn't mean, and now thinking that those same words would shape my life in dreadful ways. Recently, too, I have deliberately avoided his amorous gaze all too often. I had told him I was too tired, and myself that it was too much trouble.

"He does not have to put up with my difficult ways," I thought. "I am not necessary to him; I am dispensable. He has others."

Yet, he had told me he would do everything possible to help me. And on that fateful evening, when I looked into his face through my watery eyes, I had seen nothing but kindness and truth in his words…and desperately wanted to believe that my beseeching eyes on his had somehow repaired the damage caused by my impulsive outbursts and recklessness.

Many times that first day I dashed up the stairs leading to the ramparts, spyglass in hand. Visions of Ali changing his mind and turning back drove me there, ridiculous as that now seems upon reflection.

And oh, how I longed for the impossible: to feel his loving gaze upon me, to be forgiven, and have all forgotten, or find a place some-time past and start over again….

On the second day, long after the possibility of Ali's early return had vanished, my mind found new things to fear—a fear for Ali more intense and stronger than fear for myself.

If the mullahs rejected Ali's intervention and story, what would happen? By his appearance before them, they would know my whereabouts, whether Jamaal told them or not. There could be no hiding. And by some twisted interpretation of the law might they ensnare Ali in their unreasonable judgments? Adultery draws in two people—they would know both. Why had I let him go on this mission, exposing him to these perils? My children, his other wives, and their children needed and loved him. It was all my foolish doing. I was a deplorable disturber of the household, a spoiler of the lives of others—the gates of Jannah would surely close before me.

It was nearing dusk. Over the sea, the setting sun had slashed the waves with a sword of gold and splashed all within its sight with gilded light that held the promise of a beautiful day to come.

A small dust cloud, on the horizon, to the east. Caught by the low skimming sunlight, it twirled brightly and clearly against the darkness of distant hills. Maybe a dust devil stirred up by swirling wind, or a mirage caused by the setting sun. Or was the end of my watch at hand?

I glanced at Paeonia. Our eyes met in silent understanding. I knew what she was thinking—"Aren't you going to look through the spyglass?" I could not bear to. I desperately wanted to know, but did not want to have to understand there had been problems, things had gone wrong, and Jeddah would be my destination. A chill of dread shivered through me. Was this cloud of desert dust heralding the end of my life? Was it concealing determined men, bloated and grim with fanatical piety, unburdened by conscience, and coming to take me back with them? I could not look through the spyglass, even if my shaking hands had allowed it.

I handed it to Paeonia.

She leaned her back against the wall to steady herself.

"How many are there?" I impatiently croaked.

"Three."

"Are you sure?"

"Sapphira, I can count past three!"

"Is it Ali?"

"Yes, I can see the Saalih standard flapping high in the breeze."

"Let me see," I replied, as a wave of confidence and courage swept over me.

"It is them for certain! I can see Ali and the captain with his man holding the standard, and the three spare horses tethered behind. There is no one else in sight." My eyes followed them for a while as they traversed the *méréyé* and descended into the shallow valleys of wind-blown sand, swallowed from view, only to re-emerge on the next crest.

I softened with the inevitability of it all, powerless to change anything, and colored and warmed by the sunlight my mind recalled from long ago, in a melancholy way, the ending verse of a poem:

> *My time is like the setting sun,*
>
> *the final scene has now begun.*

I leave a cast of color too,

reflecting on the ones I knew.[2]

"Come on," urged an excited Paeonia, "as soon as the horses see Makram and the sea their pace will quicken, they will be here within the hour and we have work to do. Down you go—Topaz is waiting for you. We will make you look human and pretty again—as best we can in light of the mess we have to work with," she laughed.

They were cheerful and diligent, happy and noisy, as they bathed, brushed, primped, perfumed and oiled me. They gave me fresh clothes and put on me a little mehndi. I did appreciate their attentions, but miserably, I was unable to catch their excitement. Thoughts I had dismissed earlier in moments of confidence swept back with renewed vigor. I had been afraid for too long, fear had buried all hope and joy. I pretended to share their joyfulness, but in truth, my small smiles were too shallow to part my lips and crinkle my eyes.

"Thank you for your caring, I feel wonderfully refreshed and presentable. Thank you, you are so kind…but now I would be grateful if you left me alone to greet him."

"Of course," and they slipped away.

How would I greet him? Should I kneel before him like the chastened wife I was, or stand to one side and not obstruct his way should he want to denounce me and stride past in disgust.

He came through the archway looking robust and kind. A larger more foreboding and more handsome figure, it seemed, than when he had left—now dressed in black, wearing a kaffiyeh around his head, dusted with dry desert dust, and smelling of horses.

For a moment, I felt that he was more than I deserved and wished that his searching eyes would not find me; that he would walk on past, my guilt mislaid, forgotten, and unaccounted for. But no, he came towards me, placed his hands gently on my shoulders, and held me at bay with his arms and kind eyes.

"You are not married to Jamaal; you are not an adulteress, and there is no record of these past times. We are married; your past is unstained."

His hands slipped from my shoulders and tightened about me. I squeezed my eyes tightly closed and buried my face against him, clinging tightly to the peace that came with his embrace and words, not saying a word.

---

2. Adapted from the poem *Summer Sunset* by Donald Jeffrey.

How was it possible to fall in love with someone who has already taken your heart and all the space within you? I do not know. But I do know, with absolute certainty, with vivid recollection, that in that brief moment of peace I fell in love with him all over again, and feelings of new love flared up and surged within me.

"I shall take a bath and change out of these clothes before eating—I am famished," he said, leaving the great hall with a proud stride entitled by his immense achievement, and leaving me with the thought that he was indeed the shadow of God on earth.

A row of four slippers peeking from under one of the hanging rugs betrayed their hiding place. Those incorrigible girls had watched and heard all words, few though they were.

They emerged, bunched their arms around me, and swept me up and down and danced me around like excited children. I cried and crinkled my eyes with laughter.

How do you thank someone for saving a life—my life? What do you say? What do you do? I had few possessions of value and no money; and if I had, they would have no special meaning or value to him. I had no useful product of my time alone to offer in return, only tears, and they had long dried up. I had no wonderful surprise or carefully composed speech with which to salute his achievement. I could not reply. I was inadequate, a lice on a camel, insignificant.

His unsatiated hunger further burdened my inadequacy. All I could think of bringing from the kitchen was the couscous and falafel I had earlier left uneaten, now cold and unappetizing. Why had I not had the cook stay, made something in my idle moments, perhaps some freshly baked khobz, or kept a wholesome stew simmering on the stove? Simple things any caring wife would think to do. My tired and cold leftovers—hardly a fitting meal for my conquering hero, the master of the house, keeper of the harem, my light after darkness—my husband. My mind had been unable to see past the dark wall that blocked my existence, and I was unprepared when he demolished the wall and it crumbled and fell, and my demons fled before the light.

"What will he eat?" I cried out in despair.

"Sapphira, please! The cook and Topaz have kept their hands busy this afternoon. Topaz has made Syrian betinjan and fresh bread, and the cook has left a hearty goat stew on the stove. Our husband will not go hungry after his travels," said Paeonia, to my great relief. "We have also sent the same down to his two traveling cohorts."

In the great hall, we gathered around him and he told us everything that had happened in Jeddah.

"We rode hard and made the outskirts of Jeddah before dawn and camped there until the sun came up," he began. "We entered the city through the Mecca Gate and made our way to the residence of Sharif Hussein of Jeddah where I paid my respects and advised him of the purpose of my visit to his city, so if there were unfortunate repercussions he could squelch them. He owes me favors. Then, to avoid notice, we rode separately to the Mosque where I spoke to the cleric, the one who has counseled me, and the one who married us. I explained to him that there had been a serious error in the records and asked him to find the old declaration of adultery in the archives, and meet with the Mullahs. I would return later that day and bring a witness who would verify my words. I gave him your real name and the date of your indiscretion.

"We then journeyed on to your husband's house, my two men going ahead to conceal themselves in his stables.

"Your husband answered the door. I could see fright and suspicion in his face; he knew why I was there, and it was not to buy horses!" A smile curled across Ali's face. "He told me that he had nothing to show; the demands of war in Europe and the north had long ago depleted his stock. Most of his horses were gone and he had just a few camels. His business had fallen on hard times—too much competition from America and Ireland, and besides, he said, 'All they are buying is gun horses and mules, not Arabian racing stock.'

"Nevertheless, I wedged my foot in the door as he tried to close it, shouldered it open, and barged in. He protested that he thought it pointless to go to the stables as his stock was sold out. I told him we would walk through to the stables and look, regardless of what he thought.

"On the way I thrust the letter at him and asked if it was known to him—he ran out towards the stables, and that told me all I needed to know." Ali allowed himself a small, satisfied smile. "I blew a short blast on my garrison whistle and my two men emerged from hiding and snatched him as he ran. They brought him to me, knives held to his throat.

"He swore he knew nothing about the letter; you were long dead, lost in a desert sand storm after a visit with friends—so I nodded to my man to take off his shirt. When he did so, of course, he revealed the weapons and blacksmith tools hanging about his waist." The smile broadened. "'This man of mine has ways to restore a faltering memory,' I told your trembling husband. He fell to his knees, groveling, and pleading for mercy.

"I made it clear to him that he would accompany us to the Mullahs to tell them, convincingly and without hesitation, that an error had been made, that there had been no adultery at all, just an unauthorized journey.

"I asked him who knew about the letter and he told me that it was his idea; his wife had nothing to do with it. I took our blacksmith's iron pincers from my man's belt, brought the cold steel between your husband's legs, and told him that if I ever found out what he told me was untrue, or if he told anyone, I would come back and snip off his manhood, a punishment second only to death. He swore to Allah that he was the only one who knew.

"Before the Mullahs he swore that an error had been made, that the decree of adultery and the reward for your capture had been made on mistaken facts. The Mullahs looked at each other. A little mystified they were, and after talking amongst themselves, they said they could not remember such an event, and as far as they could recall, had never declared a fatwa or authorized a reward for the capture of an adulteress. But then again, it was a long time ago and some of the older men had died during the intervening years. They also acknowledged that their own memories had faded somewhat over the years. However, convinced by your husband's vigorous testimony, and assured by him that his testimony was given freely and not under duress, a divorce decree was written and entered in the records against your name.

"While I engaged the Mullahs in conversation, our cleric friend looked again for the offending pages in the ledger of blasphemers, but could find none. He returned it to its dusty place in the archives. There seems to be no written record of this past episode, which is indeed a blessing.

"Before we left, I had my man reinforce my previous threat to your husband. He told him again, that he would be extremely annoyed if he later heard rumors or gossip about this incident and had to make the journey back to Jeddah to attend to unfinished business. In excruciating detail he explained, that if he came back, he would have no hesitation in cutting out your husband's tongue and adding his manhood to his trophy belt. He doesn't have a trophy belt, of course, but mention of it gave life to his threat." At this point, Ali's smile grew into a chuckle. He was relishing his story as much as we were. "There will be no idle talk about this business," he added.

"We had been without sleep for two days so we made camp that evening just outside of Jeddah and when we awoke after sunrise we started back to Makram at a fast pace slowed only by the horse's stamina."

After the story had all been told, we wildly congratulated him, and I kept impulsively hugging him about his neck and kissing his cheek, probably annoyingly so—could I be guilty of giddy hankering?

While he retold parts of the story, we passed around the hookah, and by the time our happy celebration was over, we were all tired, but more so Ali—he was visibly exhausted and weary.

During the past days, I had thought a great deal about what I had done—how I had put Ali in danger and brought dishonor to his family name. On the way to the bedchamber, a rising sense of shame and remorse engulfed me, and I felt the need to submit to his anger, to pay somehow for my transgressions. I broke off a stout sapling, stripped off its leaves and concealed it behind my back. In the bedchamber, I knelt before a puzzled Ali, handed him my newly made switch, bared my back, and said, "Husband, beat me nine times, for I am a deceitful and unworthy wife."

There was a long pause—I waited for the first sting of my well-deserved lashing.

"This is nonsense! Stand up," he commanded, and threw the switch to the corner of the room. "Come to bed…I will deal with you there," he said, giving me that certain smile I knew so well and had been longing for so desperately.

I took a quick bath—I do not know why—it was not needed, and hurried to my apartment to freshen my mehndi and "give nature a helping hand". He was asleep by the time I returned to the bedchamber. In the short time I had taken to refresh myself, his weariness had found relief. I blew out the lamps and slipped into bed, careful not to disturb him. I, too, was suddenly exhausted, and wanted nothing more from the day. Content with his nearness, I curled in against him, feeling small, thankful and safe—and very married.

He "dealt with me" in the morning. I thought he might—but knew deep down he wouldn't—rape me as a conquering soldier rapes a captive, to punish me. I would not have complained if he had, but anger and punishment were far from his mind. I surrendered to him and he took me tenderly. My outburst and ecstasy were truthful.

Side by side, basking in the afterglow of passion, I spoke to him of my feelings of inadequacy about being unable to repay him for his grand intervention. He dismissed my thoughts with these words: "Sapphira, you have given me my greatest gifts in life, love, our children, and the wonderful spirit of joy and lightness that pervades the House of Saalih. Without you, these would be unknown to me—I am indebted to you. They are priceless gifts."

I swallowed back my tears.

Paeonia and Topaz came with a samovar of hot mint tea and joined us on the bed. We propped Ali against pillows and insisted he retell the story of his adventure in Jeddah once again.

In his retelling, he elaborated his story with little vignettes about acts of bravado: bandits, falling rocks, poisonous snakes that could spit in a man's eyes and blind him, and fighting off fiercely clawed night-stalkers—whatever they may be—that became part of a thrilling tale. These were dangerous circumstances and hardships, many of which I knew he made up to embellish his story. I thought I was the *raconteur*, the storyteller. It was all to the good, he had truly earned our admiration and we let him steep in it.

"Pray tell, husband, in the records if I am not an adulteress what then is the cause for my divorce?"

"Three-Day Journey,"[3] he replied.

Following a moment of silence, Ali said, "Sapphira has something to tell us. Tonight she will tell her story."

It was commanded of me.

Before I left, I picked up the switch from the corner of the bedchamber, not wanting the others to know the extreme to which my remorse had driven me, and threw it outside against the wall by the shallow reflecting pond. It bounced back into the water and floated to the edge.

That evening they gathered around me, Ali, Paeonia and Topaz, as I untied the string holding together the cover boards of my journal. I took a deep breath and started to read.

> "My real name is Mariyah, Mariyah El-Abiad, but they have always called me Marie. Marie is a fair compromise—a Muslim name shortened to a French name. Neither a Muslim cleric nor Catholic priest could be offended.
> My mother was the daughter of a senior French Embassy official and my father a Tunisian Government minister responsible for purchasing military supplies. I considered myself a fortunate woman to be born in Tunisia to a Tunisian father of Arab and Berber descent and a French mother. Although my Catholic mother embraced Islam in her marriage she never fully adopted the customs

---

3. Abu Sa'eed al-Khudri: The Messenger of Allah said: "No woman who believes in Allah and the Last Day should travel a distance of three days' journey or more unless her father, son, husband or brother is with her."

and teachings, and insisted that I, unlike most women, be given that rarest of gifts—an education....
I shall remain forever indebted to my mother...."

They were enthralled, Ali in particular, and they insisted I keep reading until the small hours of the morning, interrupted only by short breaks for water and sweetmeats.

Finally, tired out, I snapped closed the journal after the part where Ahmad had sold me to Ali, telling my audience that I would continue tomorrow.

"I am angry with you, Sapphira. You are telling me, that you made me pay that rogue Ahmad—peace be upon him and Allah's mercy and blessings—when I could have just kept you and paid nothing. You let him cheat me. I should put a whip to you!" he said, scowling.

"You don't have one!"

"If that is the case, then instead, you owe me five thousand qirsh for your deceit." He burst into laughter, the scowl passing from his face.

"No I don't. You have had your money's worth from me over the years. I owe you nothing," I countered.

"Well the least you can do is draw me in your sketches a little more generously; my manhood is shown too small."

"You are too vain, Ali, that part has already received all the favor an artist can give. It is as much as I can do."

"Let me be the judge," said Paeonia, "I am fully qualified."

They gathered around as Paeonia turned pages, studying my sketches.

"Hmm, yes Sapphira, your depictions are generous enough—no changes are required."

Ali pretended to sulk, but you know how vain men are about these matters.

The stripped switch I so carelessly discarded in the pond sprouted new roots and shoots and started life anew. The similarity struck me, for I felt I, too, was reborn and starting life anew.

I asked Hortensia to plant it in a fruitful place where it could thrive. I water it faithfully every day. We have both put down new roots and we flourish.

NOW I UNDERSTAND

I know now what I did not know then, when all this trouble started many years ago.

There never was a declaration of adultery, a fatwa, or a reward for my capture. I am now certain, that when I went back to Ahmad after my first brief stay in Ali's harem, I was in no danger whatsoever had I continued on to Jeddah to be with Jamaal. Why was the cleric unable to find the declaration of adultery in the archives? Why were the Mullahs mystified by the claim of a fatwa and a reward? Ali had used that word "mystified", I remember it well. Why was Jamaal confused and unsure about these events when confronted by Ali? Surely they would have loomed as large in his life as in mine, and not be forgotten.

Certainly, his second wife held no love for me, nevertheless, she was not vindictive towards me; my barrenness was all she needed to usurp my position as first wife. I posed no threat to her—definitely not a threat extreme enough that only my death or banishment could diminish it and satisfy her. And I truly doubt Jamaal would have permitted her to post a reward for my capture; it could not be done without his approval. He was not an evil or hateful man; even though we were separate as to bed, we were always decent and pleasant to one another. And how would she know I was an adulterer? She knew only that I had gone away to be a tutor.

Then again, at the time, the improbability of it entirely eluded me, and I thought nothing of it. But why would Jamaal send ahead a messenger to Ahmad's place to warn me about the fatwa? If Jamaal was determined in his plan—if he had a plan—why would he bother to warn me? It did not make sense. Would he not simply have let me come home to Jeddah and ride into his trap?

This I am now certain of—Ahmad had created a myth to frighten me into not returning to Jeddah. He would not want the story of my rape told and risk retribution from Jamaal, or send me back with my tutor's wages, which he would have to make good. He saw profit from his dastardly plan—to hold me captive until all was quiet, and then sell me into a life of secluded servitude, silencing me, and burying me from sight.

My request, to be sold to Ali, was an unexpected gift that played into his hands. An offer he eagerly accepted because it gave him the money he craved without any delay or risk. Furthermore, by accepting my offer there would be no nastiness, and he could truly swear before Allah that he had not done anything against my will.

In all likelihood, Ahmad told Jamaal that he had sent me on my way back to Jeddah as agreed. Jamaal would have no reason to disbelieve him, and would accept that my entourage had lost its way in a sand storm and perished—until he saw me in Jeddah.

These are the real circumstances that led to my enslavement, no others are needed.

I had reasons to hate. Jamaal was not one of them. But should I love or hate Ahmad for his lies and deceit?

FOURTEEN

He doesn't hug or kiss me easily, anymore. An awkward awareness has come between us, an awareness of the closeness of a woman's body that stiffens him to my embrace. I understand, and I am pleased—he has come of age. Isma'il will be fourteen years old tomorrow.

I remember when I first came to Ali's harem and Yasmeen told me she was Ali's first slave girl, given to him when he was fourteen. I imagined that if I were living here in that time I would have already bought Isma'il a slave girl for his bed—a nonbeliever no doubt—a Christian Oromo from Ethiopia. I would have instructed her in her duties and taught her how to please my son. She would be a virgin—every man is entitled to deflower one virgin in his lifetime—with a narrow waist swelling to comfortable hips, smoothed, with full breasts set high on her chest. Yes, I would want the best for my son. Ask any mother.

These thoughts are, however, out of keeping. I do not advocate slavery, far from it, and I have added my strong voice to those calling for its abolition. I often think of other girls secreted away in harems so far away from home, with no bright future to look forward to—only a life of servitude. Ahmad's "pearls" come to mind often.

Several months ago they publicly flogged and banished "Salim the Turk" for procuring girls. Seventy-four lashes with full force, I heard from others.

Seven girls regained their freedom.

Our supercilious government referred to them as girls destined for "forced domestic service". In their minds, slavery no longer exists in this most holy and God-fearing land.

Some years ago, we noticed Isma'il taking a more than casual interest in the female form, watching Constance in the bath and looking at the younger girls in their innocent nakedness. Since then we have kept clothes on the older girls and boys, or separated them when bathing, not wanting to inflame passions or arouse impossible desires.

Isma'il has never seen a girl with her fleece grown in. Constance has not been smoothed, but then Isma'il has never seen her naked since she changed from a girl to a woman. Or has he?

One day at the stables, I went into the feed room for a bucket of grain and found Isma'il sitting back on a pile of empty feedbags, and Constance standing some distance away hurriedly adjusting her dress.

"What are you doing here?"

"Playing house," replied Constance, blushing and shuffling her feet over her knickers that were lying on the ground.

"Playing house! You are too old to be playing house," I said—meaning too young. "Out you go; both of you, there are chores to be done. Isma'il, Shadrack needs water and your horse's stall could do with a good mucking out. And Constance, Faizah is starting her labor. Watch over her for goodness sake and don't leave till her calf is standing and butting her mother's teats."

They beat a hasty retreat through the doorway, giving me wide berth, leaving the knickers shuffled away under the hay.

I think it was nothing more than a game of you show me yours and I'll show you mine. Nevertheless, Constance heard from me later, but only to hear that my lips were sealed. I am no prude. How could I be?

Do I tell Isma'il more about women, or do I let him discover the intricacies for himself? No, fathers should talk to sons and mothers to daughters. I will mention to Ali that Isma'il is old enough to be told about women—I already answer Fatima's questions with the truth ever since she came to me and asked, "Maman, tell me about boys."

For his fourteenth birthday, we are giving Isma'il a new saddle for his horse, made from elaborately tooled leather trimmed with fine silver.

DO YOU REMEMBER ME?

Her mistress had brought her to Jeddah, tired of the slowing pace and forgetfulness of her servant slave. She intended to sell her to the slave traders who practiced their trade clandestinely in the shadows and alcoves of the city wall. However, there were no buyers for this worn out scrap of human flotsam; she had no value. In their eyes, she was worthless.

Her mistress told her to wait by the wall for her, but she never returned. She abandoned her slave, left her to her own devises, homeless and destitute. She sought refuge with the beggars, thieves, and diseased who lived in caves scratched into the hillside outside the walls of the city. Had she been younger that timeless profession of women would have provided for her, but her charms had long ago taken leave. She begged for a living.

But fighting and squabbling ensued. Others claimed that as a new arrival from far away she had no right or call on the meager alms of Jeddah, so she and several other outcasts made the journey to Makram. There the pickings would be better they were told.

Paeonia told us:

"I was in Makram with my escort buying spices and wicks for the candles and lamps when we walked past a clutch of beggars begging for alms. I had diverted my eyes from them so as not to give them hope and have them follow and bother us when I heard my name called—'Paeonia'. I stayed my walk, but the guard urged me to continue. 'They are not to be encouraged,' he said. As we started to walk away, I heard my name called again—'Paeonia'. I turned around and did not see anyone I knew. The guard again advised me to move along, or at best throw them a few coins, but to stay away from them. I reached into my moneybag and threw some coins on the ground. They scrambled and fought over them—except for one woman who ignored the coins and came closer to me.

"'I am Lashida,' she said. 'We were together in Buraydah. Do you remember me? I am the mother of Hortensia.'

"I will admit I still did not recognize her, but who else would know of Buraydah and Hortensia?

"Much to my guard's annoyance I questioned the woman further, and asked her questions that only someone from the harem of Ali's father would know the answers to. I asked her for names of other women, about the color and pattern of the unusual Persian carpet in the great hall—with its distinctive scene of trees, wild animals and hunters on horse back—and the shape of the bath. She took out her breast from beneath her rags and showed me the Saalih brand—irrefutable proof of her claim.

"We will take this woman back to the palace, I told the guard, who stoutly maintained Ali would have 'no interest in a dirty beggar.' I insisted and the guard agreed (he had no choice, Paeonia was of greater rank) on the condition 'that she stay outside the gates until Ali gave further instructions—and she is to follow twenty paces behind and not bring others with her.'"

Ali was skeptical at first, but when told of her good answers to Paeonia's questions and her mark, he allowed her to enter. He ordered her washed and groomed. "If what she says is true, then this is a joyous occasion for all—particularly for Hortensia."

Paeonia proudly asked me to bathe and groom the woman, a task I found at first to be distasteful in the extreme. She had that sour smell about her, that particular smell that lingers about the uncared-for old and poor, that tells of their neglect by others, and I took her to the far corner of the garden, near a small pool, to avoid her touching or walking on our things. Furthermore, I was ashamed of her; she was a disgrace to womanhood, and I did not want Ali to see that a woman could be this disgusting.

I undressed her—angrily and uncaringly, I shamefully admit—and placed her stained and dirty clothes in a small basket. I went about washing her with water from the pool, watching the rivulets of water running down her body roil the dirt aside, leaving lightened trails against her dark skin. Her hair smelt like a wet dog.

Looking upon this pitiful bag of bones, draped in a shroud of wrinkled skin, I found it hard to imagine that in its youth this body had rendered erotic delights to lustful men—if what she said was true.

I called for Paeonia and she agreed; we would have to shave the woman, so badly was her hair infested with lice and caked with dirt. She started to cry as I sheared the hair from her head, catching the matted tufts in the basket along with her clothes. She asked what was to become of her, was the Sheik angry with her, what would he do to her, while desperately and profusely apologizing for her condition and unkempt self.

Her tears pulled at me. It was out of keeping for a woman to go unclean, but I realized that poverty, hunger and despair, had drained her of both the means and the will to groom herself. A feeling of pity and brightness overcame me—Allah spoke to me—and I comforted her with kind words and went about my task with renewed enthusiasm, compassion and care, assuring her that Sheik Ali had only good things planned for her and that before sundown she would be smiling and happy.

Paeonia returned with a bowl, razor, and carbolic ointment and soap that she brings from the hospital to use on the children's scrapes and bruises. Together we shaved her close, and rubbed her sore, lice bitten scalp, with carbolic. We burned the basket and all its unclean contents.

Swathing her from head to foot in a large cotton cloth we led her to our baths, where we waited well on her and pampered her. We cleaned and trimmed her nails, massaged her with sweet-smelling emollient, and oiled her sore hands and callused feet. I wanted to nurture her, to sweeten her, to return her to the human race, to loosen the yoke of hardship, and give her comfort and peace of mind in her closing years.

From our care emerged a gentle woman, broken and burdened by sadness and shame not of her making and deserving of our respect. A small radiance from her thin black skin showed thanks for the brief care we had given her. A little rouge high on her cheeks, and a dab of oil of bergamot completed my tending.

I found a colorful ikat robe and African headdress scarf for her, last worn years ago by one of the harem servants, and slowly a swell of her ancestral pride and tall elegance rose to the surface surprising us all with her splendor and dignity.

Hortensia and her husband and children were sent for. "A matter of urgency and importance," was the message conveyed to her. "Be here at two hours before dusk."

We gathered in the great hall and sat the woman on a stool. Paeonia stood between her and the door through which Hortensia would come, blocking their view of each other.

A curious Hortensia arrived, family at heel, her three children wide eyed and bewildered, as they lined up in a row, side-by-side—apprehensive.

Ali gave the sign and Paeonia stepped aside.

I did not know what to expect. Had an imposter duped us with a clever charade? Would mother and daughter cry out in unconfined delight at seeing each other, or would they be unknown to each other after being lost to each other for all these years, and be disillusioned and amused by the elaborate staging we had mounted?

They were both stunned to silence. Nothing stirred, except for welling tears. Hortensia walked slowly and knelt at her mother's feet for a long moment of silent reverence that ended with streams of tears and a crushing embrace, and Hortensia's shout of joy for all to hear—"Mama, my mama!"

Over refreshments, Paeonia retold the story of the chance encounter, and Ali told all how Paeonia's remarkable astuteness had given rise to this great reunion. Paeonia took Lashida's measure for clothes yet to be made, and Ali knelt at her feet and fastened a Saalih emblem bracelet around her wrist. For the rest of her life she would shelter under the protection of the House of Saalih.

They left at sundown, a family of six, three generations strong rejoined together, never again to be broken apart except by God in his own time and wisdom. Lashida was weeping, smiling and happy. Hortensia's eyes no longer grieved.

CLOSING THE CIRCLE

Astounded is all I can say. I had thought about it often, but believed it impossible. I always quickly dismissed it from my mind, not wanting to torment myself and divert from my happiness and contentment. Nevertheless, it was always close to mind; it never went away.

Ali and I were strolling in the gardens talking of that unforgettable day when we united Hortensia's family. "I know from your journal readings that you, too, are very fond of your mother," he said. "Why not make a visit to Tunis to find your mother? Reunite with your family as Hortensia did. Take Isma'il and Fatima with you; they are ready to see other places in this world. I will send the captain of the guard with you. He is experienced in protection and can pick out bandits and thieves and other unsavory characters even in large crowds, and he sees through the lies of men."

I could not believe what I had heard; I was overwhelmed with joy, elated and excited. Even then, I ungratefully protested that I could travel alone without need of the captain, but he abruptly pulled from under me my proud assertion. "There will be no 'three-day journey' for you, the last one you took lasted fifteen years and ended in serious trouble. You will go with the captain or not at all."

At first, I believed that he insisted the captain accompany me because he did not trust me. But of course, my past record did not instill confidence and trust. It could not be easily forgotten that I had deceived many, and that Ali loved his children and would do all he could to protect them from harm. Fortunately, I kept my selfish and unreasonable thoughts to myself and thanked him instead for his vision, thoughtfulness, and precious trust.

It preoccupied our minds. Everyone was involved, joining in the intrigue, to solve a mystery, to search in unknown foreign lands for persons long lost. I had my share of trepidation and second thoughts. Sometimes, it is best to leave the past undisturbed. Perhaps a higher reason existed for why my life had unfolded as it had—perhaps I should not interfere with its course and invoke curses from above for my meddling.

Optimism overcame caution, and preparations commenced in earnest. We made clothes, bought shoes, packed trunks, and practiced sitting at a table and eating with knives and forks. Ali arranged for money. He had a deep distrust of the new-fangled paper money and sent us on our way with gold sovereigns and silver shillings—Barry assured us that these English coins were readily exchangeable into local currency when required. I packed my journal in a wooden box wrapped in oiled cloth to keep it dry. I had a secret plan for it.

Our entourage headed for Jeddah where we would embark on our journey. Ali of course came, and so did Paeonia, to see us on our way. Paeonia traveled on a camel in her colorful palanquin that Ali had had specially made for her so that the searing desert sun would not scorch her alabaster skin. Ali and I, and the captain and four guards, rode horses, and camels carried our trunks on their sides.

"Chou-Chou, I am afraid."

"That is to be expected," he said. "It will be a long journey for a woman and many things will have changed. Luckily you are a brave girl and I am sending a good man with you."

"It's not that," I said. "I was thinking, aren't we taking the same way to Jeddah that you took when you went to see about Jamaal?"

"Yes that's true; I know the best way, even at night. My secret is to keep the Goat star behind you," he proudly explained.

"When it's dark, will the fiercely clawed night-stalkers come out and will we have to kill the snakes that spit in your eye and blind you?" I asked, with coyish innocence.

He raised an eyebrow, hid a smile behind his handsome face, and pulled ahead.

Our descent onto the quayside attracted a swarm of eager porters who started to unload the pack-camels without asking for permission or waiting for instructions. A disjointed scream coming from within the silk draped palanquin—Paeonia has quite a voice when needed—halted their efforts in midstream. "Stop doing that immediately!" she shouted, and then gracefully descended from her palanquin.

Turning to us, she said in a calmer voice, "I know ships. I will check it over for you and make sure it is seaworthy before you board." She headed for the gangplank while the surprised and restless porters hustled and jockeyed amongst themselves and waited for her return.

"It was built by Harland and Wolff in 'The Merseyside' in England. Only the best ships are made there," she proudly reported back, "It is safe for you to board."[1]

Later, the captain confided. "Please excuse my boldness, but that woman who came on board to inspect my ship—what incredible beauty she possessed," he said, looking down and gently shaking his head from side to side. "Tell me, how does a woman who comes in from the desert riding on the back of a camel, know about Plimpsoll Load Lines and bilge pumps? And she inspected the sisal hawsers for rot—she even asked me when they last saw creosote."

"When she was a young girl she ran away to sea and worked on a ship," I explained.

"Well, please tell her that if she ever wants to run away again, she is welcome to join the crew on my ship. And forgive me for repeating myself—she is such a strikingly beautiful woman," he said, with a distant smile that laid bare his thoughts.

"Yes, she is. She is married to the man she was with, and has children of her own. She will not be running away," I added, with a smile.

"Such a handsome couple."

"Yes, they are," I agreed, a little sadly.

Packed to the gunnels with *Hajj* pilgrims returning from Mecca, the ship pulled out of the harbor and headed north to Suez and the canal. We stood at the rail and waved final goodbyes back and forth until the figures on the dock shrank out of site and the sea breeze dried the tears on my cheeks.

Amid throbbing engines and black smoke from the stack, clanking bells and bellowed orders, a token cotton sail fore and aft, I would reverse the journey I made years ago. It seemed so long ago, that journey from Tunis to Jeddah. Then, favorable winds pressing gently against white sails had buoyed us along silently, while a crew of skilled sailors quietly worked the rigging. It was in stark contrast to the commotion that surrounded me now—the harsh noises of a modern world.

---

1. Harland and Wolff would later build the ill-fated Titanic in their Belfast shipyard.

On the advice of Barry, Ali had reserved two cabins for us on the shady starboard side for our westward passage and on the port side for our return. This was, supposedly, first class accommodation, but in reality, the cabins were merely cramped painted steel boxes with small round portholes for light and air. A tiny brass washbasin, a mirror, a narrow bed, and a pull-down bunk completed the suite. Nevertheless, this was superior to the accommodations for the hoi polloi, the returning pilgrims, who slept where and when they could on deck and stairs, praying, cooking and washing in small territories fiercely protected and defended from fellow travelers. We took our meals with the captain and first mate and had private use of an upper deck.

The captain of the guard, Abdul-Khaaliq, and Isma'il took one cabin, Fatima and I the other. We traveled as man and wife, in name only, to avoid raising the ire of the devout about us, as no *mahram* was available to me.

First, we would sail to Port Said, where most of our fellow travelers would disembark and commercial goods would be loaded on board—a stopover of two days—before resuming our westward journey to Tunis via Alexandria, Tobruk and Tripoli.

As dusk darkened our cabin, I realized we had no candles or lamps for the night and went on deck to inquire of the first mate. "Do you have candles? Our cabins will soon be dark."

"No ma'am, but you may switch on the lights, the electric dynamo is turning."

"Switch, electric dynamo—what are those?"

"Come. I will show you," he said, in a condescending way, as though speaking to a child.

He opened our cabin door, felt for the wall inside, and *voilà!* Light bathed the cabin in a warm yellow glow—light coming from hot wire in glass globes. It was truly amazing, and frightened Fatima somewhat.

I spent the next few minutes sitting in flashing light as Fatima played the switch up and down with great fascination.

"Go next door and show your brother what you have discovered," I said, relishing a little peace from the insistent flashing and welcoming an opportunity for a proud Fatima to show her brother something he did not know, for a change.

I heard the commotion next door and saw the corridor outside lightening and darkening before an argument broke out, and a tearful Fatima returned complaining that Isma'il would not let her have a turn.

In a foolish, condescending moment, I told her she could play all she wanted with the switch in our cabin, and I spent the next hour or so on deck to avoid the persistent flashing, imagining that that was how the world would end—in flashes of bright light.

Abdul joined me on deck—also seeking refuge.

"How do those lamps work? You push the little handle down[2] and the wire in the glass ball glows hot, but there is no flame."

"They are little suns made by the electric dynamo. Modern science," I offered.

Abdul agreed. "Yes that must be it, little suns made by modern science.

"I will go down now and take up my station," he said.

I found him sitting cross-legged on the corridor floor, a short sword across his lap, guarding our rooms, looking out of place and old fashioned in this modern era. A loyal anachronism. He reminded me of the night guards of the harem of years ago who sat side by side across the entranceway into the courtyard. How I had marveled at their overnight fortitude.

"It is unnecessary for you to mount guard, Abdul, this ship is safe and the doors are steel with heavy bolts. Take your rest." I said.

"Ali would want this."

"Then you must stay only until all is quiet on deck," I replied, waving a finger at him with friendly authority.

At our first port of call, Port Said, the captain advised us to take an overnight room in town as the unloading and loading was a noisy, all-night affair, and we would have no peace and quiet. "When I have shore leave in Port Said I stay in a small lodging. It is friendly and peaceful. The owners have a lovely daughter, just about Isma'il's age," he added, with a twinkle in his eye. "I can also recommend highly a restaurant, 'The Crown', where British army and naval officers of the British Suez Contingent take their wives and lady friends. A little bit of England here in Egypt. You can't go wrong with that," he said.

"With your permission I will send a boy to tell both to expect friends of mine."

I was pleased to take his advice. We took rooms—small ones, simply furnished, and scrupulously clean—in a small yet rather splendid *pension* owned by an Egyptian family. That evening we ventured to the recommended restaurant near the souk.

---

2. British convention. Switch down for on, up for off.

Paeonia had sewn me a dark blue abaya for such occasions, and with the white hijab scarf I wore over my head and shoulders it made for an attractive ensemble. "*Très chic*," I thought. Abdul wore a dashing white thobe and *bisht*. The bulge in the cloth from his concealed dagger was barely visible, and with the children in their best clothes we buoyantly followed our chatting guides—the young girl and her mother from the *pension*—through the narrow streets to the restaurant.

The sign in English read, The Royal Crown Restaurant and Bar, but our greeting at the door was less than royal. With obvious contempt, the maitre d'hotel eyed my abaya and Abdul's thobe, spoke to us in haughty English, and informed us that no tables were available—although when I looked past him, the room was half-empty, with bored waiters standing by listlessly.

"May I recommend another…?"

"You must be mistaken. Captain Hobeika sent his boy earlier today," I interrupted in English, much to his surprise.

"Who? Captain Hobeika? My good friend. Oh, yes, now I remember. How could I forget? It is unusual to have an Arab family dine here," he said, with unfriendly emphasis on Arab. "We use knives and forks here."

"Of course, what else nowadays? And why could it be that Arab families rarely dine here? I was told you manage a high class place."

"Please follow me," he continued, my sarcasm wasted on him.

"Reserved for Captain Hobeika" read the card on our table—the captain had influence here!

It was a plush establishment with dark wood paneling and stocky chairs covered in dark red leather. A challenging array of silver cutlery graced the white cloths that covered the tables, and the beautiful crystal wineglasses did not go unnoticed. A dull floral patterned carpet covered the floor and black wooden beams set against smoke-yellowed plaster crisscrossed the ceiling, all of which made for a rather stiff and formal atmosphere.

A small orchestra and piano played Western-style music. It was something I had not heard for many years and it sounded confusing and strange to my ears—too harmonious and low pitched. Our waiter, too, gave no relief from formality, immaculately dressed as he was in black trousers and white shirt with a red tasseled fez perched on his head—a ridiculous token concession to the heritage of the host country. I wanted to tell him I knew a better place for tassels—I was feeling cheerful of mind and it would take more than a surly maitre d'hotel and our less than friendly welcome to dampen our evening.

We were addressed in English as Sir and "Madom", with emphasis on the "o",—where the "o" came from was a mystery to me—and the children were referred to as master and mistress. "Such bizarre titles for innocent children," I thought. Our table for the evening was in a choice spot, one step up from the sunken polished wood dance floor, where, to the undivided amazement of Abdul, couples were holding each other in their arms, with no chaperone in sight, moving about together, even sharing the occasional kiss.

"Would Madom care for something from the bar?"

The bar? Paeonia had never taught me about the "bar", and I stared back, confused. "Would Madom partake of a drink?" Ah that was better—a drink. "Yes, a bottle of French Bordeaux, si'l vous plaîs," I replied, in a mix of poor English and Parisian French that caused an immediate name change—we were now *Monsieur* and *Madame*, and the children *les enfants*.

"And *Monsieur*, what could I get for you?"

I translated into Arabic for Abdul, who was confused about the proceedings, the ambience, and the foreign languages being spoken. I was annoyed with the waiter for not speaking Arabic to Abdul and humiliating him and I suggested to Abdul that he order a beer.

"I have never had beer before—should I?" he asked.

"Yes, we are on holiday in a foreign country, rules can be broken."

"How do I order?"

"Raise your finger and say, 'Une bière garçon'," I advised.

Incomprehensible words followed. The waiter looked confused—or was he ignoring the demeaning *garçon* and Abdul's finger? Should I have explained better how to hold the finger? Maybe not.

"Oh, I'm sorry," I interjected, "my husband, Sheik Abdul-Khaaliq, expected you to speak Shari"—a name for a fictitious language I had quickly thought up. "All officers of high rank and the better educated in our country speak that dialect. Even the lowly slave girls in his harem have learned it; I am surprised you do not speak it. Never mind I will translate for you. Une bière, si'l vous plaîs."

"And *les enfants*?" asked the humbled and deflated waiter.

"They will have lemon water—no, we will all have lemon water to start," I corrected.

We spoke Arabic from then on. There was no need to further impress the waiter or condescend to his fanciful talk.

We sipped on yet another amazing modern invention—nose prickling carbonated lemon water with ice. Isma'il and Fatima had never seen ice or carbonated water, it fascinated them, and Isma'il soon discovered that timeless use for ice—putting it down the back of little sisters' dresses.

English roast beef for me, tender and well aged. A curious Abdul had never tasted beef. I offered him a small piece. "It has been dead too long," he said, returning keen attention to his platter of fresh lamb. Disregarding Abdul's reproachful judgment of beef, we had a delightfully different meal from what we were accustomed to, and the children ventured, but not too far, by ordering English fish and chips, avoiding the more exotic items on the menu. This rejection of exotic foreign delicacies, however, did not extend to the entertainment.

Isma'il and Abdul were equally happy to ogle the belly dancer, and sensing that she had an appreciative audience she was just as happy to oblige. She played up to them, kneeling and making the "layback" in front of them, a move I knew well—keep your knees apart, girl—and flipping and turning coins up and down her belly. Coins that Abdul was more than pleased to provide and place on her belly, so generously laid bare by her stingy costume. Then she stood up and twirled her tassels, first one way and then the other, and then both in the same direction and then in opposite direction. I assure you; this was not authentic Egyptian belly dancing, but merely contortions and costume to feed the fantasies of "the foreigners".

A second distraction caught my attention as she sashayed her way between the tables, with an unwavering approach and ridiculous costume—or am I becoming prudish and envious of the young. She wore a short black skirt, a too-small white blouse, barely buttoned closed, and a tray about her neck. Black silk stockings sheathed her long slender legs, her toes tucked into shoes with high heels—"not so ridiculous, the shoes and stockings," I conceded. She sidled up to Abdul and leaned forward to show him the contents of the tray—and her blouse—and me, a flash of the red frills of her garters as her too-short skirt rode up at the back.

"Trollop," came to mind.

"Cigarettes *Monsieur*?" she purred, "Or perhaps a cigar for the evening?"

Unsure if Abdul knew about cigarettes and cigars I interpreted, explaining that cigarettes were tobacco wrapped in paper. "Yes, I would like to try them," he said, not taking his dazed eyes off the contents of her blouse. I ordered for him, assuming it was cigarettes he wanted to try.

My mother was right. They are "irresistibly alluring" to a man. Abdul was excited; it shows in men's faces as well as other places. Catching his excitement, I removed my hijab, shook out my hair, and when he turned to look at the dancer, I raised my wineglass and secretly looked over the glass at him bewitchingly. He is a handsome man—I could see how easily one might love him and lie with him. I would not—but the thoughts were there, having enjoyed more than one glass of the fine Bordeaux at this point.

The more fully dressed dancers on the floor, swirling around in never changing circles, fascinated Fatima. She took her eyes from them only briefly to eat and sip her lemon water.

He was a distinguished looking gentleman with graying hair and an elegant stature. He stood before me, his courteous bow proclaiming his European origin.

"Please excuse me for interrupting your evening, but my wife and I couldn't help noticing your daughter's interest in the dancers. May I ask her for a dance? My wife suggested it," he added, as though apologizing for his forwardness. "She thought your daughter would enjoy it."

"Yes you may, she speaks Arabic and a little French."

"We will manage; I speak a little French too."

He turned to Fatima and in French asked. "Would Mademoiselle care to accompany me for a dance?"

Fatima was unsure about what to do, and turned to me. I nodded my approval, and she rose to accompany her beau, her prince, to the floor. At the same time, Abdul jumped aggressively to his feet, his hand searching under his bisht for the handle of his hidden dagger.

I quickly explained what was happening and he sat down again, but was restless.

"Are you sure this is right? Would Ali approve?"

"Yes," I assured him, "the man is from Europe, they do this in Europe, it is quite proper."

We watched as he showed Fatima how to hold her arms, and as the orchestra struck up a waltz, he whisked her off into the midst of the swirling couples. Abdul craned his neck, never losing sight of her.

Each time they passed us they added a twirl and spin for our benefit, which caused Fatima's hair to fly outwards as she beamed a proud smile at us. It was the highlight of her evening.

A highlight of a different sort was offered to Abdul, which I quietly thwarted.

A somewhat disheveled and crumpled figure, looking slightly out of place, moved close to Abdul and pressed a card into his hand before melting back into the crowd. Abdul looked at the card and turned it over. There was writing on the back, in English, and he handed it to me. "What does it say?" he asked. I flipped it over. On the front was printed the name—Christopher Dilworth Esq.—and on the back a message written in pencil:

> Sir: The dancing girl will be pleased to entertain you in her room. For one shilling, she will take off her clothes and give you her sweetness. I will be sitting under the bar clock after eleven if you wish to avail yourself of her kindness.

"It is a note from the proprietor. It thanks us for coming to the Crown Restaurant and he hopes to see us here again."

"That's a nice thing to say, perhaps we can do that on our way back," he replied.

"Yes, we will, if the ship stops over."

"Mama, who is that a picture of?" asked Isma'il, pointing to a framed portrait of Queen Victoria, her dour face looking down disapprovingly on the revelers beneath her. Victoria Regina 1819–1901, revealed the gold lettering carved into the black banded frame through which she peered.

"She, my dear son, was the Queen of England."

Isma'il commented, "She looks as though she is sitting on someone's hand and they have a finger up her bum." We burst into laughter, sputtering food back onto our plates; our concerned waiter hovering nearby thinking—and maybe hoping—that we were choking.

"Is the food to *Madame's* liking?" he inquired.

"Yes, the food is wonderful; we were just admiring the portrait."

"Yes, indeed. She was the Queen of England. A lovely portrait—one of her better sittings," he informed us, unaware of his unintended innuendo, and we burst into yet another round of laughter that attracted unwanted attention from nearby tables. The prospect of an unpaid bill was probably all that kept us from eviction onto the street outside.

Had Isma'il made that comment at home I would have sent him to his room, and we would have laughed in his absence and denied him credit for his humor, coarse schoolboy talk though it was. However, we were on holiday and rules could be broken.

I cajoled and prevailed on Isma'il to dance with me—his mother! We stumbled, stepped on each other's toes and bumped into decorous couples as we shuffled around the floor much to his embarrassment. Then, for the *coup de grâce*, I bribed him—with an offer of more iced lemon water—to dance with his sister. It was a study in contrasting attitudes, of displeasure and delight, and there is no need to tell where each belonged.

After escorting us back to the pension, Abdul told me that he found Egypt an interesting place and proudly announced in English that he was going back to the bar "for beer and cigarettes," to which I added, rather nastily, "and another look." At least I didn't ask him if he had a shilling.

I threw him a glance and a smile as he left. He is not anyone's husband, and I was not his chaperone. I would apologize for my comment, made no doubt by a wine loosened tongue.

Asking the children what they thought of their first time in a foreign country was a mistake. I expected thanks and accolades for what I thought had been an excitingly different evening for us all.

"Dancing is silly; riding horses is better," replied Isma'il, I being unsure of the connection—if there was any.

Fatima answered him indignantly. "Well, the dancing girl was rude, wiggling around like that."

"Better than dancing with you, and anyway you will grow titties like her."

"No I won't."

"Yes you will, all girls have them, you have already started."

"Well if I do, they are better than that silly thing boys have between their legs."

"How would you know? You are just a little…"

"Constance told me!" she shouted, abruptly ending their dispute.

Nevertheless, fearing that the conversation might resume and go in a direction that Isma'il and I would not want it to go, I intervened. "When we get back to the palace we will teach papa to dance—then we can dance whenever we want," I told Fatima.

She stared back, smiling and wide-eyed.

"Papa will be really pleased with you two!" scoffed Isma'il.

From whom does he get his sarcasm? From me, by chance? And to think I had thanked Ali so profusely for sending the children with me.

"Children, that's enough—*fini*—off to bed, it's way past your bed-time," I ordered, as the full affect of the wine took hold and I flopped down into a chair—the same one I woke up in, crumpled and stiff, in the early hours of the morning.

We boarded the boat in the morning, two sprightly children, differences forgotten, and two adults, clearly remembering and feeling the excesses of the night before, inwardly praying for calm seas.

It was a kohl black night as we slowly steamed into the Gulf of Tunis and dropped anchor offshore of La Goulette, the port city of Tunis. Tunis itself was about six miles inland, connected to the sea by a deep canal and a stone-paved road. I sat up in my bed, peered out through the porthole and saw the guiding lights on the pier, flickering their welcome. Sleep did not return—I was too excited.

At the break of dawn, I went on deck alone and watched as the sun rose over the low buildings—first catching the tops of the tall minarets, then sliding down and spilling over the white dome of the mosque—as the captain nudged the ship to berth.

From a high balcony around one of the minarets, a muezzin called the faithful to prayer:

> God is Great.
>
> I testify that there is no God but God.
>
> And that Mohammed is his Prophet.
>
> Come to prayer.
>
> Come to prosperity.
>
> God is most Great.
>
> There is no God but God.

While Abdul supervised the unloading of our trunks, I hired transportation to our hotel, the Maison Dorée on rue de Hollande. An automobile would take us there, adding to our excitement.

Abdul was leery of such conveyances. It would not have surprised me had he looked underneath for the horse's legs. There were none of these in Jeddah, and I was rather proud of the advancements my country was showing to Abdul and the children. I took an aloof, blasé view of everything, implying that it was nothing unexpected, while quietly absorbing the amazing scene before me. So much had changed.

With Abdul sitting beside the driver in the open front and the children and me in the covered cab at the rear, luggage stowed on the roof and in the boot, we chugged and rattled to the Maison Dorée.

After lunch, I dressed the children in their finest clothes and took the auto taxi to my childhood home in Ville Nouvelle, but before I did that, I went to the telegraph office and sent a message to Ali.

·ARRIVED IN TUNIS TODAY·ALL ARE WELL·OFF TO FIND MY MOTHER'S HOUSE THIS AFTERNOON·ALREADY MISS ALL OF YOU·LOVE SAPPHIRA ISMA'IL FATIMA ABDUL·

The house was as I remembered it although the wrought iron gates were not as freshly painted as I recalled and the wall leaned a little with age. And, as with me, the trees and plants had matured and were overflowing their confines.

I unlatched the gate and with the children clutching hands I proudly walked the gently rising brick pathway with its five small steps, steps that years ago as a young girl I had bounded up and down with carefree abandon, the passing years now calling for care in my stride. Steps that led to the solid wooden door, painted bright blue with rows of black iron studs, set below an arch of alternating light and dark stone. It was secure, yet inviting. I raised the black iron hand of the khomsa doorknocker and allowed it to fall sharply—demanding attention.

A young woman opened the door. Of course, my elderly parents would have a maidservant to help them, and I confidently asked for, "Madame El-Abiad."

"I am sorry; there is no one here by that name."

I was dazed—it was a possibility I had simply not considered.

Stupidly I asked. "Are you sure?"

"Definitely Madame, we have lived here for many years, at least six or seven. An elderly lady and a younger couple lived here before us; they moved to another house. I do not remember names or where they went. Would you accept a drink before you leave? It is a hot day."

I accepted her abrupt offer. The children stared glumly into their glasses—clearly disappointed and ungrateful for water without ice—while I told her who I was looking for. I asked her to send a message to the Maison Dorée should anything, even a small clue, emerge as to their whereabouts.

I retraced our steps down the pathway only to be reminded again of my stupidity. I had dismissed the driver and we would have to walk back to the hotel in the sweltering afternoon heat.

With cranky children in tow, I set out on the long walk back. At least this gave me time to think out a plan, and this time I would base it on careful consideration, not blind optimism.

Next morning I left the children with Abdul and set out for the Place du Gouvernement (Government Offices) on rue de Syrie where my father had worked. After being reluctantly granted entry by the guard at the doors, and disturbing the quiet of the young girl sitting at the reception desk, I was bounced around from office to office in a way only a well-established bureaucracy could perfect, finally arriving before an elderly graying gentleman. "Yes," he said, "I remember your father," and then he proceeded to regale me with stories of the past, eventually closing with, "I don't know where he is now.

"Fortunately for you, a man in my high position has ways of finding out things. I will put the matter into the hands of the Chief of Police; he looks for missing persons and has nothing better to do." He gave me his card and advised me to show it to the guard and receptionist when I returned, saying, "With this, you will be speedily granted audience."

"Pompous ass," I thought, but I needed him. He was the only one offering any sensible help.

"I shall convey a message to you as soon as I hear anything," he echoed, as I left his office.

Early in the morning next day a uniformed messenger boy came to the hotel bearing another of his cards. I graced the boy's open hand with coins, and read the terse message on the back of the card.

"Two o'clock, my office. I have news for you."

Returning to the Government Offices, I showed his card to the guard and receptionist, and as promised, it gained me speedy entry to his office, at two sharp.

"The chief, M. Bédard, is a meticulous man, although he does not always find good news. Going through the records, he found entries for two men with your surname, who died about eight years ago in the great epidemic. One was definitely old enough to be your father. I am sorry to convey this sad news to you. Please accept my condolences."

"On the other hand," he continued, "M. Bédard worked late into the night and has found the likely address of his widow, Madame El-Abiad."

He handed me another of his cards with an address written on the back. My heart pounded.

I thanked him profusely and turned to leave when he coughed lightly. "It is customary nowadays to pay the expenses of officials who perform nonofficial duties in their own time. The chief will, I believe, be expecting similar thanks. We are not well paid, you realize, and need to supplement our income. I am sure you understand."

"Of course," I replied, and dipped into my money pouch and handed over a gold half-sovereign, which he accepted with gleeful enthusiasm. I wondered, but didn't really care, how much, if any, of the money would find its way to the Chief of Police. I surely overpaid him—the half-sovereign would exchange into many Tunisian dinars, but I was more than satisfied with his work, although sadness over the news of my father's death clouded my thoughts.

"It was my pleasure to be of service, Madame. If there is anything more I can do, it will again be my pleasure. *Bonne chance!*"

This time I asked the driver to wait as I cautiously walked the cracked and worn steps leading to the door. I knocked on it lightly, without the confidence I had felt before.

A woman, somewhat younger than me, answered the door with a young girl peeking from her hiding place within the folds of her mother's skirt. I asked to see Madame El-Abiad.

"May I say who it is?"

"Yes, tell her it is Mariyah," I said, trying to conceal my excitement.

She returned shortly to inform me that, "Madame is resting and not expecting visitors today," and was about to close the door when I said, "Please tell her I have news from Arabia about her daughter Marie."

I could faintly hear their conversation, although I could not follow it, and time seemed interminable before she returned.

"Please come with me."

With two reluctant children at my side, we followed her into the house to an open doorway, where she graciously stepped aside to let us pass through.

I stood facing my mother.

For a moment, we just stared at each other in utter disbelief, unable to speak. I walked to her, knelt at her feet and tightened my arms around her in sobbing silence, let her go for a moment, looked into her eyes, and then again clasped her to me. We burst into tears at the same moment, startling the children and the other woman who rushed in, alarmed by the sudden outburst.

My overwhelmed mind did not come to life until Isma'il said, "Mama, what about the driver? He is waiting for us." I gave Isma'il the fare and he made a welcomed retreat, dragging his sister with him.

"How is this possible? We were told that the desert claimed you, that you took a long journey, lost your way, and were never found. Consumed by the sun. How did you get here? You must be hungry; Nesayem, please bring them food, do you have money enough? What about clothes? Are you here to stay?"

"Mother, mother, please! It is true that I took a journey and lost my way. But after that fateful journey I have managed to survived for twenty or more years; I am not about to expire. Do I look starved or poorly dressed? I have a husband and these are your grandchildren. We live in Arabia and I am here to visit with you for a few weeks before I return.

"Once a mother, always a mother," I thought. "May Allah bless her."

"Something to drink, you must be thirsty after your travels," she said with urgency, as though I had just trekked across the Sahara Desert to be with her.

"Maybe water or lemon water—with ice if that is possible," I replied.

"Nesayem, go for ice and lemons—hurry!"

I turned to the woman and countermanded my mother. "Please don't rush, it's not urgent, I do not want to put you to trouble, but the children do look forward to ice, it's a special treat, something unknown to them in Arabia."

She smiled kindly and left the room.

"Sit down, are you staying or do you have other things to do?"

"Mama, I am here to be with you and papa, and my brothers. I will come every day. I promise."

An awkward silence followed as I realized what I had said.

"Your father and brother Amenzu are dead, taken by *La Grippe* eight years ago. Your father went first, and a two weeks later Amenzu followed him. They rest in peace, side by side, in the cemetery on the road to Bizerte. My oldest and youngest are together—they were so fond of each other."

She was crying.

"I loved your father to the end. I still love him and think of him every day. He died not knowing you were alive and well—he mourned for you for so long. I want to be with him again; I will tell him the good news when we soon meet in Jannah."

"Oh mother, don't be gloomy, you have many happy years left and we all want you with us. Make papa wait, he will be the better for it. No, that is unkind. Better we tell him tonight. I will ask Mamoud to lead us in prayer; we will pray together. Papa and Amenzu will hear our prayers.

"And what about my dear brother Mamoud?"

"Oh, how could I forget? Nesayem is his wife, the little girl is their daughter and they have a son too, a little older than your boy by the looks of him. The girl is your namesake; Mamoud named her Mariyah in memory of you. The boy, Emad, is following in your father's footsteps. Both he and Mamoud work for the government. They will be home soon. This is their house; I live with them.

"There is so much to think about, I am forgetting many things," she fretted.

"Mother, we have time enough to catch up with our lives, let us not rush. Show me the garden and then we will plan a surprise for Mamoud—his dreadful sister has come back from the dead to haunt him for all those horrible things he did to me when I was a little girl. Do you remember when he…?"

Next day I returned with my still-wrapped journal under my arm, alone. Family visits quickly bore children and mine preferred to explore the crowded souks and cafes of the Medina, the old walled city of Tunis, under the watchful eye of Abdul.

I told my mother about my writings and she insisted I read them to her. I would pace it out, a chapter or two a day—there was so much for an elderly lady to absorb.

> *"My real name is Mariyah, Mariyah El-Abiad, but they have always called me Marie. Marie is a fair compromise—a Muslim name shortened to a French name. Neither a Muslim cleric nor Catholic priest could be offended.*
> *My mother was the daughter of a senior French Embassy official and my father a Tunisian Government...."*

"Now don't skip over anything, these old eyes and ears cannot be offended anymore, they have seen and heard all there is to be seen and heard."

She insisted on sitting by my side so that she could see better my illustrations, she claimed, and at the same time, I suspect, to check casually that I was not holding back words from her.

My initial embarrassment at my explicit writings faded as the readings progressed. My mother took a matter-of-fact attitude to it all as I read quietly to her each morning.

After I read the chapter about Topaz's piercing, she told me that she too had considered it once in the years when many French women were swept up by the *"anneaux de sein"*[3] (bosom ring) vogue. "Like you, I could not bring myself to do it," she told me.

"Tell me, is it true that Ali branded you?" she asked. "Or are you making up that part? because I can hardly believe all these things you have written—yet I suppose I must, because it is too much to imagine."

---

3. In Anatomy and Destiny (Bobbs-Merrill, 1974, p. 97), Stephen Kern explains that: "In the late 1890s the "bosom ring" came into fashion and sold in expensive Parisian jewelry shops. These *"anneaux de sein"* were inserted through the nipple, and some women wore one on either side linked with a delicate chain. The rings enlarged the breasts and kept them in a state of constant excitation.... The medical community was outraged by these cosmetic procedures, for they represented a rejection of traditional conceptions of the purpose of a woman's body."

"It is true, mother."

"Then show me the mark."

"No, it's rude for me to raise my skirt before others, just take my word for it."

"You raise your dress for Ali, why not for me?"

"That is different. He is my husband and lover, you know that."

"Remember you are my child. I have seen you before, *au naturel.* So show me. I am curious."

"I will…but never a word to anyone, you must promise that," I replied, as I stood up and raised my dress—rather proudly.

"Why did he do it to you? It seems to me that he was already in love with you at that time, and surely wouldn't want to hurt you."

"Custom and teachings, mother. It is true I am a victim of these relics of history and have felt the harsh heat of custom. But I am also a beneficiary of the old teachings that allowed a man to buy slaves and take four wives, teachings that made it possible for Ali to buy me from Ahmad, and make me a second wife. When I look back, I am thankful. I have a wonderful husband and children and I am content. The balance is clearly in my favor."

"All this is truly amazing," my mother said, "and yet, you know, we have heard of and do some of these things, even in Tunis! Your smoothing brings back memories from many years ago, more years than I care to count, and I have a little secret to tell you," she said, squeezing my arm tightly. "You remember Madame Leconte, the ambassador's wife. Well, for a little surprise for our husbands we would have ourselves 'done in that way' occasionally. French girls at the embassy found a woman who bared the brothel girls, and we would both sneak there together on occasion. It made us feel like 'Parisian women'[4]. I loved the naughty excitement when I showed myself to him, and it never failed to revive our husbands' enthusiasm for us. Of course it didn't last; we didn't have Ahmad's balm."

Today, in the hushed foyer of the French Embassy, we watched and waited, in apparent invisibility. Employees swiftly and silently glided back and forth before us, all it seemed, deeply burdened with self-importance and sheaves of

---

4. In France the habit of depilating fell into disuse after Catherine de Medici, then queen of France, forbade her ladies in waiting to remove their pubic hair any longer. However, courtesans continued to do it, and it is still a characteristic trademark of Parisian prostitutes.

paper. For a good quarter-hour we waiting about before an official inadvertently paused in his earnestness sufficiently long for us to impose on his day. After explaining that I was a good friend and confidant of Ambassador Leconte and had confidential papers of national importance to deliver, he reluctantly granted an appointment for us the next day to see the present ambassador, Ambassador Leconte having retired many years ago.

"His office is located…."

"I know it well, thank you. Through the double doors at the top of the stairs," I interrupted, much to his surprise. "Tell me, does the portrait of Madame Thiers still hang over the desk," I asked, recalling in my mind times when Jacqueline and I had noisily ran up and down the stairs and in and out of her father's hallowed office.

"Yes indeed, Madame. Nothing much has changed since Ambassador Leconte's time. May I advise our present ambassador of the nature of the confidential papers you will be bringing with you?"

"The papers are for his and his superiors eyes only. Some things are better not spoken of," I replied, with a wink.

"Yes, so very true," he whispered back, with a conspirator's understanding and respect.

"The ambassador will be unable to resist the pleas of a feeble old woman and her beautiful daughter, but wear a pretty low cut gown, it won't do any harm," sang my mother.

"I don't have anything like that with me."

"Not to worry, I still have French dresses in my wardrobe and they will fit you. I have no call for them now; you may take them with you when you return to Arabia."

"We will see," I replied, not at all sure that I wanted to take those memories away from her.

Next day we sat across from the ambassador, a large expanse of tidy polished desk between us. "Yes, I know Ambassador Leconte well, and how may I be of help?" he inquired.

We explained in detail our past relationship with the former ambassador and his family, how my father and Ambassador Leconte were the best of friends, and how I had played and attended school with his daughter Jacqueline at the private embassy school. With my mother kicking at my ankles under the desk, I hinted that the only reason they admitted me to the embassy school was that Ambassador Leconte was very fond of my mother, a notion that tickled the fancy of the current incumbent, but not my mother.

With the formalities and courtesies over, I started. "We have a manuscript that we dearly want to have safely delivered to Ambassador Leconte's daughter. It is valuable to us and there is only one copy in existence. It is hand-written. We were hoping that the embassy could arrange for its safe delivery through diplomatic channels."

"What is in the manuscript?" he inquired.

"It is a diary, the story of my life as a harem slave in Arabia," I replied.

He laughed heartily. "Well, I suppose I don't have to know what it is about, it is none of my business and I could never bring myself to peek at a lady's diary. All I need is your assurance that it is not a manifesto supporting independence for Tunisia or other subversive nationalist diatribe."

We convinced him that the manuscript was nothing more than a private diary and not, "subversive nationalist diatribe," and he agreed to arrange for its delivery. He rang for his adjutant, and a smartly dressed man promptly appeared, who cagily wandered his eyes over my décolleté while the ambassador instructed him to receive a parcel from us next week and to arrange for its delivery to Paris via diplomatic pouch.

"I believe we may have met before many years ago," said the adjutant after receiving his instructions. "Are you not the girl who was always with Mademoiselle Jacqueline Leconte?"

"Yes, that would be me. I am surprised you recognized me after so many years."

"A schoolboy's first attractions stay forever in his mind," he replied, shifting his flirting eyes to mine and giving me a secret wink.

After our successful meeting we made our way to the Maison Dorée, gathered up the children and Abdul, and after meeting with Mamoud and Emad, we went to fulfill our appointment at a photographer's studio. A family portrait and one of Abdul was in order, taken against a faux background of the Roman ruins in Dougga. I wanted people to know we were worldly and had traveled to exotic places far away!

I went for a long walk today—alone. A woman could do this in Tunis these days; it was commonly done. I did not want anyone to know where I was going. Not that it mattered to them, but because I myself did not know why I was going, should they ask. I felt perhaps that I should be ashamed and was deceiving Ali in some way, or being unfaithful.

I stood outside my old house in a thoughtful mood. It had changed little from when Jamaal and I spent our first years there in youthful optimism of a life of love and contentment, touching for the sake of touching when we passed closely, laughing easily at small things, chasing each other through rooms and up the stairs. I did love him then, I have come to realize. Not with the same overwhelming love I first found with Ali, but a more subtle love that spoke in a lowered voice that went unheard for what it was. But who could have known how our lives would unfold, indeed unravel, and how we would separate and years later learn again of each other after mistakes had been made. What if Jamaal had been the father of Isma'il and Fatima, how would life have turned out for all of us, and where would I be now?

The years have erased the particular feelings I had for Jamaal, yet I was thankful that when Ali found him in Jeddah he did not hurt him and damage that part of my past, although of course I said nothing at the time. He and the house were part of my life and always would be. Perhaps that is why I had this urge to revisit this place. Who can tell?

Although I had already bought gifts for everyone, on my way back to the Maison Dorée I bought three more: a book and two pocket watches. "No, they are Geneva Chronometers," the jeweler corrected me. They came with compasses and a flip-up dial for "shooting the sun." He told me that with them you could tell where you were in a featureless desert, and in which direction Mecca lay. Modern science. I bought a gold one for Ali and a silver one for Abdul. And the book? *Teach Yourself to Waltz.*

While sitting with my mother I have brought my *Journaux Intimes* up to date and today I take it to the embassy. I have no further use for it, and maybe, just maybe, it will find its way to Jacqueline and be of interest to her and others.

I have removed all sketches and drawings of Ali and myself from my journal. I shall accord my family anonymity this way.

Furthermore, Sheik Ali bin Shareef al-Saalih is not his real name.

Tomorrow evening we sail for Jeddah. It will be a hard and tearful goodbye, for I have come to know my mother again, and accept that this will be the last time I will see her in this life. Nevertheless, my visit has been incredibly uplifting and has brought conclusion and contentment to both of us. New peace and lightness has settled on our lives.

I have closed the circle.

I am going home.

Fin

ÉPILOGUE

by Jacqueline Beauvais-Leconte.

This short letter accompanied the manuscript I received in Paris, forwarded from the French embassy in Tunis.

Dear Jacqueline:

So much time has passed since we lay together on my bed in Tunis dreaming of being harem girls. Foolishly or otherwise, I went beyond this dream and found it in real life and this "Journaux Intimes" records the events that followed.

Why write letters, I have reasoned, when everything is in these pages? Besides, I have no further use for them except that as an aspiring writer I suffer from that common delusion of wanting to see my work published and acclaimed and not set aside and disregarded. Do you think it has merit?

The modern wonder of the telegraph has come to us in Arabia. Send a message to Sapphira Marie c/o Anglo Arabian Oil Exploration Company in Riyadh. This is Ali and Barry's new venture. It will find me; I think there is only one Sapphira Marie in all of Arabia!

I miss you, and think of you often.

Fondest love,

Sapphira Marie Saalih-El-Abiad.

The fact that you are reading this book tells you much about the final disposition of Marie's journal.

My father received it via diplomatic pouch, screened from the scrutiny of those at our borders inclined to impose their high moral values on the more prurient populace of France. He passed it along to me unopened.

All the mainstream publishers considered it too risqué to publish, but I found a small printers shop willing to do the work.

Marie and I have exchanged messages via the telegraph and I have arranged to visit her in Makram. I am so looking forward to that day.

I shall be taking gifts: shocking French lingerie, long silk stockings, and high-heeled shoes for the girls.

Ali will no doubt derive as much if not more fun from these gifts, nevertheless I have for him a leather bound set of the complete works of Jules Verne, including of course, *20,000 Leagues the Under the Sea*. Marie will have some reading to do.

And most importantly for Marie, a first edition print of her book.

That is not all. Ali and I have colluded via telegraph and unknown to Marie I will be bringing a houseguest—Madame El-Abiad.

Jacqueline Beauvais-Leconte

THE HAREM

❦

YASMEEN	His 14th birthday present. First slave of the harem. Visayan—known today as the Philippine Islands—and Chinese parentage. Pirate booty, first sold into a harem in Baghdad and later bought by the Master's mother. Christian.
BLACK PEARL	His 15th birthday present. Nubian, kohl black with gorgeous full breasts and buttocks. Captured by a raiding party from Upper Egypt. A Christian.
CAPUCINE	His 16th birthday present. From Aden—now known as The Yemen. Sold into slavery as punishment for an offense committed while a free girl in the service of the Sultana of Sana'a. Named after a flowering plant of the region.
BRIAR ROSE	His 17th birthday present. Asian from Zamboanga—a town in the Philippines. Indentured as a household servant by her unsuspecting parents. Catholic Christian.
KATANA	His 18th birthday present. Deceased.
PAEONIA	His 19th birthday present. English. Ran away to sea. Later sold by the captain to an Arab slave trader in Dublin Ireland. Named after a flower that grows wild in the Atlas Mountains.
NADYA	His 20th birthday present. Fair hair and blue eyes. Nadya means "moist with dew". Abducted from Northern Europe—Sweden. A Christian.
ZAHRA and NOSZAHRA	Sisters from Iberia (Spain or Portugal). Zahra means "flower". Almost identical in appearance. Christians.

HORTENSIA	Christian from Southern Ethiopia. Kohl black/brown. Named after a local flower.
TOPAZ	Syrian. Sold into slavery by her uncle. Won by Sheik Ali as part of a wager. Named after the horse that won the race.
SAPPHIRA	Your journalist and diary keeper.

CHRONOLOGY

1863	Emancipation Declaration abolishes slavery in the United States.
1869	Yasmeen, Sheik Ali's first slave girl, is born in the Philippines.
1875	Sheik Ali is born.
1876	Suez Canal officially opened.
1881	French colonize Tunisia displacing the Turkish Ottomans.
1886	Marie is born in Tunisia.
1895	Sheik Ali's mother dies.
1899	Sheik Ali's father dies.
1900	Marie is fourteen years old. Her journal writings begin here.
1902	Marie is married.
1903	Sheik Ali migrates from Buraydah to Makram.
1904	Marie moves with her husband to Jeddah.
1909	Marie enters the harem of Sheik Ali.
1912	Marie gives birth to Isma'il.
1914	Marie gives birth to Fatima. World War I starts.
1916	Arab revolt against the Turks. "Lawrence of Arabia" helps Arabs.
1918	World War I ends. Arab revolt ends. Spanish Flu (La Grippe) epidemic sweeps the world killing 20,000,000 people.

1922	Turkish Ottoman Empire ends. The great harem in the Topkapi Palace is closed.
1924	Ibd-Saud unites Arabia's warring tribes.
1926	Marie visits Tunis with Isma'il and Fatima.
1927	Marie's book is published in Paris.
1930	Oil discovered in Arabia.
1932	Abdul Aziz Ibn-Saud becomes king of Saudi Arabia.
1935	Slavery officially abolished in Somalia.
1936	King Ibn-Saud of Saudi Arabia restated the teachings of the Qur'an. Required owners to register slaves with the government and licensed slave traders.
1962	Slavery officially abolished in Saudi Arabia.

GLOSSARY

Abyssinia	Old name for Ethiopia, a Christian country in northeast Africa.
Abaya	A loose robe worn by Muslim women covering the body from neck to toe and often worn with a headscarf or veil. See burqa.
Bijoux indiscret	Dildo.
Bin/bint	Arabic—son of/daughter of.
Bindi	Small crystals or sequins that are individually gummed to the skin in patterns or lines of glitter.
Bisht	A sheer outer cloak worn over a thobe.
Burnt umber	Natural earth pigment. Deep reddish brown. A mehndi for the eyes. Also used to darken a brand.
Burqa	Somewhat like the abaya except that it covers all of the body, and sometimes has only a mesh screen for sight. Usually made from black light-weight material that has two layers.
Called/calling	Chosen or selected by the harem master for intimacy.
Chalwar	Trousers tied at the waist and gathered at the ankles into a cuff or with a drawstring. Harem pants.
Choli	Short waisted upper garment that often has sheer sleeves. Bolero jacket or blouse. Usually laced or buttoned in front and drawn tight.

Chou-chou	French term of endearment. Much as we would use the nonsensical terms "honey" or "sweetie pie". Literal translation—cabbage-cabbage.
Cochineal	A red dye made of the dried and pulverized bodies of female cochineal insects.
Djellaba	A long loose garment with full sleeves and a hood.
Erga	Torture chamber for administering punishment, especially for females. Derived from the Latin word Ergastula meaning private prison. Roman emperor Hadrian abolished them citing "liable to great abuse in the hands of tyrannical masters."
Excise	Cut away the clitoris, sometimes with the inner labia minora.
Ferman	A Sultan's written edict.
Gelded	Castrated in the Semivir way, effeminated man or boy.
Gendarmerie	French police force.
Ghutrah	Male Arab headdress worn along with a double coil of black cord wrapping on top called an Iggal.
Glans	The bulbous end of the penis. Latin, meaning acorn.
Hajj	Muslim annual pilgrimage to Mecca.
Halaal	Allowed, legal.
Haraam	Forbidden, illegal.
Haseki	A Sultan's harem favorite.
Hijab	Scarf worn over the head, usually with the abaya.
Houri	One of the beautiful maidens that in Muslim belief live with the blessed in paradise. A voluptuously beautiful young woman.
Iggal	Double coil of black cord to hold the ghutrah in place.
Jambiya	Yemenese ceremonial dagger with a sharply curved blade that men acquire at reaching manhood.
Joy-girl/boy	Slave kept aside for sodomy.
Jannah	Jannah literally means "garden". In the Qur'an Jannah is also used to mean "The Garden" or heaven/paradise.

GLOSSARY

Kaffiyeh	A cloth headdress fastened by a band around the crown and usually worn by Arab men.
Kasre-el-Nouzha	Castle of Pleasure.
Kava	Explorer Captain James Cook gave this plant the botanical name of "intoxicating pepper". Used for over 3,000 years for its medicinal affects as a sedative, muscle relaxant, and as a remedy for nervousness.
Keening	A lamentation to the dead uttered in a loud wailing voice or wordless chattering cry.
Khamsin	A Sahara wind that carries with it fine sand.
Khobz	Arabic flat bread, similar to Pita bread.
Khomsas	Hardware, usually a doorknocker, in the shape of a hand, which according to legend wards off evil.
Kilim	A hand woven rug or covering made in Turkey, Kurdistan, Iran and western Turkestan.
Kif	A Moroccan mixture of marijuana and tobacco.
Kohl	For centuries, the secret of sparkling eyes. Jet-black powder mixed with almond or castor oil. Chemical composition: Antimony sulfide.
Kris	Sword with curved blade, scimitar style.
Lady position	The "69" position where lovers lie head to tail over the other and each gives the other oral stimulation.
Mahr	Traditional gift from the groom to the bride after her acceptance of his proposal.
Mahram	Males of her immediate family to whom a woman cannot be married, such as a father, brother, or a married uncle, who are allowed to be a woman's escort when travelling.
Mehndi	Arabic—cosmetics, makeup. Also means "henna".
Méréyé	Low waves of dunes in parallel ridges set a few hundred yards apart.
Niqaab	A lightweight veil that has a tie that fastens behind the head. Covers the face from the top of the nose down leaving the eyes seductively exposed.

Nubia	A Christian country largely incorporated into Egypt since the fourteenth century. The Nubian people have retained their heritage and remain a distinct race within the region.
Oil of hamamelis	Witch Hazel. A mild astringent extracted from the hamamelis tree.
Pearl of Allah	Female virgin.
Pleasuring	Sexual stimulation using the mouth. See also Sangara.
Pronged	The use of an iron prong to bring about an abortion.
Purdah	A Muslim practice that secludes women from public observation by means of concealing clothing. From the Hindi word Parda—screen or veil.
Qanass	Falconry. (Saker or Perigrine females are the best hunters).
Qirsh	Old Saudi copper currency. Replaced in 1960 by the riyal.
Salwar-kameez	Northern Indian. A long tunic, falling to about mid-calf, called the kameez, and usually worn over salwars, loose, drawstring pants tapering to a cuff at the ankle.
Sandali eunuch	A fully castrated man, clean cut.
Sangara	Hindi word meaning "swallowed whole". Oral sex to completion. In today's ugly raw vernacular—a "blow job".
Semivir eunuch	Man who has been rendered sexless by the removing of the testicles or by their being crushed, or seared leaving the penis intact. From the Latin for half man.
Smoothing	Removal of all body hair from the neck down. Enjoying resurgence in North America with the growing popularity of "Brazilian bikini waxing."
Tajine	A Moroccan stew that gets its name from the traditional cooking vessel in which it made, an exotic-looking pot with a heavy base and conical lid.
Tantra	Tantric lovemaking incorporates the teachings of the Kama Sutra. Kama Sutra in turn translates as "Guide of the Hindi God of Love".
Thobe	Long white robe worn by Arab men. A sheer outer cloak called a Bisht or Mishlah worn is over the Thobe. This attire represents the official dress code for Arabs in the Arabian Peninsula.

Threading	Persian technique for removing hair whereby individual hairs are entwined with two cotton threads and pulled out.
Tilth	The finely worked top layer of soil made ready for seeding.
Tugra	A Sultan's own monogram in stylized script.
'Ud	Al-'ud is a long necked pear-shaped stringed instrument with 10 to 12 strings played with a plectrum. It is considered to be the predecessor of the guitar and lute.
Ultramarine	A bright blue pigment made from finely ground Lapis Lazuli from Afghanistan.
Umm	Arabic—mother of.
Vernix	A cheesy white substance that covers a baby's skin at birth.
Ylang-Ylang	An essential oil with an exotic floral fragrance used traditionally as an aphrodisiac. Sweet to the taste. In Indonesia, the yellow flowers of the ylang-ylang are spread on the bed of newly married couples.
Zills	Popular Turkish name for finger cymbals, metal discs slipped over the fingers and used to make a musical sound while dancing or singing.
حريم بنت	Arabic script—Harem girl.

ABOUT THE AUTHOR

❦

A degree in, you guessed it, metallurgy, from a second rate college, made the author eminently unqualified to write a book—never mind one about life in a harem. Fortunately, no one told Mariyah, and in many moments of blind optimism and delusion, *Harem Girl* was written.

Born in England, Mariyah Saalih traveled extensively in Europe and the Middle East before settling down to relative obscurity in North America where a large part of Mariyah's life is spent playing personal assistant to the family cat Sasha.

A tour of the grand harem in the Alhambra Palace in Granada, Spain, inspired the writing of this first full length novel.

Contact the author at:
mariyahsaalih@haremgirlreview.com

978-0-595-31300-6
0-595-31300-0